THE FURY
OF RACHEL
MONETTE

Peter Abrahams

PUBLISHED BY POCKET BOOKS NEW YORK

POCKET BOOKS, a Simon & Schuster division of
GULF & WESTERN CORPORATION
1230 Avenue of the Americas, New York, N.Y. 10020

TO DIANA

PROLOGUE

It was one of those winds that have a name. The *chergui* they called it, a hot summer wind that blew from the east. At dawn it was already gathering strength, picking the crests off the dunes and driving the sand through the air like sparks from a grindstone.

There was no escaping it. The sand forced its way up the soldier's pant legs, stung his wrists and neck, filled his ears. Hunched over the steering wheel he guided the jeep slowly south, seeking the firm rocky patches which provided the only traction in the ocean of loose sand. You will be back in time for lunch, the French liaison officer had promised. How far can a pregnant woman go in the desert? Farther than I want to, thought the soldier.

He stopped the jeep and stood on the seat to look ahead. He was a big man with thick shoulders and the kind of beard that can never be shaved into invisibility no matter how sharp the blade. His eyes were tearing, leaving muddy tracks on his dark cheeks. There was nothing to see, nothing except dunes and rocks. Nothing was what he expected to see: that was why all the others had been sent north. It is improbable that she will go south, the Frenchman had explained rather superfluously—it was almost three thousand kilometers to the next town. Still, she does not know where she is to begin with. We must consider the irrational.

He had driven south.

The wind blew harder, darkening the sky with sand, screening out all color. The sand was gray, the sky was gray, the sun was gray. For a while the wind made the soldier forget the heat, but the wet stains under his arms spread quickly to join those on his back and across his chest. His undershorts clung damply to his groin. The Frenchman loved the desert; he said he found something fascinating about it. The soldier drank from his canteen and drove on.

In the early afternoon he thought he saw a movement on the horizon. It made him try to go faster and that was a mistake. Rounding a dune the jeep slid suddenly into a large expanse of deep sand. There was nothing to do but press the accelerator to the floor, hoping that speed would carry him through. He saw firm ground to his right and turned toward it. As he did the front wheels bit into the sand, and the rear ones at first spun wildly and then not at all, as the jeep sank to its axles. The soldier got out and drank more water. Again he saw something moving to the south. He could free the jeep—he had a shovel, sand ladders, a jack—but hours would be lost, and perhaps the woman too. Slinging his rifle over his shoulder he started after her on foot.

Two walkers in the desert. The small one moved slowly, sometimes stumbling. The big one had a long steady stride and drew nearer with every step. The wind didn't care. It threw sand in both their faces.

She reached the edge of a *sebkha*, a large dry salt lake depressed fifty or sixty feet below the desert floor. As she walked she kept looking at the blue light that shimmered in the center of the lake bed. She is wondering whether it's water, thought the soldier behind her. He was near enough now to see that she wore a dark blue robe, the hood pulled over her head. Again she stumbled, and drew away from the edge. She's ready to collapse, the soldier thought. That's why she doesn't hear me. She'll probably be glad to go back.

He removed the canteen from his belt. Stop, he called to her. She turned quickly. The veil she wore hid everything but the fear in her eyes. She was breathing heavily: the robe stretched taut over the swell of her stomach. He held out the canteen. Without hesitation she took a step and jumped off the edge of the sebkha. There was no attempt to land feet first, or in any other way. It was a random fall and a random landing. She lay broken and still in the lake bed.

The soldier ran along the top of the depression until he found an incline. Scrambling down toward the bottom he lost his balance and slid the rest of the way on his back. He reached the body, turned it over and pulled aside the veil.

She seemed to be grinning at him. That was because someone had cut off her lips. Her nose was gone too, and there were other things. The soldier looked away and vomited until his stomach muscles ached.

After, with the toe of his boot, he rolled her over so that she lay face down. It was then that he noticed the rings on her fingers. There were five, all diamond. The soldier knew nothing about diamonds, but a few of them seemed very big. The woman had hidden them somehow, he thought. She had been given the diamonds because she was going to be free.

The soldier sat on the lake bed until nightfall. There was no wind in the depression, no sound at all. Finally he rose and took off all his clothing except the boots: he would chance the boots. Then one by one he removed the rings from her fingers. One would not come; he left it. Trying not to look, not to see anything, he stripped off her robe. With his hands he dug a shallow grave, and gripping the ankles pulled the body inside. He threw sand on top until she was gone.

The moon, a golden crescent, glided slowly across the sky, not standing straight, as it did in northern latitudes, but lying on its back. The sky was full of stars, millions of lights without heat. Suddenly it was very cold. The soldier put on the blue robe, slipped the rings in an inner pocket, and began walking north, north to the mountains and the cities beyond.

1

Outside it was still dark. Snow was falling heavily. The individual flakes seemed bigger than usual and they descended in dense hordes as if they were in a hurry to get the driveways blocked before anyone woke up. The Eskimos have more than a hundred words to describe the different kinds of snow. Rachel Monette, née Bernstein, hated them all.

With a loud click that wasn't mentioned in the brochure the clock radio signaled it was ready to talk: ". . . instead think of the fun you can have building snowmen with the kids. And remember folks—today is the first day of the rest of your life. Think about it. Sports, Jim?" "Right, Bob. First action last night in . . ."

Rachel shut it off but it hadn't finished communicating. Its red fluorescent digits, shaped in the style computers like, were relaying the news from the fourth dimension. Six fifty-six they declared, thought about it and switched to 6:57. The black modular oblong didn't harmonize with the old New England pine furniture in the room, but try to find an antique clock radio. So few of the shoppes are making them these days.

Rachel got out of bed and stood before the full-length

mirror as she did every morning. She saw a tall big-boned healthy female who in a ten-years-earlier and ten-pounds-lighter version had played some good basketball for Bryn Mawr. The strength of her nose and jaw had always kept people from calling her face pretty, but in the last few years others had begun to see in it what she had almost given up hope they would: a kind of beauty.

Rachel fought another battle with her thick dark hair until it submitted grudgingly and temporarily to the will of her comb. She pinched here and there at her flesh trying to determine what was fat and what was muscle. Deciding that the fat was hard and the muscle soft, she gave it up. Goose bumps began to roughen the texture of her skin. She poked through a pile of clothes on the floor until she found a worn terry-cloth robe. She put it on, inserted a small gold ring in each earlobe and turned to leave the room.

"I wanted to hear what happened in last night's action," her husband called from the bed.

"Tie ball game."

"No overtime?"

"After what you had to drink?"

Adam, or Adman as he often called himself, wasn't in his room. He had already made the bed, smoothing away the wrinkles on the duvet that showed woolly sheep hovering over red fences. Adam had tidy habits like his father. Parked with precision in the corner was a fleet of huge yellow trucks, ready at a moment's notice for a wildcat walkout.

She found him in the playroom at the end of the hall, building something post-modern with blocks, his tongue stuck out between his teeth. He had Scotch-taped his paintings all over the walls. When he first got the paint set he had done many versions of his parents, singly and together, or Garth. Now he was at the height of his hockey period and the gaudy uniforms of the players loomed at her from every side. He knew all their names because he and his father watched the games on television. Each figure was identified in large black letters, sometimes printed on the backs of the sweaters where they belonged, but also on the shorts, the stockings or even the blades of the sticks. Lupien, Schmautz, McIlhargey. They hooked, elbowed, speared, tripped, and slashed just as in real life.

Rachel bent down and kissed the top of his head, feeling the impossibly fine blond hair on her lips. As she carefully picked the sleep from the corner of his eyes, Garth came in and knocked the blocks all over the floor.

"Down, Garth, down."

"Don't shout at Garth, Mummy. He won't love you if you shout."

"He's got to learn."

"Then say nice Garth, nice Garth. He'll learn," said Adam, stroking the animal's tail. Garth picked up a block and trotted out the door.

Rachel looked out the window, which gave a view of the backyard, the frozen pond, and the fields beyond. The daylight had brought a slight wind which was putting the snowflakes through their paces, directing them this way and that in a fanciful choreography. They were as synchronized as the June Taylor dancers.

Rachel went downstairs to face the living room. It had borne the brunt of last night's party the way the Carolina beaches had that of Hurricane Hazel. Someone had ground chocolate into her Persian rug while winding up to pitch spaghetti into the stone fireplace. It sounded like fun but it wasn't.

Rachel had planned it as a celebration of the announcement in Paris the day before that Dan's book had won the Prix Gobert. She had remembered to invite the history faculty, the French faculty, spouses, Dan's senior students, their girlfriends and boyfriends. She had remembered to buy a case of California Chianti, to hide the good wine in the cupboard under the kitchen sink, to pick up her black dress from the cleaners, and to make two sauces for the spaghetti since some of the guests were vegetarians. She had forgotten to reckon with envy, envy of the subspecies academicus, which had arrived uninvited at the party and goaded everyone into drinking too much, laughing too much, and spilling things too much.

She had placed two copies of the book on a glass coffee table, one the English version, one the French. They looked nicely done up in their bright blue dust jackets. On the back of the English version was a photograph of Dan, his sandy hair rumpled in the breeze, wearing a plaid lumberjacket and playing with Garth. On the back of the French one he wore his glasses, a dark suit, and a sober face. It had become a minor *cause célèbre* in France and in other parts of Europe too, because it made some people recall what they wanted to forget and taught others things they didn't wish to learn. *The Dreyfus Disease: France and the Jews 1939 to 1945. La Maladie Dreyfus: Les Juifs en France 1939 à 1945.* The media loved it: two film crews had already come from Paris to interview Dan and a speaking tour of French universities was in the works. It was an excellent piece of research but she didn't understand the passion it aroused. It all seemed long ago. That bothered Dan. "You're the one who's Jewish," he had said. And she was Jewish. The way Werner von Braun was American—for official purposes. She didn't deny it, or feel badly about it, or wish to change. It wasn't that important.

Dawkins, head of French, who spoke it very correctly but with an Arkansas twang, had ferreted through the French copy querying some of the usages Dan had chosen when he did the translation. Holding the book at arm's length in case it had germs he said, "Sorry, Monette, even if a Frenchman ever had that thought he'd never express it like this. He'd turn it upside down and use the reflexive—it's the very essence of the way they see things, for Christ's sake." Ethel Dawkins, a plump, rich woman whose knowledge of French was confined to proper nouns like Givenchy and Louis Vuitton, nodded in support.

"How the hell would you know how they think?" Dan replied in a pleasant voice, sipping armagnac. He was having a great time. The success of the book made him feel invulnerable. "I was born in Paris. I was speaking French before you emerged from your backwater and heard proper English for the first time."

"Dan," Rachel said. "Don't let Garth do that." Garth was eating spaghetti off Ethel Dawkins's plate. She raised a fleshy helpless forearm in defense.

"No, Garth," Dan said in the firm voice he used on Garth. Garth lowered his head and growled. Ethel Dawkins wound some more pasta around her fork and popped it into her mouth.

"I'm grateful for my simple origins," Dawkins resumed, running a big hand through his gray crewcut. He took pride in being the last surviving male in the western world with a crewcut, a quixotic sort of achievement, like being the last dodo bird. "You people with roots in two civilizations can never intuitively grasp either. You have to analyze, analyze, analyze. It's the price that cultural mongrelization exacts."

"Bow-wow," said Dan. Garth growled sympathetically and began to tear at the laces of Dawkins's brogues. Dawkins kicked him away, not very gently. Garth looked cross and skulked behind a couch, overturning an ashtray en route.

A chubby balding boy named Andy Monteith, who was one of Dan's best students, cleared his throat. "What do the minutiae of the translation matter, compared to the content?" He had an expressive, porcine nose which now turned up to test the wind for the scent of danger. "Surely what the book says is what counts."

"Sensible boy," Dan said.

"Sensible?" said Dawkins. "Anyone who has taken grade two phenomenology knows you can't separate the two." He looked at Andy. "How did he get admitted to this college with ideas like that?" The boy blushed.

"His father donated the French building," Rachel said. "An illiterate, but he had a knack for applied phenomenology." Everyone laughed, even Dawkins.

"Okay then, Dan, in terms of the content," said Henry Gates, his heavily bearded and rather unkempt colleague in European history: "I don't see where you tackle the question of the lack of physical Jewish resistance."

"I thought Dawidowicz took care of that pretty thoroughly, Henry." He sighed. "First of all, I think people who ask that question are really asking 'Why aren't Jews tough?' like Gurkhas or something. I don't mean you, Henry—you're just asking it to bait me. But it's a wholly spurious issue. Resistance movements all require a support system—money, supplies, safe houses, weapons, pockets of public sympathy—and if those don't exist there is no resistance. You've got to have something to work with. So, what happened in France? In the majority of cases French Jews were protected. Their lives anyway, if not their property or dignity. But Jews living in France but born outside were handed to the Germans gift wrapped. A trade-off, as a sop to French pride, French sovereignty. Is that something to be proud of? Can they be proud that of the ninety thousand Jews in France who were killed, most weren't born there?"

"Easy, Dan," said Henry Gates. "I was three years old when the war started."

"That's not enough protection when you get Dan started on this subject, Henry. It's his obsession," Rachel said.

"Right you are, Rachie. Every man needs one, like a five-cent cigar." Dan held out his glass. "How about a weensy bit more?"

"Number five, Dan?"

"So who's counting?"

She poured him another. "I just don't want you to suffer any tissue damage," she said.

"Oh, it takes years and years of drinking to reach that stage," said Andy, who had the facts from family history.

But Dan knew she was talking in code about erectile tissue, and he left his drink untouched.

"Jews are tough," he said when they were in bed.

"It pays in the end."

Later, with her head on his shoulder, she had thought about the book. It had been with them for a long time, almost like another child; a child that needed special attention from both of them. Now Rachel hoped that Dan would regard it as the culmination of years of work, and move on to something else. She said so as they drifted off to sleep. Dan sighed:

"I don't think I'm finished with it yet, Rachie. There's always more."

Someone, Rachel saw, had discovered the wine cache under the sink. A cigarette butt was floating in a half-full bottle of Gevrey-Chambertin, taxing her level of tolerance to mess. It was high, but it had limits.

"Dan," she called up the stairs, "come help me clean up."

"Can't. I'm engaged." That meant on the toilet. Rachel sighed and went to the phone. Mrs. Flores would take care of it.

Rachel went into the morning routine, an orderly progression which finished when she was back where she was the morning before. First, hygiene: floss teeth, expectorate blood. Brush teeth because they don't feel clean without toothpaste, no matter what the dentist says. Step into shower. Regulate water with rotating retracting swiveling control lever. Scalding. Screaming. Freezing. Scrub every square inch of skin with transparent English soap. Skip the middle of the back. Rinse. Step out. Shiver. Dry. Second, clothing: always from the bottom up. Wool socks, blue cotton long underwear, jeans. A sensible brassiere for sensible breasts. Irish sweater. Fur-lined suede boots to the knee. Third, food: her turn to make breakfast. Reheat last night's coffee. Squeeze fresh orange juice. Dan always used frozen and in that Dan failed as a nurturer. Yogurt into bowls, blueberries onto yogurt, brown sugar on Adam's blueberries. Set table in breakfast nook. Fix Adam's lunch: BLT on brown bread, sweet pickle in Saran Wrap, banana. Apple juice in thermos. Pack it in lunch box with Porky Pig on the front. Sip coffee. Look out window. See Mrs. Candy across the street open door, clutch pink gown at fat throat, stoop for newspaper, straighten with effort, reveal glimpse of white sagging thigh, close door. Fourth, departure: stuff into briefcase tapes, notes, pen, stopwatch, apple. Put on blue down jacket, leather gloves, wool headband. Open door.

Garth was relieving himself against Mrs. Candy's garage. The houses in their neighborhood near the edge of town stood about fifty yards apart but Garth seldom ventured into the wide open spaces alone, preferring a man-made environment.

In their red sweatsuits Dan and Adam were pushing at the trunk of the oak tree, stretching their calf and thigh muscles. Adam enjoyed the warm-up as much as the run.

"Limbered up, Adam?" Dan asked.

"Not yet, Daddy," Adam grunted, red in the face.

"No one goes anywhere until the driveway is cleared," said Rachel. "Shoveling is the best limbering exercise there is."

"It is not."

"It is. Bill Rodgers says so."

"He does not, Mummy." They went to fetch the shovels, too late to be of any use to the mailman, a gaunt Vermonter who was making his way with difficulty up the walk.

"You should get this walk cleared," he said, handing Rachel a letter. "The law says the mailman is not obligated to negotiate an uncleared access."

"Sorry." She took it from him. The return address said Leonine Investments, 1550 Fifth Avenue, New York. It would contain a quarterly dividend. Leonine Investments was her father's frozen fish.

Quickly the shoveling degenerated into a game which involved tossing snow high into the air and watching

Garth jump at it, snapping. Rachel brushed the snow from the windshield of the little Japanese station wagon.

"You're really going in this?" she asked.

"Sure. It's what makes tough guys tough. Right, Adam?"

"Right." They leaned on their shovels.

"Okay, tough guys. Breakfast's on the table and there's fresh O.J. in the fridge." She walked over to Dan to kiss him goodbye. There were dark smudges under his eyes.

"You didn't sleep well."

An odd look surfaced in his eyes. "Not very." He lowered his voice so Adam wouldn't hear. "I even had a nightmare, if you can believe it."

"I'm not surprised, with all the booze you drank. What was it about?"

"Nothing really. I'll tell you later."

"Was Tom Dawkins in it?"

He laughed. "It wasn't that scary."

She kissed him on the lips. "The run will do you good. Don't be late for school, Adam." The school was a few hundred yards away, on the road to town.

Rachel backed the car out of the drive. As she drove off she saw them in the rearview mirror, running along the road: Dan in the lead with his long-legged lope and Adam falling behind but going as quickly as his little legs would carry him, more graceful than his father. Garth stayed right beside Adam.

2

Rachel touched the play button and the girl said, "I gave up the baby because my father beat the shit out of me when he saw it was half black, you know?" It was a problem. Using the fast forward Rachel searched through the tape until she heard the girl saying, "It's all a load of crap no matter what the social workers tell you." With her hands on the reels Rachel slowly moved the word "crap" across the tape head, bracketing it with a grease pencil. She lay the tape in the editing block and cut along the two lines with a razor blade. She spliced the tape with a piece of adhesive, rewound to "beat the shit," isolated "shit" with the grease pencil, excised it and replaced it with "crap." "Crap" was half an inch longer than "shit": she supposed it was due to the girl's drawl. She stuck on the adhesive, rewound and heard, ". . . father beat the crap out of me." The intonations matched. "Crap" wasn't as strong, and it wasn't what the girl had said when Rachel held the microphone in front of her in the dingy room, but it would play in the high schools of Massachusetts and "shit" wouldn't. That's what they meant by editorial judgment.

Rachel rubbed her eyes. The fluorescent lights hurt

them. As did, come to think of it, the flaking yellow paint on the walls of the editing cubicle, and the poster advertising a forgotten concert by a forgotten folk singer. Once, in her last year of high school, she had an orgasm while listening to one of his songs. More than any adolescent longing it had probably been due to the two-hundred-dollar earphones her father had given her, or marijuana bought in the girls' washroom. The episode seemed incredible to her now.

Andy Monteith opened the door and leaned in. "Thanks for the party last night, if that's what it was." He moved his chubby body a step farther into the room, and lifted his nose inquiringly toward the Ampex.

"Adoption in the Commonwealth of Massachusetts."

The nose turned up. It did a lot of his talking, like a dog's tail. "Sounds dry. But I loved the one you did for NPR."

"Which one? I've done two for NPR."

"You know. The one on skin flicks, or whatever excuse you found to air all that titillation."

"It wasn't meant to be titillating—it was meant to be frightening. Now vamoose. I've got work to do."

The nose drooped and Andy backed out of the room, neglecting to close the door. Everyone remembered skin flicks, no one mentioned commodity futures, a much better piece. Sex sells, even in documentaries for nonprofit radio.

Blues drifted in from the control room. For some reason WMS, the college radio station where she did her editing, liked to devote mornings to scratchy blues recordings. Bessie Smith was singing:

> I ain't gonna play no second fiddle
> I'm used to playing lead

in a threatening voice and young Louis Armstrong was blowing into his cornet as if he couldn't agree more.

Rachel threaded the tape through the timer. The

standard length for a half-hour documentary was twenty-eight minutes and fifteen seconds. She had thirty-two fifty. It was too much work to do before lunch. She left the tape on the machine and went home, as she often did when Dan had no afternoon classes. They would eat in the study while Dan marked papers or read monographs for a while before she lured him into bed. "Just for a quick nap." There were many of these quick naps during the winter, and often they lasted until Adam came home from school.

The snow had stopped falling as Rachel drove home. It lay everywhere in puffy pure white carpets, as in the Christmas cards of yesteryear. It made the branches bend and the roofers rich. The whole town was very quiet, and she could hear the deep-tread tires gently compressing the snow beneath. Then the bell on the old white Congregational church rang one peal, signifying 12:15, and the streets filled with hungry students on the way to lunch, and then more classes, study, labs, writing letters home, sleeping, reading comic books, watching TV, drinking beer, smoking marijuana, having sexual encounters, stealing money from the lockers in the gym. The Ephs, they were called, after Colonel Ephraim Williams, a minor performer in the Revolutionary War and founder of the school. An Eph did not have the formidable sound of an Eli, to say nothing of a Sooner, a Razorback or a Fighting Irish; but many parents paid good money to make sure their child became one.

She passed the airplane hangar that called itself a New England Inn and turned the corner that led by Adam's school to the house. The new inn had replaced the bona fide one which had become a residence when the college finally began admitting women. In the dark paneled bar of the old inn, on a warm spring night with the birds singing and the waiter dispensing free drinks, Dan had asked her to marry him. She had said yes. The waiter was fired soon after.

The plow had already been by to wall off the driveway. Rachel left the car by the side of the road, climbed over the snowbank, feeling the snow infiltrate her boots, and walked up the unshoveled path, taking advantage of the footprints that led to and from the house.

Rachel turned the doorknob and pushed. The door didn't open, which was strange because they never locked it, not in a small place like Williamstown. She remembered the front-door key she had on the ring that held the car keys. She tried it; the door wasn't locked, only stuck. Rachel pushed again, harder. The door yielded an inch. She put her shoulder against it. It refused to open until she had strained with all the power in her strong legs. The difficulty was Mrs. Flores lying against it on the other side.

"Mrs. Flores?" Rachel bent down. Dark red blood was spreading slowly through Mrs. Flores's iron-gray hair. A pool of it no bigger than a peanut butter cookie had dripped onto the shiny black tile floor, where it quivered with surface tension. Rachel heard a sound from above. She didn't even stop to discover if Mrs. Flores was breathing.

"Dan? Dan?" She tried to control her voice as she bolted up the stairs, leaving little pads of snow on the deep blue runner. "Dan?" she called, throwing open the door of one room and then another.

She found him in the study. Still wearing the red sweatsuit, he knelt on the floor with his back to her, surrounded by a sea of books and papers. Very slowly he turned to face his wife. She saw the gold handle of the letter opener sticking out of his chest. The letter opener she had bought in San Francisco, she thought stupidly. Chinatown.

"Danny." Not taking her eyes off him, Rachel ran to the desk, picked up the phone and dialed the operator. No sound came from the other end of the line. Frantically she tapped on the depressor button until she noticed that the line to the wall plug had been cut. It dangled in the air, ending in a fray of copper wire.

Outside she saw Mrs. Candy shoveling snow. She tore at the window catch but it was jammed. Seizing a dictionary she heaved it through the window with both hands. The glass shattered and landed in the snow without a sound. She leaned into the opening and screamed: "Mrs. Candy. Call the ambulance. My husband is badly hurt. Quickly." Mrs. Candy stared up at her for a second and ran into her house.

With a soft groan Dan slumped down on all fours. Rachel gently turned him and propped his back against the wall. She felt his blood on her hands. Despair filled his eyes and he opened and closed his lips as if to speak. Rachel put her ear to his mouth.

"Adam," he said. She could barely hear him. And then something else that sounded like, "it can't happen."

"I can't hear you, darling." He tried to take a deep breath but could not. She held him. "Oh, Danny; oh, Danny." He was trying to push her away.

"Get Adam," he said in less than a whisper. His vocal chords could not make sound with the tiny volume of air that was passing over them.

"Yes, darling, after the ambulance comes." She heard the siren. His hand squeezed her arm with desperate strength.

"Now, Rachel, now." He struggled for breath. "Get him now." His eyes were pleading and his face tense with effort, or pain, or both. Suddenly she understood and felt something that made her whole body shake. The siren was very loud. She tried to find her normal voice.

"All right, Dan." She wanted to say something hopeful, to forge a link with the future, but she couldn't think of a word. Rachel kissed his forehead, feeling a cold dampness on her lips. Slowly she stood up, and left him sitting against the wall with the letter opener in his chest and his eyes staring into the middle distance.

Rachel ran down the stairs. In the front hall Mrs.

Flores sat on a little bentwood chair, dabbing her head carefully with a dish towel.

"Mrs. Flores, are you all right?" Mrs. Flores murmured something in her own language. Her dark eyes seemed unfocused. "Don't worry, the ambulance is coming." When Rachel opened the door she saw it had already arrived. Two young men were carrying a stretcher up the path.

"Hurry," she said. "He's upstairs and he's been stabbed. And the housekeeper's in shock."

"We always hurry, ma'am," one of them said as they passed her.

"Please," she said. They looked at her for a moment before they entered the house.

In her mind she began running the block and a half to the school, running along the snowy road as fast as she could. But she continued to stand outside the house. She realized she was holding her breath, had been holding it for some time.

She let it out and ran. She ran in the tread marks she had left a few minutes before, ran with long swinging strides that risked a slip or a fall. But she didn't slip. An approaching car honked at her; Rachel stayed in the track and the car pulled to the side of the road, stopped and honked again.

The schoolhouse, a two-story white frame structure with a parking lot in front and playing fields behind, had a main entrance which Rachel ignored. Automatically she ran to the rear of the building, to the door that led directly to the kindergarten. She turned the handle and burst into the room.

A dozen children sat at a long table eating lunch and making noise. They looked at her in surprise, stopped eating, and became still. She saw fair faces and dark faces and faces streaked with mayonnaise. She didn't see Adam's face.

"Oh, Mrs. Monette." Miss Partridge, the tiny white-haired teacher appeared in the doorway of the small kitchen at the rear of the class. She crossed the floor and nudged Rachel toward the windows, away from the children. She spoke in a hoarse whisper.

"Mrs. Monette, I'm so sorry to hear about your husband." Miss Partridge's tongue moved nervously behind her yellow teeth. Her breath smelled of coffee and cigarettes. "The rabbi came and took Adam twenty minutes ago. He should be home by now. I hope someone's there." Tentatively she reached out and patted Rachel's hand.

"What do you mean, Miss Partridge? What rabbi?"

Miss Partridge's liver-spotted bony hands began to tremble. She raised them to her thin chest and held them in a position of prayer. "I'm afraid I don't remember his name, Mrs. Monette. I'm sorry. I'm not Jewish myself."

Rachel grabbed the little woman by the shoulders. "Miss Partridge! What are you talking about?" One of the children started to cry.

"Please don't raise your voice, Mrs. Monette. I know how upset you must be, but it's not fair to the children."

"What rabbi?" In trying to moderate her voice she was squeezing the old woman's shoulders very hard.

"Why, the one you sent to take Adam home." Rachel wanted to shake her and she almost did. Miss Partridge saw it in her eyes and went on quickly. "He said you phoned the synagogue from the radio station and asked if someone could call for Adam."

"There is no synagogue in Williamstown, Miss Partridge." Rachel suddenly pushed her away, thrusting her against the wall, which kept her from falling. Her hands left red stains on Miss Partridge's white blouse. More children were crying. Miss Partridge's whole body trembled, afraid of Rachel and afraid of something else as well.

"Maybe there's one in North Adams," she said. Her pointed tongue appeared and moistened her lips.

"Jesus Christ," Rachel said. She walked toward the door, suddenly feeling very big and very awkward in the room with the little chairs and the little blankets and the little people. On the windows hung snowmen the children had cut out of thick paper. By the door Rachel saw one with Adam written on it. The snowman held a hockey stick. Rachel took it, folded it carefully and put it in her pocket. The folding seemed to take a very long time. As she went out Miss Partridge said, "He was the religious kind of rabbi, Mrs. Monette, with the black robe and the beard and the funny hat. Like at that wall in Israel."

Again Rachel ran.

Several cars were parked outside the house. She was stunned to see the ambulance still there. How could they be so slow, so irresponsible? The attendants came out of the house, supporting Mrs. Flores on either side as she walked to the ambulance. A well-groomed man carrying a black bag followed them.

"Mrs. Monette?" He came forward and took her arm. "Better not go in just now." He looked closely at her, then reached into his bag and quickly fitted a needle into a plastic cartridge of colorless liquid. "Can you take your coat off for me, Mrs. Monette?" he asked gently.

"Not now," Rachel said. "I've got to find my boy." Garth appeared at the doorway and rubbed his head against her leg.

3

"Please don't vacuum," Rachel said to Ethel Dawkins.

"Oh, it won't be any trouble, dear," Ethel Dawkins replied, dragging the old Hoover across the rug. Mrs. Flores hadn't had time to fix the mess in the living room but Ethel Dawkins had arrived and immediately set to work dusting, sweeping, washing dishes, and laundering clothes, some of which would never be needed. Rachel couldn't push that idea from her mind: she thought of Dan's brown corduroy suit hanging in the closet, his old-fashioned white boxer shorts folded in the top drawer of the dresser, his snowshoes in the basement.

Police Chief Ed Joyce stopped writing, closed his notebook, and placed it on his broad leg, just above the knee, in case he needed to refer to it. He returned the ball-point pen to the vest pocket of his navy-blue uniform shirt, settled his large body deeper into the brightly patterned and very comfortable couch, and peered through the fading light at Rachel, sitting across from him in a wooden rocker.

"So," he said in a deep raspy voice, "on the one hand we have a murder, and on the other, a suspected kidnapping." Ethel Dawkins switched on the Hoover, inhibiting

24

any further conversation. Ed Joyce looked at her with mild annoyance. Back and forth went the machine, ruffling the nap of the old wine-colored rug in various geometric patterns. The little light on the front sought out any dust that might try to hide; the little motor whined steadily like an air raid warning. Or a siren. Rachel hadn't wanted to hear that noise but she did not have the strength to stop Ethel.

The light shone on the police chief's enormous black shoes as the Hoover poked around behind and between them until he finally saw what was happening and lifted his feet in the air. Rachel thought she had never seen bigger shoes. In a strange vivid way she seemed to be seeing shoes for the first time. The soles were very worn and one of the leather heels had been replaced with a rubber one. Stuck to the rubber heel was a small flattened piece of dirty pink bubble gum. The tops were scuff free and glowed with the impasto of frequent polishing; the laces were neatly knotted and bowed. The effect was a most respectable compensation for the seediness underneath.

Ethel switched off the vacuum cleaner and led it away. A tangible and disturbing silence moved into the room to replace the noise.

Ed Joyce watched the woman sitting motionless in the rocker. Her dark liquid eyes were unaware of his gaze, or if they were not, uncaring. What rotten timing, the chief found himself thinking. He was two months short of the mandatory retirement age of sixty and what the retirement community brochures promised would be the secure and happy sunset years of his life. But it was a selfish and unworthy thought and he drove it away and gave himself a black mark for having it.

"So, because of the suspected kidnapping, we've had to call in the FBI." Which meant some corporate type with a monogrammed shirt and a head full of ambition would soon arrive. "Which means that one of their agents will be here shortly. I know it's a lot to put up with at a time like this, but every minute can be vital in an investigation of this nature. Vital. I'm sure you understand that."

A young policeman with broad shoulders, a deep chest, and a droopy mustache appeared in the arched entrance to the living room. "Hey chief, got a sec?" he asked.

"Excuse me, Mrs. Monette," said Ed Joyce, standing up. The huge shoes toed out across the rug, leaving a track of deep depressions regularly spaced in the pile. Rachel knew that Ed Joyce was a man who never varied the length or pace of his stride, good weather or bad, indoors or out.

She got up and went to the window. Andy Monteith was shoveling the snow from the walk. He wore a long purple muffler which he couldn't keep from tangling with the shovel. There seemed to be no rhythm or system to his work. He stuck his shovel in here and there, casting the loads at the snowbank. But the wind had risen, and it lifted the snow into the air before it could land, shaped it into little clouds and blew them away.

"What a winter," Ed Joyce said behind her. "I can't remember when we've had so much snow. Not since the war, anyway. What part of the country are you from, Mrs. Monette? I mean originally."

"New York."

"Oh, New York. My wife loves going to the shows. Two in the same day, sometimes." Rachel heard him sit down, heard him take his notebook from his shirt pocket, heard the soft plastic click as he pulled the top off his ball-point pen.

"Now, Mrs. Monette, we're starting to get these times nailed down." Rachel turned and looked at him, and saw his tired gray eyes and his tired gray skin. If he would go away she could imagine it was yesterday. She returned to the rocker and sat down.

"Here's the sequence so far." Ed Joyce opened his notebook. "At eleven forty-five Mrs. Flores arrives. She doesn't knock or ring, and the door is never locked. According to her that's the usual procedure." He looked up, his face inquiring. Rachel nodded. "So, she goes into the kitchen, puts on an apron, and starts doing the dishes. When she's finished one rackful, she goes into the hall and starts dusting. That way she doesn't have to dry the dishes, they dry themselves, and when they're dry she empties the rack and washes another load.

"Okay, I had one of the boys wash enough dishes to fill the rack. It took him twelve minutes. Now maybe, being a man, he's slower than Mrs. Flores." He smiled at her; she stared blankly back. "Let's say it took her ten minutes. Add two for coming into the house and putting on the apron. That makes it eleven fifty-seven when she goes into the hall." Joyce made a short notation in his book.

"While she is dusting the cabinet in the hall, she hears voices upstairs." Rachel's hands gripped the arms of the rocker very tightly. "She says that isn't unusual—students often came to the house to see the professor." Again he looked up and again Rachel nodded. "One of the voices she recognizes as Professor Monette's. The other is a male voice that she doesn't know. She can't hear the actual words, but she forms the impression that they aren't speaking English. Now, Mrs. Monette," Ed Joyce turned to a fresh page, "do you know what languages the professor spoke?"

When Ed Joyce used the word *spoke* he set off a sudden shift in the balance of Rachel's mind. A fundamental realization settled in her at that moment, and although she did not understand it, and might never, it had entered and waited patiently to be dealt with. The newspapers like to use the adjectives *shock* and *disbelief* when describing first reaction to the death of a close relative. Perhaps if the newspapers thought about it they would describe the second stage as one of shock and belief. It was because Rachel had just arrived at this point that she was slow to answer Ed Joyce's question. None of this was she willing to admit out loud: she didn't want to say "he spoke" or "my husband spoke" so she gave the police chief a list:

"French, of course, and Spanish, some Portuguese, some Italian, good German."

"Thank you, Mrs. Monette." Joyce added the details to his written account. "That could be a big help, especially if we assume Mrs. Flores would have recognized Spanish if they'd been speaking it. We can probably strike it off the list, you see."

"I believe Mrs. Flores is Portuguese," Rachel said. As she said it, she felt a keen self-hatred, for allowing herself to play an active role in this petty alignment of detail, as if they were involved in a parlor puzzle to while away the day. Who cares about the minutiae, Andy Monteith had said, was it only last night? It's what it says that counts. Sensible boy, Dan had said. She looked at Ed Joyce. He would never find her son.

Ed Joyce felt abashed. He had made an assumption and been tripped up by it, a beginner's mistake. "We'll have to check that out," he said.

Ethel Dawkins came into the room, carefully carrying a tray in her plump hands. "Tea, anyone?" she asked. She began moving magazines aside to clear a place on the table for the tray.

"Thanks, Mrs. Dawkins, love some."

"You're very welcome, Mr. Joyce. And try the chocolate chip cookies. I made them myself." Ethel looked around. "My, it's dark in here," she said, and did a quick circuit of the room snapping on the lights.

Ed Joyce poured a cup for himself and stirred in cream and sugar. He poured another for Rachel and slid it across the coffee table to her, arranging the cream, sugar, and cookies in a little group nearby. She didn't touch any of it. Joyce held the Wedgewood cup delicately in his immense hand, his little finger stuck out for balance. The chief liked the pattern on the cup—it showed a cherubic swallow hovering over a floral scene that made him think suddenly of the Garden of Eden. He sipped carefully.

"Eleven fifty-seven," he went on, holding the cup in front of him, "she's in the hall, hearing voices. She dusts the marble-top table, the vase that sits on it, and the bentwood chair. She dusts the doorknob of the hall closet. She goes to the front door and starts to work on the big brass handle. That's the last thing she remembers until you came down the stairs." The chief leaned forward, reached across the table, took a cookie and bit into it. His jaw muscles bulged as he chewed. He washed the debris down his throat with a mouthful of tea.

"Time spent in the hall, at least by the young fellow I had duplicate all that dusting—four minutes. That brings us to one minute after twelve." Ed Joyce turned a page in the notebook and pulled the floor lamp closer.

"Now, the kidnapping. Miss Partridge's class always starts eating lunch at twelve sharp. Miss Partridge estimates that they had been eating for ten minutes when she heard a knock at the door—the main door, not the one that leads out back. She opened it and was beckoned out into the hall by a tall, black-bearded man wearing a robe of some sort. At first she didn't realize that he was a rabbi. In fact not until he introduced himself as such. She doesn't remember the name he gave her but thinks it sounded Jewish." Ed Joyce closed his eyes and sighed.

"This rabbi told her that Adam's father had just been killed in a car wreck, and that you had sent him to bring Adam home." Rachel began to rock the chair slowly; one of the old wooden joints made a regular creaking sound. The chief didn't look up from his notebook, but he tried to make his voice sound softer, although he knew it was little suited to the task.

"Miss Partridge was puzzled by one thing, and I think she came close to upsetting the whole scheme right there. She didn't understand why you would send a rabbi. 'Why not?' he kept asking her. Finally, he cottoned on, and explained that you were Jewish. Evidently that did the trick. Miss Partridge went back into the classroom, got Adam dressed in his outdoor clothes, packed the remains of his lunch in his lunch box, told him that you had asked the nice man to take him home, and sent him off. When she turned from the door she noticed the clock on the wall said twelve fifteen." The creaking noise grew louder. Ed Joyce put down his notebook.

"I hope you're not thinking too badly of Miss Partridge. I'm sure she knows she's acted like a foolish old woman, but she said the man seemed very understanding and compassionate, even sad, she thought. He was very good at what he was doing, Mrs. Monette. And besides, she thought of him as a man of the cloth: that kind of thing means a lot to someone like Miss Partridge."

Rachel said nothing. She was thinking of Adam's lunch box with the picture of Porky Pig on the front. She got out of the chair and went to the liquor cabinet. She had been debating with herself for some time the question of whether she should have a drink. She wanted one but it seemed self-indulgent, frivolous. And yet what would it prove if she stopped eating, stopped drinking, stopped eliminating, withdrew from the chain of life, or whatever they called it in grade school? That was the question of course—whether to go on living. To go on living felt immoral.

"Have a drink, Mrs. Monette," said Ed Joyce quietly. "I wouldn't mind one myself, whatever you're having."

Rachel opened the cabinet and took out two glasses. She seldom drank anything other than a glass or two of wine at dinner, and perhaps beer at lunch. As she reached for the Scotch she glimpsed the dark frosted green glass of the squat armagnac bottle. She paused, bent over the cabinet, one hand around the neck of the bottle of Scotch. There was really no question at all, not while Adam was out there somewhere. Would she know if something happened to him? She had read of mothers sensing that their sons had died in far-off battles at the moment the deaths occurred. She didn't believe in psychic power; at the same time she could think of no reason why anyone would kill a five-year-old boy.

The doorbell rang. Hard shoes walked across the hall. Rachel heard a murmur of male voices and then a man said, "Hello, my name's Trimble and I'm from the FBI. May I come in?"

Rachel turned to face him. He was young, even younger than she perhaps. A barber had neatly trimmed his dark hair, a dry cleaner had neatly pressed his dark suit. An optician had sold him expensive aviator-style spectacles and the family genetic pool had given him small even features, even teeth, a light tenor voice, and faint acne scars.

"Yes," she said. He entered and sat in the rocker.

"I'll take a rain check for now, Mrs. Monette, if you don't mind," said Ed Joyce. Rachel closed the liquor cabinet and remained standing in front of it. No drinking with the FBI. To Trimble he said, "I'm Joyce, chief of the force here. Have you seen the preliminary report?"

"What there was of it."

Joyce took a deep breath before he cleared his throat and resumed: "I've been explaining the details to Mrs. Monette. I was about to go over some of the questions they raise in my mind." Trimble held out his hand, palm up in invitation to proceed.

"First, no sign of a car. Mrs. Flores didn't see one in front of the house. A fellow walking around in that getup would attract a lot of attention. But no one remembers seeing him. Therefore either he had someone drop him off in a car, or he took off the robe when he walked to the school."

"Or he walked wearing the robe and no one saw him," said Trimble trying to make his high voice sound bland.

"It's possible." Ed Joyce rubbed his fleshy nose with the side of his fist. "We do know he left the house by the back door. There was no way he could have gone out the front with Mrs. Flores lying there on the floor. And one of the boys found tracks in the snow in the backyard. They weren't very good, with the wind and all, but we took impressions anyway and sent them to North Adams. The tracks lead to the side of the house, so he probably went around to the road. It's unlikely he went through the fields—at this time of year he couldn't make it to the school in nine minutes, not without skis or snowshoes."

"This is all very interesting," said Trimble. "But the big question raised in my mind is motive. Why?" Joyce and Trimble gazed at each other in silent contemplation.

Rachel left the living room. She went into the kitchen and opened the door to the basement stairs. She touched the light switch before she remembered that it was broken. They had been making do with the other light switch, the one at the foot of the stairs. The light from the kitchen cast a faint illumination in patches high on the opposite wall of the basement, but the corners and the lower parts lay in complete darkness. She had never been afraid of darkness before, and almost turned back before it occurred to her that fearing shadows was a luxury: she had reality. She slowly descended the stairs, her ears alert for any sound. Quite clearly she heard Ed Joyce saying, "How the hell should I know about the God-damned papers? Half of them aren't even in English, for Christ's sake." It must be a trick of the pipes, she thought as she reached the bottom of the stairs. She switched on the light and quickly looked around.

The basement was the way it always was—crates of books, old trunks, broken bicycles, skis and ski poles, Dan's snowshoes still leaning in the corner. The pipes gave Trimble's high voice a sharp metallic tone. "I'll want to examine all of it anyway. It could be no more than a mess caused by the struggle. Or it could be the reason for it. Anything reported missing?"

"Just the kid," said Ed Joyce.

Rachel picked up one of the snowshoes, feeling the smooth worn ash of the frame and the tough rawhide of the netting. She stayed there a long time.

When she went upstairs they were gone—Ed Joyce, Trimble, the policeman, Ethel Dawkins. The tea tray had been returned to the kitchen counter and against the teapot was propped a note from Ed Joyce.

Dear Mrs. Monette, Thank you for your time and trouble. We are putting a tap on your telephone so we can record any possible ransom call. Try and get some sleep. Yours faithfully,

E. Joyce

In the living room Rachel found Andy Monteith asleep on the couch, one arm shielding his eyes from the light. Rachel threw a mohair blanket over Andy and shut off all the lights. She went to the window and looked at the night sky. The moon was almost full, and very bright. How could anyone ever think it was made of green cheese? It was cold hard stone, she could see it with her own eyes.

4

Some time before dawn Rachel heard the muffled thump of a closing car door. Under the street lamp she saw her father's silver Cadillac, and her father inspecting the doors to make sure they were locked.

"Oh, Rachie," he said when she let him in the house. Tears welled up in his eyes as he took her in his arms. "Poor, poor Rachie." Even in her slippers Rachel could look down on her father's head and notice the careful way he combed his hair to hide the expanding baldness. He snuffled on her shoulder for a while, quieted, and then a thought brought on a fresh wave of emotion and he said in a choked voice, "You're too young for this. I was fifty-two when we lost your mother and even at that age I couldn't cope. I still can't, Rachie."

She wasn't surprised. Except in business, coping had never been his strong suit. Away from the office Jack Bernstein was a man who cried easily and not always with great significance. To avoid waking Andy in the living room, or having to sit in the study, Rachel led her father to the kitchen and sat him at the table.

"Coffee, Dad?"

"It doesn't matter. A glass of milk maybe, two percent if

34

you've got it." She set the milk and a plate of Mrs. Dawkins's cookies on the table. He wore a red silk tie, a white silk shirt, and a hand-tailored pinstripe suit that seemed too big for him. Once a burly man, her father had begun to shrink inside his skin.

"Eat something, Rachie."

"I'm not hungry."

"You've got to eat. Regardless."

"Not now." She said it more sharply than she had intended. They sat in silence. After a while he took from his back pocket a red silk handkerchief cut from the same material as his tie and blew his nose.

"What do the police say?"

"Wait for a ransom note."

"I meant about the—about Dan."

Rachel shook her head. "What difference does it make now? It's only important if it leads to Adam."

Her father folded the handkerchief and replaced it in his pocket. "No rabbi would ever do a thing like that."

"Oh, shit, Dad."

"What did I say, for Christ's sake? Rachie?"

Rachel went to the bathroom to get away for a few minutes. She spent them in a sort of trance in front of the mirror, staring deeply into the reflection of her dark eyes. The reflected eyes stared back at hers, but neither pair was seeing anything. She jumped at a knock at the door.

"Rachie? You all right?" said her father.

"Yes."

"I'm sorry. For whatever it was, I'm sorry."

"Forget it, Dad."

When she returned to the kitchen her father was asleep at the kitchen table, his head in his arms. Rachel turned off the light.

In the morning Ed Joyce telephoned. He was one of those people who hold the perforated speaker against the side of the face, and Rachel could barely hear him.

"Mrs. Monette? You get some sleep last night?"

"No."

"You should. Listen, we've got what might be a lead on the boy. An insurance man from Putney, who was driving north on seven, says he saw a man and a boy walking through the fields behind the school, going toward the highway. He figures this was some time between twelve fifteen and twelve thirty. He's certain that the man was not wearing a robe. He doesn't think he had a beard either. But he only had a glance at them. Two glances really. When he looked the second time, just before he went around the corner, the man was carrying the boy. He also noticed that the man had some kind of small suitcase or attaché case. He remembers it because he thought the man was having trouble carrying the case and the boy both."

"Meaning what?"

"Meaning it was hard walking in the deep snow, or maybe the boy was making it hard."

"Does it matter?"

"I don't understand you, Mrs. Monette."

"Does it matter whether Adam was struggling? In terms of finding him?"

"Well, if he was a bit older resistance can be a factor. A two-sided one. It can lead to escape, or . . . or it might not. But at his age I don't think it matters, no. Anyway, we have a feeling the man had a car waiting. The insurance guy thinks he saw a black car parked by the side of the road. He didn't notice if anyone was in it. We've sent out a six-state bulletin on the car. It's a little late, but you never know." He paused, waiting for her to say something. "I'll keep in touch, Mrs. Monette. And try to keep your line open."

"Mr. Joyce?"

"Yes."

"Do you really think a murderer would risk making ransom demands?"

There was a silence before the chief replied, "It's happened, Mrs. Monette. You never know."

When Rachel went into the kitchen to make breakfast

she found Andy there scrambling eggs. He glanced at her in what she thought seemed a normal way. Everyone else was trying to peer into her soul, to measure the pain inside.

"Garth seems better today, Rachel," he said. "I took him for a walk. By the end of it he was even chasing squirrels."

"Back to his old self already?"

"Not quite." With a sure-handed economy of movement he chopped scallions into thin discs and stirred them in with the eggs. "But dogs don't live very long; I guess they've got to telescope everything."

"That's one way of looking at dog behavior." Rachel poured herself a cup of coffee and sat down. It tasted hot and bitter. She realized she had made it the night of the party. "Sometimes people don't live very long either," she said.

"I know," Andy replied quietly. He cut four slices from a loaf of rye and put them in the toaster.

"While we were out I saw Tom Dawkins. Garth tried to bite him, by the way. Evidently someone, it must have been someone who was at the party, called the FBI man and told him about the conversation that night. The guy actually went to Dawkins's house and questioned him about it. Dawkins told him that improper French syntax constituted justification for assault perhaps, but not for murder. Dawkins was livid. Apparently the FBI man wanted to take him to the station until Joyce intervened."

"That's funny," Rachel said. Some other time she might have laughed. But all the same, something in Andy's tone prevented the story from upsetting her.

Jack Bernstein entered the kitchen. Bruised circles had settled under his eyes and thin strands of hair hung over his ears, exposing the hairlessness on top.

"I just spoke to the office," he said. "I used the car phone to keep the house one free. I've got to go back to the city. There's no getting out of it." He waited for Rachel to say it was all right. She didn't. "I'll be back for the funeral," he added, stepping forward to embrace her. She thought he was going to cry again, but Andy's presence restrained him.

"When is it going to be?" he asked. "I don't know much about these things." He meant as they are handled in non-Jewish families.

"I haven't thought about it," Rachel said. "I'll let you know."

"Hadn't you better notify his folks?" Andy asked.

"Dan was brought up by an aunt in Boston. His mother's dead and his father lives somewhere in the south of France. I don't think Dan has—Dan saw him in the last twenty years."

"Still," said her father, "it's the right thing to do."

Rachel agreed. Her father kissed her and simultaneously pressed something into her hand: a folded stack of hundred-dollar bills.

"I don't need this." She looked at him and saw how much he wanted her to have it. "Goodbye, Dad," she said. He nodded his head at Andy and went away.

Rachel climbed the stairs to the study. It looked the way it always did. Books were on shelves, files were in cabinets, and no bodies were on the floor. Rachel opened one of the desk drawers and removed Dan's address book. Beside it lay an old snapshot of her undergraduate self about to throw a snowball and laughing with pleasure.

In the address book she found the entry she was searching for and copied it on a clean sheet of paper: Xavier Monette, rue de St. Jean-Baptiste, Orange, France. She lifted the telephone receiver and dialed Western Union.

5

There had not been a night in forty years when Simon Calvi slept more than five or six hours. In his youth he remembered sleeping until nine or ten o'clock; had he even on a Sunday sometimes lain in bed till noon? But that was forty years ago, and since then there had been armies and ghettos, a great war and a migration, a little war, and another and another. Israelis have no time to waste, not even in bed.

Calvi slipped quietly from the sheets, leaving Gisela undisturbed. All her friends on the kibbutz called her Sooki, she told him, but he couldn't bring himself to do it. It was a pet's name, and not an especially good one. Anyway, she had no friends, none that he had seen in the two months since they had met. She seemed to cut her ties to the kibbutz when she moved in with him.

Gently Calvi brushed aside the blond hair that had spilled across her face during the night. It was a face which bore little resemblance to the one she wore awake. They could almost have belonged to two different people. In sleep it was heavy and inert; it required wakeful energy to make it younger, and transform the excess flesh into something sensual. But in its peacefulness he preferred it. She slept deeply: she was German, not Israeli.

In the bathroom Calvi washed what needed washing: a splash of cold water in each armpit, one to the groin. It had nothing to do with any Spartan sense of self-denial—the water heater was broken. He soaped the cold damp skin, then rinsed until his feet felt how wet the floor was. The sink, a small target, had captured little of the deluge. That many of the hairs he saw in it were white still surprised him, but in the mirror his muscular chest and broad shoulders were reassuring. Some people went gray prematurely. It didn't mean anything.

How marvellous the Americans were when it came to the science of razor blades, he thought. For hundreds of years the field had been dormant, caught in the grip of a dark age. Suddenly new designs were in the drugstores every week. The one Calvi used this morning to remove his dark beard was particularly ingenious. It did its cutting with two parallel steel blades, mounted in a piece of plastic that was shaped like a prop from a film about the twenty-third century. This two-blade configuration worked very cleverly. The first blade made a neat incision in the skin; the second handled the flaying. Why did he bother with this rite? Even on a good day it was only a matter of hours before the persistent little hairs sprouted once more through the skin and cast his jaw in shadow.

February mornings in Jerusalem can be raw, but Calvi loved the little walled garden that lay behind his villa in the old suburb of Rehavia, and unless it was raining he drank his coffee there, and read the papers.

Because the villa sat on a gentle slope he had a view of the Old City to the east. Until recently it had been an unobstructed view, but now, like growths that were somehow sterile and malignant at the same time, modern towers eclipsed segments of the old limestone town. If the apartment blocks had stood there when David first came he would have turned away and we wouldn't be in this mess, Calvi thought.

But his garden was serene. He had a grapevine creeping over the end wall, he had dark brown irises growing by the villa, he had a comfortable chaise longue to recline in while he read. He also had his picture on the third page of the *Jerusalem Post*.

It was not a bad photograph. It showed him on his feet in the Knesset, right hand in the air, forefinger extended, head thrust forward: pugnacious. Whatever point he was making did not amuse his colleagues. The ones seated near him in the photograph stared straight ahead, their mouths set.

An accompanying editorial took a similar position: THE SEPHARDIC MOVEMENT: THE ENEMY WITHIN? "No one," it went on to say, "questions for a moment the integrity or the commitment to Israel of Simon Calvi, one of the leading spokesmen for the Sephardic and Oriental Jews since the fifties. And few quarrel with his argument that the Ashkenazim, or European Jews, have long enjoyed an economic ascendancy over the Sephardim. There are serious social and economic problems here which must be dealt with and are being dealt with, if at a speed too slow for men like Mr. Calvi. But, to say, as he has been recently saying, that it is government policy to keep the Sephardim in a state of second-class citizenship is to ignore two decades of government attempts to establish equality. And to bandy about terms like cultural genocide and Sephardi Power is to drive a wedge into the heart of Israel.

"Negotiations are under way to determine our borders, at a moment in history when the Arabs have never been stronger. Do they need Mr. Calvi to make them stronger still?

"Mr. Calvi said yesterday in the Knesset that an Israel which is middle eastern in behavior and outlook may have more success in negotiating with the Arabs than an Israel that acts like a western nation. Has he forgotten already what his own life was like in the mellahs of Morocco? In Morocco he was a Jew, a second-class person often living in fear. In Israel he is a citizen enjoying the full protection of the law. Yes, many of his fellow Moroccan Jews are poor, but there is opportunity here. Does not Mr. Calvi himself sit in the Knesset?"

Simon Calvi sipped the sweet black coffee. One success cancels a thousand wasted lives. He had read an article in an American magazine about something called the black man in a Cadillac syndrome. It was an argument that only the haves found convincing. Calvi knew that his followers couldn't be bought with someone else's Cadillac. The *Post* editorial preached to the converted. His troubles would come from other sources.

The complaining squeaks of a rusting bicycle made Calvi look up from the newspaper. The height of his garden wall hid the bicycle itself, but not the head of the approaching rider—his speech writer, executive assistant, and friend, Moses Cohn. Somehow in the soft but very clear golden light of the early Jerusalem morning Moses Cohn's face seemed much closer than it really was, as if Calvi had the aid of a telephoto lens. He knew that Cohn must still be almost a block away, and yet he fancied he could see the details of the thin face, the strong straight nose, the russet hair, the strong tendons which underlay the taut cheeks, the incisive mouth, the intelligent blue eyes. Perhaps this heightened visual sense was brought on by a subconscious reaction to the editorial, Calvi thought. But when Cohn had pulled the bicycle through the old iron gate and sat down Calvi saw that there was more to it. The image itself was radiating an overabundance of visual data—of color, of tension, even of violence, Calvi thought. He could see it in the flushed spots on the pale skin, and the movements of the wiry neck.

"Coffee?" Calvi asked. Long ago he had learned patience. He poured some into his own cup and handed it to Cohn. Cohn drank some, put the cup on the grass, and pinched the bridge of his nose, hard; the kind of pinch that drives out demons. He looked at Calvi in an odd way, almost, Calvi thought, as if he were trying to see him totally anew, as if they hadn't known each other for twenty years.

"Do you know a man named Grunberg?" Cohn asked finally.

"I don't think so. Why?"

"Major Grunberg."

Calvi waited. A fat red-eyed pigeon landed heavily in the garden and began to peck among the flowers, its head, neck, and breast pumping in a grotesque modern dance.

"He's with Army Intelligence. So he told me about an hour ago. Very efficient fellow. Managed to enter the apartment without waking any of us. No need to worry about the knock at the door. Just wait for the tap on the shoulder while you're sleeping." His fury had knotted the sinewy muscles in his forearms. "To get away from that sort of barbarity is why I came here." The Hebrew gutturals tore at his throat.

"What did he want?"

"I don't know."

"Well, what did he say, Moses?" Calvi asked, more aggressively than he had intended. It was the wrong way to get information from Moses Cohn. Cohn made that very point by suddenly noticing that the pant legs of his old gray flannels were still rolled up for bicycling. Giving the matter all his attention he carefully rolled them down, smoothed out the wrinkles and gave each leg a quick shake. He'd been bullied once already, he wouldn't allow it again.

"Maybe he dropped a few hints, at least." Calvi was a politician after all and knew how to give ground.

Cohn allowed a little smile to move across his face, like a ray of light, but when it had passed he looked worried.

"He asked a lot of questions about you."

"What kind of questions?"

"Questions," Cohn snapped. He was very angry. "How long I had known you. How we got together. That sort of thing. He sat right there on the bed, with Sarah and me still in it, under the covers. It was humiliating: worse than being taken into the back room."

Calvi knew the comparison was not accidental. The British had interrogated Cohn twice during the dying days of the mandate. The little man was a member of the Irgun and could have told them a lot. But he didn't. Perhaps it was more humiliating when it came from one of your own.

"So?" Calvi prodded.

"So I told Grunberg how we got together. What is there to hide?"

"What did you say exactly?"

Cohn made an impatient gesture. "That I was working on the settlement program for new immigrants. That you were an immigrant with a bit of money who was interested in politics. What kind of politics, Grunberg wanted to know. I didn't understand what he meant. So he read me something from an interview you gave in the late fifties: you said that immigrants should be assimilated into a western life-style as soon as possible. Do you see? Then he asked me about the rally in Tel Aviv last month. Did you really say that the Oriental Jews have more in common with Arabs than they do with the European Jews? Did you really say that the survival of Israel lies to the east, not the west? So, what are you getting at, I asked him. It's a matter of public record. He agreed. It's public record."

In the sky a cold west wind was pushing a dark cover of cloud over the city. The sunlight shone on the leading edge of the cloud like a gold vein in a coal mine. Calvi blew on his fingertips. It was going to snow.

"He wanted to know if I agreed with everything you said."

Calvi looked up sharply. Cohn returned the look.

"I told him yes, so don't get nervous."

"It's not a question of that. Why should he know about our internal business, that's all I'm saying."

Cohn looked thoughtful. "Why indeed?"

Calvi reached inside his shirt pocket for one of the fat

short cigars he liked to smoke. He was trying to cut down to two a day, one after lunch, one after dinner. But he felt like one now. He struck a cardboard match and said around the cigar:

"Was that all?"

"Almost. He asked a few questions about your life in Morocco. I told him I know little about it. It's true."

"How little?"

"You come from Fez. You lived in the mellah. Your ancestors came from Spain. You left Morocco after the war. So did two hundred thousand others."

"So we did." He puffed on his cigar and glanced at Cohn to see if he was listening. "We landed in Haifa on a hot day in August. They put us into trucks, about a hundred of us, right at the docks, and drove us into the Negev. By the time we arrived it was almost dark. A little village of huts had been thrown together. Okay, everybody out, they said. Here's your new home. Happy farming. We looked at the rocks and the sand. We stayed where we were. So they fired a few shots in the air, and someone yelled it was an Arab attack, take shelter. We ran and hid in the huts. The trucks drove away. The next morning we divided the land and began to plow."

Cohn appeared unmoved by the story. His eyes were far away, on the Old City. The clouds had hidden West Jerusalem in an obscure gloom, but they had yet to cover the Old City. By an accident of light and shade the centuries were rolled back like cheap rugs, and the walled city seemed more than a tourist attraction. But in a moment the vision was gone, and the golden Dome of the Rock looked once again like gold paint, and the limestone towers, churches, and synagogues like rubble.

Calvi realized that he had probaby recounted the whole episode before, perhaps even in a speech somewhere; a speech written by Moses Cohn. And he realized too that this time he had told the story with no real bitterness. No sense pretending: he had been so grateful to be in Israel he would have happily planted apple trees in granite.

Cohn had been the radical in those days, a European socialist who believed in the impossibility of comparing cultures. Therefore no one could be superior to another. Just different. Did Cohn regret the political tutoring he had given him? He could see it on his face, feel it in the tension between them. They were like a married couple growing apart: united only by a contract and the accumulation of common property.

Cohn's clear blue eyes looked closely at Calvi. "What's behind Grunberg's heavy-handed little visit, Simon? Why this pressure?"

Before Calvi could answer the rear door of the house opened.

"Oh, I'm sorry," Gisela said. "I didn't realize you had a visitor."

For one who had been in the country for less than a year her Hebrew was excellent, but neither man paid much attention to her speech. She wasn't wearing any clothes. She showed no trace of embarrassment, although she and Cohn had never met. No haute couturier would look twice at her body, but other men would. It was unfashionably heavy, especially in the hips and legs, but still retained remnants of the springy underpinning of nubility. With old-fashioned politeness Cohn looked away.

"Do you want breakfast?" she said.

"Breakfast?" Calvi asked Cohn.

"I really haven't the time this morning. But thank you."

"He can't stay," Calvi said to Gisela. In some way her nakedness required him to become an intermediary in the conversation. "But I'd like something, please." Gisela turned and disappeared in the house.

"British?" Cohn asked.

"German. They are rather easy to attract in this country, you know. It must be some form of restitution." Instantly he regretted the facetiousness of his remark. He felt more for Gisela than that.

"It doesn't bother you?"

"Why should it?" His cigar had gone out and he relit it. "She wasn't even born during the war."

Cohn shook his head, the way faithful married men often do at their bachelor friends. Especially bachelor friends who are pushing sixty. He rolled up his pant legs and remounted his bicycle.

"I'm going to tell Grunberg all about this," he called over his shoulder as he rode away. "Now you've gone too far."

Calvi laughed and turned to the newspapers. Politicians read the news avidly, the way actors read theatrical reviews. Calvi was not aware of the first few snowflakes that drifted through the trees into the garden, melting as they touched the ground. He scarcely noticed Gisela return, dressed in old jeans and a woolen sweater and carrying a breakfast tray. Politics are serious in Israel and the word *crisis* means what the dictionary says it does. Gisela sat beside him eating her breakfast. After a while she ate his, too. When she felt cold she went inside to do the dishes, or at least to stack them in the sink.

Because he read each paper from beginning to end it was some time before Simon Calvi reached the classified page of the *International Herald Tribune*. Among the personals his eye caught a brief notice addressed to Walter D. In his armpits the pores opened suddenly.

"Walter D. Did you get my present? Marie."

He went quickly into the house, into the little study on the ground floor, and locked the door. Taking a French edition of *Crime and Punishment* from the shelves he sat at the desk and began marking numbers on a sheet of paper.

Walter D. was meaningless. It was just to get his attention. He began with *did*. *D* was twenty, page twenty, fourth word, first letter. *I* was forty-five, ninth word. *D* again. It was an elementary code. All you needed was the right edition of the right book.

6

Simon Calvi stood near the Damascus Gate wishing he weren't. It wasn't the cold, he had been cold before, many times. It wasn't the night, night didn't bother him either. Perhaps it was age. He had never been old before. He knew he wasn't going to like it.

He looked up at the crenellated wall that topped the gate. The half moon was doing a terrific lighting job on the old stones, cutting centuries off their age. No Hollywood director with all his fancy filters could have done better work for his fading star. In the pale light Calvi could almost see a real fort, with Crusaders lurking behind the wall getting ready to shoot their arrows through the slits. In the daytime it would be a Crusader's dream come true from up there: the square packed with peddlers, beggars, tourists, housewives, and donkeys, like the cast and crew of *The Ten Commandments* on a break. Now Calvi had the place to himself, except for an emaciated old Arab sleeping behind his felafel stand.

Calvi sank deeper into his fleece-lined duffel coat. A muezzin, in a dyspeptic voice that told listeners it was just a job, and not a very good one, began singing the last call to prayer. The scratchy notes heralded the arrival of two soldiers who came through the gate quite suddenly, Uzi submachine guns slung over their shoulders. Groggily the old Arab got to his feet and stood behind the pile of dirty orange crates that served as his stand, his eyes on nothing. From a distance of thirty or forty feet the soldiers gave Calvi a careful look. Indifferently he turned his back on them and slowly walked over to the felafel stand. He felt the soldiers' eyes on his back while he asked the old man in Arabic if he had anything left to sell. The old man had white cataract smears on both eyes. He reached into a crate and pulled out a little lump wrapped in shreds of greasy newspaper. Calvi dropped a coin into the man's hand and forced himself to bite off a piece and chew it. He heard the soldiers start walking away, their heavy boots making hard sounds on the unyielding stone.

When he turned around, they were gone. Around to the Jaffa Gate and back inside the walls, he reckoned. They probably patrolled the Old City quarter by quarter. He tossed the remains of the felafel away and resumed his position near the gate. It was hard to feel inconspicuous when your face was in the morning paper.

Calvi heard the old man mutter something and saw him walk stiffly into the square to retrieve the felafel. He returned to his stand, wrapped it in another tatter of newspaper and tucked it out of sight. Calvi leaned against the wall and thought about the trouble between the Arabs and the Jews.

From the Nablus Road came the rough sound of a car motor that needed tuning. Calvi looked north and saw the approaching headlights. Slowly a dusty, dark-colored Volkswagen entered the square and swept around the perimeter until its beams fastened on Calvi by the wall. Then the lights were shut off and the motor cut. It was very quiet. The old man slept on the stones.

Calvi waited for a minute before he walked across the square to the car. He opened the passenger door and sat inside. Immediately the car began a startling high-pitched buzzing. The driver turned to Calvi and said, "Seat belt." He said it in English but the barely detectable lilt came from Germany, perhaps Austria. Calvi, a polyglot, knew accents.

Calvi fumbled with the mechanism but could not manage it. He had never fastened a seat belt in his life, except in airplanes, and this seemed far more complex.

"God in heaven," said the driver with some impatience as he switched on the interior light. Calvi thought it a mild oath when he saw the face it came out of. A face enormously broad, with a thick sweeping bony crescent of brow, two slabs of cheeks and a nose like a redoubt between them. The blond hair was thinning, the blue eyes were somewhat wide and in the mouth the teeth that weren't missing didn't match.

The blond man leaned across Calvi's body and reached for the seat belt. Calvi had never seen a thicker wrist, and the nylon fabric of his cheap jacket stretched tautly across his back. Not until the blond man had finished with the seat belt and sat straight did Calvi notice how close to the floor pedals the seat was pushed. The blond man could not have been more than a few inches over five feet. Standing, Calvi imagined, he would look like a being adapted to a much more massive planet than earth. Here he was in the wrong place. The thought was restorative.

"You're late," Calvi said.

In answer the blond man started the motor and turned the car south, toward Mount Zion. He drove like a good citizen, obeying all the lights and signals and staying under the speed limit. Calvi patted his pockets until he found the one that held his cigars, and lit one, dropping the match on the floor. He drew smoke into his mouth and forced it out through his nose. The sting in his sinuses brought tears to his eyes. Despite the cold the blond man lowered his window two or three inches.

Outside the city, on the road to Beersheba, the blond

man began to drive faster. At first there was a little traffic, but after the Bethlehem turn-off none. In the Judean hills the blond man pressed further on the accelerator, and Calvi knew that no Volkswagen could go so fast.

"What sort of motor have you got in this thing?" he asked.

"Porsche." The blond man spoke the word as if it were the name of his baby daughter.

Calvi twisted around to see the back seat. There was no back seat; in its stead a thin metal casing had been hastily banged into place to hide the hypertrophied engine. He listened to the sounds of the spinning steel. It wasn't out of tune at all, not in the sense he had thought at first.

Calvi stared out the window as they climbed through the olive groves of Judea. The dusty leaves were silver foil in the moonlight. Calvi tried to play back in his mind the arrival of the Volkswagen at the Damascus Gate, and in this review he saw what his eyes had seen the first time, but his mind had missed: the very wide, very deep-tread tires of the car. He wondered now where they were going.

Ahead Calvi thought he could make out the round dark shapes of the bare hills of Gush Etzion. Two kibbutzim were sheltered in those hills, populated in part by descendants of the two hundred and forty Jews who had been killed on the same site in the '48 war. Fourteen, Calvi remembered, had blown themselves up in their armored car rather than be taken by the Arab Legion. In the end even the trees had been uprooted by the Arabs. It made the present inhabitants determined.

With a quick movement the blond man switched off the headlights, and slowed the car by half. He put his face almost against the windshield, squinting ahead. In the distance Calvi thought he saw a light, but he could no longer trust his eyes for that sort of thing. The blond man braked the car to a creep, and began peering into the vineyards that bordered the side of the elevated road bed. Then, with a suddenness that caught Calvi by surprise he jerked the wheel, and sent the car flying off the road. They landed with a sickening jolt that cracked the top of Calvi's head against the roof. He felt thankful for the seat belt.

The blond man drove the car in a quick circle, snapping the vine stocks beneath. He parked at the foot of the embankment which supported the road, and switched off the engine. The vines would not afford much cover at this time of year, Calvi thought. He's counting on the superior elevation of the road. But Calvi was certain the top of the car would show.

Calvi rubbed the top of his head, and realized that his mouth had a death grip on the cigar. As he puffed it back to life he felt the muscles of the blond man stiffen. Calvi too saw it—a point, no, two points of light in the south.

The blond man turned to Calvi to show him that he had his finger over his lips. Then he did something that Calvi did not like at all: with his short broad fingers he took the cigar from Calvi's mouth and put it in the ashtray. Calvi started to protest.

"Silence," the blond man hissed.

They waited. Calvi tried to think of a credible explanation for why he was sitting in a vineyard in the middle of the night with a man whose name he didn't know. He couldn't. They watched the headlights bob up and down and sometimes slip out of sight as they moved through the hills. In about two minutes they were very close, although it seemed much longer to Calvi. He heard the throb of the engine, and mixed into that sound a metallic rattle of the kind a jeep frame might make. The yellow beams illuminated the vineyard behind them, and Calvi saw how bare it looked. For a very long moment the light flowed into the Volkswagen showing Calvi the beads of sweat on the blond man's upper lip. From six feet away the din hit their ears, the pounding pistons and the high-pitched wail of eroding rubber and asphalt. Then the Doppler effect bent the noise like a blue note and it was gone, leaving a wake of noxious fumes.

"Dear God," said the blond man softly. But he made no

move to start the car. A dark green gecko ran along the windshield, stopped, dipped up and down a few times like a push-up fanatic, and rested motionless, its reptilian feet clinging to the glass.

From very near Calvi was surprised by the faint susurrus of slow rolling tires on the road, followed by the almost undetectable purr of a lovingly treated engine. No headlights this time, no rattle. It went by like a ghost. The blond man checked the luminous dial of his wristwatch and waited exactly two minutes before he started the car. He was very good.

Before they reached Beersheba the blond man turned the car off the road, and barely slackening speed, using only the light of the moon, he began to maneuver across the rock and sand of the Negev. At first the way was very bumpy. Rocks, some big and unyielding, struck at the axles. Wiry bushes clung to the bumpers. Occasionally the fat tires lost traction in drifts of soft sand, but the blond man always slid through. Finally he found the hard-packed bed of a *wadi* winding south, and he followed it. In the distance Calvi could see the dark shape of a massive plateau rising straight off the desert floor. He had been a soldier, he had learned the soldier's art of falling instantly to sleep when there was nothing to be done. He slept.

When he awoke the moon had gone down. He could see little except the profile of the blond man, sickly green in the light from the instrument panel. Again they were on very uneven ground and the lines of strain on the blond man's forehead were etched in a deeper green. As his eyes adjusted, Calvi saw that they were beginning the climb up the massif. Around him loomed hulking twisted rocks; robbed of their yellows and pinks and browns by the night, they took on the shadowy shapes of the prehistoric monsters that once walked the earth. He guessed that they had entered the land that had made the Hebrews so fed up with Moses on the trek to the Promised Land. Cohn had told him Isaiah's description when they had toured the area once in the fifties. Cohn liked to take him on little educational trips and his hobby, which he admitted was somewhat nostalgic, was the geography of the Bible. Isaiah had called the place "a land of trouble and anguish, from whence came the young and old lion, the viper and fiery flying serpent." Calvi saw no sign of the fauna but he didn't quarrel with the first part.

The climb was very slow. Several times rocks as tall as trees forced them to backtrack. During one stretch they crept along the edge of a deep gorge. Calvi could feel the cold wind rising in a steady current from the dark and arid plain below. One of the rear tires slipped off the sand, and it spun wildly over the abyss before the blond man could fight the car back to safety.

Calvi guessed that they had climbed only a few hundred feet when the blond man stopped the car and peered at the solid rock wall that rose to his left. He took a flashlight from under his seat and got out of the car. Calvi saw that he was even shorter than he had guessed. With his hand over the lens like a visor, the blond man shone the light for two or three seconds at a time at different sections of the rock. Calvi saw nothing but a shadow that might indicate an indentation further up. The blond man returned to the car and drove on.

When they reached the shadow in the wall the blond man stopped the car and turned off the ignition. He motioned for Calvi to get out. Calvi unfastened the seat belt—in this respect it resembled those on airplanes—climbed out and closed the door quietly.

There was no sound except the faint brushing of the wind in the whorls of his ears. The cold dry air sharpened his senses. He walked softly to the indentation in the rock face. Only when he stood right before it could he see that it was not an indentation but a narrow natural passage through the thick stone wall. At the end of the utterly black corridor he could see the deep grays of open space. He walked through.

He supposed that he had entered a small boxed canyon.

On all sides he felt the vertical presence of the cliffs. He had taken two steps inside when he sensed a man behind him. He whirled, and faced a robed Bedouin, as tall as he, but not as broad. In one motion Calvi crouched and turned sideways, watching for a knife. But the Bedouin reached out his hand, and gently touched Calvi on the upper arm. Calvi relaxed slightly, and the Bedouin ran his hand softly over his arm, under it, down the side, the leg, the inside of the leg, the other side. How careless, Calvi thought. If guns were a worry the blond man should have searched him long before.

He took a cigar from his coat pocket. To hell with these people. He struck a match, and in the glow of the light saw the rifle held loosely in one hand, the bandoliers that formed an X across the man's chest, and the *keffiyeh* pulled across the lower half of the face against the wind. But above the keffiyeh, the face, although dark, looked soft, very soft for a Bedouin. And between the keffiyeh and the round neck of the robe Calvi saw the starched beige collars of a uniform. Why are they taking such chances, Calvi asked himself. Angrily the man leaned forward and blew out the match.

The hand that had been so gentle turned Calvi with surprising strength toward the end of the canyon. There in the shadow of the wall he thought he could make out the darker patch of a Bedouin tent. The hot red embers of the cigar end gave him comfort. He knew he would see the Captain tonight. It had been a long time.

As they reached Jerusalem dawn was bringing out all the right colors in the limestone. The stones that lay on the ground were ready to be chipped and shaped and piled on top of each other in buildings and walls; the ones already in piles were falling down. The battle against rubble had been fought for three thousand years, but no one was winning.

The blond man dropped him at the Jaffa Gate, under David's Tower, and drove away without a word. Calvi gazed at the tower, making sure he had memorized the license number of the car. It wasn't much of a tower—a stunted cylinder like a primitively sculpted rook. David had had nothing to do with it. It was a good place for the staging of sound and light shows in English, French, and Hebrew. David had nothing to do with them either.

Calvi walked west, into the new town. An old man was hosing the part of the sidewalk that he borrowed from the city for his outdoor café. The chairs were stacked on the tables, upside down, and there were no customers. The water ran across the sidewalk and sluiced along the street, moving a cargo of torn wrappers, yesterday's papers, used cinema tickets, banana skins, dust, and dirt. The water swept everything along its course, except a few mounds of donkey excrement which refused to budge. Calvi took a chair off one of the tables and sat down.

The old man laid down the hose and went inside the café. In a few moments the water came out of the hose in one last gurgle, and stopped. The old man returned.

"Yes?" he said. He had taken the trouble to wrap himself in a clean white apron.

"Coffee, please," Calvi said. "Black and strong."

"A little sugar, maybe?" the old man asked.

Calvi looked up. The old man's eyes were very clear and very blue. He was probably no older than Calvi himself.

"Yes. Sugar."

The old man disappeared into the café, and Calvi heard the sucking sounds of the coffee machine. He came back carrying a tin tray. With hands that shook slightly he carefully arranged the cup and saucer, sugar, spoon, and paper napkin on the table. When he reached forward his white shirt sleeve slid up his forearm and Calvi saw the tattoo, bluer than any vein. S4106. Many people in this town could tell from that the name of the camp and the week he had arrived, but Calvi wasn't one of them.

He drank his coffee but he forgot about the sugar.

As he felt in an inner pocket for his wallet he touched the folded sheets of paper. He hadn't read them yet, but he knew they bore a letter from a girl named Marie to a man named Walter D.

He also knew that after the letter had been translated into the language of *Crime and Punishment* it would become a speech calling on the Oriental Jews of Israel to stage a general two-hour work shut-down one afternoon in early April. In an age when workers set fire to their factories it sounded like kid stuff.

Simon Calvi told himself that a few times but it didn't help.

From the soft fragrant breezes that drifted lightly through the pine trees in the cemetery and the dirty crusted snow that lay melting slowly by the gravestones, Rachel knew that winter was ending. They stood around a hole in the wet ground—her father, Andy Monteith, the Dawkinses, the bearded Henry Gates from European history, the college chaplain, Rachel. The sun shone warmly, making up for lost time.

The service was nonsectarian. There was little to say but the chaplain stretched it to a suitable ceremonial length. He wore a well-cut suit of thick black-and-gray tweed, and black wing-tip shoes of richly shining leather. He was perfectly turned out except that he had forgotten his rubbers, and the damp grass was getting the tops of his shoes wet. From time to time he rubbed them against the backs of his pant legs, standing like a stork while he gave his version of the meaning of life and death. He said something about contributions and something about loss, but Rachel wasn't really listening. She was watching a robin sitting on a nearby gravestone watching her. At her side her father dabbed at his eyes with the sleeve of his vicuna coat. It was unlike him to forget a handkerchief. Perhaps he did not want to bother digging it out.

After a while she heard a change in the tone of the chaplain's voice and she sensed that things were winding up. Two men wearing down vests stepped forward and lowered the box into the hole with ropes. When they had it down one of the ropes would not come free, and the man had to tug at it carefully, the way one does with a snagged fishing line. An old New Englander with a runny nose tossed in a shovelful of earth. Because it was wet it landed on the wood with a heavy plop. That sound was what Rachel remembered best from the funeral.

As they walked slowly, funereally she supposed, along the path that led to the cemetery gate, Rachel saw a tall man carrying a small suitcase. He was coming their way, striding quickly in a loose-jointed manner that was so close to Dan's that it made her heart race. As he drew nearer she realized that he was a much older man. The skin of his thin face was a deeply weathered red-brown leather, and contrasted strangely with his hair, which was as white as chalk dust and fine as a baby's. But the shape of the face resembled Dan's—the long firm jaw line, the prominent cheekbones, the determined mouth. At the same time it was very different—more Gallic she thought, the nose more prominent, the whole structure not so used to what? To laughing? And the eyes, observant and clear walnut-brown like Dan's, but far more experienced. Maybe that's what aging does.

"Ah, no," he said, addressing his remarks to Tom Dawkins, oldest in the party, "I am not too late?" His faint French accent went well with his musical voice.

"You're Dan's father?" Dawkins asked, and in his words, following directly on the other man's, Rachel heard more of Arkansas than she had in the past.

"Dan?" The tall man seemed puzzled. "Of course, yes. Daniel. He was called Dan in America?" He caught sight of the gravediggers and looked thoughtful for a moment.

"I'm very sorry, Mr. Monette. It's a bad time for all of us," Tom Dawkins said.

The tall man nodded his head. Dawkins held out his hand. Monette removed his from the pocket of his gray trench coat and clasped Dawkins's lightly and briefly in the French style.

Dawkins turned to Rachel. "I understand you never had a chance to meet Dan's wife Rachel." Rachel and Monette looked at each other. Rachel appreciated what a good organizer Dawkins was being, but she had no idea what to say. She wasn't even sure what to call him. Were they expected to embrace, she wondered.

Monette helped. "I hope I have not upset you by being late," he said to her.

"Oh, no."

"I found that this is not an easy place to reach," Monette said. He looked slowly around, taking in the scenery. "It must be pleasant in the summer."

"It is very pleasant," said the chaplain, perhaps a little stung. "In fact, in my opinion it much resembles the Vosges region of your own country."

Monette's brown eyes moved without haste from Rachel to the chaplain.

"Really?" he said. It wasn't a question.

"Where did you fly in? JFK?" Rachel's father wanted to know.

"Yes. I did."

"That's a shame. If I'd known I could have given you a lift up." He gestured to the long silver car outside the gate.

"Bad luck," said Monette.

She decided on his full name. "Xavier Monette," she said, "this is my father, Jack Bernstein." Again the hand emerged from the coat pocket and did its duty. Her father took the opportunity to develop Tom Dawkins's theme.

"What an awful time. Awful. And the police are getting nowhere. Fast. I'm losing all my respect for the FBI."

The others were beginning to move away. Rachel, her father, and her father-in-law walked toward the gate.

"In your telegram you said that the little boy was missing. Is there any word?"

"Not yet. I'm calling the police as soon as we get home."

"Then let us go, by all means."

The means they went by was Jack Bernstein's silver Cadillac, Jack driving, Rachel in front and Monette in back.

As they drove home Rachel saw that the whole town seemed to be shaking off its winter lethargy. People were shoveling the remaining snow off their lawns and onto the streets, and then poking doubtfully at the brown grass with various tools. She heard the sound of a baseball smacking into the deep pocket of a well-oiled glove. Baseball had been Dan's favorite sport. She would try to keep away from thoughts like that.

"What is the boy's name?" Monette asked from the back seat.

"Adam," she told him.

"That's a good name. I like biblical names."

"Me, too," said Jack Bernstein, twisting to look at Monette. "The Bible's full of them. Both testaments," he added. Rachel guessed that her father associated the name Xavier with Christianity but was not certain where it came from.

There was a quiet buzz and Rachel's father reached for the telephone receiver that hung below the dashboard.

"Hello." He listened for a few moments. "Listen, I can't talk to you now. I don't . . . No insurance? They must be crazy. Look. I'll call you tonight. Where will you be?" He put his fingers over the mouthpiece. "Rachie sweetheart, could you take down a number for me? There's paper and pencils in the glove compartment." She wrote down the number that he gave to her. It reminded her of her childhood. Jack Bernstein replaced the receiver and turned again to the back seat.

"I'm in frozen fish," he said. "It never stops."

"That's interesting," Monette replied. "I don't know very much about it."

"What line of work are you in, Mr. Monette, if I may ask?"

"I am retired," Monette said. "Before I was in the army."

"Dan told me Mr. Monette was with the Free French in North Africa," Rachel explained to her father.

"Is that so?" Jack Bernstein said. "You fought the Desert Fox?"

"In a very minor capacity."

"Did you see any action?"

"I was with General LeClerc," Monette said quietly.

"You're kidding. Were you part of that march from Lake Chad?"

"Yes."

"Don't tell me. January of forty-three. Am I right?"

"Yes."

Jack Bernstein shook his head in wonder at his own power of memory. "I know that stuff backwards and forwards. God knows I had plenty of time for reading the papers in those days." He glanced in the rearview mirror to see if Monette was paying attention. "I'm a navy man myself. Just for the war, of course. I volunteered for sub chaser duty, hoping to blow a few Nazis out of the water, but it didn't work out that way. I spent most of the war in Honolulu. The worst thing that happened to me was a bad case of athlete's foot. Spent a week in the hospital. That's the military for you. I guess it's the same all over." In the back Monette said nothing.

They were almost home when Rachel felt him lean forward and grip the top of the seat back.

"Would it be possible to make a slight alteration in plan?" he asked.

"Of course," she said.

"That is very kind. I would like very much to see something of my son's surroundings. You know that I last saw him when he was six years old. I really know little about him as an adult, how he lived and worked. Naturally his book has been much talked about at home, but that kind of thing is so . . . impersonal. Do you understand what I'm saying?"

Rachel turned to look at him. He seemed very intense and serious. "I think I do, Mr. Monette. What would you like us to do?"

He thought. "Perhaps he had an office that I could see?"

"Of course. Would you like to go there now?"

"If it is not too much trouble. You see, I haven't much time. I must leave tomorrow."

"Back to New York?" her father asked.

"Yes. I fly to Paris in the afternoon."

"Perfect. I can drive you down in the morning."

"You're very kind."

Rachel directed her father to the old brick mansion that contained the European history offices. Dan had spent very little time there, but she didn't think it necessary to tell him that. The father had a right to assemble his memories without her interference.

Dan's office was a large room on the third floor, overlooking a seedy tennis court that no one used. There was a wide bay window on one side. Dan had placed his desk in front of it. On it lay his pens, pencils, rulers, and erasers, neatly aligned and ready for action. The room seemed the same as she had seen it last, two, perhaps three weeks before. Along one wall were shelves of books, floor to ceiling. By another stood a line of gray metal file cabinets. On the third wall hung a large framed blown-up photograph of Chamberlain on his return from Munich. Monette looked at the photograph for a while and then turned to Rachel.

"It's a pretty room, isn't it?" he said. It had never struck Rachel that way.

"It's quiet," she said, choosing an aspect of the room she could approve with honesty.

Monette walked over to the old pine desk and ran his hand over it softly. He gazed out the window.

"You never know if you've done the right thing."

"No," Rachel said. She saw that he was rubbing his hand back and forth over the surface of the worn pine. "Why did you decide to send Dan over here when his mother died?" Rachel asked him quietly.

The hand stopped moving. Monette continued to face the window, his back to her. She heard him take a deep breath as though he would need extra oxygen to think about it.

"It was the most difficult thing I have had to do in my life," he said finally. "How can I explain it? It was only three years after the war when Margaret died. Daniel was a little boy. We lived in Paris then. We had no money. No one did, of course, but it meant I had to work all the time, and when I wasn't working I was looking for work. I worked as a waiter in Les Halles, I sold shirts in Faubourg St. Honoré, I delivered messages on a bicycle." He stopped talking and once more ran his hand along the desk.

"But in America people had money," he continued in a somewhat sharper tone. "When Margaret died, I assessed my potential for taking care of the little boy, and concluded that in the next few years at least it was very poor. I knew Margaret had a younger sister in America, of whom she was very fond. Angela."

"I know her."

Monette went on as if she had not spoken: "A married sister, husband a dentist, if I remember, no children. She was very happy to come and get him. In America he would have a better start, I thought. Then, when things were better . . ."

His voice trailed away. He continued to stare out the window.

"Stay here for a while if you like," Rachel said gently. "Come back to the house whenever you want. You can sleep in Adam's room."

"You are very considerate."

She gave him a key to the front door in case they went to bed before he arrived, and turned to leave.

"Oh, you'll need directions, won't you?" And she told him the way.

8

"My dear," said Dan's Aunt Angela when Rachel came into the house, "you'll just have to forgive me for skipping the funeral. I can't stand them and that's that." Angela put her arms around Rachel and hugged her tightly, patting her on the back without losing grip of the cigarette wedged between her fingers. And Rachel suddenly felt tears coming to her eyes, tears she could do nothing about, so they ran down her face and onto Angela's pink cashmere sweater. They didn't bother Angela. She kept patting.

Gradually Rachel became aware of the subtle scent of the perfume Angela wore: Angela always enveloped herself in her own atmosphere; she was a planet where the air always smelled of sandalwood, or myrrh. For a long time they both breathed it.

"Well, then, let's have a look at you," said Angela, and she pushed Rachel back to arm's length. Rachel never knew what to do with her face when people said they'd like to have a look at it, so she looked at Angela's. The same arched eyebrows, the same inquisitive blue eyes, the same rosy skin; the color of the hair changed, the jewelry changed, the clothes changed, but Angela didn't.

"You look god-awful," Angela said. "If you're going to be out of fashion at least do it aggressively. Come, I'll make you a drink. I'll bet you haven't had one since it happened. I know, I was the same when Henry died. I remember thinking that if I had a drink it would prove I hadn't loved him. Well, that's hooey."

Rachel smiled. "Okay, but first I've got to call the police station."

"I've done it already. Nothing to report. What a plodder that chief is." Angela saw the look in Rachel's face. "Maybe it's an asset in something like this."

They went into the living room and had a drink.

"What I detest is the drivel at the cemetery," Angela said. "Was it drivel?"

"I think so." The Scotch felt good, in the mouth, in the throat, in the chest. It was a plain fact.

"It always is. Oh God: get that repulsive creature away from me."

"Garth," Rachel called. He trotted over and sat at her feet. She stroked him between the ears; from his throat came a low growl which was unmistakably sensual.

"Dan's father was there," Rachel said.

Angela's mouth opened in surprise, and when she spoke her cheeriness seemed brittle. Perhaps it had been brittle from the start.

"Really?" She set her glass on the coffee table. A little wave of whiskey broke over the side and cascaded to the table, forming a golden pool.

"You seem astonished."

Angela picked up her glass and drank half of it down. "That a father should attend his son's funeral? No." She searched through her alligator purse until she found cigarettes, set one on fire with a gold lighter, and inhaled the fumes. "Where is he?"

"He wanted to see Dan's office. You know him, don't you?"

"I've met him. When I went to Paris to get Dan." Angela sat on the couch with the drink in one hand and the cigarette in the other, balanced like the scales of justice. "Is he staying here? In this house?"

"I think so."

"Well, what are the arrangements?" Angela said sharply, crushing her cigarette in a copper ashtray. "Oh dear, forgive me. I'm sorry." She patted Rachel's hand. "Don't listen to me. I've always resented him. It's a failing on my part, I know. Margaret and I were very close."

"How did she die?"

"Of drowning." Angela finished her drink and went to the liquor cabinet.

"In Paris?"

Angela paused at the liquor cabinet and looked at Rachel. "Yes, you could say that, I suppose. Drowned in Paris." She took the bottle from the cabinet and carried it to the table. She filled her glass and poured a little in Rachel's.

"Margaret fell from a bridge into the Seine some time before dawn on New Year's Day 1948. She was on her way from one party to another. Evidently it was some kind of stunt. Margaret had a wild streak. We were very different."

"Was her husband with her when it happened?"

Angela looked deep into the liquid in her glass. "Yes. Dan was there too."

"Dan?"

"That was Margaret for you. She had a lot of theories about how a child's first few years should be rich in experience. Partly it was to make up for what she considered her own deprived childhood. If you can call private schools, music lessons, and sailing at the Cape deprived. Somehow Margaret could. That's why she went to Paris in the first place."

"Dan never told me."

"He never knew. At least he was never certain. He must have been half asleep at the time. He asked me about it once or twice when he was very young, and I told him he'd been at home in bed. No sense in giving him a thing like that to brood over, I thought. Anyway, he forgot about it after a while."

"Still, it seems odd to drag a little boy around on New Year's Eve."

Angela laughed. "Oh, Margaret didn't do the dragging herself. She hired a babysitter to come with them. She had a highly developed sense of style. That's how I heard the whole story: from the babysitter. I met her when I went to take Dan home."

"It sounds like they had some money."

"They weren't rich. But they weren't poor, either. Margaret had an allowance. It wasn't very big, but it was in American dollars. They went a long way in Paris in those days." Angela shook her head. "Now you have to own an oil well to afford to stay there overnight."

The late afternoon sun slanted into the room in low-angled rays that illuminated the dust hanging in the still air. Rachel felt claustrophobic, as if she were trapped in a paperweight of the kind that snows inside when you turn it upside down. She had a sudden clear picture of two widows sitting in a paperweight and talking about the past. She didn't like it. She thought that her life could start again. Especially if she found Adam.

"I realize that I have no business at all resenting him," Angela said, returning to her earlier thought as though it were a train that had disappeared for a while in a tunnel. "I only met him the one time. It's just that he didn't seem very upset by her death. It's always bothered me, but it shouldn't. That's one of the hardest things there is, to know how upset a man is about something. They have such crazy values. They'll fly off the handle about the littlest thing, and then with something big they'll tuck it in an inside pocket and you'll never know. I suppose that's the way he is. Also he must have seen a lot of death in the war. The war changed a lot of men I knew. When they came back they were like icebergs, seven-eighths under-water." She smoked her cigarette and thought about it.

"In fact, I'm rather grateful to him. Henry and I

couldn't have children of our own, you know. The years we had Dan, before he went away to college, were the happiest years of our lives. For the first year he even slept in the bed with us. In the beginning it was on account of his nightmares but then it got to be a habit."

"I didn't know Dan had nightmares," Rachel said.

"Oh yes. Almost every night when he was little, and then off and on until he went away to college. After that I don't know. If he never mentioned it to you, I guess he outgrew them. Thank God. I've never seen a child so frightened. Screaming inconsolably. The strange thing was it was the same nightmare over and over. He dreamt he had shrunk to a tiny size and he was in his sandbox. His parents stood in the sandbox towering above him and shouting at each other. He thought he was going to be trampled."

In the night Rachel had an uneasy dream of her own. She lay on a narrow cot in an endless maternity ward. She felt desperate because she was twelve months pregnant. No one paid any attention to her, huge and bloated on the cot. Finally she began to push. She pushed and pushed as hard as she could, her muscles knotting with the exertion, but it was no use.

She woke up to find that she had wet the sheets. Webs of a drugged sleep—Angela had made her take a strong tranquilizer—still clung to her mind and a few moments passed before she was aware of what had happened. A pang of self-disgust hit her above the stomach where those pangs do, and she was about to get up to change the bedding when she heard a sharp metallic noise from somewhere in the house.

The sound caused a spurt of adrenaline to pass through her, washing out the remnants of sleep. She lay on the bed, listening, feeling the dampness against her thighs. She heard another sound, softer, like the shuffling of papers. She got up, put on her robe and went into the dark hall as quietly as she could.

There was nothing to see except a narrow band of weak

yellow light that had managed to squeeze under the door of the study at the end of the hall. Rachel walked carefully to the door, her bare feet soundless on the carpet. Slowly she turned the doorknob and pushed the door half open.

Xavier Monette stood beside a filing cabinet, still wearing his gray trench coat. In his hands he held a copy of the American edition of Dan's book. He was staring at the photograph of Dan and Garth. After a few moments Rachel felt him become aware of her presence. He sighed and turned very slowly toward her.

"It's so sad," he said in a whisper. "So sad. I was a fool to imagine I could reconstruct a whole life from silly pictures." His eyes filled with tears and he averted his head.

"You should get some sleep," Rachel said.

"I am not very tired," he replied, keeping his head turned away.

"Are you hungry? There's some ham in the fridge. I can fix you a sandwich."

Monette looked at her in surprise. "Ham?" he said.

"Yes."

"You have ham here?" Rachel nodded, feeling slightly puzzled.

He studied her face. "You're a Jew, aren't you?"

"Yes. I'm Jewish. Some Jews eat ham."

He reached up to replace the book on the shelf. A corner of the dust jacket caught and made a ripping sound. In the silence that followed Monette spoke softly: "But they are still Jews."

"Of course," Rachel said, surprised at his naiveté. "It's like any other religion. Some people practice it and some don't."

"I see," he said.

When Rachel awoke for the second time it was mid-morning. As she rolled over to get out of bed she remembered something, almost as if the physical act had spilled an image out of her brain. It was Dan on the front lawn, smudges under his eyes, telling her about a nightmare. The image shocked her. Dan was gone, but still his personality seemed to be capable of disembodied change and growth. She was afraid of losing her fix on him, and of losing herself too, in the nightmares of a dead husband.

When she got up she found that she was alone in the house. There was no sign of her father, Angela, or Monette. Like strangers who had gathered to attend a wedding they had gone their separate ways after the ceremony. Rachel went to the telephone to call Ed Joyce.

9

On the night of March 15 blue and white posters were
pasted on walls and telephone poles all over Israel. In the
morning people awoke to find them stuck on tar-paper
shacks in the little villages of Samaria, to the glass and
steel doors of boutiques in Tel Aviv, to the crumbling
limestone of Jerusalem. In Hebrew and Arabic they said:

Major Rally of the Sephardic Movement
Special Speaker Simon Calvi
11:00 A.M. April 2. The Hebrew University
Jerusalem
Defend the Rights of Oriental Jews!

That morning Simon Calvi went early to his office near
the Knesset. It was a suite of simply furnished cubes in a
new government building which contained hundreds of
other cubes just like his. He rode in the elevator with a
young man in a hurry and a young woman carrying three
cups of coffee. One of them was wearing too much
perfume.

Sarah Cohn was already at work, typing a letter and
dealing with someone on the telephone, the receiver

wedged between her uplifted shoulder and tilted head. She was always first to arrive, usually the last to leave. A trim fit-looking woman crowned with tight auburn curls, she ran the office in the same pleasant efficient way she ran Moses Cohn's life. He thrived under it, and so did the office.

As Calvi moved toward his inner cube Sarah held up her hand to catch his attention and then pointed with exaggerated significance at his private door.

"Who?" he mouthed, approaching her desk.

She wrote a word on a sheet of paper and turned it so he could see: Grunberg. Calvi nodded. Sarah crumpled the paper and tossed it into a wastebasket.

On the lemon-colored walls of Calvi's inner office were hung framed photographs. All were handshaking studies: Calvi with Ben-Gurion, Dayan, and Golda; with chairmen of the United Jewish Appeal; with the chief Sephardic rabbi; with five of the last six presidents of the United States. Richard Nixon was represented by a lighter colored rectangular patch on the wall. Sarah had removed him the day the American people had done the same.

A big uniformed man was standing before the picture of Eisenhower. He turned when Calvi entered the room. He was not as tall as Calvi but as broad, perhaps broader, and at least twenty years younger. He was deeply tanned with thick black eyebrows hanging over sunken dark eyes that had seen it all. On his epaulets he wore the single oak leaf of a major.

They looked at each other.

"Do we have an appointment?" Calvi asked in a polite but slightly puzzled tone.

"We should."

"Then we shall, by all means," said Calvi affably. He gestured toward one of the old wooden armchairs by the desk. The Major sat down. Calvi eased himself into the dilapidated swivel chair on the other side.

"What should we talk about, Major . . . ?"

"You know who I am," the man replied in the kind of bored voice people use on children when explaining something for the twentieth time.

Calvi didn't like it. "I suppose you must be Major Grunberg, Army Intelligence. My friend Moses Cohn told me what an early riser you are. Still, I think that even rudimentary security procedures require that I see some identification."

The Major gazed thoughtfully at Calvi. There was not the least sign of anger, fear, or even annoyance in his black eyes as he unbuttoned his shirt pocket. He handed Calvi a photostat encased in plastic. Calvi looked at the picture on the photostat. He saw the same calm deep-set eyes, eyes that seemed capable of penetrating any screen his own eyes could raise, eyes that Calvi would not easily forget.

"You're very photogenic, Major Grunberg," said Calvi, handing it back.

"So are you, Mr. Calvi. I've had many opportunities recently to see your face in the newspapers. You must be pleased with all the publicity."

"Yes, I am," Calvi said. He reached in the desk drawer where he kept his cigars and came out with two, offering one to Grunberg. Grunberg waved it away. Calvi lit the other and blew a little cloud into the air between the two men. "But not for me personally. I am pleased for the movement. I myself have no political ambitions. Furthermore, Major Grunberg, I never have had any. I am here by circumstance. I hope you believe that."

Grunberg's head moved slightly forward on his thick neck, perhaps no more than a millimeter or two, but it seemed to Calvi as aggressive as a shaking fist. "I don't give a damn about your career, your politics, or you," Grunberg said. "On all that I am neutral. Absolutely neutral." But Calvi knew he was lying from his tone. Grunberg despised him and he wondered why. "All I'm interested in is the effect you have on our Arab neighbors."

"And what is that?"

"Don't pretend to be naive. It doesn't go with your face. The Arabs have been watching you for a long time because they dream of turning the Oriental Jews into a fifth column. They want you to be a big success. But I don't have to tell you that."

Calvi brought his chair forward and put his elbows on the desk, further narrowing the space between them. "Are you calling me a traitor?" he asked quietly. "Are you making that accusation of a member of the Knesset?"

A long moment passed before Grunberg said no.

"I'm glad to hear that," Calvi said. He didn't feel glad.

They watched each other through the smoke. From the street rose a short auditory drama—a honking horn, colliding steel, shattering glass, and a policeman's whistle, after the fact. Calvi heard, but it was only unrelated noise.

"Anyone who thinks that the Sephardim could be used as a fifth column doesn't know us at all," Calvi said. "I'm surprised you would treat such an absurd notion seriously. Have you ever seen us fight the Arabs?"

For the first time the dark eyes looked annoyed. "I've been in every war since 1956."

"Then you know that the Sephardim are without doubt the cruelest in battle. If the Arabs think they can use us they should talk to their own soldiers."

"Then why have you said that Oriental Jews should look to the east?"

"I'm talking about eastern culture in general, not the Arabs. You should look at the map more often, Major, and see where we are."

Grunberg slapped the back of his hand through the smoke. "Eastern culture?" he said. "Forty percent infant mortality? Wasteland instead of orchards? Is that what you want?"

Calvi stood up angrily. "I don't have to listen to this bigotry in my own office. Get out."

Grunberg rose and approached the desk. He faced Calvi. "Very well. But before I go I'm sure you'll be interested to hear a little piece of information which came my way. The Egyptians have decided to agree to no further commitments at the peace talks until after April the second. It's a secret, of course. They plan to attend, to seem enthusiastic, to be friendly. But to do nothing."

Calvi felt his mouth go dry.

"April the second." Grunberg spoke like a man musing idly to himself. "That's the day of your next rally, isn't it?"

Calvi ignored his question. "How do you know about this—this secret, as you call it?"

Grunberg laughed in his face. "That's my job, the way yours is making philosophy out of lines on a map. Let's just say that someone in Cairo has a secretary who likes to talk."

"You don't get information like that from secretaries."

"No," Grunberg admitted.

"Who, then?"

"Who?" Grunberg repeated. "Now we're entering the area of my own little secrets." He leaned forward. "Every man is entitled to keep some things to himself, isn't he, Mr. Calvi? Such as where he goes on cold dark nights?"

"You're not making much sense, Grunberg," Calvi said. In his mind he saw two soldiers. But it could have been the waiter. Or the felafel vendor. Or all of them.

Grunberg leaned across the desk, looking up from under his luxuriant eyebrows: "Must everything always make sense? Does it make sense that a man who says he's not political becomes more radical than his mentor? Does it make sense that a man who arrives from Morocco at the age of twenty-eight, and with enough money to soon buy his own farm, brings no family?" Grunberg pushed himself away from the desk and walked toward the door.

"Life wasn't easy in Morocco," Calvi said to his back.

"Remember that when you write your speech," Grunberg replied as he went out.

Calvi sat at his desk for a while and then stood up and began pacing past the American presidents on the wall. He paused in front of the one showing him and Kennedy saying hello or goodbye on an airport runway. Kennedy was smiling warmly. He had taken Calvi for someone else. He looked at the photograph for a long time before an idea came to him.

The telephone rang. Calvi went to the desk and lifted the receiver. It was Cohn.

"What the hell is going on?" His voice was tight and angry.

"Nothing."

"Nothing? Those posters weren't supposed to go up until next week. And I thought we had decided on a small printing. They're all over the God-damned place. Why this big production?"

"It's not a big production. I thought it was important to attract a big crowd, that's all. You always say that yourself."

"What about paying for all this? Where is the money going to come from?"

"Don't worry. We'll be more economical from now on. I promise."

"I just don't understand the way things are being done lately. I don't like being kept in the dark."

Calvi could hear the shreds of other conversations in the wire. The voices sounded distant, and had the tinny high-pitched tone of mice in American animated cartoons. He wondered whether his telephone was tapped.

"It's nothing to get upset about, Moses. Calm down. It's just the usual sort of speech. You know that. Consciousness raising—isn't that what you called it?"

"Who's writing it? You?"

"Me? I can't do half the job you can. What a question."

Calvi waited for a response. He heard only the mice, far away.

"Don't you want to write it, Moses?" he asked finally. He listened to the mice and had a sudden thought. "Is Grunberg there?"

"Of course not," Cohn said quickly. "Why would he be?"

"I don't know. You sound strange, that's all."

"I'm thinking about the peace talks a lot these days."

"What about them?"

"They seem to be going well. I wouldn't want to do anything to spoil them. Every war seems so much worse than the last."

"Do you think that I want to spoil them, Moses? Do you think that I want to get my ass shot at in another war?"

"It's not likely that you'll be sent to the front the next time, Simon," Cohn said drily.

"That's unfair. You're the one who always told me that anyone who waited for his rights until Israel was secure was a fool."

"That's true."

"So I don't understand you. It's just the same old stuff. We'll even tone it down a little. It might get us a few points from some of the hostile press. Why don't we work on it tomorrow morning?"

Cohn sighed. "All right," he said, and hung up. Calvi held the receiver firmly to his ear, listening for any sign that the line was tapped. But he heard nothing unusual. Even the mice had gone away.

In the late afternoon he walked home. The sun was low in the sky, radiating through the air above the city a heavy, tangible golden light that made everything seem solemn and peaceful. It even affected the pedestrians, making everyone walk slower, except the middle-aged American couple who jostled past him. He heard the man say, "The nerve of that God-damned waiter. I came this close to telling him what we give to the UJA."

"I don't think it would have helped, dear," his wife said gently. "You can't buy politeness."

"Then what can you buy?"

A black-bearded Armenian priest in a pointed cowl caught the conversation as he approached from the other direction. He directed a big white smile at Calvi as he passed. Calvi smiled back as the priest walked away, chuckling happily to himself.

On an impulse Calvi went into an American-style drugstore. He walked up and down the sterile aisles, not sure of what he wanted. In the end he bought a small round hot-water bottle. It had two eyelets in the rubber rim and the stopper was placed in the center of one side.

"That will take care of all your aches and pains," said the girl at the cash register.

At home he found Gisela in the bath. He bent down to kiss her on the lips. Her pubic hair, a shade darker than the hair on her head, waved gently under the water, like seaweed on a calm day. She followed his gaze.

"Come in with me," she said.

"In this little tub?" He laughed and went to the study. It was time to work on Marie's letter to Walter D. He looked in the bottom bookshelf where he kept his copy of *Crime and Punishment,* but its space was empty and the surrounding books leaned inward as though trying to cover up. He quickly scanned the other shelves, then tried the desk, and its drawers. He felt his heart beat faster. He clearly remembered replacing the book in its usual spot.

He found it in the bedroom, on the floor by the bed. By the side of the bed where Gisela slept. He ran for the bathroom but outside the door he forced himself to stop and turn away.

"Have you changed your mind?" she called through the door. "Hurry, I'm just getting out."

"Never mind then," he said.

He waited until they lay in bed with the lights out before he said, "Are you enjoying *Crime and Punishment?*" He felt the tone of her skin change beside him.

"It doesn't seem to be the kind of book you enjoy," she said. "But I've only read a few chapters."

"I suppose it isn't." He remembered how Raskolnikov took an axe to the old woman. He wished he could remember more so that he could question her on the content, but he had read the book at the age of sixteen and everything but the murder was locked up out of the reach of his memory.

"Why didn't you buy a German translation?" he said. "I'm sure one is available here."

"I can manage the French," she said.

They lay quietly in the dark. After a while she touched him, and they clung together. But for the first time in his life, Calvi found himself unable. They both pretended it was not important, and Gisela soon fell asleep. Calvi lay beside her, but not touching, thinking about Raskolnikov. Much later he left the bed and went to the window. On the street below he watched a man in a broad-brimmed hat emerge from the shadows, walk through the cone of yellow light under the street lamp, and merge with the shadows on the other side. In five minutes he came walking back the other way.

10

"Mrs. Monette?" The manager of the little bank on Spring Street stood in the doorway of his frosted-glass office opposite the teller's wickets and crooked an arthritic finger. "Have you got a minute?"

"I'll be right with you, Mr. Kettleby," Rachel said. She performed the ritual of the deposit slip under the watchful gaze of the teller-priest who, satisfied, banged a purple stamp of approval on the dividend check from Leonine Investments and accepted the offering.

Rachel went into Kettleby's office. Kettleby sat behind an ugly mahogany desk which dwarfed him.

"Please sit, Mrs. Monette," he said. He leaned forward to counter the divisive influence of the desk. Under the translucent skin of his face delicate capillaries formed patterns like red spider webs. Two necks like his could have found room in his shirt collar and the pinstriped jacket of his old-fashioned suit would have hung just as well on a scarecrow. He was an old man stripped of extras like a Mississippi paddlewheeler before a big race.

"We at the bank were all very sorry to hear about your husband." Even his voice sounded spare, as if he were down to one vocal chord. But the blue eyes were un-impaired, and they were kind. "Is there any news of the boy?"

"Nothing definite," Rachel said.

"Well, it's only been a few weeks . . ." Kettleby said, his voice trailing away. He looked down at his pink blotter. Three weeks and two days, Rachel thought. Kettleby's eyes stayed on the blotter. There were no interesting inkblots to study because it had never blotted anything. He looked up quite suddenly and blinked at her, as if he had been startled.

"In any event, Mrs. Monette, we've been reorganizing your affairs here at the bank as we always do in situations like this. On the instructions of your family attorney we have transferred the funds in your husband's accounts to yours. These funds amount to $892 from his savings account and $136.70 from his checking account. The total is $1028.70."

He had the figures in his head. She wondered if he had been meandering through a forest of numbers when he fell into his stupor over the blotter.

"We have transferred the entire sum into your savings account." He looked up. Rachel nodded to show she had been following.

"There is one other matter." Kettleby paused, and licked his lips nervously. "Your husband's safety-deposit box." From a drawer he removed a locked tin box and set it carefully on the desk.

The sight of it sent a chill through her body. Again Kettleby's eyes went to the blotter. She guessed that it was common banking knowledge that husbands often had safety-deposit boxes that their wives knew nothing about. Rachel felt something tugging at her inside, very deep, like a strong current on an anchor. Her dead husband was changing the way they had lived.

"Your attorney has instructed me to turn the contents over to you, Mrs. Monette." He removed a key from his vest pocket and opened the small padlock. He opened it carefully, his head slightly back, as if he suspected that a prankster had placed a jack-in-the-box inside.

All he found was a sealed manila envelope, eight by eleven. There was no writing on it, no stamp, no marking of any kind. He handed it to Rachel, looking relieved. As she left she wondered what he had found in other men's safety-deposit boxes.

She drove home with the envelope on the seat beside her. What had he hid from her? A secret romance? She thought about the women they knew, and couldn't imagine him with any of them. But there were female students in his classes she knew nothing about. An approaching car honked angrily and she swerved back onto her side of the road.

She parked in the driveway. In March all the snow melts in the valleys of the Berkshire Mountains, leaving the sickly brown grass to recover slowly under gray skies. Across the street a fair-haired gardener with a squat body was scattering seed over the bare patches on Mrs. Candy's lawn. His shiny black tool box lay in the mud by the telephone pole. Rachel walked across her own lawn to the door; with sucking noises it tried to pull her boots off.

She sat at the kitchen table, the envelope in her hand. She tried to picture Dan's face, at a picnic, playing tennis, in bed. But she could only see him in front of the house, with smudged unhappy eyes.

Her hands shook as she opened the envelope. Inside she found no secret telephone numbers, no love letters, no sickening Polaroids. There were only two sheets of paper folded together and beside them a small envelope addressed to Dan care of the history department and postmarked in Nice on the tenth of January.

The smaller envelope contained a yellowed piece of paper, partly torn. She unfolded it. There were two short typewritten paragraphs, but Rachel couldn't read them because they were in German. Only the letterhead, a single swastika, required no translation.

The two sheets of paper made up a letter handwritten in French on history department stationery. It began "Mon père," and was signed "Daniel." The neat even lettering was Dan's and the date on the letter was February 18, six days before he died.

French had been her major in college, and she had retained more than enough to translate the letter in her head. A word or two gave her trouble, but with the help of a Larousse dictionary she arrived at a fairly accurate English rendering. She copied it onto a note pad. It read:

> *Mon père,*
>
> *How strange it is for me to write those words. How can I call someone father whom I last saw as a child? And yet I can honestly say that for the last few years at least I have borne you no resentment whatsoever. That has not always been the case: as a boy I felt that you had rejected me, and tried very hard to understand why; I even supposed for a while that you had blamed me for mother's death—I had myself convinced that I had been on the bridge with the two of you and even less likely had somehow caused mother to lose her balance. Thank God Aunt Angela straightened me out on that!*
>
> *As I say, I have finished with all those childhood difficulties. I owe my good luck in this to two sources of strength, one from outside and one from within.*
>
> *The first is my wife Rachel. (I wrote you shortly after our marriage, if you recall. Perhaps you didn't receive the letter.) She has taught me what loving someone is all about. At one time that phrase would have seemed like gibberish to me, and it may to you, but I assure you it is not. From Rachel I know that love is not some mushy feeling for your parents that you are both with, or a romanticized sexuality you learn from magazines. It is action. If you know what love is you can never be in doubt about whether someone loves you or you love someone. And we*

have no doubts. In case you form the impression she is an ultra-serious type, let me tell you it took me a long time to discover the seriousness in her. (She and her father have a routine that is priceless!)

Anyway, I'm rambling, the way my students do. We also have a five-year-old boy. He's a delight. He wants to be an ice hockey player.

Secondly I mentioned an inner source of strength. My work of course. For a number of years I have been narrowing in on the behavior of German-occupied countries during the Second World War. I suppose it has the same sort of fascination for me that the character of Macbeth has for students of drama. The book, which you must know about ($17.95 over here, I don't know what that is in francs these days), is a culmination of the years I have spent in the field. Although Rachel thinks it's my obsession, I really want now to get on with something else; the publication made me feel like a fat person who has lost a lot of weight.

The book has unleashed bundles of correspondence from France, some of it quite nasty. It happens that I have received one letter with which you might be able to help me. Not a letter at all, really—it's a document that seems to pertain to North Africa. I know you were there during the war and you may have come across information that might help to explain it. I will make a copy of it in the morning when the secretary arrives, and enclose it with this letter.

Incidentally, I hope you read German. If not, any student with a few years of German can translate it for you without difficulty. There is no hurry on this, but I find it rather intriguing. Perhaps there is an obvious explanation that I don't see.

Hoping that you are in good health, I remain,
Your son,
Daniel

Rachel read the letter three times. She didn't cry; she had finished with that on Angela's shoulder. But she felt deep shame at the thoughts she had allowed herself to have at the bank and in the car.

At the same time she was more convinced than before that the Dan she had known was not precisely congruent with the Dan that was. The thought still made her uneasy, but it also awakened her curiosity, a curiosity related to the one that she felt for the subjects of her documentaries, but far more urgent, and darker. She wondered why he had not sent the letter, and thought of sending it herself, in the hope it would console his father. But there was also the risk it would further upset him. It was unfair to take that risk when someone else would suffer.

Rachel got up from the table and heated coffee on the stove. When it was ready, she poured some into a large mug and read the letter again. Dan had left a legacy of problems. The big ones of course were his murder and the kidnapping of Adam, a kidnapping, she realized, that he knew was going to happen before he died. So she took a fresh sheet of paper from the note pad and wrote at the top, "How did D. know about kidnp.?" And underneath that she wrote, "Has Joyce made this conn.?"

Then came the difficulties raised by the yellowed German paragraphs. There was nothing to suggest that these smaller problems in any way related to the two big ones, so she wrote her questions on a separate sheet of paper: "What intrigued D. about doc.? Who sent doc.? Did D. know who sent doc.? Why safety dep. b.? When s.d.b.? (letter pstmkd. Jan. 10)."

Rachel had little hope that the answers would lead her to Adam. Yet she thought that they were answers she was capable of finding. And Dan had sought them too. He had considered it necessary to rent a safety-deposit box. She was following his footsteps, she realized, and it gave her a cold-blooded feeling she had never experienced.

She picked up the telephone and dialed Andy Monteith's number. He lived in a student residence. The girl who answered yelled that she would try to find Andy. She put the phone down on something that made little burping noises from time to time. In the background Rachel could hear the sounds of five thousand drunks having fun. She remembered that it was Friday, but she hadn't thought they began so early.

"Hello," Andy shouted.

"Hello, Andy," Rachel said. "How's your German?"

"Not bad. Why?"

"I've got something I'd like you to translate. It's very short and it should be no trouble for someone with a few years of German."

"What? I can't hear a word you're saying."

Rachel repeated what she had said in a louder voice.

"Okay," Andy said. "What is it, by the way?"

"If I knew what it was we wouldn't be yelling at each other like this." She thought Andy laughed, but she couldn't be sure. There was a lot of laughing going on. "It's something of Dan's," she added.

"Drop it off at my carrel," he told her. "Three ninety-one. I should be there by nine."

"How can you think of studying when you've had so much to drink already?"

"Study? I'm going there to drink in peace." He hung up and the party was over.

Rachel looked at her watch: six-thirty. The bank closed at six, but someone might still be there. She dialed the number and let it ring. It rang twenty times. On the twenty-first someone picked it up.

"Yes?" said a voice that meant anything but.

She recognized the thin dry tone of Kettleby. "Mr. Kettleby. I'm so glad I caught you. It's Rachel Monette. I wonder if you can tell me when my husband began renting that safety-deposit box?"

"He didn't rent it, Mrs. Monette. That service is free to all holders of your husband's bank credit card."

"When he started using it then."

She had allowed too much impatience to enter her

voice and she guessed he was trying to imagine what
marital bombshell she had discovered in the box.

"There's no one here now. Perhaps if you'd call on . . ."

"Please, Mr. Kettleby."

"Very well." His footsteps clicked away on the stone
floor, and she heard nothing but the stillness of the empty
bank. And very far away tiny voices that made her think
of the cartoon characters Adam liked to watch on Saturday morning television. The footsteps came clicking
back out of the silence.

"Mrs. Monette?"

"Yes."

"Our records show that your husband signed for the
safety-deposit box on the fifteenth of January of this
year."

"Thank you very much, Mr. Kettleby."

"You're welcome," he answered, in a puzzled voice.

Rachel picked up a pen and ran a stroke through
"When s.d.b.? (letter pstmkd Jan. 10)" on the questions
sheet. The information wasn't surprising; it had been easy
to find, but she felt better than she had in three weeks and
two days.

Rachel placed her notes, the document, and Dan's
letter to his father in her briefcase and carried it out to the
car. A fine drizzle hung in the air; it was hard to say
whether it was going up or down. It didn't bother Mrs.
Candy's gardener, busy replanting a rose bush under the
darkening sky. He looked up as Rachel drove away.

The library was deserted except for a student librarian
with corn-colored hair gathered in uneven pigtails. She
stood behind the long wooden counter chewing gum.
Rachel broke her rhythm by asking to use the copier.

"Copying facilities close at six o'clock," the girl said,
pushing the gum into her cheek.

"But there's the Xerox machine right behind you."

The girl didn't bother to deny it. She just put her gum
back in action. The little popping sounds she made with it
did her talking for her.

Rachel opened her briefcase and took out the document.

"I only want to make one copy," she said reasonably. They looked at each other for a while. Finally the girl held out her hand.

"I'd prefer to copy it myself," Rachel said. "It's not in good condition."

Rachel could see that the mere thought was causing alarm. Boldly she pushed open the waist-high swinging door that divided the counter in two, entered librarian territory, and marched on the machine. It was a master stroke. The enemy sued for peace.

"It'll cost you a dime."

Rachel dug two nickels out of her pocket and dropped them in the girl's hand. She made her copy and departed in modest triumph.

She climbed the broad marble staircase to the top floor of the library where most of the space was used for senior graduate student carrels. The doors to the little cubicles were set closely together along both sides of long corridors. The students had named it the Ant Colony. From somewhere in its depths Rachel heard frantic typing, punctuated by low groans. She found three ninety-one and slipped the copy of the document under the door.

When she descended to the main floor she saw pigtails in urgent conference with a fat gray-haired woman wearing half-spectacles. They watched Rachel out of the corners of their eyes. All the signs indicated they were girding their loins. She left before they were ready to do battle.

She spent the evening in the study, searching through Dan's files for anything that would explain his interest in the document. She found information on Bosnian politics, a series of letters from a nitpicking professor in Australia and classroom notes going back to the tenth grade. She was relieved when Andy finally telephoned. She heard restrained excitement in his voice.

"Rachel? I think I'm making some sense out of this thing."

"What does it say?"

"I'm not sure yet. I've got to find an atlas and a few other books first. Why don't you come by in an hour?"

"Okay."

"And by the way, what did you do to Mrs. Mallow?"

"Who?"

"The chief librarian. A fat old lady. I asked her if she'd seen a tall dark-haired woman and she almost bit my head off."

"It must be the way you said it."

Rachel went into the kitchen to fix dinner the way Garth liked it. An inch of kibble at the bottom of the bowl, canned dog food in the middle, and an attractive topping of fried eggs and cottage cheese. She opened the front door and called him. In a minute or two he bounded out of the darkness, gave her face an extravagant lick and trotted into the kitchen.

Before she drove to the library Rachel wrote a note to herself: "Talk to Ed Joyce first thing in the morning. Call Trimble, FBI." Garth was savoring the last morsels in his bowl so she left him behind. She took her briefcase from the kitchen table and left the house.

11

Rachel opened the heavy oak door of the library. Across the large entrance hall Mrs. Mallow and the pigtailed girl were drinking coffee out of styrofoam cups. Rachel's presence turned them to stone. Before they were transubstantiated back to flesh and blood Rachel had turned and gone up the marble stairs.

The long corridor on the top floor was very quiet. The groaning typist had given up for the night, or forever. Most of the ceiling lights had been turned off, probably by an automatic timing device, Rachel thought. One in every five burned dully. They bracketed the shadows between like blurred parentheses.

The door to three ninety-one was closed. Rachel knocked softly. There was no response. Dan had often said that the carrels were ideal for sleeping.

"Andy?" she called.

She opened the door. It was almost completely dark in the windowless room. With her hands Rachel felt along the walls until she found the switch. She turned it on.

Andy sat at the gray metal desk in the corner with his head resting in his arms. Like bedposts on either side of him were a typewriter with a little notebook balanced on the carriage and a pile of books which included a large atlas.

"Andy?" She nudged his shoulder. His head lolled to one side. His eyes were open wide. They bulged. A broken vessel in one had turned the white bright red. His face, so bloated that the skin looked ready to burst, was a deeper crimson. Two sluggish red trickles ran out of his snubbed nose, over his upper lip and onto his protruding tongue. All this was caused by a guitar string wound so tightly around his neck that it almost disappeared in the flesh. Andy was dead.

Rachel backed slowly away, toward the open door. When her leg brushed the doorjamb she whirled with a start, and looked quickly in both directions along the dark corridor. The only sound she heard was the beating of her heart. And she could hear it, distinctly, the same way she could here a fly buzz. It was no figure of speech.

Rachel wanted to run away, down the stairs, to be with Mrs. Mallow and the pigtailed girl, but she forced herself to reenter the carrel. She had to see if the copy of the document was still there. She searched through the books, and among the pages of the notebook on the typewriter. All the pages remaining in the notebook were blank. She got down on her hands and knees to look under the desk. She found a plastic wastebasket. The balls of paper it contained were now ashes; she smelled traces of the fire. As she replaced the wastebasket she saw a wet smear where she had grasped it and it occurred to her that she was leaving her fingerprints on everything.

One possibility remained—the part of the desk hidden by Andy's head, chest, and arms. She tried to lift him carefully with a hand under his arm, but she could not control her jerky movements and ended by using too much force. Andy came straight back in the chair, sat squarely for a moment, then slowly slumped to one side and fell heavily on the floor. Rachel's hands went to her

mouth and her eyes opened wide with fear as if she had
accidentally killed him herself. It was a high price to pay
for nothing on the desk.

Fifteen minutes later Rachel and Andy were still in the
little cubicle but they no longer had it to themselves. Two
policemen in uniform were sprinkling a white powder like
icing sugar here and there. Another was taking photographs. A doctor was sitting beside Andy making notes in
a black book. And a campus cop rocked on his heels in the
corner. Ed Joyce had arrived and shooed Mrs. Mallow
into the corridor. When she went out she gave Rachel the
kind of look people must have given Lizzie Borden. Anyone who could make unauthorized use of the Xerox machine was capable of anything.

Joyce had a pink blazer on his beefy torso and liquor on
his breath, but he had left his party mood outside. He
looked at Rachel and his eyes were grim. They were telling
her that he didn't blame her for any of the trouble, but it
seemed to find her. He was barely a month from retirement and wading in unsolved capital crimes. Rachel
didn't know about his retirement plans; she sensed in him
something close to kinship with Mrs. Mallow. But she
remembered the way he had looked at her teacup, and
changed her mind. There was no malice in him. It was
frustration—he was a toothless, clawless bear forced to go
on living in the wild against his will.

Partly for this reason she omitted any mention of the
document. Instead she decided to inform Trimble of it in
the morning, with the thought that the FBI was better
equipped to deal with it than the town police. She did tell
him that the body had been in the chair when she found it.
She had assumed Andy was asleep, and the gentle poke
with which she tried to wake him had knocked the body to
the floor. Joyce asked her a few simple questions, listened
to her answers and rumpled his hair.

When Rachel left she passed two ambulance attendants
carrying a stretcher along the corridor. For a moment
their faces seemed familiar. She thought she had seen

them before, and then she remembered when. They didn't seem to notice her at all.

A few small clouds sailed in state across the night sky. Standing on the broad lawn in front of the library Rachel watched them go. Fish must watch the hulls of ships in the same way, she thought. Like a gossamer seine net dragged by the clouds, a soft breeze touched her skin. It almost felt warm: the first night in months that she couldn't see her breath.

Rachel stayed there for a few minutes, until she began to hear the distant throb of jukeboxes from different parts of the campus. Like tribal drums in the jungle they brought a clear message, and it threatened to spin somewhere inside her for a long time, the way a tune in the head sometimes refuses to go away. It was guilt. Guilt for involving Andy, who should now have been drunk and happy. She sighed deeply a few times, but she couldn't blow it away.

Rachel drove home with the window rolled down. A few students were walking unsteadily to the next party, following a route through the night that led from oasis to oasis. Her headlights exposed a boy and girl walking together along the road. They were talking loudly but their minds were on the other's buttocks where each had placed a hand.

Rachel felt very tired, but the night air streaming in the window revived her. As she neared home it began to carry a scent like burning leaves; but when she pulled into the driveway she saw smoke billowing from the upstairs windows, and behind the smoke occasional bright flashes like dancing revelers at a costume ball.

Halfway to the house Rachel remembered her briefcase on the front seat, and ran back to the car. She didn't want to leave it there, or risk bringing it into the house. She slid it under the chassis.

When she opened the door the house coughed hot smoke on her face. The cough was very contagious. From within she heard the popping and cracking sounds of the fire's movements. She couldn't see it but it was near: she could feel its breath on her skin.

Rachel knelt on the threshold, keeping her head below the main stream of the smoke.

"Garth," she called, "Garth."-

She thought she heard a muted whimper under the noise of the fire. She called again and waited, but he didn't come. Rachel crawled into the house.

She crept slowly through the hall, stopping every few feet to call Garth and listen for his reply. She was sure she could hear his whimpers, but they seemed to come from different parts of the house at the same time.

She felt her way to the staircase. Her eyes could see nothing in the thick blackness. They had become organs of touch instead; they felt the greasy smoke and it made them water.

Rachel reached the staircase and tried to go up, but waves of heat flowed down the stairs like lava and drove her back. She was coughing uncontrollably and her clothes were soaked with sweat. From above she heard a loud cracking followed by a tremendous crash, as if someone had driven an enormous poker into the house. It seemed to madden the fire. Rachel heard it raging around her like a wild beast. On the second floor the bannister suddenly burst into flame. In its light she saw files and papers scattered on the blue runner that carpeted the staircase. They too caught fire, and then the runner, like a blazing tongue reaching for her.

Rachel scrambled toward the front door.

"Garth," she shouted. Again she heard whimpers that came from all sides. Then she remembered the trick of the pipes, remembered standing by the snowshoes and hearing Joyce and Trimble in the living room. She crawled into the kitchen, where the melting tile burned her hands, and opened the door to the basement.

"Garth," she called down the stairs. From below she heard him whimper, very distinctly. "Come," she said.

She heard the nails in his paws scraping frantically on the cement floor. She started down.

The heat was less intense in the basement and the smoke was not as thick. At the bottom of the stairs she felt for the light switch on the wall and pressed it. To her amazement the naked bulb in the ceiling came on.

Garth was in the corner. A length of plastic-coated clothesline wire was tied in a slipknot around his neck. The other end was fastened with a simple granny knot to a vertical copper pipe that came through the ceiling and joined a main under the floor. Rachel untied the granny knot and knelt to slip the line over Garth's head. As she did he tensed and growled angrily. Behind her she heard a footfall on the basement steps.

A man wearing a gas mask stood on the stairs. He was massive, so broad that he had to stand sideways on the staircase. In one hand he held a large aluminum pail. In the other he had Rachel's briefcase. He swung the pail forward and let it go. With a dull ring it fell on the cement floor, splashing a honey-colored liquid across the room. Some of it wet Rachel and Garth. The rest formed a pool on the floor. Rachel smelled gasoline.

As the man reached into his pocket Garth snarled and sprang up the staircase. He hit the man at knee level, just hard enough to make him lose his balance. He rolled to the bottom clutching the briefcase. Garth yelped and lay panting on the stairs.

Rachel grasped one of the snowshoes that leaned against the wall and went for the man. He bounced to his feet with incredible speed. Now that he stood on common ground she saw that his body had a freakish density: he was not much more than five feet tall. As she raised the snowshoe he darted sideways with quick crablike steps. She brought it down at his head with all her strength. Without releasing the briefcase he lifted his left arm to block the snowshoe, stepped forward and smashed her in the face with his right fist. The force of the blow lifted her off her feet and knocked her against the wall, where she fell in a pile of skis and poles.

Her mouth filled with blood. She was dimly aware of loud cracking sounds very near, and fingers of flame creeping down the basement stairs. The man moved slowly toward her, his face unreadable behind the mask. Rachel grabbed a ski pole and got to her feet. She backed away from him until she was in a corner. She brandished the ski pole in front of her with both hands. It made the man laugh—she could hear him behind the mask.

The sound acted like a signal on Garth. He leaped down the steps and sank his teeth into the man's thigh. The man twisted around and brought a corner of the briefcase down very hard on the top of Garth's head. At the same time Rachel drove the ski pole at the man's side. But he was already turning back to face her and it caught him in the chest. She felt the steel tip push through bone.

The man dropped the briefcase and staggered back, taking the pole with him. He put his hands around it and pulled it out. It was like uncapping a well of red oil. Pointing the ski pole at Rachel he took a step forward and toppled onto the floor. His blood flowed into the gasoline that was already there. It also stained Garth's coat, but that didn't matter anymore.

The flames probing into the basement had now engulfed the stairs. They brought smoke so thick that she could barely see the hanging light bulb. Quickly she bent over the man and removed his mask. At first she didn't recognize the broad face, the blond hair. But then she remembered the gardener on Mrs. Candy's lawn, and his black tool box by the telephone pole.

Rachel patted the man's pockets. In the back one she felt paper. She reached in and found Andy's copy of the document and some notes in his handwriting. She didn't stop to read them. The flames had almost reached the pool of gasoline. Rachel picked up the briefcase and ran into the furnace room.

There was a small window at the top of one of the walls.

Rachel dragged a trunk underneath, stood on it and opened the window. She lifted the briefcase through and set it on the lawn. With her hands on the sill she lifted herself up, but her shoulders were an inch too big. Behind her she heard the roar of the fire. She retrieved the briefcase and struck it against the wooden window frame until it split from its hinges, giving her the extra space. She tossed the briefcase outside, pulled herself through the opening, picked it up and started running.

The explosion caught her like a tidal wave and blew her over the lawn until the earth's gravity reasserted itself and sucked her back down. She lay on her back struggling for breath. Around her the night turned red. It made a siren scream, far away.

12

Rachel awoke in heaven. Someone had made a mistake. They had sent her to the wrong section. She was in thirteen-year-old-girl heaven. The walls were pink, the ceiling was pink, and so were the sheets on the bed, the quilt, and the silk fabric on the headboard. What clinched it were the posters. They all showed skinny young men with translucent skins and yearning faces covering their groins with electric guitars.

Heaven hurt her eyes. But they hurt anyway. Her face hurt too, and her neck was so stiff she could barely move her head. She hurt all over. Gingerly she touched her nose with the tips of her fingers. Once was enough.

Rachel pushed back the covers, releasing an odor of smoke, sweat, and gasoline that made her feel sick. Her toes gripped the thick pink broadloom and she stood up. Through a pink haze she caught a brief mirrored glimpse of a bruised and grimy woman. She sat down hard on the bed, and remained there for a minute with her head between her knees.

Someone tapped on the door.

"Rachel, dear. Did I hear you up and about?" The door

opened and a plump manicured hand entered, followed by the plump made-up face of Ethel Dawkins. Rachel sat up.

"Oh, God," said Ethel. "You're a mess. I'll get a hot bath going on the double."

It was exactly what she needed. Ethel helped her into the tub.

"My, where did you get such a lovely figure, Rachel?"

The water was very hot and Ethel had added a bubbling solution. Rachel sank in and closed her eyes.

"Bloomingdale's basement."

Ethel laughed a little harder than necessary. "What I meant was I've met your father now, and he's a very nice man, but not really very tall, is he?"

"My mother was."

"Oh, that's good," Ethel said, sounding pleased. "I knew it had to come from somewhere."

The heat began to work on her body, undoing the knots in her muscles and soothing the soreness in her joints. It almost made her enjoy her achiness.

"This bath is perfect, Ethel."

"There's nothing like a hot bath, dear," Ethel said. "Do you want me to scrub your back?"

Rachel opened her eyes, and saw behind the make-up the concern in Ethel's face. "Not right away," she said.

"Well, then, I'll just sit here and keep you company." Ethel lowered the cover of the toilet, sat down, and crossed her thick legs. She twisted her wedding band while she thought of a good topic for conversation. She played it safe.

"How do you like Amy's room? Isn't it sweet?"

Sweet was a stomachful of cotton candy, Rachel thought. "Very," she said.

"Of course I think it's a bit young for her now that she's gone away to graduate school, but she doesn't want to change it. Kids are funny sometimes."

Adam's room appeared suddenly in Rachel's mind. She

saw it clearly—the woolly sheep on his duvet, the big yellow trucks, his drawings of hockey players on the walls. It was gone. All of it. She sat up quickly, sloshing water on the floor. Ethel hadn't played it safe enough.

"Ethel. Where is my briefcase?"

"Why, I think Tom put it in the front hall closet when Mr. Joyce brought you here last night."

"And some notes. I had some notes on a few sheets of paper."

Ethel looked at her gently. "Yes, you did. You wouldn't let go of them. I took them out of your hand when you fell asleep. They're on the desk in Amy's room."

Rachel didn't recall a desk. Neither did she remember seeing her clothes. She asked Ethel about them.

"Oh, I threw them in the garbage. No amount of washing would get them clean again."

"But I've no other clothes," Rachel said, thinking of the closets and chests of drawers that had been full of them.

"Don't worry, dear. Amy's about your height, and she leaves plenty of things here. She hasn't got your figure of course, but they should do for now. Take what you need." Ethel went to make breakfast.

Her clothes were beyond cleaning, but her body and hair were not. When she had done she sent a black stream swirling down the drain.

A dainty desk sat in front of the window in Amy's room. It looked like a pretty imitation of the sort of desk every little princess just had to have in the days of some Louis or other. Wrapped in a thick red bath towel Rachel sat down on the matching chair. The chair emitted a shocked creak, outraged that anyone dared take such liberties.

The dirty papers lay on the desk. They smelled of last night. She unfolded them. There were three sheets, the first the copy of the document she had given Andy, the second his translation, and the third had a few notes in his handwriting. She read the translation:

                                January 18 1942
To : Lieutenant Hans Kopple (der Leutnant)
From: Headquarters, 90th Light Infantry Division
Subject: Transfer
This is your notification of immediate transfer to
Camp Siegfried ten kilometers SW of Mhamid.
Requisition supplies necessary from the
quartermaster of C Company and proceed at once.
On arrival report to commanding officer. Duties
at Camp Siegfried: Supervision and maintenance
of security. You are to detach from your company
and take with you the following men:
    Corporal Joachim Shreyer
    Private Victor Reinhardt
    Private Max Feldbrill
Your destination is secret.

On the third sheet of paper Andy had written:

90th Light Inf.—Rommel. Where Rommel:
18/1/42?
Fr. surrender June 22 1940
Allied landings N. Afr. Nov. 8 1942
Vichy?
P. 137

Rachel reread the translation and Andy's notes several
times. She looked at the swastika and the German words.
Kopple, Shreyer, Reinhardt, Feldbrill. And Rommel.
Rommel's name she knew although she would have failed
the simplest quiz about him. The other names were
meaningless. The men were probably all dead by now. But
a conviction grew inside her that those orders, written
before she was born, had somehow not died with them.
    An unformed thought was hiding somewhere in her
mind and she couldn't quite flush it into the open. After a
minute or two she gave up trying. It will come, people
said. Or sometimes they said, if you can't think of it it

musn't be very important. That was how folk wisdom dealt with the problem. Rachel squeezed into a pair of jeans she found in the closet, pulled on a purple and gold football sweater, number twenty-two, and went down to breakfast.

"Not that awful thing," Ethel said. She had a big breakfast ready. Pancakes with maple syrup, scrambled eggs and bacon, hot coffee. Rachel remembered that her last meal had been the morning before. She ate ravenously. Ethel ate ravenously too, although she never missed her three squares a day.

When nothing was left but a few scraps, Ethel said, "Mr. Joyce asked if you'd call him when you felt up to a visit. He wants to come over. And your insurance agent called this morning. He said there's nothing to worry about."

"I'll call Joyce later," Rachel said.

She sat back and sipped her coffee.

As if her brain had been holding the unformed thought as a hostage for food, it now released the memory of the atlas sitting on the desk in carrel three ninety-one. Rachel stood up quickly, startling Ethel, who was reaching for a piece of bacon that had fallen off her plate. Her hand jumped back into her lap as if she had been caught shoplifting.

"Where's my car?" Rachel asked.

"I think Tom parked it in the laneway, but oughtn't you to take it easy, Rachel? I can drive you if you really have to go somewhere." But Rachel was already on her way out the door. Ethel retrieved the piece of bacon and offered it up to her mouth.

The shortest route to the library led past her house. Rachel barely slowed down as she went by. Smoke rose in the air from a soggy ruined pile that separated the front yard from the back. The lawn had been turned into a muddy battlefield by the water from the hoses and the boots of the firemen.

Rachel hurried through the library doors. There was no

sign of Mrs. Mallow or the pigtailed girl. She ran up the stairs, and along the corridor, now brightly lit, to the carrel. She hesitated outside the door. Down the hall the door of another carrel opened and a pasty-faced student peered out like a pearl diver coming up for air. He saw Rachel.

"It's okay, you can use it," he said. "They've got it all cleaned up."

Rachel went in. The events of the night had made no lasting impression on the room. The books remained on the desk. Someone had repiled them more neatly.

Rachel opened the atlas to page 137. It showed a map of Morocco, green at the top, brown and wrinkled in the center, and flat yellow at the bottom. Deep in the yellow, near the crosshatched line resembling barbed wire that marked the Algerian border, a circle had been penciled around an isolated word written in very small letters. Rachel lowered her head to the page and read it. Mhamid, it said.

The Dawkins's house stood behind a line of spruce trees about a mile out of town. They had designed it themselves. The trees made it hard to count all the levels into which it had been split, but they didn't hide the two wooden footmen flanking the path. They had silly red smiles on their black faces and they were getting ready to bow. When Rachel arrived she found Ed Joyce sitting on the steps between them wearing his blue uniform. He had a foil packet of potato chips in his big hand and was tossing crumbled bits of them at a squirrel on the grass. The squirrel faced him on its haunches, forepaws raised to its face like a fighter, and didn't move a muscle. The four of them had a nice act going but Joyce dropped out when Rachel walked up the path. He got to his feet. The squirrel ran up one of the spruce trees and jumped onto the roof.

"You look like you've just gone fifteen rounds with the champ," Joyce said watching her closely. Rachel thought she heard a new respect in his tone.

"Nothing's broken."

"Glad to hear it," Joyce said. "I'm real sorry about your dog. I know how it feels. I lost mine a few months ago. A God-damned kid ran him over. We were going to retire down to Florida next month." Joyce rolled the potato chip packet into a ball and put it in his pocket. "What was your dog's name again?"

"Garth."

"Garth," Joyce repeated. "Mine was Wally." He stared down at one of the footmen but he wasn't getting any sympathy from that quarter. The footman went on sharing a private joke with his buddy. Rachel didn't know the joke but she was sure they were laughing at the Dawkinses. Maybe it had something to do with their taste.

Ed Joyce took a long deep breath and let it out with a sigh.

"Mind if we sit out here for a while?" he said. "It's a nice day."

They sat together on the steps. The squirrel ran back down the tree and glared at them from a safe distance.

"I went down to the morgue in North Adams to have a look at the body this morning," Joyce said. "What was left. It won't be easy to identify. There's nothing to take prints of."

"What about Mrs. Candy?"

"Oh, we've gone into all that." He removed the potato chips from his pocket and threw a few more at the squirrel. It kept glaring. "She says the guy came to her door a couple of weeks ago. Said he was a graduate student from a university in Munich, working his way across the states. Hoped to write a book about it, he said. He asked her if he could work on her lawn. For a buck an hour. Well, Mrs. Candy has a regular gardener, but the price was right. She said okay."

"Did she find out his name?"

"He gave her a name all right. Gurt Weiss, she thinks it was." Joyce spelled it for her. "I called Trimble in Boston and he telexed the name to the university in Munich. But I'm not expecting much. He had no reason to give her his real name, and a lot of reasons not to." Joyce made clicking sounds in his mouth to encourage the squirrel.

"Was he staying at Mrs. Candy's?"

"No. He rented a room on Water Street. We searched the room last night. Nothing there that would identify him. Some clothes. A cheap suitcase. And his tool box." He shook his head. "That was some tool box."

"He tapped my phone with it, didn't he?" Rachel said.

Joyce turned sharply. "How did you know that?"

"I didn't know, really. I guessed."

"That's a hell of a guess." He looked at her thoughtfully.

"I wonder where his passport is," Rachel said. "It's hard to imagine something like that being completely destroyed in the fire."

"It could have been."

"Even so, why would he risk carrying it with him on a night when he's out murdering and burning houses. You're sure it wasn't in his room?"

"Yes," said Joyce. "We even looked under the mattress."

She looked at his face to see if he was making a joke, and decided he was. "If it wasn't in his room and it didn't burn in the fire—let's just say for now it didn't—where is it?"

Joyce rubbed his jaw and pushed it to one side, holding it there with his mouth open. He was watching a big squirrel with a bushy tail that had appeared on the far side of the road. It suddenly dashed across and went straight for the potato chips. The other squirrel stopped glaring and began running around in little circles. The big squirrel chased it away and went back to the potato chips.

"I don't know," Joyce answered finally. "It could be buried in Mrs. Candy's backyard, or stuck in a locker in the bus terminal in North Adams. It doesn't matter much now."

"Of course it does," Rachel said, raising her voice slightly. "Did you ever think that maybe there is no passport?"

Joyce threw a potato chip to the big squirrel. It got its paws on it and shoved it in its mouth. "I don't see what you're getting at."

"Just that perhaps he wasn't German after all."

Joyce shook his head. "He was German all right. Both Mrs. Candy and the landlord on Water Street say he had a distinct German accent. He had to, really. It explains the whole case."

"How?" Rachel said quickly.

"The guy was obviously some sort of pro-Nazi, a fanatic. Your husband's book comes out, and makes a big splash in Europe. This guy is already unbalanced, and something in the book pushes him over the edge."

"But the book's not about Germany. It's about France."

"Not entirely," Joyce said. "Chapters eight and nine relate changes in the behavior of the Vichy government to events in Germany."

"You've read it?" Rachel asked in surprise.

A hurt look rose to the surface of his gray eyes. It reminded her of the tension that always existed between town and gown. Like a fault in the earth it divided the community.

"I'm sorry," Rachel said. "I didn't mean that the way it sounded."

Joyce went on as if she hadn't spoken. "Another fact to remember is that on the dust jackets of the German editions it said that your husband was planning a book on resistance movements within Germany during the war."

"It wasn't definite," Rachel said.

"That wouldn't matter to our boy. The way I figure it he started thinking about putting an end to all this research. And remember, he's a bit weird—when he finds out that the author of all this has a Jewish wife, and that would have been easy, there were many articles on him in the German papers—he gets the idea of using this rabbi disguise."

"But that can't be right," Rachel said. "Miss Partridge said he was a tall man."

"Remember how short Miss Partridge is," Joyce replied patiently. "And she was upset. And the guy, although short, was very broad. She formed the false impression that he was tall. Witnesses do that kind of thing all the time."

"What about the insurance salesman?"

"Who?"

"The one who saw a tall man struggling with a small boy in the field."

"He was too far away to be reliable, Mrs. Monette."

"He was close enough to see that they were struggling," Rachel said, and suddenly felt close to tears. Joyce sat quietly for a minute and then resumed.

"So he flies over and does what he does. But he doesn't finish the job." He cleared his throat. "I think he meant to kill you from the very beginning."

"Why?"

"You're Jewish. He was a Nazi," Joyce said simply. "When things got quieter around here he came back. Listening in on you and the Monteith boy he probably thought you were continuing your husband's work. He killed the Monteith boy, and the rest you know."

Rachel shook her head. "You haven't explained why he took Adam."

"He was crazy, Mrs. Monette. Some things you can't explain rationally."

Rachel stood up, walked a little way down the path and turned to face him. "I don't understand where all this leads."

"It doesn't lead anywhere, Mrs. Monette. You finished it in the basement last night."

"What are you talking about?" Rachel said angrily. "Nothing's finished until we find Adam."

Joyce got up and walked slowly over to her. He laid his hand on her shoulder and spoke very gently. "I don't think that's possible."

Rachel jerked her body away from his hand. "Don't be ridiculous. He has to be somewhere." Joyce looked at her sadly.

"Yes, he does," she shouted at him. She saw the curtain in the living room twitch. Ethel Dawkins's face peered out. Rachel tried to lower her voice. "You're asking me to believe he's dead, based on nothing more than a flimsy theory. You don't even know all the facts."

So Rachel told him about the safety-deposit box, the document, and Camp Siegfried. He listened carefully but the look in his eyes didn't change. It remained sad.

"We can't assume that other people attached the same importance to this document that your husband did," he said quietly. "He was a professor doing historical research, not an agent for the CIA."

"Don't you even want to see it, for God's sake?"

"Yes, of course I'll look at it," Joyce said.

"And then call Trimble in Boston and see what he can dig up on the camp."

Joyce gave her a weary look. "All right," he said. They went into the house.

When Joyce finished talking to Trimble, Rachel signaled that she wanted to speak to him as well. Joyce handed her the receiver. She covered the mouthpiece with her palm, and said to him, "Do you mind if I talk privately?"

"Not at all," he said without emotion, and left the room.

"Mr. Trimble?" she said into the mouthpiece.

"Hello, Mrs. Monette," said the tenor voice. "I hear you handled yourself very well last night. Are you feeling all right?"

"Yes, Mr. Trimble, but I'm not happy with the way the investigation is going. Mr. Joyce seems to think that the whole thing was the work of one maniac, the man in the basement last night. I think he's wrong."

"You do?"

"Yes. I think there's some sort of large conspiracy involved, and the German document is the key to it."

"We're checking on the document, Mrs. Monette. But there was no big-time conspiracy. If there was, you wouldn't be around to talk about it."

13

Saturday night March 20, Moses Cohn rode his bicycle to Simon Calvi's villa to finish writing the speech. He had the collar of his baggy tweed jacket turned up to guard against the chill of the night air, and he carried a bottle of Scotch whiskey in the pannier to guard against something else.

They sat in the dining room, Cohn at the typewriter and Calvi pacing around the table. These speech-writing sessions were usually noisy and full of argument, but this one was subdued. Calvi paced and drank and hardly said a word. Cohn typed and drank and composed almost all of it himself. On the other side of the arch that separated the dining room from the living room they could see Gisela lying on the couch, lit only by the flickering blue light of the television. She was watching a program about seal hunting in the North Atlantic and eating chocolates from a box on the floor. Above the soft percussion of the typewriter they could hear the little voices in the television yelling at each other. If they looked they could see Gisela's strong heavy thighs naked below the hem of her short skirt. From time to time they did look. They thought different thoughts. None of this made an impression on

Gisela. Except for the opening and closing of her eyes and mouth she was inert.

"That's that," Cohn said finally. He shuffled the papers together and laid them on the typewriter. "You're sure you don't want a little more punch in it, Simon?"

"Aren't you the one who has been nagging me about the peace talks?" Calvi asked testily.

"That doesn't mean we have to emasculate ourselves."

The annoyance drained from Calvi's eyes and for a moment his gaze seemed to be directed inside. He picked up the bottle and emptied it into the two glasses. "Let's leave it like this, Moses," he said quietly. "It will get the job done."

"Whatever you say." Cohn shrugged. Calvi took him to the door and switched on the front light. Outside the man in the broad-brimmed hat peered down the street, as if he were expecting someone any moment. Cohn mounted his bicycle and wobbled into the night. He wasn't a drinking man.

Neither was Calvi. When he awoke in the morning his insides felt bruised and his head throbbed. The soft golden light that the tourists raved about made his eyes water. He groaned to himself, and groaned again more loudly to discover if anyone was paying attention. But he lay alone in bed.

Shakily he got out of bed and walked down the hall. Gisela was on the telephone in the kitchen, speaking in German. She had pinned her blond hair back off her face. Her skin had a smooth healthy lustre. The little T-shirt she wore stretched tightly across her breasts. She waved at Calvi as he came in, glancing at his body. Something in the glance made him feel old as the hills.

She replaced the receiver. "Who was that?" he asked her in German, without thinking.

She looked up in surprise. "I had no idea you spoke German," she said. "Why didn't you tell me, you silly thing?"

Suddenly he didn't feel his hangover anymore, as if the

surge of fresh blood that swept through him had washed it away.

"I don't really," he said. "Just a few words, that's all."

"But your accent was excellent! Say some more."

"I don't know more."

"You must. Come on, Simon, talk to me in German."

"Auf Wiedersehen." He pronounced the words very badly.

She pouted. "You're not trying."

"How can I? I don't know the language. I speak Hebrew, English, French, and Arabic. And Mughrabi. Isn't that enough?"

"Don't be angry, Simon," she said. "I got excited, that's all. It would be nice if you could speak German. There are things I could say to you in German that I can't say in any other language."

He walked across the kitchen and kissed her on the mouth. He would make use of that surge of blood. "Like what?" he said.

She wriggled herself against his skin and held him. After a while she said, "Not here, Simon."

"Why not?"

"It's not comfortable. Let's go to bed."

"If you want."

"Carry me."

"For God's sake."

But after she had not forgotten. "I'm amazed that you could learn any German at all in Morocco," she said.

He reached across her and took a cigar from the drawer in the bedside table. "I didn't," he said. He lit the cigar and laid his head back on the pillows. "The few words I know I learned here. There are a lot of Germans in Israel."

"Do you mean German Jews? I thought they spoke Yiddish."

He drew deeply on the cigar. He felt much better. "And German. They're very snotty."

He left her sleeping soundly, her mouth a little open. Sunday is not a holiday in Israel, but Calvi had come to believe in the American-style weekend and he usually spent Sunday mornings walking around the city. He dressed in his old green corduroy suit with patches on the elbows, and wore the stout leather shoes he had ordered from a British manufacturer of outdoor equipment.

When he stepped outside a warm breeze touched his face. It ruffled the leaves of the carob tree across the street. Its branches extended far over the road in one direction, but almost not at all in the other, making the tree look as if it had an avant-garde coiffeur. In its shade a man had set up an easel and was gazing with intense concentration at the walls and trees that enclosed Calvi's villa. The man wore a broad-brimmed hat. Calvi wondered when he slept. Perhaps several men shared the hat.

Calvi crossed the street and walked right by the man. Under the brim was an olive-toned, middle-aged face that needed a shave. The man wore thick spectacles, but they didn't hide the fatigue in his eyes. He appeared not to notice Calvi at all. As Calvi passed he turned to look at the painting on the easel. He saw a study of his house and garden that, even unfinished, projected a mood of quiet and peace. He thought it was very good, and had a wild notion of offering to buy it.

He walked on, moving in the direction of the Old City. After he had gone a few hundred feet he looked back, and saw the man walking about half that distance behind him. He still held the paintbrush in his hand. Calvi didn't alter his speed, or look back a second time.

Two fat American women were having their picture taken in front of the careless arrangement of stones known as Herod's family tomb. The photographer, a little man with a thick guidebook stuck under his arm, clicked the shutter, preserving for eternity their affable pose, each with a flabby arm over the other's shoulders.

"So is Herod in here, Mervin?" one of them asked.

"Good question, dear," the little man said. "Apparently it's only members of the family. In fact he ordered most of them killed himself." He consulted the book. "If you want to see Herod we have to go to Bethlehem." But the women had stopped listening and were talking about something else.

Calvi walked around them and entered King David Street. As he approached a bus stop the number fifteen bus arrived, headed north. He timed his arrival so that he reached it just as the last passenger boarded. He slipped through the closing door, paid the driver, and sat down. Three stops later he got off and hailed a taxi going the other way. From the passenger seat Calvi saw the man in the broad-brimmed hat running clumsily past the King David Hotel. His wet paintbrush touched the arm of the woman who wanted to know where Herod was. She looked at the green smear it left and yelled something after him.

The taxi took Calvi to a dilapidated garage in the southeastern part of the city. As he opened the car door he nearly knocked over an Arab woman who was panting under a large bundle of firewood she carried on her back. A few feet ahead her husband rode on the back of a tiny donkey that wasn't having an easy time either. The wife, bent almost double, had a view of the donkey's hindquarters, and not much more. The man's thin sculpted features were composed in an expression of dignified benevolence, as if he had just taken the city.

Around the single gas pump a few scrawny chickens fought over bits of oil-soaked feed that lay in the dirt. A toothless Arab wearing a stained and shiny red suit emerged from the bare room inside and looked inquiringly at Calvi. His eyes gleamed. Calvi glanced through the cracked panes of the window and saw two other men, sitting around a bubble pipe. Calvi told him what he wanted.

The man went back inside and returned bearing an iron key of the size you would need to open the cathedral at Chartres. He led Calvi into an alley, where they walked beside a head-high cement wall covered with lurid movie posters. They showed bare-chested Arabs with jeweled belts waving curved swords and glaring hotly at each other. The only thing wrong with them was that they didn't look like Arabs; they looked like Rudolf Valentino in harem pants.

They came to a thick wooden door in the wall. A beautiful barefooted little girl with thick black hair and big brown eyes sat in front of it, doing nothing. In an angry voice the toothless man said something that Calvi didn't catch and she ran away.

The man placed the key in the lock and turned it. It opened without a hitch. The man removed the key and put it in his pocket. He was proud of that key.

They stepped through the doorway and into a small dirt yard surrounded on all sides by cement walls. In the center was a dry and cracked stone fountain surmounted by a curly-haired marble god who looked Greek. Decaying around the fountain were four automobiles. Two of them had no wheels, the third had wheels but no doors. The fourth was a rusty ambulance with broken headlights. It had the right number of wheels and doors.

"What do you want for the ambulance?" Calvi said.

The toothless man looked shocked. "I can't sell the ambulance," he said. "Never."

"Why not?"

"It's too valuable."

After a while they returned to the garage to talk further. The toothless man fetched a chair that was less broken than the others for Calvi. The two other men at the table smiled at him. They shared the bubble pipe. They talked about the weather and kids today. They praised his command of Arabic. A woman entered bringing sweet coffee and little cakes that tasted of powdered sugar and motor oil. They smoked some more and watched the flies go after the cake crumbs. Soon Calvi's hangover began to make a comeback. When the toothless man saw that his eyes were sufficiently glassy he named an absurd price. Calvi accepted at once. Calvi and the toothless man shook hands. Calvi and the other two men shook hands. The three Arabs shook hands.

Calvi paid the money and got ready to leave. Before he did he asked that the ambulance be repainted, in the same ambulance colors, and that the flashing red roof light and siren be in good working order.

"Ah," groaned the toothless man as if his appendix had burst. He thrust the wadded bank notes back across the table with a revulsion that suggested they were leprous. They settled on a new price.

Calvi told him that it must be ready by the end of the month, and told him who would come to call for it. He stood up and they all shook hands again. When he left they seemed genuinely sad, and Calvi knew they were.

14

The drunks had finally gone to sleep or passed out. In the oval window of the airplane Rachel saw a sallow reflection of her face. Beyond it there was nothing but the blackness of the Atlantic night.

She reclined her chair as far as it would go and closed her eyes but she was unable to sleep. She thought of her last telephone conversation with Trimble.

"Of course we're keeping the case open," he had said. "We haven't given up on tracing the black car, and something may turn up on the blond man." But the FBI had found no record of a graduate student named Gurt Weiss enrolled in any university in Munich, and no one had ever heard of a German encampment named Siegfried in a place called Mhamid or anywhere else in North Africa.

On the drive to Kennedy Airport her father had reiterated these facts. "Let the professionals handle it," he told her.

"Adam's been missing for over a month. That's not handling it."

"But—"

She gripped his shoulders hard. "Adam is alive. I'm going to go find him."

At the last minute he offered to go with her. "But who would take care of the fish?" she had said. She meant it lightly but it brought a hurt and slightly shameful look to her father's face. She leaned forward and kissed his forehead.

"Have you got enough money, Rachie?" he asked.

"Yes." She kissed him again and went through the glass doors where a tired young man waited to search her bag.

To the east the sky began to lighten. A band of red gold appeared on the horizon dividing space into two endless halves of navy blue. Rachel pictured herself sitting in a padded chair bolted to a hunk of metal speeding over the cold sea. She hated flying.

Dawn brought the stewardesses in fresh make-up, applied thickly enough to hide signs of fatigue, or anything else. They woke up the passengers to give them tepid, bitter coffee and jellied rolls of the sort a tongue could feel but not taste. Everyone was eager to get off the plane; she could hear it in the captain's voice when he told them it was he speaking.

True to his word he landed the plane on the runway at Mohammedia Airport, north of Casablanca. Then he drove it around the tarmac for a while giving the stewardesses a chance to walk up and down the aisle ordering everyone to remain seated. They were released at precisely 8:32 in the morning, Tuesday, the twenty-third of March. Rachel knew that because she was adjusting her watch on the captain's instructions.

Inside the terminal a fat man in a gray uniform held out his hand for her passport. He opened it to an unmarked page and stamped it hard, so it would stay stamped. She was admitted into the country.

The first place she visited was the luggage carousel. A dark youth with a broken zipper beat her to her suitcase and in English demanded a four-dirham ransom. She explained in French that she had not yet had opportunity to change money, consequently she herself had no dirhams. Her accent sounded strained and arrhythmic in her ears, but the boy didn't seem to notice. He smiled and handed her the suitcase.

"You owe me," he said in French.

"The next time," she answered. Despite everything she felt excitement at being in a strange place.

On her way to the car rental counter Rachel made a detour and entered a door that had the word for women written on it in five languages, and also displayed a black plastic silhouette that looked like a man wearing a dress. She went into one of the cubicles, closed the door, wiped off the seat with the course brown tissues which the tin box dispensed one at a time, and sat down. On the inside of the door in front of her face she saw fingerprints etched in human waste. Rachel laughed out loud. She had left the deodorized world of the west far behind, but she knew the culture shock had come and gone, passing through her in that one moment. She was glad it had happened while she was still in no-man's land.

At the car rental counter, operated by an international agency, Rachel asked for something with four-wheel drive. At first she spoke French, but the attendant, a dark woman with dyed blond hair who weighed less than she was meant to, held steadfastly to English, so Rachel gave up. In English she felt more muscular, and she needed all her strength to wrest the automobile from the woman. It was almost noon before she drove away in a dusty Land-Rover with an ashtray full of date pits.

On the flight Rachel had studied a detailed road map of Morocco. She had plotted the route from Casablanca to Mhamid and added the figures that marked the distance in kilometers from point to point along the way. They came to a total of six hundred and ninety, slightly more than four hundred miles. She had planned to complete the drive in one day, but she did not reach Mhamid until Thursday morning.

She couldn't blame the car—it ran without difficulty.

Or the roads—except in the High Atlas, where children waved raw chunks of amethyst at her, they were straight. Only the last ninety kilometers, from Zagora to Mhamid, were they not paved as well. It was her own fault. A tiredness overcame her on the journey that made her sleep for fourteen hours in an expensive dirty hotel in Marrakech and twelve more in an expensive clean one in Zagora. Even on the road her eyes constantly felt heavy, and she didn't exceed fifty miles an hour.

Soon after Zagora the mood left her quite suddenly. Perhaps it was dispelled by the sight of the first sign pointing toward Mhamid. Rachel followed the graded dirt road which clung for a while to the west bank of the Oued Draa, a mean trickle that managed to sustain narrow bands of palm groves on both sides. The green of their fronds, in the midst of the surrounding waste, seemed more succulent to her than any green she had known before.

The road turned away from the valley of the Draa and led her across a plain of sand and pebbles. Bare brown mountains ringed her on all sides; whenever Rachel looked at them they receded before her eyes. She did not see another person until the road rejoined the Draa.

She smelled the date palms long before she saw the trees themselves, surrounding a small village walled in reddish stone. A group of little boys sat barefoot beneath the trees, each holding chalk and a slate and facing a bearded old man who stood in front of them. The boys watched Rachel pass. Many of their faces were black, but some were lighter than Rachel's. Rachel waved. The old man said something in a sharp voice and the boys turned their heads away.

Beyond the village the road ran once again along the bank of the Draa, now completely dry. The trickle of sluggish brown water had become a line of polished stones. As if in sympathy the road, too, grew rougher and began trying to shake the Land-Rover apart. Rachel found it easier to leave it completely in favor of the hard-packed plain.

After a while the first dunes appeared, forcing her to return to the track. Then, divided here and there by the sand came a last resurgence of palm groves. Through the trees she could see small villages, some of them fortified. Suddenly the rutted track became smooth black asphalt and the noise of rattling metal was replaced by the quiet hiss of the tires.

The palm groves ended and Rachel found herself in the central square of a small town. Several jeeps of various manufacture stood at different angles in the middle of the square, more abandoned than parked. The whole town had that forsaken look. There were no people or animals in sight. The doors of the faded yellow-cement buildings that surrounded the square were closed, and the windows covered with crude wooden shutters. Two buildings slightly taller than the others faced each other across the square. One was the gendarmerie, the other the Hotel Mhamid. Neither looked inviting.

Rachel drove on, her destination ten kilometers beyond, somewhere in the southwest. Beyond the square the road continued for a few hundred feet before the asphalt stopped abruptly. No dirt track replaced it. Rachel stopped the car and got out. A dirty cloud of flies circled her head and came to rest on the windshield. She gazed into the distance. Two faint trails led north and northwest. To the southwest Rachel saw a plain of sand and stone that gave no sign that anyone had ever set foot on it.

She looked back toward the town. Two men, one wearing a white robe, the other in khaki uniform, stood in front of the gendarmerie, watching her. She climbed into the Land-Rover, noted the number of kilometers recorded below the speedometer, and drove slowly into the southwest. The flies stuck to the windshield like barnacles.

There were no clouds in the sky but that didn't mean it was blue. It seemed to be filled with fine dust made honey-colored by the warm sun. In the golden light her eyes were unsure of distance and direction. She took a pocket compass from her bag and set it on the dashboard.

When she had gone ten kilometers she got the binoculars out of the glove compartment and stood on the roof of the car. She scanned the world around her. Nothing moved. There was no sign of any building, old or new. On the northern horizon rounded hills rose out of the plain. To the west it continued unchanged, stony and flat. In the south fields of sand appeared, covering parts of the rocky surface, and beyond she saw columns of dunes marching into Algeria.

In her notebook Rachel drew a diagram of what she had seen, and then began a methodical reconnaissance of the area. Using the place she had stopped as a mid-point she made a two-kilometer square in the desert. When she had completed it she began a second, twice the size.

On the southern leg she began encountering sand dunes. Keeping to the shallow sandy patches, she picked her way between them until she was blocked by a long line of dunes, running east to west without a gap. She drove west until she found a dune less imposing than the rest, then circled back across the sand. From a distance of about three hundred yards she accelerated toward it, the tires whining at the lack of traction. Nevertheless when the jeep hit the dune it was moving fast, fast enough to twist its way to the top and drop off the other side. It landed with a heavy jolt that knocked the wind out of Rachel. When she had recovered she got out and crawled under the chassis. Nothing dangled.

She stood up and brushed the sand from her clothes. A man was singing. He sounded like Frank Sinatra. He was singing "Fly Me to the Moon." Frank was fighting a large smothering string section for possession of the melody, and losing. The sound of the battle came closer.

A huge yellow smile appeared at the crest of a dune. It belonged to a camel that lumbered over, looked right through her and kept on going. The man sitting on top, resting his bare feet on the camel's neck, wasn't as friendly. He didn't turn in her direction at all. He was too busy adjusting the aerial on the big overseas radio that hung on a strap from the small leather saddle, beside a long and very old rifle. Frank wondered about the quality of life on Jupiter and Mars.

"Wait," Rachel called, trying French and English.

The camel halted. The two heads swiveled slowly. Two sets of eyes rested on her, one brown, one yellow. She walked close to the camel, but not too close, and spoke to the rider in French.

"I am looking for an old settlement called Camp Siegfried," she said. The camel made a loud sniffing sound and turned away, but the man kept his eyes on her. His skin was very dark, and tinted indigo by the dye in the robe he wore. He had prominent cheekbones and a thin-lipped mouth. "Campement Siegfried," she repeated.

The fine mouth opened and the man spoke rapidly for a minute or two in a language Rachel did not know. He ended on an interrogative note. She squatted and with her finger drew a picture in the sand. A flat-topped block-house. A tent. A flagpole with a flag sticking out at the top. A circle around it all to indicate the wall.

The man laughed happily. He switched off the radio and made a clicking sound in the back of his mouth. The camel knelt. Gracefully he slipped down, landing lightly close beside her. He drew several new buildings in the sand, and outside the circle added a few palm trees. The palm trees pleased him. He chuckled to himself and drew a few more. Against one of them he sat a little stick figure. That did it. He clapped his hands like a four-year-old and laughed until tears rolled down his cheeks. After a while she joined in. Gradually the fit subsided. He dabbed at his eyes with the tips of his finely shaped fingers.

"Where is it?" she asked in French. He smiled at her encouragingly. Rachel assumed a questioning expression and pointed with exaggerated tentativeness in different directions. He began to like this game as well as the other. Each new direction struck him as funnier than the last. He was getting set to go into the hand-clapping bit.

"Stop it," Rachel said in an irritated tone.

His laughter ceased immediately. Gently he laid his hand on her shoulder and turned her toward the north-east. With a slow gesture he raised one of his beautiful hands and pointed in the direction she had come from.

"Merci," Rachel said, clasping her hands in a thanking gesture.

She thought of one more question: "How far?" She repeated it a couple of times. He pointed again with the same elegance. She shook her head, and held her hands apart as if she were telling fish stories. He giggled and held his hands apart, a little wider.

"Merci," she said again.

From an inner pocket the man drew several grimy dates and offered them to her. Because she had read that refusing food was a cardinal rudeness in the eyes of primitive people she took one and ate it, expecting him to do the same. But he returned the rest of the dates to his pocket.

"Merci," she said again, holding out her hand. Instantly she saw that he did not want to shake it. He clasped the tips of her fingers for a moment, stepped on the neck of the camel and sat lightly against the hump. The camel stood, bobbed its head and strode away. Two French female voices began discussing their favorite detergent.

Rachel made a detour of several kilometers to the west before she found a path through the dunes. Then she drove in the direction the man had pointed, stopping several times to look about with the binoculars. She saw nothing resembling the drawing in the sand, nor any sign at all of human existence, until she reentered Mhamid. He had sent her back to the town. A late afternoon breeze nipped at the Moroccan flag on the pole in front of the police station.

Rachel parked by the hotel and carried her handbag and suitcase inside. A ceiling fan in the tiny lobby revolved with barely enough speed to keep the flies off it. Behind a linoleum-covered counter a pale woman slightly older than Rachel was pouring Pernod into a glass. She wore no make-up but compensated by what she did to her hair. It was twisted into the kind of knots found on uncombed poodles, and reddened with henna. The eyebrows had been plucked away so there was no problem getting them to match.

Rachel asked for a room and the woman opened a stained register and asked her to sign. The way the woman squinted at the entry Rachel made in the book suggested that the Pernod was not her first of the day.

"Ah, Madame Monette," she said. "You are French? Me too."

"No. American," Rachel said.

"Truly? You speak French very well."

"Thank you. My husband was French." Rachel had not spoken more than a few words to anyone in the past three days and she found herself becoming voluble.

"So were two of mine," said the woman, with a rueful laugh.

"They're not dead?"

"Oh, no," said the woman, "in fact I was not really married to either of them. I only told people I was because I am a respectable woman." She drained her glass, found a somewhat clean one behind the counter and filled the two of them. "Here," she said, sliding the new glass across the counter. "It's on the house."

"Thanks."

"It's nothing. How often do I get to talk to another European woman?" Rachel let the inaccuracy pass. The woman gulped more Pernod. "We don't have many visitors at this time of year."

"When is the busy season?" Rachel asked.

"Never." She patted Rachel's hand. Her fingernails came in several lengths and colors. She looked at Rachel with small eyes that probably were not very smart even when they were sober.

"It's good to see a European once in a while, instead of all these stinking Arabs."

The door opened and a handsome young Moroccan came in. He appeared not to have heard the woman's remark, but she suddenly became nervous anyway and rubbed her fingers on the rim of the glass.

"Bonjour," he said in a way that included both of them. Then to Rachel he added, in French, "Be careful. Madame Ratelle likes to turn people into drunkards like herself."

"Be nice in front of the lady, Rashid," the woman said. "She's come all the way from America. Give me a kiss."

The young man ignored her. "What state in America?" he asked Rachel in good English.

"Massachusetts."

"Oh, New England," he said.

"Yes, have you been there?"

"Not yet," Rashid said. "But I lived for a year in England."

Madame Ratelle's eyes moved quicky but uncomprehendingly from one to the other, as if she were a spectator for the first time at a tennis match.

Rashid introduced himself and they shook hands.

"I am helping Madame Ratelle with the hotel for a while," he explained, "but in the summer I must return to Agadir. I'm the assistant to an important British travel agent."

"What are you saying about me?" Madame Ratelle asked sharply.

"Nothing. I was telling Madame of my work with Agatours."

Madame Ratelle laughed sarcastically. Rashid turned his back on her.

"How long have you been in Morocco?" he asked Rachel, resuming the conversation in English.

"Three days."

"And you are already here? Most tourists never get this far at all. Where did you enter the country?"

"Casablanca."

"Ah, Casablanca," Rashid said, smiling broadly. "I love Casablanca. 'The problems of three little people don't amount to a hill of beans in this world. You're getting on that plane.' Fantastic. I've seen it twenty times.' I adore that phrase 'hill of beans.' Are there many like it in English?"

"Some," Rachel said.

"Tell me."

"Ocean of tears." It was the first one that came to mind. His face grew solemn.

Rachel reached for her suitcase. "I'd like to go to my room now," she said.

"Of course. You must be tired. I'll show you the way." Rashid turned to Madame Ratelle. "Number eight," he said in French.

"I've put madame in number twelve," said Madame Ratelle defensively.

"Why? The hotel is empty. Give me number eight."

She handed him the key and he carried Rachel's suitcase up the stairs.

"Here we are," he said, pushing open the door to number eight. The floor was purple linoleum, the bed was lumpy, the bedspread had holes in it burned by cigarettes, there were no pillows. The heat was so stifling that the flies were enervated.

Rashid crossed the room, pushed aside the yellow plastic curtains and opened the window.

"It's not Claridge's," he said.

"That's a good thing. I can't afford Claridge's."

Rashid laughed and laughed. She seemed to have that effect on the locals. "I adore witty women," he said, turning his dark liquid eyes on her. They all do, thought Rachel.

"We have dinner in the dining room at eight o'clock,"

Rashid said. "Whatever else one thinks of Madame Ratelle she is an excellent cook."

"I'll be there."

"The bathroom is at the end of the hall."

He seemed reluctant to leave the room. She wondered if he expected a tip.

"Have you come to see the rock drawings?" he asked.

"I didn't know there were any."

"Oh, beautiful ones. Crocodiles, elephants, lions—they're everywhere." He waved his arm toward the window. "Professor DePoe from Paris has been here studying them for the whole week. I can introduce you to him."

"Does he know the terrain very well?"

"Yes," he said, slightly puzzled. "But not as well as I do. I've been working as his guide since he got here. I was born in Zagora. But I'm not Berber. I'm pure Arab."

"Have you ever heard of something called Camp Siegfried? In the southwest?" Rachel asked.

"No. There is no such place around here," Rashid said.

"Are you certain?" Rachel pressed. "It may be in ruins."

"Ruins?" Rashid's face brightened. "Yes, there are ruins. I can show you them. They are in the southwest as you say, less than an hour's drive. I can take you to them."

"Can we go now?" Rachel asked, unable to keep the excitement out of her voice.

He laughed. "It will be dark soon. The ruins will still be there in the morning."

"All right," Rachel agreed.

"You may be disappointed," Rashid warned. "There is not much to see. It's not like the rock drawings. And it is not called Siegfried. They are the ruins of the fort of the slave traders."

Rachel felt her excitement ebb. "They sound much too old to be what I'm looking for."

Rashid looked at her closely. "There are still slave traders in Morocco, madame."

15

Rachel awoke soon after dawn. The hotel was quiet. She took the tiny threadbare towel from the wall hook and walked softly down the hall to the bathroom. Behind the closed door of number five she heard the low murmur of a male voice, and then Madame Ratelle saying distinctly and angrily, "You are going nowhere until I tell you." The male voice murmured again in a higher pitch. Rachel went into the bathroom.

Rachel liked long showers, but not in cold salt water. When she went downstairs she was wide awake. In the dining room Madame Ratelle was serving sticky buns to a bald, plump European man who didn't need them. Rashid sat alone in a corner stirring his coffee with a distracted deliberation that suggested he might go on stirring it forever. Somehow he managed to appear quite un-American in his tight white jeans and black nylon jacket with "New York Yankees" written across the front.

"Good morning," Madame Ratelle said with loud cheeriness. "You slept well?"

"Yes, thank you," Rachel said.

"You see?" Madame Ratelle said to the bald man as if Rachel had settled a dispute. "Our guests sleep well." The bald man spread a thick coat of butter on top of a sticky bun and took a big bite.

"I'm trying to persuade Professor DePoe to move in here," Madame Ratelle explained to Rachel. "He insists on staying with the caid instead of me, his own countryman. They get lice, people who sleep in the caid's beds, every one of them."

Rashid rose and left the room, leaving his cup full. Madame Ratelle turned to watch him go. Spots of pink appeared on her pale cheeks. Although she stood by his elbow Professor DePoe seemed oblivious to her presence. His small blue eyes glanced quickly at Rachel before he reached for another sticky bun.

Madame Ratelle showed Rachel to a table and gave her a tangerine, coffee, and sticky buns.

"So Rashid is taking you to see some ruins," she said suspiciously.

"That's right." Rachel peeled the tangerine.

Professor DePoe twisted in his chair. "There are no ruins here, madame, in the strict sense of the word." His French was imperiously clear Parisian, but difficult to understand when his jaws were glued together with sticky bun. "We speak of rock engravings," he added.

"I've been told of ruins nearby, dating from the Second World War perhaps," Rachel said. "Have you ever heard of anything like that around here?"

"Very strange," said Professor DePoe, shaking his head. "You must tell me if you find something."

Outside, Rashid was putting things into the Land-Rover—two shovels and four long strips of corrugated steel.

"Sand ladders," he told Rachel. "Never go into the desert without them."

She let Rashid drive. He went in the same general direction she had gone the day before. He was a poor driver. Once when the jeep began to lose traction in a patch of loose sand he put his foot on the brake and almost buried them. But Rachel did not think it was a good time to give him driving tips. His face was puffed and sullen, and when he wasn't biting his lower lip with his upper teeth he let the lower teeth go to work on the upper one.

"When did you say you were going back to Agadir?" Rachel asked after a few kilometers, remembering something he had seemed happy about.

"I'm not going back," he replied gloomily. "Never."

"But what about your job, assisting the travel agent?"

"She doesn't want me anymore," Rashid said. "I am stuck down here in the desert."

"How long were you with the travel agency?"

"Eleven months."

"With that experience I'm sure you'll have no trouble finding a job at another agency," she said encouragingly.

Rashid laughed bitterly.

When they reached the line of sand dunes in the south Rashid made no attempt to penetrate, as Rachel had done, but followed them toward the west. In a little less than three kilometers they came to a narrow *oued* which cut straight across the plain from the stark gray hills in the north and disappeared among the dunes. Rashid drove the jeep onto its hard-packed bed, and followed it. The oued wound a serpentine course through the dunes before emerging on a small flat plain bounded on three sides by the dunes and on the fourth by a stark outcrop of russet-colored rock rising sharply from the desert floor.

On the plain the oued resumed a straight path, leading toward the outcrop. Halfway there it began quite suddenly to narrow, and soon vanished under a grave of worn stones. Rashid drove to the base of the outcrop.

"Over there," he said, using his nose as a pointer.

In the shadow of the outcrop Rachel saw a small gray pile of rubble. They got out of the jeep and walked closer. It was a heap of broken cement. Rachel picked up a piece and found that one side had a smooth half oval carved in it. If she found the matching piece and fitted them together she would have part of a concrete block.

"This is all that is left of the fort of the slave traders," Rashid said. There wasn't enough to build a tool shed.

"What else do you know about it?"

"They were very cruel."

Rachel dropped the piece of cement. It broke into several fragments on the unyielding sand.

"How was it destroyed?" Rachel asked.

"I don't know," Rashid said. "It has always been like this."

"Have you ever heard of Germans in this area?"

"Germans? I've seen many of them. They come every summer, in the worst heat. They love the engravings."

"I don't mean tourists," Rachel said. "I mean soldiers, German soldiers. During World War Two."

Rashid looked puzzled. "There was no war here," he said.

"Are there any more of these piles?"

"This is the only one I know."

Rachel walked around the debris. She could have found it near any demolition site in the world. In its banality she tried to see some link to Adam, but couldn't.

"Do many other people know about it?" She was running out of questions but she didn't want to leave.

Rashid thought about it. "The nomads of course," he said. "They know the desert, every little stone. But others, no, not many. No one comes here. There aren't even any engravings on these rocks." He waved at the outcrop contemptuously. If his prehistoric ancestors had considered them unworthy of decoration he had no respect for them either. "They are the only rocks around here that don't have engravings," he said.

Rachel sighed and looked away to the south, where the Sahara began. "If this was a fort where did the people who lived in it get their water?"

Rashid looked at her. "Are you a scientist like Professor DePoe?"

"No."

"You are very curious for a tourist."

"I'm not really a tourist," Rachel said. "I'm a sort of historian."

"Ah," he said. The information put him in a better mood. "I knew you were educated. I cannot resist educated women. Do you know that I am more educated than Madame Ratelle?"

"No."

"Yes. She knows practically nothing about literature or art. She grew up in Paris and she has never been to the Louvre. Can you imagine that? When I lived in London I went to the Tate every Sunday."

Rachel tried to imagine Rashid at the Tate.

"I knew every painting. I explained them to the American girls."

That helped her.

"What about the water?" she said.

"It's very simple." Rashid said. "You dig a well. Whenever there is a oued like that you find water." He pointed across the small plain. "Sometimes you have to dig deep, but you always find it. Where are you going?"

Rachel was running toward the jeep. "To get the shovels," she called over her shoulder.

Rashid took off his Yankees jacket and laid it down carefully before he began to dig. He worked enthusiastically. The March sun was not oppressive, just warm enough to encourage a light sweat. Rashid had a thin hairless torso with well-defined muscles. They looked good but they hadn't much staying power. After a few minutes he dropped the shovel, stretched his arms and sat down.

"Coffee break," he said.

Rachel took out the shovel. Rashid glanced at her in surprise, but said nothing. Rashid's exertions had produced little change in the dimensions of the pile. Rachel stood on top of it, bending her knees as she dug, and straightening them as she scooped each shovel load away, letting the big muscles of the body do the work. Sometimes she laid the shovel aside and moved the larger cement chunks with her hands. Her body found an easy steady rhythm. It encouraged her pores to open. The sweat they released her clothing absorbed, and it soon clung to her uncomfortably. She felt Rashid's eyes on her back, and thought of removing her cotton shirt, just to show what educated women were capable of.

After an hour she had moved the debris aside, exposing a rough circle of stony sand which differed from the surrounding sand only by its thin covering of gray dust. Her body felt loose and relaxed but blisters were forming on the inside edges of both palms. She turned to Rashid and saw he had fallen asleep beside the Land-Rover, his Yankees jacket over his face to protect it from the sun.

Rachel dug her shovel into the hard sand. The crust resisted penetration. To break it she had to place her foot on the upper edge of the blade and push with all her strength. But when she had dug away the crust the work was easier. The sand became less stony, less dense, and, it seemed to her, very slightly moist.

When Rashid awoke Rachel was up to her waist in the pit she had made. Rubbing his eyes he approached her and glanced down into the hole.

"Maybe I was wrong," he said.

Rachel looked up at him. "I don't think so," she said. "This earth is moist." She tossed a shovelful up for him to examine.

He ignored it. "Aren't you hungry?" he asked. "We could come back tomorrow."

"No," Rachel said. "I want to dig a little deeper. I'm happy to pay you, Rashid."

He jerked his head back as if she had slapped him.

"I came with you out of friendship," he said hotly, and walked away.

"Come back, Rashid," she called after him. "Only a fool works for nothing." He kept walking. "What kind of person would I be if I took advantage of a friend to save a little money? Come back."

He stopped and turned to face her. They gazed at each other. "Okay," he said.

He came to the edge of the hole and extended his hand to help Rachel climb out. "But not for long," he said, looking at his watch. "I don't want to drive back in the dark."

"Why not? The car has lights."

"It's no good to be in the desert at night," Rashid insisted. "The vipers come out."

"I'm sure we'll be safe in the car," Rachel said. Rashid shook his head.

Rachel went to the jeep for the canteen while he began digging. She tilted her head back and let the tepid water flow down her throat. She was about to pour some on her head when she heard the clear sound of steel striking steel.

"Come here," called Rashid, but she was already there. Rashid knelt in the pit. With his hands he was clearing the earth from a thick brown metal ring which bore a silver gash from the shovel's blow. Rachel got in to help.

As they moved the dirt aside they saw that the ring was bolted to a round block of wood, slightly bigger than a manhole cover. To lift it they had first to widen the space at the bottom of the hole. They dug quickly, flinging the earth out so carelessly that much of it slid back down.

When there was enough room for both of them to stand in the hole without placing their feet on the wooden cover they leaned their shovels against the earthen wall and bent together to grasp the metal ring. It required all their strength to lift it.

The odor of decay that rose from the well made them both sick where they stood. Hands on their knees they vomited, pouring their insides into a well of bones and teeth and skulls. The well brimmed with the hard remains of the dead, jumbled together in an obscene and secret intimacy.

Rachel heard Rashid scrambling to get out. He was making a small high-pitched noise in his throat, and he was having trouble gripping the edge of the pit to pull himself out. She placed her hands on his buttocks, pushed, and followed him up. He ran to the jeep and leaned against it, sucking air into his lungs. Rachel laid her hand gently on his back. He was shaking. She looked for his jacket and saw it on the ground by the edge of the pit.

When she bent to pick it up a faint glimmer in the well caught the corner of her eye. She peered down but saw nothing more than she had seen already. Reluctantly she entered the hole and looked more closely. Nothing glimmered.

With the toe of her shoe she poked gingerly into the well. One of the skulls seemed different. She pried it loose with her foot and rolled it out of the well and onto the earth at the bottom of the pit. A perfectly round piece of bone was missing from the top of the skull. In its place there was a very thin steel plate. Rachel knelt to examine it. She was still there when she heard the sound of a motor.

She climbed out. Halfway across the plain she saw three jeeps approaching, moving in single file along the oued. Rashid was watching them. She handed him his jacket.

"Who are they?" she asked.

"The army," he said. His eyes were frightened.

"They're not going to accuse us of doing it," Rachel said, gesturing at the well.

"You don't understand," Rashid said impatiently. "We are probably not allowed to be here. This is very close to Algeria. We may even be in Algeria."

"Don't worry," she said to calm him. "Everyone knows that tourists make silly mistakes."

They watched the jeeps come. When they were about fifty feet away they stopped. Men in khaki uniforms jumped out, holding rifles in front of their chests. They quickly formed a wide circle around Rachel and Rashid: A tall man in khaki stepped unhurriedly from the first jeep. Rachel thought she had seen him before, standing with another man in front of the gendarmerie. His eyes rested for a moment on the pile of dirt they had dug, then moved to Rachel. He crossed the sand to her and held out his hand, palm up.

"May I see your permit, madame?" he said politely in French.

"What sort of permit?" Rachel asked.

"You must obtain a permit before making archaeological excavations, madame. They are available from the Ministry of Antiquities in Rabat." He was still polite but his eyes were hard.

"I'm sorry," Rachel said. "I didn't know. I'm a tourist. In any case, I was not digging for antiquities. But if you'll come with me I think I can show you evidence that a serious crime took place here." She led him to the well. He looked in, but he wasn't really interested.

"You are right, madame," he said. "Desecration of old burial grounds is a very serious crime."

"Don't be silly. This is no burial ground."

"Are you informing me about the customs of my own people, madame?" he asked her coldly. He turned and nodded to one of his men.

"Of course not," Rachel said. "But—"

The soldier walked up to Rashid and swung the butt of his rifle into his stomach. When Rashid doubled over the soldier was waiting to drive a knee into his face. Rashid fell backwards on the sand.

Rachel put her hand on the officer's sleeve. "Stop it," she said to him. "He hasn't done anything." The officer jerked his arm away from her and with the back of his other hand slapped her hard across the face.

"You bastard," she said in English. There was a shine in his eyes that hadn't been there before, the dark shine of the inner spirit that had made the hard cruel eyes. Rachel fought down her anger.

"I want to speak to the nearest American consul at once," she said to him in French.

"Of course, madame," he said, his eyes very bright. "There is a telephone behind this rock. Shall I tell one of my men to show you?"

Behind him a soldier snickered. The officer turned and gave him a cold look. When he turned back to Rachel the shine had vanished beneath the surface of his eyes.

16

Rachel held on as long as she could before going to the stinking little hole in the floor. Her reluctance was due not so much to the filth as to the presence of the guard seated in the walled courtyard beyond the bars. She could not see him in the darkness but he could see her by the yellow light of the greasy bulb in the ceiling of the cell. The light that had no switch.

The only piece of furniture in the cell was a wooden pallet. Rachel lay on it and tried to sleep, but her eyes would not stay closed. They watched the glow of the guard's cigarette in the night. The ember made quick tiny movements like a firefly trapped in a very small cage. After a while it escaped and dropped in a long arc to the ground. The fall killed it. In a few minutes the guard had trapped another one.

By the first light of dawn Rachel saw that he had fallen asleep on the stones, his back to her and his knees drawn up to his chest. A stooped woman with blue dots tattooed around her eyes like a mask entered the courtyard bearing an earthenware bowl. When she noticed the guard she made a clicking sound of disapproval and kicked him smartly in the back. With a groan he got to his feet, and fumbled with a ring of many keys fastened to his belt. He carefully considered several of them before making a final choice. He and the woman approached Rachel's cell. The guard unlocked the barred door and pushed it open. The woman slid the bowl inside and the guard relocked the cell. Without looking at her they turned to leave.

"I want some water," Rachel said in French.

Their faces were blank. "Water," she repeated. She made drinking motions. Comprehension lifted their heads back as if it had tapped them on the chin. The woman went away and returned with a can of Coca-Cola. She reached between the bars and set it on the floor.

Rachel pulled off the metal tab and drank the syrupy contents of the can before she looked inside the earthenware bowl. Two frayed lumps of gray meat floated in a brown swill. She left it untouched.

Rachel sat on the pallet and waited. In the late morning Madame Ratelle appeared, carrying Rachel's suitcase and handbag. The guard let her into the cell. The licorice scent of Pernod accompanied her. She looked at Rachel's face.

"My God," she said. "They hit you, too."

"Just once."

"Pigs," Madame Ratelle said. Through the bars she made a spitting sound at the guard curled up on the stones. "They're all pigs." Rachel was not sure which group she meant, soldiers, Arabs, or men.

"How is Rashid?"

The mention of his name bunched the skin of Madame Ratelle's forehead where the eyebrows should have been. "Fine. He is in bed at the hotel," she said. "He is a stupid boy." The focus of her eyes lengthened as she gazed into the beyond, of space or time. "Too stupid for the hotel business, I think," Madame Ratelle added.

"He didn't do anything wrong," Rachel said.

Madame Ratelle expelled air through her compressed lips, making a rude vibration loud enough to stir the guard in his sleep. "Entering Algeria was the act of an idiot. He is the one who should be in jail."

"Did we cross the border?"

Madame Ratelle waved impatiently to the south. "The desert is the border. There is fighting all the time. Phosphates." She said the word again, sarcastically.

"But I'm a tourist. Doesn't that mean anything?"

"It does if they believe you."

"Madame Ratelle, I want you to do me a favor."

"What favor?" Madame Ratelle said warily.

"Telephone the nearest American consul and tell him what has happened. There should be one in Marrakech. If not try the embassy in Rabat."

Madame Ratelle shook her head. "What you ask is impossible. If I tried it I would be in here with you before I spoke two words."

"I don't understand," Rachel said.

"There is one telephone in Mhamid, the only link to the outside. It is in the caïd's office at the gendarmerie." She pointed through the rear wall of the cell.

Rachel wrapped her hands around the bars and looked up at the sky. A dark brown buzzard circled high above, dropped down for a better view, then rose cumbersomely and flew away.

"In that case I'll need a lawyer," Rachel said. "I don't know if I've been charged with any crime, or whether I'm to have a trial. Or how long they can keep me here."

Madame Ratelle touched Rachel's arm. "There are no lawyers in Mhamid," she said. "The law here is the caïd."

"Then I have to see him."

"You will," Madame Ratelle said. "But first he will make you wait. Perhaps a day or two, perhaps a week." She took a package of Gauloise from the pocket of her skirt and lit one with a cheap plastic lighter. She squinted at Rachel through the blue smoke.

"If you want my advice, make the first move."

"How?"

Madame Ratelle came closer and lowered her voice. "Wait until tonight. Then call the guard and offer him a bribe. Give him enough to make it worth the beating he will get." Her eyes became thoughtful. "Two hundred dirhams should be sufficient. Go to two hundred and fifty if you have to."

"I'll pay whatever it takes," Rachel said in an excited whisper. "Will he do it?"

"I think so," Madame Ratelle said. "Have you got enough money?"

Rachel groped quickly through her handbag. Her passport was there and so was her notebook. The money and traveler's checks were gone.

"That proves I am right about the guard," Madame Ratelle said.

"He took the money?"

"No. Someone who did not want you bribing him took it." Madame Ratelle walked to the corner and flicked her cigarette into the hole in the floor. "Can you have money sent to you in Marrakech?" she asked Rachel.

"Of course," Rachel said. "I could give you a telephone number in the United States and you could make the call from Marrakech. No one here would know."

"No. They will find out if I help you." Madame Ratelle's eyes moved to the corner of the cell where a thin plume of smoke rose out of the hole. "After you have gone I still have to live here. If you can call it living." She lit another cigarette. "But you can have money sent to Marrakech when you get there?"

"Yes. But how do I get there?"

Madame Ratelle's thin lips curved in a little smile. "There is another way to bribe the guard."

"That's out of the question," Rachel said angrily.

"Is it? You may change your mind after a few days." They both looked at the bowl on the floor. "I'll bring you something to eat," Madame Ratelle said more gently. She turned toward the guard to be sure he was still asleep, and quickly took a small folded envelope from between her breasts.

"From Rashid," she said, handing it to Rachel. Rachel saw jealous suspicion in her eyes. "He insisted I deliver it to you." The envelope was sealed. Madame Ratelle waited for Rachel to open it, but she put it in her pocket instead.

Madame Ratelle shouted at the guard. Wearily he got up and unlocked the cell. Madame Ratelle took out her plastic lighter. "When you have read it use this. I don't want the boy beaten again." She stepped outside.

"Where is my jeep?" Rachel asked before she went away.

Madame Ratelle gave her a knowing smile. "In front of the hotel. The keys are in the ignition and there is a full can of gasoline inside."

The guard turned the key in the lock and stared through the bars at Rachel. The features of his face were little, except for the ears which were large and stuck out from the skull. His head was too small for his pear-shaped body. He turned away and walked across the courtyard. On the other side he blew his nostrils empty one at a time and lay down on the stones. When he was asleep Rachel opened the envelope. The note was hand-written in English.

Dear Madame (she read)
I am so very very sory. Do not eat the food they give you. It will make you sick. Jeanne will bring food. That place is *not* a bearial place. I have herd of an old man who nos.
I will pray that you are soon free.

Rashid

Rachel lit the corners of the letter and the envelope and dropped them burning to the floor. She lay on the pallet and slept. She dreamed of the well. It was the same as before except that she could hear Adam calling her from far below.

The turning of the key in the lock woke her. A short man wearing a white robe and a white skull cap was standing in the doorway. The guard went away without locking him in. He took a position in the middle of the courtyard and stood alertly.

Rachel sat up. The white-robed man watched her. He had large intelligent dark eyes and a neatly trimmed white beard. His skin was almost completely free of wrinkles. He could have been forty, or sixty. Under the robe his shoulders were muscular.

"I am the caid," he said in French. "That is something like a mayor," he explained, "but more like a chief. Madame Ratelle says that you wished to see me." His tone was polite and slightly pedagogical, like a doctor's.

"I want some explanations."

"Explanations?"

"Why am I here? Have I been charged with a crime? Which one of your men stole my money? Those will do for a start." Rachel's voice rose and the guard stepped forward. The caid motioned him back.

"I am sure none of my men would take your money, madame. But the law prohibits prisoners from having any." He spoke in a way that implied he would change it if he could.

"Then I should be given a receipt. That is how these things are done in civilized countries."

The caid's head jerked back as if his hair had been yanked. His eyes narrowed. Without turning he spoke a curt command to the guard, who ran off immediately. Rachel and the caid watched each other until the guard returned. He held up a hand full of coins and bills and traveler's checks. The caid gestured toward Rachel. The guard entered the cell and handed it all to her. A coin fell to the floor. It landed on edge and rolled across the stones to the corner, where it disappeared into the little hole. The caid said something angrily to the guard. The guard walked to the corner, stooped and fished about with his hand for the coin. When he found it he wiped it on his trousers and brought it back to Rachel on his palm. She took it. The guard looked at her feet. The caid dismissed him and he resumed his post.

"Now, madame," said the caid in a flat voice, "I, too, would like an explanation."

"There is nothing to explain. I went to look at the desert. I did not know we were near Algeria. I wasn't even aware that there was trouble between the two countries."

"Why did you dig a hole in the sand?"

Rachel suddenly felt the whole story begin to well up from her chest. But as she opened her mouth her eyes rested on the white beard and she realized that the man was probably old enough to have been caid in 1942. "To see if there was water," she said.

"Were you thirsty?" the caid asked in a neutral voice.

"I was curious. My guide told me that the nomads often look for water near those dried riverbeds. I wanted to see if it was true."

"Unfortunately, Lieutenant Moutassim reports that you have desecrated a burial ground." He sighed. "Moroccans are a very religious people." It could have been a statement of fact but she took it as a threat. He called to the guard, who brought a wooden office chair and placed it in the cell. The caid hitched up his robe and sat down. He wore leather sandals on his stubby feet.

"May I see your passport, madame?"

"Haven't you seen it already?" Rachel asked. He ignored her and held out his hand. She gave it to him. He took a pair of silver-rimmed spectacles from a pocket in the side of his robe, put them on and examined the passport. His face assumed a puzzled expression.

"Excuse me, madame, but what is the English word for religion?"

"It's the same."

"Your passport does not include that category on the page devoted to personal description. Why is that?"

"Under American law, government and religion are kept separate."

"How strange," said the caid. "Is that, too, a mark of civilization?"

"Some people think so," Rachel said. The caid's eyes told her that they weren't his kind of people. He handed her the passport.

"May I ask what is your religion, madame?"

"I am not a religious person."

"That may be true," he said, watching her face closely. "Here in Morocco there are many Muslims who say they are not religious. But if you ask them they will tell you that their religion is Islam. It is in that sense that I am asking you."

"In America we don't see it that way," Rachel replied.

"You are a Jew," he said, bringing his hand down sharply on his thigh. "Why not admit it? It is nothing to be ashamed of. The Prophet said that the Jews are a special people." The caid began to adopt his lecturing tone. "A quarter of a million Jews used to live in this country, side by side with us. In my own lifetime. Their lives and property were protected by law." A brief smile passed across his face in memory of this golden age, but it didn't reach his eyes. "Now, of course, most of them have gone to Israel. And despite Zionist efforts to silence them we have heard that they are clamoring to return."

"I don't think that's true," Rachel said.

"Of course you don't." He leaned forward. "Why would you? You are a paid agent of the Zionists."

"You're crazy," Rachel said. "I've never even set foot in Israel."

He laughed sarcastically. "Do you take me for a fool?" he asked. She saw again the intelligence in his eyes. He was no fool, but if he believed what he was saying he was far more dangerous. "The Zionists have a gift for strategy and tactics," he went on. "How clever to send a woman. If she is captured she will be dealt with less harshly." He touched her knee with the tip of his forefinger. "They do not know Lieutenant Moutassim," he said.

Rachel drew back. "I want to telephone the American ambassador. He is a friend of mine."

"Very well. I will place the call. What name shall I ask for?"

Rachel glared at him.

"The American ambassador to Morocco is a woman," the caid said.

Rachel felt herself blush at being caught in the lie, and at her stupidity. She couldn't afford to be stupid.

"I meant friend in the sense of countryman. I apologize for my bad French."

"On the contrary, madame, it is excellent. You speak it far better than any American I have met. Far better." The caid stood and smoothed his robe. "Thank you for this interview," he said. The guard came to carry the chair away.

Rachel got up from the pallet. "But what is happening? Am I charged with a crime?"

The caid turned to her. "You will be in due course."

"Then I want to see a lawyer."

"One will be provided at the proper time."

The caid stepped outside and the guard locked the cell. As the caid was walking away Rachel suddenly crossed the floor, poked her head through the bars and called to his back. "If I am tried as a spy where would the trial take place?"

He stopped walking, turned and stroked his beard. "Possibly Marrakech. Perhaps Rabat."

"But not here?"

His eyes tried to probe hers. "No, not for something of that magnitude," he said finally.

"Then I am a spy," Rachel shouted at him. "Do you hear me? A spy."

He left the courtyard but not before Rachel saw the worried look appear in the big brown eyes. The guard went to his favorite spot, lay down and made himself comfortable. Rachel sat on the pallet and waited for nightfall.

17

Evening. Hunger grew in her stomach. Thirst dried her tongue. But Madame Ratelle did not come. A crust of flies formed over the earthenware bowl. They were big brown flies that made no buzzing noise when they flew, moving around the cell in silent smears. In the shadows the guard smoked a cigarette, resting his back on the far wall of the courtyard. Rachel lay on the pallet.

She awoke with a start, and went to the bars of the cell. The sky was black, except for the strange moon, a reclining yellow crescent too lazy to get up, and the cold white stars as far away as far can be. In the darkness of the courtyard she saw the light of the guard's cigarette. She realized that the naked bulb in the ceiling had gone out.

Rachel listened carefully for sounds from the jail or the town beyond but she heard nothing. She felt through her handbag for the bank notes. By holding them close to her face and squinting she was able to count out two hundred and fifty dirhams.

"Guard," she called in a hoarse whisper. There was no response. "Come here," she said in a louder voice. The cigarette burned in the night. Rachel tapped her wedding band on the steel bar and called again. The little fire moved. It rose a foot or two and slowly approached the cell.

The guard stood a few feet from the bars of the cell. She could see the vague shape of his khaki uniform, but his face was lost in the night. He held the cigarette at his side. It coated his hand in red light. It was a very powerful hand for a man like him.

"I will give you two hundred and fifty dirhams to let me go," Rachel whispered. He didn't answer. She mimed the act of unlocking the door, and held up the money. She hoped he could see her better than she could see him. "Two hundred and fifty dirhams," she repeated, offering the money between the bars. "Please."

Without haste the hand lifted the cigarette to his mouth. It spread red light across his face. The hard eyes shone with it, but the shine came from inner fires. They were the eyes of Lieutenant Moutassim.

With his free hand Moutassim took Rachel's wrist and pulled. Her face struck the steel with a force that made her dizzy. She tried to draw away but he held her tightly with enormous strength, her breasts crushed against the bars. He raised the little fire and touched the back of her hand with it. She dropped the bills. He released her wrist and she stepped back out of reach. He kicked the money onto the stone floor.

Lieutenant Moutassim withdrew into the night. He began pacing the courtyard, rapidly at first and then more slowly. Huddled on the pallet Rachel listened to him breathing and watched the glow of his cigarette. She did not take her eyes off it. After a while he walked across the courtyard and did not return. Rachel heard a door close, and then another, very faint.

She got off the pallet and gathered the money from the floor. As she replaced it in her handbag she thought she heard a footstep in the courtyard, very close. She whirled and was hit in the face by the narrow beam of a flashlight. It was shut off immediately, leaving Rachel blind in the darkness. Her hands found the heavy bowl. She picked it up and moved softly to the rear of the cell.

"Madame Monette?" whispered a male voice that she remembered hearing before. She didn't answer. "It is I," came the whisper. "DePoe. I have a key."

She heard the key scrape in the lock, and felt DePoe in the cell. "Where are your things?" he said. "We must hurry."

Rachel still held the bowl in her hands. "How did you get the key?"

"I bribed the guard." His face was very near but she couldn't see it. She smelled toothpaste and onions on his breath. "We must go. I will explain later."

"But the guard isn't here. Lieutenant Moutassim took his place."

There was a silence before DePoe said very quietly, "I didn't see him. But in that case we are in great danger. Quickly."

Rachel put down the bowl and reached for her suitcase and handbag. She felt DePoe's hand on her back. He guided her out of the cell and across the courtyard. He opened a small door in the wall and led her outside.

They were in an unpaved unlit street. A small open jeep was parked on the far side. DePoe took Rachel's suitcase and handbag and wedged them behind the seat.

"Get in," he said. She hesitated. The moonlight cast a faint gleam on DePoe's bald head but left his eyes in shadow. "He will kill you," he whispered urgently. Rachel got in.

DePoe turned the key in the ignition with a delicate touch, as if that would make the engine catch more quietly. Without switching on the lights he drove quickly through a series of dark streets bordered by high clay walls. The last of these alleys opened quite suddenly on the flat plain to the west of town.

"Where are we going?"

"I want to see what you found in the desert," DePoe said. He pressed on the accelerator. His left hand reached for the headlight switch, hesitated and returned to the steering wheel. He hunched forward as far as his soft belly would allow.

"What makes you think I found something in the desert?"

"Logic. You told me at the hotel that you were interested in some ruins from the Second World War. I'd never heard of such ruins. But the same day you are brought back by Lieutenant Moutassim and thrown in jail. Therefore you found something that someone did not want found."

The jeep sped across the sand. In front of them the moon hung low in the skyline like a cupped hand bearing an unknown offering.

"Besides," DePoe added after a while, "I am staying with the caid. You have managed to make him very upset."

Rachel turned in her seat, trying to see his face. But the night painted every shape in featureless gray and shaded all the edges in black; except for the moon and its golden reflection on the curve of DePoe's bald head.

"How well do you know him?" Rachel asked.

"Who?" DePoe replied after a pause.

"The caid."

"Not well. I met him for the first time last week, when I arrived. The university arranged that I would be his guest."

"What university?"

"Aix-en-Provence."

"Rashid says you taught in Paris."

"He is incorrect."

DePoe glanced in the rearview mirror. "It must be safe by now," he said. He switched on the headlights. They drilled an expanding cone of light across the desert. In the distance a glowing pair of topazes hovered above the sand. When the jeep drew nearer Rachel saw that they were the eyes of a large brown hare. It bounded out of sight in two leaps.

"Can you remember the way?" DePoe asked.

"I don't understand why you are doing this," Rachel said. "They can easily find out you were involved."

"It won't matter. By dawn we can be at the airport in Marrakech. When they realize what has happened it will be too late."

"But why are you taking the risk?" Rachel pressed him.

'Shall we say it's my job?" he replied. "I am an employee of the government of France."

"Doing what?"

"France still has many interests in North Africa. I help protect them."

"So you aren't really a professor?"

"But I am. Anthropology. It's been my passion since childhood. And it provides an excellent cover.".

"What is France's interest in this?"

DePoe sighed. "How can I know until I've seen what you've found?"

Rachel told him the way.

They rode in silence. Gravity tugged the moon lower and lower in the sky until it sank from sight. No more topaz glowed in the yellow tunnel. The cold night air flowed over Rachel's face, powdering her hair with fine dust. DePoe found the oued and followed it through the dunes. They rose up on all sides like ocean waves frozen during a midnight storm.

The yellow beams touched the face of the outcrop on the far side of the plain. "Over there," Rachel said. They swept across the sand in a short arc. The pile of broken cement was gone. So was the earth that Rachel had dug out of the hole. And the hole.

"Stop," she said. She got out and walked toward the outcrop, examining the ground where the hole had been. "Come closer," Rachel called to DePoe. The light grew stronger, throwing Rachel's shadow against the rock. It also cast lines of thin parallel shadows across a patch of sand not much bigger than a pitcher's mound. They resembled miniature furrows.

"Someone's been over it with a rake," Rachel said over the sound of the motor. DePoe shut it off and walked over to Rachel. In front of his stomach he held out a shovel like a ceremonial object.

"I hope you won't think me ungentlemanly," he said, "but I have a heart condition."

Rachel hesitated.

"I have to see with my own eyes," DePoe said patiently. "Otherwise I can't help you."

"Help me how?"

"You tell me. After all, you haven't yet explained what you are doing here."

Rachel took the shovel. "I'll show you," she said. She dug the hole again.

It was easier the second time. The earth, looser and drier than it had been the day before, offered little resistance to the shovel. DePoe stood to one side, hands in the pockets of his tweed coat and the collar turned up. In less than two hours Rachel reached the round wooden cover. She leaned on the shovel and rested. She had spent most of her strength and energy, converting it into matter, the dirt that lay in mounds around the hole. She tried to remember her last meal. Sticky buns, almost two full days ago.

"Is anything wrong?" DePoe asked, looking down at her.

"I'll need your help to lift this cover," Rachel said. "It's very heavy."

"I'm sorry. Lifting is out of the question. The doctor was adamant on that." In the movies secret agents never had bad hearts, Rachel thought. "Why don't you use the shovel to pry it off?" DePoe suggested.

"All right," Rachel sighed. Wedging the blade of the shovel between the cover and the edge of the well she leaned all her weight on the handle. The cover began to lift. "Be ready," she warned him. "The smell is awful."

But the smell was gone too. When the cover slid off the top of the well it released only the scent of damp earth, coupled with a faint suggestion of cool fresh water. Rachel peered down in the empty blackness. DePoe shone his flashlight into it, but the beam didn't reach bottom. It expired somewhere in the void.

"Is this a joke?" DePoe asked in a hard voice.

"Not by me."

The yellow beam climbed backwards out of the hole, curved in a slow arc the way a rifle follows a moving target, and fastened on Rachel's face.

"You'd better explain," came the voice quietly from behind it.

Standing in the pit Rachel raised a hand to shield her eyes. "First get that damned thing off my face." In the silence which followed she heard DePoe's rapid shallow breathing. The light left her face, trailed down her body and came to rest at DePoe's feet like a heeling dog.

"Go on," DePoe said.

"I'm not trying to play games with you. I want to find out what's going on just as badly as you do, believe me. More so." And she told him about Dan and Adam and Andy and the document. She left out the blond man.

"The connection seems rather flimsy to me. It might help if I saw this document."

"I don't have it with me."

"Is it at the hotel?"

"No."

"Where then?"

"In a safe place. But I've got an English translation in my pocket. I'll show you." She moved to climb out of the pit.

"Stay right there," DePoe said in a tone that sounded cold and frightened at the same time. His right hand moved out of the shadows and pointed at her head. It held a small black gun.

Some people have reported that their life stories unreeled in their minds when they thought they were about to die. Rachel watched a shorter film. She saw DePoe eating sticky buns in the dining room of the Hotel

Mhamid while she discussed the planned drive to the ruins with Madame Ratelle. She saw the three jeeps coming without hesitation across the desert, as if they already knew where they were going. She saw Lieutenant Moutassim pacing in the night outside her cell.

"So you couldn't get Moutassim to do your dirty work for you," Rachel said, and she heard her voice as if it were another person's. It sounded hard, and calm. "No, that's not it. He was willing. The caid was the one who said no." DePoe did not speak. His breath wheezed quietly in his throat.

"Surely you don't believe the caid can keep this a secret much longer?" She gestured at the pit around her.

"Place your hands on your head," DePoe said nervously.

She did. "Think of all those soldiers who saw the well," Rachel continued. "Are you going to kill them too?"

"If it is necessary." But the quaver in his voice said it wouldn't be that easy.

"It was clever the way you asked for directions," Rachel said. "As if you didn't know the place at all. I bet you knew it when it was a going concern." She felt adrenaline pumping through her as if it had a heart of its own. "Who are you? Kopple? Shreyer? Reinhardt? Feldbrill?" De-Poe's forehead wrinkled in a puzzled way. Suddenly his eyes opened wider and Rachel was sure that they held a look of recognition.

"I don't know what you're talking about," he said, breathing very loudly. He made a flicking motion with the gun. "Now lift the shovel and place it slowly and carefully on the ground."

"You haven't got the strength to bury me," Rachel said, remaining motionless.

"Shut up," he said shrilly. "Do as I tell you."

"All right. But if I'm going to die anyway why not tell me where Adam is?"

"Is?" DePoe said. He shone the light into the pit. "The shovel. Now."

Rachel slowly lifted the shovel forward, off the ground. In the same motion she scooped a bit of dirt onto the end of the blade. She brought it even with the lip of the hole and as she stepped forward to set the shovel down she flung the dirt upward in DePoe's face. The gun went off. Rachel drove the blade at DePoe's groin. With a cry he fell backwards. She scrambled out of the pit. DePoe was crawling toward the gun, which lay on the sand a few feet away. His breath made a high whistling sound. Rachel grabbed the shovel and went after him. As his hand curled around the gun she brought the flat of the blade down hard on the back of his head.

Rachel dragged the body to the pit and tumbled it in. It hung on the lip of the well. She climbed into the pit and rolled it over the edge. After a few seconds she heard the hollow echo of a distant splash. She threw in the gun and the flashlight. Then she replaced the wooden cover, climbed out and began to fill in the pit. The well had been free of bodies for only a day. Rachel realized with horror that she was on the side that was putting them in.

She smoothed the earth over the top of the pit. With the edge of the shovel she tried to duplicate the furrows made by the rake. Then she put it in the back of the jeep and drove toward Mhamid.

18

Rachel drove the jeep across the plain until she saw the squat gray blocks of Mhamid thrust against the blackness of the night sky. She left it in the desert. As she walked toward the town she thought of Rashid's vipers, and wanted very much to be racing through the night on the road to Zagora, up the valley of the Draa, and over the mountains to Marrakech and the airport. She had very little time.

No lights shone in the town. The streets were empty. Behind the clay walls of the houses no one muttered in his sleep. Like a thief Rachel walked softly through the shadows.

She tried the door of the hotel. It opened with a squeak of the hinges. Quickly she turned to look at the gendarmerie across the square, but it remained dark and still. She entered the lobby and felt her way up the stairs. Keeping one hand on the wall she went along the corridor until she came to the second-last door on the right. Her fingers reached for the brass numeral screwed to the wood and traced the metallic shape of the number five.

Rachel knocked three times, quickly and almost noiselessly. There was no response. She counted to thirty before turning the knob and stepping inside.

She could see the shape of the bed under the narrow window. On the white pillows lay two heads, one dark, the other light. Rachel went to the dark one, found a shoulder, and prodded it gently.

"Rashid," she whispered.

On the other pillow the light head came awake with a jerk. "Who's there?" said Madame Ratelle in a high scared voice.

"Shh," Rachel said. "It's me."

"You? How dare you break into my room like this?" Anger pushed the fear out of her voice, and made it louder.

"Be quiet," Rachel hissed.

Rashid rolled over and sat up, rubbing his eyes. Sweeping away the covers with a furious motion Madame Ratelle leapt from the bed and pressed the switch of the lamp on the dressing table. It stayed dark. Madame Ratelle swore at it, quite loudly.

"It's the generator," Rashid explained. "They've gone back to shutting it off at night."

"Merde," said Madame Ratelle. Rachel heard the dresser drawer open, hands fumble in jewelry and tissue paper, the scrape of a match. Madame Ratelle lit a candle and faced Rachel across the bed. Her long thin breasts pointed to the curved scar on her lower abdomen. Her pale body shook very slightly.

"I see your bribe was acceptable," she said. "But you are crazy to come here. If they find out we'll all be in that stinking jail. You have no right to do that to us."

"I'm sorry," Rachel said firmly. "I need Rashid. Not for long, but I need him now."

"Why? You weren't satisfied with the guard?"

"Don't be a fool." Rachel turned to Rashid. "I want you to take me to see the man you mentioned in the note."

"Tonight?"

"It's the only time I've got," Rachel said. Rashid looked at Madame Ratelle.

"If you go, you don't come back," she said.

"Madame Ratelle, please. A boy's life may depend on it."

"What about Rashid? He's a boy too."

"Shh," Rachel whispered fiercely. "I'm talking about a five-year-old boy. And if you cared so much about Rashid you wouldn't tell him not to come back." Madame Ratelle had no answer. Her eyes went to Rashid, and they seemed to want him to say something. But he kept silent. "Please don't make it difficult," Rachel went on. "I can give you both money if you want."

"No," Rashid said. "Some things I do for free."

"Shut up," Madame Ratelle told him. She turned to Rachel, holding the candle in front of her breasts the way nuns do in processions. "How much money are you offering?"

"I don't know. Five hundred dirhams."

"Make it a thousand each."

"I don't know if I have that much in cash. I can sign some traveler's checks."

"That's very funny," Madame Ratelle said. But not enough to make her laugh. "What happens to us when we cash them?" She snorted. The haggling improved her mood. "How much cash have you got?"

"About thirteen hundred dirhams."

"Very well." She held out her hand.

"It's in the jeep."

"Go get it."

"There isn't time," Rachel said impatiently. "The jeep is outside the town. You have my word that I will give the money to Rashid before I leave."

"I won't take it," Rashid said.

Rachel gripped his bare shoulders very hard, digging her nails into the flesh. "You will," she said quietly. "You can solve the problem of what to do about your pride some other time. Now let's go."

He got out of bed and searched about the floor for his clothing. Madame Ratelle bent over him extending the candle. Huddled together their naked bodies looked defenseless, but in some way suggested to Rachel that their relationship had a better basis than she had first suspected.

When Rashid was dressed Madame Ratelle hugged him and kissed him on the mouth. "You are a stupid boy," she said. He turned to Rachel.

"I'm ready," he said.

In the eyes of each of them Rachel saw fear. They were afraid of loneliness, poverty, each other, Moutassim, the caid, the west, the east. And of her. She was struck again by the predatory feeling that had come to her as she smoothed the sand over the well.

Rachel left the hotel door open to avoid risking a second squeak. Rashid saw the Land-Rover parked in front of them. He put his mouth very close to her ear and spoke in a voice so light that the words seemed to bypass her auditory passage and enter her mind directly.

"You lied to us."

She shook her head and cupped her hands around his ear. "I have another jeep," she said, reaching inside the Land-Rover for the spare gasoline can. They took turns carrying it into the desert.

Rachel was worried that she might not be able to find the jeep in the darkness, but her steps led her directly to it. It was much closer to the town than she had remembered.

"This is Professor DePoe's jeep," Rashid said suspiciously. Rachel did not respond. "How did you get it?"

"He lent it to me."

"When?"

"Tonight, of course." She sat in the driver's seat and glanced at the luminous dial of the dashboard clock. It said twelve forty-eight. "Get in. We haven't got much time."

Rashid refused to budge. "I don't believe you," he said

stubbornly. "Why would he do that? He is a friend of the caid."

"I thought they just met last week."

"That's what he wants people to think," Rashid replied. "But when he arrived I took him to the caid's house. They looked at each other in a very strange way. They had met before." He said it with certainty. "So how did you get the jeep?"

"I stole it," Rachel said impatiently. "The keys were in the ignition and I didn't want anyone to wake up in the night and wonder where mine had gone."

"I still don't believe you," he said.

"You wouldn't believe the truth either."

"Give me a chance."

"No, Rashid. It wouldn't do you any good to know, and it might do you a lot of harm."

He sighed and got into the car. "Drive north," he said. "Toward the hills."

The temperature continued to fall and the open car gave little protection. Rachel adjusted the heater to its maximum, but the warm air barely had time to touch their feet before the cold wind reached in and blew it out the back.

"Tell me about this man," Rachel said.

"There is not much I can tell you. After they took you to jail I was very angry. I went to Zagora and talked to a friend of mine. He is a school teacher, and knows the history of this region. He said he has an uncle who once told him a story about that place."

"What story?"

"He didn't say." Rashid paused. "His uncle is not an educated man. I don't think my friend takes him seriously."

"He hasn't seen what we saw."

The rounded bulks of the hills seemed to float on the plain like icebergs on a calm sea. Rachel slowed the jeep.

"Over there," Rashid said. "Where the tents are."

Rachel saw no tents, but she steered in the direction he pointed. After she had driven a short distance her eyes were able to separate two low shapes from the shadows of the slope.

"Stop here," Rashid said. They left the jeep and approached the tents on foot. A sharp voice called to them in a language Rachel did not recognize. Rashid quickly responded in a placating tone. Rachel heard a rustling sound and two robed men stepped forward from the shadows. Both carried rifles. When they came closer Rachel saw they were no older than Rashid. He spoke to them for a few minutes. She did not understand a word he said, but the polite soothing way he said it was unmistakable. One of the men grunted and turned on his heel. Rachel and Rashid followed him to the nearest tent. The other man followed them.

The first man lifted a flap in the tent wall and went inside. Rachel heard a brief, muffled conversation. The flap reopened and a line of women, children, and babies paraded out and walked to the second tent. The man behind them nudged them forward with his rifle.

Inside the first man had lit two oil lamps that looked like they had been handed down by Aladdin: the smoky flickering light illuminated the worn rugs overlapping on the floor and the goatskins and sheepskins lying in little piles where people had been sleeping. On the edge of the thickest rug was a powerful overseas radio. Sitting beside it was the man who liked drawing pictures in the sand. Rachel smiled at him. He smiled back, but without a hint of recognition. He raised his fine hands above his head, palms up, and lowered them slowly to the rug. Everyone sat.

"Tell him why we are here," Rachel said to Rashid, "but don't mention what we found in the well."

Rashid spoke to the man in a questioning tone. He answered, talking rapidly and making vigorous gestures, most of them toward the south. Rashid turned to the two younger men and said something in a language that sounded different to Rachel. One of the men shook his head.

"Is something wrong?" Rachel asked.

"He speaks a dialect of Berber I've never heard."

"Can you understand what he says?"

"Most of it. I don't recognize some of the words. His grandsons speak Arabic, but he does not. He has no education."

Rachel had supposed they were his sons. While he and Rashid talked she watched his face. Like the caid's it did not betray his age.

After a few minutes Rashid turned to Rachel. "He says that he comes from far away, deep in the desert. Many years ago there was a very bad summer. The wells went dry. People died. He took his family and camels and came north. It was a hard journey. His first wife died, and a baby. He slaughtered a camel and the rest of his family drank its blood to stay alive. They reached the lower Draa, which is always dry, and followed it toward the source. One night they camped within sight of that rock in the circle of dunes. He knew there would be water nearby—he smelled it, he says—and before dawn he got up to have a closer look.

"There were two buildings near the rock. One was very low, and had no windows. The other was smaller and had windows. He saw two sentries so he hid behind a sand dune. They wore gray uniforms and had very fair skin, the fairest he had ever seen. He says that he had never seen a European before that time."

"Does he know what year it was?"

Rashid asked the man a question and he nodded eagerly and replied.

"It was the year his youngest son was born," Rashid said.

"How old is he now?"

Rashid and the man exchanged a few words. "He died the same year."

"Tell him I'm sorry."

Rashid did. "It's the will of Allah, he says. Do you want to hear the rest?"

"Yes."

"He says that while he watched the sentries he heard the sound of an airplane. He had seen them before, flying over the desert. He heard it long before the sentries did, and wondered if they were deaf. The airplane landed on the plain and rolled to the buildings. The two sentries went into the small building and he didn't see them again. Three men with rifles came out of the big building. They were fair-skinned like the others, but wore black uniforms. The door of the airplane opened and some steps were lowered. Many women, more than a dozen he thinks, got off the plane. They wore robes but were also fair-skinned. The three men in black marched them to the big building. Out of the small building came two men wearing khaki uniforms. He did not know at the time, but realized later, that they were French. He knows because they wore the képi. One of the men was tall, the other quite fat. They went into the airplane, the door closed and it flew away to the north.

"Was the fat one also bald?" Rachel interrupted. Rashid translated. The man said something and slapped his thigh. He began laughing. He repeated what he said to his grandsons. They smiled politely. He made a little bow to Rachel. He seemed to recognize her now.

"What's so funny?"

"He says how could he see if the fat one was bald? He was wearing a képi," Rashid replied. The man looked at Rachel expectantly, but she didn't play along. He stopped laughing and assumed a somber expression.

"After the airplane left a man in a white coat came out of the big building. He walked along the line of women. He looked at them very closely, making some of them open their mouths or lift their robes. The old man was very impressed by their pink nipples." Rashid seemed suddenly embarrassed. Rachel knew he was thinking of Madame Ratelle.

"And then?"

"They all went into the big building—first the man in

white, then the women, and the men in black. After a while the two sentries came out of the small building and began patrolling again. He didn't like it. He went back to his camp and led his family west. They stayed for many years near Tarfaya, by the ocean. When they returned he went back to the rock and found only the pile of cement. He told one or two people what he had seen, but no one was interested."

"That's all?"

"Yes."

"Ask him if there were any markings on the plane."

Rashid asked. Rachel could see right away how much the question pleased him. Not like the one about the bald man, but it was a good question all the same. He nodded happily.

"Tell him to describe them."

The man extended a lean forefinger and traced a rectangle on the rug. Then he divided it in thirds with two vertical lines. He pointed to each section in turn, each time saying a different word.

"What did he say?"

"Blue. White. Red."

Rachel drove back across the hard sand. The clock said six minutes before two. There were almost three hundred miles between her and Marrakech.

"Stop here," Rashid said. "I'll walk the rest of the way."

"Are you sure?"

"It's safer. No one will hear me."

"All right." Rachel put her hand on his arm. "When you get back you have to forget this night ever happened. Don't do anything about the Land-Rover. And tell Madame Ratelle to bring food to the jail for me in the morning."

"Professor DePoe is dead, isn't he?"

Rachel reached in the back for her handbag and counted twelve hundred dirhams. "Here. Don't make a fuss."

"I don't want it."

"It's not for you. It's for her. We made a bargain."
Rashid took the money and got out of the jeep. "Come
here," Rachel said. He walked around to her door. She
put her hand around his neck, brought his face close and
kissed him on the cheek.

"I hope you find the boy," Rashid said.

Rachel drove away. She headed straight north until she
reached the track that joined Mhamid with Zagora. She
stopped the jeep and got out. Behind the back seat she
found a coil of thin rope and a tire iron. She knotted one
end of the rope to the tire iron and walked underneath the
single telephone wire that sagged from pole to pole along
the track. She swung the tire iron like a pendulum until it
gained momentum and let it go. It cleared the wire by
inches. Both ends of the rope hung from the wire. Rachel
untied the tire iron and looped the ends of the rope
around the rear bumper. She maneuvered the jeep until it
was perpendicular to the wire, and then ran it forward.
The wire gave with little resistance. It fell writhing in a
shower of sparks, like a fiery severed snake.

At dawn she began the descent through the mountains,
still more than fifty miles from Marrakech. She wore a
coat of encrusted dust and sweat. Her eyes were opened
unnaturally wide. She knew that if she closed them they
would remain that way for a long time.

During the night she had encountered no traffic at all,
but now a few cars appeared. She watched each one
warily, looking for a colored light on the top, or a uniform
behind the windshield. In a foothill village a rusting green
bus was parked outside a tar-paper cafe. Rachel drew up
beside it, and took her baggage from the jeep.

"Marrakech?" she asked the driver. He nodded behind
the sports pages of the morning paper. Rachel paid him
and sat by a window at the back.

The bus stopped at ten villages on the way to Marrakech. Rachel counted them. People got on and off. They
carried live chickens, dried salt fish, and dead rabbits.
They ate a lot and got sick, sometimes out the window,

sometimes on the seats. The bus entered Marrakech just before noon.

Before it reached the station an enormously fat woman sitting in front of Rachel shouted to the driver. He stopped the bus and opened the door. The fat woman got to her feet and made her way along the aisle. Thinking it would be a good idea to avoid the bus station, Rachel followed in her wake. The fat woman gave the driver a dirty look and lowered herself to the ground. Rachel got off behind her. She found a taxicab rank and hired the first taxi.

At the airport a small but noisy crowd of French tourists assailed the clerks behind one of the ticket counters. They wore cameras around their necks, tans on their faces, and many had added henna to their hair and adopted Moroccan dress as well. None of it made them happy.

A disembodied voice announced that flight five thirteen to Paris would leave in thirty-five minutes. The announcement stirred the crowd like Mark Antony's oration at Caesar's funeral. Rachel waited behind them until they had been pacified with tickets and herded to a boarding gate. Then she bought a ticket to Paris.

"Hurry, madame," the clerk said, handing her the ticket. "There isn't much time."

A uniformed man sat behind a desk in the passage that led to the gate. He didn't want to see her passport or find out how long she had been in the country. All he cared about was whether she had enjoyed her visit.

Rachel boarded the plane and fell asleep.

19

Sunday morning the twenty-eighth of March a blue delivery van parked in front of Simon Calvi's villa. A painter wearing a broad-brimmed hat to shield his face from the bright sun put aside his brush and took a small notebook from his paint box. In it he recorded the license number of the van, a description of the driver who carried a large rectangular cardboard box to the front door, and the time, ten twenty-two. The painter wrote that Calvi himself opened the door, that the delivery man held out a piece of paper for him to sign, and once he signed, gave him a copy, that he handed Calvi the package, that Calvi said something which made the man laugh as he closed the door.

Simon Calvi carefully unfolded his new suit and threw the cardboard box away. He could not remember when he had last bought one. The new suit was splendid, far more luxurious than any clothing he had ever owned, and far more expensive. He had paid almost four thousand shekels for it, less a ten percent discount from the shop beside the King David Hotel which encouraged patronage by members of the Knesset, and anyone else who got his picture in the paper without breaking the law. For the best suit of his life he had chosen a fine charcoal gray worsted, with a very thin red stripe that would be visible only to someone crying on his shoulder in direct sunlight.

Calvi carried it in his arms to the upstairs bathroom and locked the door. He hung the suit on the shower-curtain rod, beside the white silk shirt and navy blue tie which were already there. It was the best-dressed shower-curtain rod in the Middle East.

Calvi stripped to his socks and undershorts. He opened the towel closet and stood on the tips of his toes to reach the back of the top shelf. His fingers found the small circular hot-water bottle he had bought on the way home from his meeting with Major Grunberg, and a thin leather strap with a simple fastening mechanism fitted to the ends.

After passing the strap through the two narrow eyelets on the rim of the flesh-colored water bottle Calvi held it under the tap until it was half full of warm water. Then he fastened the two ends of the strap together and slipped the water bottle over his head and shoulders. He adjusted the strap so that the flat rubber container sat tightly on his sternum. In the mirror it looked like an ugly tumor. He also saw in the mirror that he had forgotten something.

He unlocked the door and stepped into the hall. The house was quiet. Gisela had left to go to the market after breakfast. Wearing socks, undershorts, and the hot-water bottle Calvi went downstairs to the kitchen. From a drawer beneath the counter he took a sharp, thick sewing needle and a short piece of string. As he was closing the drawer he heard the tumblers revolve in the lock on the front door. The door faced the bottom of the stairs. Calvi spun around, raced from the kitchen, grabbed the bannister and catapulted himself up the stairs, the water sloshing wildly in the container on his chest.

"Is that you, Simon?" he heard Gisela call.

"Yes," he said from behind the locked bathroom door.

"Come help me carry in the packages."

"I can't," he yelled down. "I'm in the bathroom."

"I don't know how you can spend so much time in there. If you want to read you have a very comfortable study."

"I'm not reading. I just this minute sat down."

Gisela said something Calvi didn't quite hear. Holding the rubber stopper of the water bottle in place, he poked a hole through it with the sewing needle. He passed the string through the hole, knotting one end and letting the other dangle against his groin. He put on the trousers of his suit. They were fancy enough to have an inner buttoning flap as well as an outer one. You had to pay for that kind of absolute guarantee against accidental self-exposure. Calvi tied the string to the inner flap so that it was not quite taut.

He put on a silk shirt, and the navy blue tie, which he tied carefully in a Windsor knot. It required three tries. In the mirror he could barely detect the bulge on his chest. When he slipped his arms through the sleeves of the jacket and fastened the middle button he was unable to see it at all.

Calvi looped his fingers in his belt, the way men do when they are talking tough. He leaned back slightly and pushed down gently with his hands. A dark stain spread slowly over his chest. It wet the silk shirt, the blue tie and the charcoal gray jacket with the tiny red stripes. He felt the warm water trickle across his stomach and under the waistband of the trousers. He undressed, dropped the suit, shirt, and tie in the clothes hamper, replaced the hot-water bottle on the top shelf and dressed again in his other clothes.

"Simon, I've got to use the bathroom," Gisela said from the other side of the door, startling him.

"Coming right out."

"That took long enough," she said when he opened the door. But she gave him a long kiss on the mouth to show that she was his lover, not a nagging wife. After a few moments they both stopped thinking about why they were kissing; Calvi's big hands were drawn as if by magnets along her back and up the slopes of her strong buttocks. Once Cohn had told him that fondness for large buttocks denoted an infantile mentality. And what is grownup, Calvi had asked him. The elbow?

Gisela pushed him away. "Wait for me," she said a little breathlessly as she went into the bathroom and closed the door. Calvi entered the bedroom, took off his clothes again and lay in bed. Gisela came naked into the room. She could have stepped out of a Titian if her hair had been redder and her desire less obvious. Over terrain which never became completely familiar they fought a not too gentle combat, and then like soldiers after a battle slept dreamless sleeps.

The late afternoon sun shone steadily through the bedroom window onto Calvi's eyelids, making him see red until he opened them. The room was full of gold. Calvi sat up and lit a cigar. The rising smoke coalesced with the gold to form a shimmering sfumato thick enough to stop time. Beside him Gisela lay still in the twisted sheets. He didn't love her, she didn't love him, but it was better than he had any right to expect. After a while the sun sank below the window, taking the gold and leaving a room full of smoke behind. Calvi stubbed out the butt of his cigar. The earth spins on its axis. It circles the sun. The sun revolves around the center of the Milky Way. The Milky Way races the other galaxies to the edge of the universe. Calvi understood why time marches on, but it didn't make him like it any better.

He reached under the sheets and patted the fleshy rump. "Gisela," he said. "How would you like a holiday? You and me."

She murmured, "Wonderful," rolled over and put her arms around him.

"Good," he said. "I haven't had a holiday in years. I thought we'd go to Germany. Stay for a long time. You can really give me the grand tour."

Gisela opened her eyes. "Oh, Simon, what a good idea." She hugged him tightly. "I'm so happy I don't know what to do." But she thought of something. It led to something else.

When his heart returned to its normal rhythm Calvi wanted to sleep again, but Gisela was hungry.

"Take me out to dinner, Simon."

"But you just bought groceries."

"They'll keep. Let's go celebrate." She gave him a series of quick pecks on the forehead to drive the idea home.

"Celebrate what?"

"The trip, of course," Gisela said. "How about Rubin's?" she suggested, naming a small restaurant bar on the roof of one of the new hotels on the Mount of Olives. "I've never been."

"You're not alone," Calvi said. "No Israeli has ever been there either. It's for tourists."

"Please, Simon."

"Very well," he said, wondering whether his artistic friend could afford it.

But when they left the villa the man in the broad-brimmed hat made no attempt to follow them. He didn't even look up as they passed, oblivious, it seemed, to everything but his canvas, his brush, and the dying light of the day. It made Calvi uneasy. He hadn't taken Grunberg for one who hires careless or lazy men. His mind tossed up the thought that the painter might not be Grunberg's man at all. There was only one alternative, and Calvi liked it less. The painter had to be Grunberg's man.

Three decorators had tried their luck on Rubin's. As at Troy, or Jerusalem itself, they did not throw away what had gone before; they built on top. Rubin's was an Arabian Nights version of an English men's club as seen by a Scandinavian minimalist on LSD.

You paid for the view. From their table they looked down on the Mount of Olives, touched here and there by the last rays of the sun. The Mount of Olives was a hill, a hill of gravestones—weathered, cracked, overgrown, submerged. A few even stood upright in the rubble.

The souls underneath were said to have first crack on

Judgment Day. The waiter, a middle-aged Arab whose wet eyes had but one expression, eagerness to please, fed them the whole tourist spiel when he came to take their order.

"There," he said excitedly, leaning over the table to point. "Between the bottom of the slope and the Old City walls. You see? The Valley of Jehoshaphat. That is where we will all be judged on the last day. All of us," he repeated, in case anyone was clinging to the hope of exemptions drawn along ethnic or class lines. "Both the Koran and the Bible agree," he added rapturously.

"I guess that settles it," Calvi said, ordering Scotch for himself and dry sherry for Gisela.

But it didn't. With an impatient movement the waiter waved Calvi's request into thin air.

"Both agree on what will happen," he said. "But—" He held a stubby finger to the tip of his nose, indicating that he had arrived at the tricky part. "But," he continued, forgetting for a while to drop the gesture, "on how it will happen there is not the same agreement." He began an analysis of differences in the two accounts. He was unable to disguise his preference for the Koranic.

"Look over there," he commanded. "The Dome of the Rock. Like a golden hat, I like to say to those who sit at my table. On Judgment Day the Prophet will sit on top of the hat. A wire will be stretched from here on top of the Mount across the valley to the Prophet. All mankind, all, will walk that wire. The wire to eternity. The faithful will cross in safety. The rest will fall and perish in the Valley of Jehoshaphat." He lowered his face to Calvi's. "Perish," he repeated in a hushed voice.

Calvi didn't like the waiter's chances. His breath reeked of cheap wine and the Koran took a categorical position on that subject. But he kept his mouth shut. He wanted dinner. As for himself he felt little concern. He had been on a high wire since childhood.

They drank two bottles of overpriced Sancerre, and ate fresh shrimp, overcooked roast lamb, and mocha cake that was so full of brandy it could barely stand up. Gisela had two pieces.

"I don't know how you do it," Calvi said.

Gisela looked worried. "Should I go on a diet?"

"No. Don't do that."

She scraped the last sticky remains of icing onto her fork and licked it clean with her pink tongue. She lifted her face and said seriously, "You're very good to me."

"You've had too much to drink."

"No. You are," she insisted. "We don't have to go to Germany just for me."

"It's not just for you," Calvi said. "I want to go too. I've already bought tickets to Munich." His eyes searched the room for the waiter. He was talking about golden hats to two very drunk American businessmen. Their condition didn't matter to him: he was drunker than they were. When Calvi attracted his attention he ordered two glasses of cognac.

"Unfortunately," he resumed, "we have to fly separately. I've booked you a flight on the thirty-first and one for me on the third."

"Of April?"

"Yes."

"But that's impossible. I'll miss your speech." Gisela seemed quite upset.

"It's not going to be much of a speech. It's very mild. You can read it if you want."

Gisela drank her cognac in one gulp. "It's not the same."

"I know," Calvi said. In the near darkness he saw the round cerebellum-shaped roofs of the Old City, and the television antennae sticking into them like probes. He turned to Gisela and covered her hand with his own. "I want you to do a favor for me. That's why you must go on the thirty-first."

"What favor?"

"I am sending a large package to Munich by air freight the night of the second. I want you to pick it up."

"What's in it?"

"I can't tell you," Calvi said. "It's a surprise."

"For me?"

"Yes, partly for you," Calvi answered. "I know you will like it. Don't spoil it by making me tell."

"All right, Simon."

"You'll do it, then?"

"Yes," she said, gazing across the valley at the Dome of the Rock. No one was sitting on it yet.

Smiling broadly the waiter presented Calvi with the bill. Perhaps he was amused by its sheer audacity. Calvi paid it and added a tip that was audacious in its own way.

They waited in front of the hotel for a taxi, standing slightly apart. When one arrived Calvi opened the door for Gisela but did not get in himself.

"Do you mind going home without me?" he asked her through the window. "I won't be long."

"What do you mean?" Gisela said, annoyed. He realized he was about to ruin the evening.

"There is a meeting I couldn't avoid."

"At ten o'clock at night?"

"That's the way this business is."

"Where is it?" she asked. "I don't mind waiting outside."

"That's not a good idea."

"Why not?"

The driver twisted around in the front seat. "Make a decision," he said.

"Drive," she told him. He slipped the car into gear and rolled away with Gisela looking straight ahead in the back seat. Calvi waited for another taxi. He knew the fare would be ridiculous but he didn't see his former wife very often.

___

20

The taxi dropped Calvi in front of a block of workers'
flats in the northwest part of the city. It stood on grassless
and treeless level ground among a herd of other blocks
which had all come from the same litter. Law compelled
the builders to use native limestone on the outsides of
all new structures. The intent was to blend old and new,
but all it did was make the workers' flats tawdrier than
those in other cities, like plain women wearing too much
make-up. Jews from Morocco, Yemen, Iraq, Kurdistan, and Tunisia lived in these flats. Calvi was visiting
his constituency.

Before entering the building he looked back along the
road the taxi had come. No one followed. Calvi went
inside. A sign on the elevator said out of order. Under it
someone had written what he thought of that. Calvi
climbed four flights of dreary unswept stairs. On the last
landing he trod carefully around a cluster of teenagers
singing along with the pop tunes vibrating from a tinny
little transistor radio. They made no effort to clear a
passage; he was too old for them to see.

They were waiting for him on the other side of the
flimsy pressed wood door. It opened at the first touch of

his knocking hand. A dark young man of his own height closed the door after him. Calvi turned with the idea of embracing him, but modulated the movement to a handshake instead. Then he crossed the bare wooden floor of the living room and shook hands with the two other men, younger and shorter than the first, who stood up from the worn couch.

"So," Calvi said, calling each one by name, "you all look very well." None of them had his bulk, or the prominent brow ridge and strong wedge-shaped nose, but the sensitive full-lipped mouths were almost identical.

"We are well," the oldest one said. "And you?"

Calvi shrugged. He didn't have time to give a true answer. "You become a resident soon?" he asked the eldest.

"By September if I get through the exams."

"Did you hear that?" Calvi asked the other two, trying to strike a light note. "If he gets through, with that brain of his." None of them saw the joke. He abandoned levity. "And you two," he said to the younger ones, "are you studying hard?" They nodded. "Good," Calvi said, perhaps overemphasizing the approval in his tone.

An inner door opened and a small thin woman who looked old enough to be Calvi's mother came into the living room bearing a tray.

"Why don't you all sit down?" she said in a voice that was quite deep. All sat except Calvi, who approached the woman and stood opposite her.

"Hello, Aziza," he said, watching her eyes. They were dark and quick-moving, and seemed much younger than her face. They didn't meet his.

"Hello, Simon," she said. "Take your tea."

He lifted the cup and saucer from the tray and sat on the couch between the two younger men. The scent of mint rose from the tea, tea sweet and fragrant in the Moroccan style. Calvi sipped it and sighed with satisfaction. In truth, on top of the rich dinner, it threatened to make him sick.

"Yours is still the best tea, Aziza," he said.

Aziza said nothing. She sat on a wooden chair by the kitchen door. The two younger men sat beside Calvi. The eldest leaned on the wall by the front door. They had waited for him to arrive. Now they were waiting for him to talk. He stared intently into his cup as though the script floated on the surface of the thick green tea.

"I have some news," he said. He looked up at Aziza. "From now on I am not going to be in a position to give the boys money to pay—to help with their educations. Instead I have brought with me tonight a lump sum." He took a long envelope from the inner pocket of his jacket and handed it to Aziza. "It is all I can afford."

Aziza opened the envelope and counted the money without removing it. The three young men watched her carefully. She nodded. "It is generous."

"I know," Calvi said. "But the boys have to earn it."

Aziza's eyes narrowed. "What do you mean?"

So Calvi told them about Grunberg. He told them about the ambulance by the broken fountain in the walled yard, and the hot-water bottle on the top shelf in his bathroom. He told them about schedules, and flight numbers and undertakers. He told them just what they had to know. And then he told them what he wanted. They didn't like it.

"Can't you simply retire?" the eldest asked him.

Calvi shook his head, smiling. "This is the only way."

"Why? I don't understand."

"You'll just have to trust me."

"Why should I?" the young man said hotly. "Why the hell should I? You've got your nerve coming here and asking for trust." Calvi saw angry tears in the young man's eyes.

"Don't trust me, then," Calvi said, his voice rising. "The question is, will you help me or not?"

The three young men looked at each other and in some unseen way came to a decision. He could see that the answer was no. The eldest opened his mouth to speak the word.

"They will help you," Aziza said.

"Mother—"

"They will help you," she repeated firmly.

"How much money is in that envelope?" sneered one of the younger men.

"How much is not the point," she said. "But don't belittle money, either."

"And don't take that tone with your mother," Calvi put in stupidly. It roused fury in the three young men. The two sitting beside him jumped up and faced him. The eldest stepped forward.

"You'd better keep your mouth shut," he said in a shaking voice.

Calvi knew he had been wrong to say it, but he wasn't going to be talked to like that, either. He got to his feet, making them aware of his size and strength, and looked at each of them in turn.

"You have to grow up some day," he said very quietly.

The front door opened. A wiry little gray-haired man stood in the entrance. He wore filthy blue overalls and the hands that dangled from his thin wrists, almost as if they were foreign objects, were the swollen, calloused hands of a man who had worked at hard labor all his life. His wrinkled face was gray with fatigue. He looked shyly around the room and went into his kitchen without a word. The three young men followed him, closing the door behind them.

Calvi and Aziza remained together in the bare living room. Calvi's eyes were fixed on the kitchen door.

"I have to get dinner ready, Simon," Aziza said quite gently. He remembered that tone. It was like a lullabye. He turned toward the door.

"Goodbye, Simon."

"Yes," he replied. "Goodbye." He opened the door.

"The boys will help you," she said. "They are good boys. They're your boys, Simon."

"No, they're not," he said softly and went out.

* * *

The basement in which he stood was really a cavern cut into the limestone foundation of the city. He heard an echo of dripping water which seemed to come through the walls, and he felt the dampness in his nose and under his feet. Two naked bulbs hung from the ends of wires which were taped crudely to the ceiling. Damp currents set them swaying above his head. Their light rose and fell along the walls making him slightly seasick. Perhaps he would have felt sick anyway. The room was filled with coffins, some stacked in piles to the ceiling, others lying randomly on the floor. Several of these had open lids. The bodies in them were dressed for a formal party. They had straight parts in their hair and a waxy composure on their faces. Men and women alike wore exotic perfumes. He smelled sandalwood, lavender, rose hips, and laurel, and another scent the others couldn't hide.

"You're late," whined the Arab undertaker sitting on a coffin in the shadows, his legs casually crossed. He rose and approached Calvi. He had arranged his full lips in a pout like Clara Bow's, but it didn't look cute on him. Perhaps the large, flat, fleshy ears spoiled the effect, or maybe the pallor of the recently shaved head. Calvi noticed that his eyebrows too had been shaved; no hair at all was visible on him, other than the long curling lashes and the few dark ones that emerged from the pits of his nostrils. "I've been waiting and waiting," he added in a hurt voice.

"And you're getting paid for it," Calvi said sharply. His anger reverberated through the cavern. It buffeted the Arab enough to make him step back, but not enough to take the peevishness out of his tone.

"When?"

"Tonight, if you've done what I asked."

"I have." He turned and led Calvi into the depths of the cavern. His big hips engaged in a rolling struggle with the fabric of his tight blue jeans. He stopped beside an olivewood coffin which lay at the rear of the cavern near the worn stone steps leading to street level.

"Here," he said, with a hint of pride in his tone.

The coffin was big and solid. Ornate brass handles were screwed into both ends, and all the corners had been reinforced in brass as well. The Arab opened the lid. The coffin was lined in red silk, and a soft red silk pillow lay at one end. On the inside of the lid, near the head, was another brass handle, smaller than the others but equally fancy.

"Watch," said the Arab. His hand grasped the ring, twisted it a half turn, and pulled. It came away in his hand. Calvi saw that the ring was attached to a square block of wood, the size of a man's head. A dozen or more small cylinders of olivewood were glued to the face of the wooden block. There were now a dozen or more small round holes in the lid of the coffin. The Arab replaced the wooden block and closed the lid. Calvi leaned forward to look closely. He saw no sign of the holes in the highly polished lustre of the wood. He ran his hand carefully over the surface. He felt nothing that interrupted the smooth flow of the grain.

"It's good," he said.

"Good?" cried the undertaker. "It's perfect. Perfect." He caressed the wood with his hand.

"Open it again," Calvi said. The Arab lifted the lid. Calvi climbed inside the coffin and lay on his back. The big unshaven head loomed over him. "Close it," Calvi ordered.

The lid closed, shutting out the Arab, the cavern, and the sound of dripping water. Calvi lay in complete darkness, his head on the soft pillow. A peaceful sleepiness crept over him. He fought it off and reached above his face for the brass handle. To grip it he had to tuck his elbow into his chest and cock his wrist under his chin. He turned the ring and pulled, the way the Arab had done. The block came loose. Carefully he moved it along the length of his body and placed it by his hip on the floor of the coffin.

At first there was plenty of air, even some light. Then,

quite suddenly, no more light filtered through the holes in the lid. No fresh air. Calvi inhaled deeply but the air in the coffin seemed thin and impoverished. It made him breathless. He felt sweat break out all over his body.

"Open it," he shouted. There was no response. He felt the air holes with his fingers. They were too small to allow the entry of any but his smallest finger. He stuck it into one of the holes. The fingertip touched the blockage on the far side. It felt like rough cloth, denim he realized, the denim used for making blue jeans. Struggling for air Calvi banged on the inside of the lid, but he was too cramped to bang with any force. "Open it, you bastard," he yelled again.

He heard a faint crack, close to his face. He smelled an odor. Quickly it filled the coffin, displacing whatever air remained. It sickened him. The Arab, sitting on the air holes, had farted.

The lid swung open. Fresh damp air flowed over his soaked and panting body. The unshaven head above him was thrown back in hysterical laughter. The meaty jowls shook with it. The wild laughter bounced off the lime-stone walls, sweeping back and forth through the cavern. Calvi felt that he lay inside a laughing bell.

He sat up and pulled himself from the coffin. Unstead-ily he stepped in front of the Arab. Something made him stop laughing. Calvi grabbed the man by his shirt and lifted him onto his toes. He felt his fingers sink into the soft flesh of the Arab's chest. The man yelled in pain. Calvi drew back his right fist.

"Don't, please don't," the undertaker pleaded. "It was only a joke."

Calvi struck him hard on his Clara Bow lips. The lower one split, releasing a trickle of blood which ran onto his chin.

"Stop," the man cried. "I won't help you if you strike me again."

Slowly Calvi relaxed his grip, lowering the Arab's heels to the floor. Both men were breathing heavily. Fear and hatred fought for possession of the Arab's eyes. Calvi felt his anger ebb, too late.

"I didn't mean to hit you. But you shouldn't have done that."

"You shouldn't have hit me," the man said sullenly. "You have no sense of humor."

Calvi was prevented from arguing that point by the sound of a door opening above. Footsteps approached on the stone steps. Out of the shadows appeared a slender boy of sixteen or seventeen, wearing white sailor pants and a black T-shirt. His heavily lidded eyes moved carefully over the two men. They stopped on the bloody pouting lip.

"Is something wrong?" he asked in a voice still not secure in its lower register.

"No," replid the undertaker. "Nothing. Please go upstairs and fetch Mr. Calvi's urn." The boy turned and ascended the steps. The undertaker kept his eyes on the boy's buttocks until they disappeared in the shadows.

In his back pocket he found a soiled handkerchief. He dabbed his lip with it, wincing at the touch.

"You shouldn't have hit me," he repeated in a tone that seemed at once both hurt and menacing.

"I'm sorry," Calvi said. "But you provoked me." The undertaker shook his head.

"That's the trouble with you Jews. You provoke too easily."

It made Calvi laugh. He was still laughing when the boy returned. It turned out to be a good place for laughter. First the undertaker, now him.

In his hands the boy held a tall ceramic urn decorated in a mosaic of white and navy blue squares. He set it gently on the stone floor. The undertaker gazed at it in admiration.

"Beautiful isn't it?" he said. "It's our most expensive model. We only sell about four or five a year."

Calvi stood over the urn and peered into it, but beyond

the circle of light at the top he saw nothing but darkness. "Have you put the ashes inside?"

"Not yet. We're waiting for a new shipment." His voice teetered on the edge of a laugh, but when he saw that Calvi and the boy weren't in the mood he bit it off.

"What about teeth?" Calvi asked.

"We grind up anything the furnace doesn't burn, and throw it in with the rest."

"That's important," Calvi said. "They are sure to ask about the teeth."

"Don't worry. Everything will be perfect."

"Why cremation?" Calvi asked in a catechistic tone.

The undertaker rolled his eyes. "Must we go through this again?"

"Why cremation?" Calvi persisted.

The undertaker sighed. "The boy made a mistake," he answered wearily. "He didn't know cremation was forbidden to Jews."

Calvi looked at the boy. The boy nodded. He had intelligent eyes under his heavy lids. Calvi took a starter's pistol from the pocket of his coat and handed it to the boy.

"Do you know how to use it?"

"Yes."

"Show me."

The undertaker covered his ears. The boy raised the pistol over his head, closed his eyes and pulled the trigger. The report sounded like a cannon firing in the stone cavern. The noise crashed against the rock walls trying to escape, then folded back on itself and its family of echoes and slowly died away. The undertaker removed his hands from his ears.

"Good," Calvi said to the boy. "Remember you have very little time to get here. Ten minutes at the most." The boy's eyes showed that he remembered. "And ten minutes after that," Calvi said, turning to the undertaker and jabbing his finger at the coffin, "this is on the road to Lod."

"Stop worrying. If they come, all they will find is ashes, just ashes."

"They'll come," Calvi said grimly. "Don't fool yourself about that."

"It makes no difference. We are ready."

Calvi nodded.

"Perfect," the undertaker said. "Is there anything more you want of the boy?"

"No."

"Good." He turned to the boy. "Take the urn upstairs." The boy lifted it and went up the steps. "So," the undertaker said to Calvi. "The fee."

This had been a problem. The undertaker had no use for Israeli cash, which might be devalued at any time, and Calvi could not risk an attempt to buy foreign currency. But they had found a solution. From the front pocket of his trousers Calvi drew a little jewel box, covered in purple velvet. He handed it to the undertaker, whose fingers opened it eagerly. A single cut diamond rested on the velvet lining. Immediately it began to play with the yellow of the light bulbs and the purple of the box. It was almost the size of a pea. The undertaker couldn't take his eyes from it. They radiated a gleam of their own, empty of the stone's beauty but just as hard. Reluctantly he closed the box.

"And the other one?" he asked.

"You'll get it later."

"When?"

"When I know that the job has been done."

"But you promised tonight."

"Stop whining," Calvi said. "You'll get it."

The undertaker shrugged. "Whatever you say." He reopened the box and gazed again at the stone. Calvi went up the stairs. "Send the boy down on your way out," the undertaker called over his shoulder.

Calvi walked home. A light rain fell and he had the streets to himself. Worries bubbled through his brain. They had the run of the place. He was too tired to argue with them. He wanted a glass of milk to quiet his stomach and a long sleep to quiet his mind. But he knew that any sleep which came would bring images of cremated Jews and hard diamonds and the nothingness that waited inside a coffin.

. The rain had driven off the painter in the broad-brimmed hat. Calvi saw a black four-door car parked in front of his villa. He walked past it and opened the gate.

"Mr. Calvi," a voice called from the car, a voice he knew.

He turned from the gate. "Yes, Major?"

"Would you come here for a minute, please?" Grunberg spoke in a cold tone which belied any courtesy in the words.

"Can't it wait till morning? I'm very tired."

"I am afraid not."

Calvi walked around the car and sat in the passenger seat. Grunberg was behind the wheel, and a very large man in an old tennis sweater occupied most of the back seat. Grunberg switched on the overhead light and looked impassively at Calvi.

"A man your age shouldn't keep such late hours," he said. Calvi didn't answer. "Would you mind telling me where you've been?"

"At dinner."

The thick black brows which hung like cornices over the sunken eyes lifted slightly. "Your companion has been back for more than four hours."

Calvi stiffened. "I'm getting sick of you spying on me," Calvi said angrily. "I am a legally elected member of the Knesset and I have a right not to be subjected to these Gestapo tactics."

Grunberg's eyes remained calm but his quiet voice sounded very dangerous. "Let's not throw that word around loosely, Mr. Calvi."

They sat in silence for a minute or two. The rain danced lightly on the roof and fog spread over the windows. The car was too small for the three of them. Calvi rolled down the window, letting the rain dampen his shoulder. He needed the fresh air.

"What makes you think I'm spying on you?" Grunberg continued.

Calvi snorted. "Don't toy with me. Your man Picasso is rather obvious."

Grunberg laughed. "Picasso. He'll appreciate that. He loves Picasso. But you've made a mistake. I didn't send him here as a spy. I sent him to protect you. I shouldn't have kept it a secret from you, that's all."

"Protect me from what?"

"Enemies. Your movement has made many enemies for you. The rally that you plan has made more. It is making people nervous. And not only in Israel. I am receiving reports of odd movements of Syrian men and armor along the border. Have you heard anything like that?"

"How would I hear that kind of information?"

"Tell me. I'd like to know."

Calvi grabbed the door handle and jerked it open.

"Just a minute." Grunberg's voice froze his hand where it was. "Close the door." Calvi closed it. "Thank you," Grunberg resumed. "As I was saying, I have a duty in these circumstances to protect you. A man in your position has a right to a bodyguard. Twenty-four hours a day."

"No thank you."

Grunberg shook his head. "You have no choice in this matter. My department is responsible for your security. From now on, at least until after the rally, you will be accompanied by a bodyguard whenever you leave your house."

"The hell with that," Calvi said, raising his voice.

"Let me introduce the man taking the first shift," Grunberg said, ignoring him. He turned to the man in the back seat. "Sergeant Levy, this is Mr. Calvi." The huge man bared his teeth at Calvi in a big cheerful smile. He held out a hand that looked capable of crushing melons. Calvi let him hold it there. Grunberg touched Calvi's arm.

"Please try to cooperate, Mr. Calvi. If you should happen to disappear, on a bus near the King David Hotel for example, Sergeant Levy is under orders to notify the police, who go on a full-scale alert until you are found. Don't make us waste the taxpayers' money like that."

Calvi got out of the car and walked toward the villa. Sergeant Levy got out too, and went to stand under the carob tree across the street. Grunberg drove slowly away.

No lights shone in the villa. Calvi entered the bedroom. Gisela slept on the far side of the bed, her back toward the middle. Calvi undressed, leaving his clothes in a pile on the floor, and lay down. He closed his eyes and saw everything he feared he would see, and more.

21

"Wake up madame," a female voice urged her. "We are on the ground." Rachel opened her eyes and slowly focused them on a face that was ready to play the role of Carmen at a moment's notice. All the woman had to do was take the little stewardess cap off her pile of hair. "That's the way," she said, smiling. She had missed a tomato seed caught between her front teeth, but you had to be front row center to see it. "There's no time for sleeping in Paris."

But sleep was all she wanted. She felt a filament of saliva against her cheek and wiped it away with her sleeve before moving to stand up. The seat belt kept her firmly in place. The stewardess found it amusing. "What have you been doing to get so sleepy?" she tut-tutted, reaching down to undo the buckle. She led Rachel off the empty plane.

A sodden sheet of gray had been thrown across Paris, hiding the sky. It dripped steadily on the city, making the old buildings look just plain old. It couldn't do anything to the new ones that hadn't already been done. The taxi careened around the Arc de Triomphe, splashing any pedestrians it could get near, and braked to a violent stop in front of the Hotel Lancaster. It was the only hotel Rachel knew in Paris; she and Dan had stayed there on their trip to Europe. She was too tired to worry whether it would bring back memories.

Rachel remembered the doorman. He had a neatly trimmed white moustache and the face of a benevolent king. He remembered her too and seemed happy about it. "Mrs. Monette, isn't it?" he said, taking her suitcase. "It's been a long time."

"Four years," she replied, wondering what kind of tip Dan had given him.

"As long as that?" He looked at the departing taxi. "And the professor? He will be coming later?"

"No."

They gave her a room on the top floor, overlooking the courtyard. She opened the French windows which led to the balcony. The last time she had seen the courtyard it had been full of people drinking champagne and nibbling homemade potato chips. Now black tarpaulins covered the wrought-iron furniture and wet pigeons pecked at the marble flagstones, searching for crumbs. The hum of traffic barely reached her ears, although the Champs Elysées was only a few yards away.

Turning back into the room she saw herself in the full length mirror on the bathroom door. She was filthy. A grimy film covered her clothes, skin, and hair. She stripped and examined herself closely. Bones showed where they had not shown in years. She had bruises she couldn't remember getting, except for the one on her jaw.

She started a bath. While the water poured into the white tub she called room service and ordered two ham and cheese sandwiches and a half bottle of red wine.

When the waiter arrived she had finished bathing and was standing beside the tub watching the brown tepid water swirl down the drain. She had dirtied the bathwater like that once before. A man died that night, too.

She wrapped herself in one of the white terry-cloth robes that lay folded like towels on a shelf above the toilet, and left the bathroom. The waiter had placed the tray on the bedside table. The fresh rich smell of the baguettes reached her nose, and the scent of vinegar from the Dijon mustard. A copy of *Le Monde* lay beside the wine glass. Rachel ate the sandwiches, sipped the wine once or twice, and left the newspaper folded where it was. For a few minutes she sat on the edge of the bed, very still. Then, dropping the robe on the floor she pulled back the covers and got into bed. She had no idea what she should do next. In a few seconds she fell asleep.

Rachel awoke shortly after dawn the following morning, Monday March 29. She rolled over and looked through the window at the sky, a luminous silver-blue making a color-coded promise of a fair day. As she got out of bed she felt the soreness in her muscles and the stiffness in her joints, but her mind was fresh and clear. It even offered a thought. Perhaps it had come from her memory of people drinking champagne in the hotel courtyard, or *Le Monde* neatly folded on the tray: ebbing sleep had left it behind on the shore of her consciousness.

On the Champs Elysées busboys swept the dirt from the patches of sidewalk used by the cafés to those that weren't. A jogger in a red track suit loped by on his way to the Bois de Boulogne. The busboys shrugged their shoulders at each other. "Crazy Americans," one muttered. Rachel watched the jogger cross the circle to the Arc de Triomphe, pass the grave of the unknown soldier, and disappear.

She sat at a table on the perimeter of the territory of a large café, a café which clung to a fading fame as a gathering place for the chic, although the chic had long ago moved on. Her choice of table annoyed the waiter. It forced him to walk an extra thirty feet on each round trip. On top of that he could tell at a glance that she wasn't one of the chic. He kept hoping that one day they would return, like migrating geese, but they never did. The recurring disappointments made him surly with the customers.

In revenge he served two businessmen who had arrived after Rachel. They each ordered coffee and cognac. While they waited for the waiter to return, one of them began complaining about a television producer who had double-crossed him before he had time to figure out how to double-cross the producer. His companion tapped his fingers on the table and looked at different parts of Rachel's body. When the waiter reappeared the second man said something to him. The waiter sighed and went back inside. After a few minutes he returned, carrying a glass of cognac. He walked all the way to Rachel and set it on her table.

"What's this?"

"From that gentleman," the waiter explained in a bored voice. He raised his arm and pointed at the second man. The second man beamed at Rachel. The happiness in his face didn't mean that the mere sight of her had brought joy into his heart; it meant that it takes some kind of a lover to pick up girls at seven in the morning.

"Thank him," Rachel said, "but I don't drink at breakfast. You have it after I'm gone." The offer made the waiter see Rachel in a new light. He asked if there was anything she wanted. She wanted scrambled eggs, bacon, and toasted rye bread. She settled for croissants and brioches. The saga of betrayal which appeared to center around a program called "Uncle Renard's Magic Farm" drew to a close. The two men drained their cognac and stood up. As they left, the second man gave Rachel a pitying look. She had lost her chance with one of the lords of amorous life, it said. Nothing could expiate the sin of frigidity.

Rachel took a taxi to the Sorbonne. The driver had dandruff on his shoulders and a pornographic magazine on his lap. He studied it at every red light, but there weren't enough: it would take the stop-and-go traffic of rush hour to make him an expert. When she paid him he grumbled for a few moments about the size of the tip, but his spirit wasn't really in it. They both knew where it was.

She and Dan had spent an afternoon trailing one of Dan's colleagues on a tour of the Sorbonne and she remembered it quite well. She went straight to the library and followed the signs to the periodical department. A young black man with lively eyes and tribal markings on his cheeks found the reel of microfilm she wanted. He wound it deftly on the spools of the viewer and switched on the rear screen light. Rachel sat down in front of the screen and began reading what *Le Monde* had printed on New Year's Day 1948.

It must have seemed important at the time but she saw nothing in the grainy light of the screen that made New Year's Day 1948 worth preserving on microfilm. She rolled the film ahead to January 2. Near the bottom of page five, beside a story about a fire in a restaurant kitchen, she found what she was looking for. She translated as she read.

YOUNG AMERICAN WOMAN DROWNED

At approximately 2:20 on the morning of January 1 a tragic accident took the life of a young American resident of Paris. The victim has been identified as Madame Margaret Monette, aged 30, wife of M. Xavier Monette, former officer in the army of France and resident at 298 rue de Millet, apartment three, first arrondissement. Police report that Mme. Monette fell from the east side of the Pont Neuf and apparently died of drowning. The body was recovered a few hours later. Mlle. Lily Gris of 298 rue de Millet, apartment five, employed as babysitter by the deceased, was taken to hospital and placed under mild sedation.

Rachel copied the French text into her notebook. She unwound the reel and returned it to the young man.

"Do you know a rue de Millet in the first arrondissement?"

"No. I've only been in Paris a month." But he knew how to find it. He took a street atlas from his back pocket and began thumbing through it.

"Here it is," he said, stabbing his finger at a spot on the page. He turned the book to show her. "In Les Halles." He snapped the book shut. He was an energetic, efficient young man. She wondered how long he would be happy at the library.

Les Halles was the old market district of Paris but town planners moved the market to a new location. When Rachel's taxi arrived she saw they had replaced it with a chic imitation of downtown Houston. The rest of the neighborhood, including rue de Millet, stubbornly went on looking like Paris.

The taxi dropped her in front of 298. It was a four-storied dun-colored structure. Brown children stared at Rachel from the open windows. Over the door a marble lintel with three roses in bas relief made a plea for respectability that the pigeons were obliterating.

No amount of scrubbing could wash away the years of seediness; but the old woman on her hands and knees hadn't given up. She had covered the stone steps with a thick lather which she rubbed into the stone with a wire brush. Her exertions made her buttocks wobble and hiked her worn cotton skirt up to her thighs, revealing varicose veins like worms under the gray skin and sparse patches of white hair.

"Excuse me," Rachel said. Still on all fours the woman twisted her head to look over her shoulder at Rachel. Her small, faded eyes were lost in flesh. Maroon circles under the eyes cut into the puffiness. Each was a sunken pit undermining her face from the lower eyelids to the cheekbones.

"He's not here," the woman said in a coarse loud voice. "And I don't know when he'll be back."

"Who?"

"Don't bother with any of your tricks," the woman said angrily. "I can smell a social worker a block away."

She tapped the side of her nose as if it were a secret weapon.

"I'm not a social worker."

"Sure. And I'm not the mother of a forty-two-year-old boy who hasn't worked a day in his life." She turned away and began scrubbing furiously. "He hasn't even learned to make his own bed," she shouted at the steps. The brown children in the windows giggled.

Rachel walked up to the landing and sat on her haunches facing the woman. "I'm not a social worker," she repeated, "and I don't know about any forty-two-year-old boys. I'm looking for a woman named Lily Gris. I understand she used to live here."

The woman stopped scrubbing and looked up. She tried to make her face cagey but it was too far gone to have that capability. "Is that so?"

"Yes. I know for a fact that she lived in this building in January 1948. Apartment five. Were you here that long ago?"

"I was born in this God-damned pigsty," the woman said. Her voice softened slightly. "Of course it wasn't a pigsty then. We had fine tenants who kept the place clean."

She raised her eyes to the stained facade, seeing it the way it used to be, or the way her young eyes had seen it. The expression on her face made the brown children giggle again. She shook her fist at them. "Now all we get are filthy blacks and filthy Arabs. I work my fingers to the bone cleaning up after them."

"Was Lily Gris one of your fine tenants?"

"Yes," escaped from the old woman's lips before she could clamp them shut. She bent over the scrub brush, hiding her face.

"I'm not going to cause you any trouble," Rachel said. "I just want to talk to Lily Gris, that's all."

"I told you our fine tenants are gone. They're all gone, long ago."

"When did Lily Gris go away?" The old woman

continued to scrub the steps. Through the thin wisps of her hair Rachel saw the skull underneath, as white as bone. "Was it soon after Margaret Monette died?"

The brush stopped moving. The old woman looked up at Rachel, her eyes narrowed with suspicion. "If you know, why ask?"

"Where did she go?"

"I can't remember," she mumbled, and began working the brush. Rachel stood up and stepped on it.

"You're not trying," she said quietly.

"Why is it so important?" the old woman whined. A sudden thought wrinkled her brow. "Did her paintings end up making her famous?"

"That's it," Rachel said.

"Are they worth money?"

"Some."

"How much?" Excitement rose in her tired eyes.

"It depends on the painting."

"How much for one about this size?" The old woman held her hands apart.

"I'd have to see it before I could tell you." The old woman's eyes went to a pigeon on the lintel but it didn't give her any prompting. With a grunt of effort she got to her feet and wiped her hands on the front of her faded skirt.

"Come inside."

The woman led her through the doorway and down a narrow flight of poorly lit stairs. The numeral one was painted on the door at the bottom in chipped white enamel. The old woman opened it and stood aside for Rachel to pass.

She entered a dark and smoky room. The only light came from two small windows in the top of the wall on the street side. Through them she could see the treading feet of passersby. The smoke rose from an unfiltered cigarette held loosely between the yellow fingers of a man seated in a lumpy armchair. He wore a cotton undershirt and cotton briefs. Both had once been white. They bore the scars of frequent repair, like an aging fighter's face. The man's own face was not a fighter's: he had buckteeth and a receding chin. The chin needed shaving and the teeth were coated in nicotine. His soft brown eyes looked at Rachel with interest. He crossed his skinny legs and brought the cigarette to his lips. Anyone guessing his age might easily have said forty-two.

"Get dressed, Guy," the old woman said. "This lady wants to see the painting. She says it might be worth money."

"What painting?" His voice was no lower in pitch than hers, and just as loud. They lived in a world where the sound was always turned up.

"How many paintings do we have? The one Mademoiselle Gris left behind, of course. Go get it."

"I always said it was a good painting, didn't I?" He rose from the chair. "How much money are you talking about?" he said to Rachel.

"I can't say until I've seen it."

His protruding teeth gnawed his lower lip. "It may not be for sale. It has a lot of sentimental value."

"Then I won't buy it," Rachel said. "But I can give you an idea of what it's worth."

"Stop trying to be clever and get the painting," the old woman snapped at him impatiently. He left through a doorway at the back of the room. "It's true he was very fond of Mademoiselle Gris," the old woman explained. "She used to keep an eye on him when I was out. Naturally I took a little off her rent. That was how she made ends meet, babysitting Guy and the little Monette boy."

The thought of Dan and the man in the underwear being boyhood friends gave Rachel a jolt. "Did she often take care of him? The Monette boy, I mean."

"Yes," the old woman answered. She looked thoughtful. "But I don't see that has anything to do with the painting."

"I think it does." The old eyes went far away.

"They were kind people, the Monettes," she said at last. "Of course Madame Monette was very high spirited, but underneath she had a good nature. A lot of the time I think she had Mademoiselle Gris help with the boy because it was the only way she could give her money without making it look like charity. Often they would go out before dawn for an hour or two and put the child in number five with Mademoiselle Gris. They didn't have to. They could easily have saved the money by leaving him asleep in his own bed. The Monettes had number three. It was our nicest apartment in those days."

"Where did they go for an hour or two before dawn?"

"To the market." The old woman gestured impatiently toward the street, then abruptly stopped her hand and let it fall to her side. She went on more quietly: "Madame Monette loved to eat onion soup and watch the market open."

"It sounds like they were well off."

"No. Not well off. No one had money in those days. Not around here. But they had a little more than most. And they were generous with it." The thought of money combined with generosity brought the old woman's eyes back to the present. "No one has ever had any money around here," she said bitterly.

Guy returned to the room, still in his underwear. He carried a painting carefully in his hands. It had a plain wooden frame and wore a thick layer of dust. He handed it to Rachel. She blew the dust off and held the painting up to the light.

It was a night scene, lit by a full moon partially obscured by clouds. The clouds had an eerie translucence. The moonlight shone dimly on a still river. Out of the depths of the water rose the blurred shape of a black bridge, like a prehistoric sea monster.

"Well?" said the old woman.

Rachel gave the painting back to the man. "I may want to buy it. But first I have to know a few details."

"What kind of details?" the woman asked impatiently.

"Anything that would authenticate the painting. For example, I need to know when it was painted."

"I remember that," the man said quickly. "She painted it just before she left."

"When was that?"

The buckteeth gnawed again at the lip. "I don't know exactly. I never thought much about dates when I was a kid."

"You still don't," his mother said.

"Don't start on me."

Their voices rose, buffeting each other like clubs. "Stop it," Rachel said. She turned to the old woman. "You must remember approximately when she left."

Closing both eyes she raised her hands to her face and gently rubbed the maroon pits with the tips of her fingers. "It must have been in the spring of 1948. April, I think, or May."

"Was it after Madame Monette died?"

"Yes." The old woman opened her eyes. They seemed wearier than they were before she closed them. "It was a great tragedy. Monsieur Monette cried like a baby. And poor Mademoiselle Gris. She was so upset they had to take her to the hospital."

"Is that why she left here?"

"No. She left to get married."

"To whom?"

"A friend of Monsieur Monette's. I can't remember his name. It was a long time ago." She took the painting from her son. "Now are you going to make me an offer or not? I haven't got the whole day to waste."

"I'll give you two hundred and fifty francs for the painting."

"It's not enough," the man said angrily.

"You stay out of this," his mother told him. "I'll handle it." She turned to Rachel. "It's not enough."

"I'll give you two hundred and fifty more if you remember Lily Gris's married name."

The old woman's head hunched forward aggressively.

"If her paintings made her famous like you said why don't you know her married name already?"

Rachel sighed. "I lied to you. She's not famous. But her paintings are good and I'm interested in them." As she said it she realized the painting was very good indeed.

"You mean there's no market for it?" Disappointment reduced the old woman's voice to a monotone.

"Not yet."

"Then we'll hang on to it until there is one," the man said defiantly.

"It may be twenty years."

"You'll be sixty-two," the old woman sneered at him. "And you'll be worms."

"Sometimes I can hardly wait." Tears welled up in the old woman's eyes but they didn't overflow. "Give me the money," she said to Rachel.

Rachel handed her two hundred and fifty francs and took the painting. The woman counted the money twice. "And what about Lily Gris's married name?" Rachel asked.

"I told you I can't remember. It's no use asking me over and over like that."

"Is there anyone else living in the building who was here then?"

She shook her head. "They've all gone away. Didn't I tell you that, too? You've got your painting. Why don't you go away and stop bothering us?"

Rachel moved toward the door. "Wait," the man said. He turned to his mother. "What about Monsieur Tremblay?"

She shrugged. "It's possible."

"Who is Monsieur Tremblay?"

"He's a clerk at the post office," the man explained. "He's been there forever. She might have left him a forwarding address in her new name."

"Let's go talk to him."

"We can't. He's on his holiday."

"Where?"

"I'm not sure. I think he goes to Italy. He takes a bus from one camping spot to another, and sleeps in a little tent." He lifted his hands palm up: there was no accounting for the man's eccentricity.

"When does he return?" Rachel asked. Mother and son conferred. They appeared to know the precise amount of holiday time the clerk had coming to him. They counted on their fingers.

"Thursday," the old woman said.

"Good. Ask him Thursday morning." Rachel took more money from her handbag. "Here are fifty francs. I'll telephone you Thursday afternoon. If you've found out the name I'll give you two hundred more."

"You said two hundred and fifty before."

"That's right," the man backed her up.

"Two hundred and fifty includes the fifty I just gave you," Rachel said sharply. "Now tell me your name and telephone number so I can reach you."

The old woman told her. Rachel opened her notebook to a new page and wrote April 1, P.M., and under that the name and phone number.

"How can we get in touch with you, if we have to?" the son asked.

"Don't worry. I'll call."

"But we don't even know your name," he pressed her. He put his hand on her forearm and moved it very slightly across the skin. She thought of the social workers.

"That didn't keep you from taking my three hundred francs."

The old woman cackled at him. He dropped his hand from Rachel's arm and left the room.

Outside Rachel walked slowly through the streets where the market had been. She thought of Margaret Monette, and felt a sudden hunger for onion soup.

22

Ed Joyce's voice, a voice she knew to be deep and rumbling, sounded weak and thin as if the weight of the ocean pressing on the cable were squeezing the life out of it.

"Hello," he said to the long distance operator. "Ed Joyce here."

"Mr. Ed Joyce?" she said in her Parisian accent. "You have an overseas call from Paris."

"Paris?" But the operator had already left the line.

"It's Rachel Monette, Mr. Joyce."

"Oh. I thought you went to Morocco." He didn't sound thrilled to hear from her.

"I did." She heard noises like pounding surf and shrieking winds, far away.

"What are you doing in Paris?"

"Looking for Adam." In the pause that followed the storm grew louder. "Is there anything new?"

"No."

"What about the FBI?"

"Nothing new there either, apparently. I'm sorry."

"Are you still working on it?"

"We never close a case like this, Mrs. Monette."

"That's not what I asked you." Suddenly the storm abated, reduced in a moment to a faint hiss on the edge of her hearing. Ed Joyce's voice, too, became very faint.

"We're doing our best," came Joyce's reply, smothered as though he held his hand over his mouth. "But nothing has happened to change our original analysis."

"That's what you think."

"What? I can't hear you very well, Mrs. Monette. You'll have to speak up."

"I'll be in Bristol next Thursday," an aristocratic English voice said very distinctly. A rush of blended conversations followed. Rachel pressed her mouth to the perforated disc and shouted through the babble:

"What about the document I left you? Has anyone asked about it?"

"I can't hear you." His tiny cry cut through the din.

"The document," she yelled at the top of her lungs. Her free ear heard a knock at the door. Her other ear listened in on an anarchists' convention.

"Still in the safe," she thought she heard Ed Joyce say.

"Has anyone asked you about it?" she screamed. The knock was repeated, more loudly.

"Negative," he said, and then something else she didn't catch.

"Wednesday's no good at all," the Englishman said with annoyance.

"Goodbye, Mr. Joyce."

"What?"

She hung up the phone. The door opened and a worried chambermaid peeked into the room. "Is something wrong, madame?"

"No." The chambermaid didn't believe her but she withdrew and closed the door anyway.

Rachel reached again for the receiver. She noticed the sweaty imprint left on the black plastic by her palm, and wiped it dry on the bedspread. The hotel operator connected her to the information operator in Orange. The number for Xavier Monette was unlisted.

Rachel caught the night train to Lyon. The couchettes were all taken. Rachel bought a first-class ticket which entitled her to share a compartment with a gray-robed nun, whose sharp nose and cold blue eyes forestalled any conversation. After the conductor inspected their tickets they lay full length on the padded seats that faced each other across the compartment.

The train drummed its way south. As sleep closed slowly around Rachel's mind she heard the door slide open. She looked up quickly and saw by the light in the corridor two girls dressed like hikers. They carried large backpacks on aluminum frames and each had a wineskin slung around her neck. Rachel and the nun sat up. The two girls hoisted their packs onto the luggage rack and took places on either side of Rachel. The nun remained sitting. One of the girls leaned across Rachel and said in English to the other:

"I told you it was easy, didn't I?"

"You were right, Mindy," replied the other. Their accents were Californian. They laughed together at the easiness of it, and the one who wasn't Mindy unslung her wineskin, and tilted it to her mouth. The nun rose and left the compartment, closing the door after her.

"Do you think she's coming back?" the drinking girl asked. "I'd sure like to lie down."

"Go ahead." The drinking girl took a last swallow and crossed to the opposite seat. As she lay down the conductor opened the door and stepped inside.

"Tickets, please," he said to the two girls in French.

"No speak French," Mindy said, shrugging in apparent hopelessness.

"Your tickets, please," the conductor said in English. The girls retrieved their packs and took a long time searching through little zippered compartments before they found their tickets.

"These are second-class tickets. You must leave this compartment."

Mindy opened her eyes wide and gestured around the

room. "But look at all the space there is," she said. "And it's so crowded in second class. Can't you make an exception just this once?"

"Please do not make difficulties." He beckoned them toward the door. The girls picked up their packs.

"This sure is a dumb way to act for a country that depends on tourists," the drinking girl said loudly to her companion as they went out. His face impassive, the conductor led them away.

"You bet it is," Rachel heard Mindy reply before the steel door at the end of the corridor slammed shut. She lay down. Once again the door slid open. The nun entered.

A nifty bit of work, Rachel thought. The cold blue eyes rested on her face for a moment: they seemed disappointed that the conductor hadn't removed her as well. The nun lay down. Rachel closed her eyes and tried to remember the story of the Spanish Inquisition. The train played its percussive symphony through the night.

When the music came to an end Rachel awoke. The train stood motionless at the station in Lyon. She heard the air brakes venting steam. On the floor of the compartment, facing the window, the nun knelt in prayer. Outside the steam rose into the night air in little white clouds, sure to beat prayers to heaven in any race Rachel could imagine. She changed trains.

Dawn of Tuesday March thirtieth cast a warm clear light on Provence. Blue mist nestled in the hollows of the eastern slopes, safe for an hour or two from the rays of the sun. Most of the brown sheaths had fallen from the buds on the vines, and the first tender shoots, which would become leaves and grapes and strong Provencale wine were green speckles on the moist red earth of the vineyards. A few of the higher slopes were topped by stone ruins of old forts, forts which had once made the farmers believe in the feudal system. Now they made the photo-processors rich, and their mortgages were enough to make the farmers believers in the system.

At Orange, Rachel was the only passenger who got off

the train. She left her suitcase with the clerk at the baggage claim counter and crossed the square to the Hotel Terminus. The manager unfolded a map of the town. Handling his gold pen with pride he drew arrows pointing to the Roman triumphal arch, the Roman theatre which he assured her was not only the best preserved in France, but in the whole world, and finally rue de St. Jean-Baptiste, which was what she had asked for. Rachel ran her finger along the almost straight line that marked the course of the street from the center of town to the outskirts where it became a minor departmental highway.

"Can you show me where Xavier Monette lives?"

The gold pen wavered above the map like a bird unsure of its landing spot. "Are you a friend of his?"

"Family."

"I didn't know he had any family," the manager said. The tip of the pen settled gently on a point beyond the outskirts of town. "We don't see him very often."

"Why not?"

"He's retired. He likes to stay at home and tend his vines." The pen made a little circle around the point in the road. "He makes good wine. You will see." He gave her directions to the house. It was less than three kilometers from the hotel. She asked the manager to send a taxi for her in an hour, and set off on foot.

A high stone wall enclosed the house and grounds, and some of the fields in the distance. The iron gates were closed. Through them Rachel saw the house set far back from the road in a grove of peach trees. It was a big solid house, white with black trim, and an orange tile roof. Several outbuildings were scattered nearby. One of these seemed to be a miniature Greek temple. It had broad marble steps leading to a shallow portico. The undecorated pediment was supported by four columns which any ancient Greek architect would have rejected for their squatness. A faded sign tacked to the trunk of a tall cypress near the gate warned of a bad dog. Rachel's eyes were still searching the grounds for it when a rifle shot cracked behind her.

She whirled about and saw Xavier Monette striding toward her through the vineyards on the far side of the road. He held a rifle in one hand; a small reddish animal dangled by its tail from the other. The clothing he wore, a faded pink shirt and white duck pants, accented his deep tan. The soft breezes ruffled his pure white hair in the way that hair ruffles when it has just been cleaned. Stepping onto the road he looked as healthy as a senior citizen in a yogurt commercial.

"I finally got the little vandal," he said to her cheerfully in French. And then he seemed to notice who she was. The walnut brown eyes, so like Dan's in appearance yet so different in effect, opened wide in surprise. The jaw, finer than Dan's and not quite as strong, dropped slightly before the mouth settled into a smile. "What an unexpected pleasure," he said in English. The little fox dripped blood from the hole where its head used to be. It made a red puddle on the road.

"I tried to call you but your number is unlisted."

"How stupid of me not to have given it to you. I'll write it on a piece of paper the moment we get inside." Tucking the rifle under his arm he took keys from his pocket and unlocked the gate. He held it open for Rachel. A telephone was set in a small nook in the far side of one of the stone gateposts. Monette put it to his ear and listened for a few moments.

"Mademoiselle Hoff? We have a visitor. Would you please bring coffee to the terrace?" He dipped the mouthpiece below his chin and said to Rachel: "Are you hungry?"

"Not very."

He spoke into the telephone. "That will be all, Mademoiselle Hoff. Please be quick."

Monette faced the house and whistled once, sharply. An enormous Doberman, the largest Rachel had ever seen, burst from the peach grove and charged toward them, scarcely touching the ground. Monette flung the dead fox in a pinwheel through the air, scattering drops of blood like sparks from a Roman candle. The Doberman leaped to head height and took the furry body in one sure and savage chomp. Rachel heard the bones crush. It was torn to ribbons almost before the dog landed. The fun over, it started running back toward the house, but became aware of a scent, turned and saw Rachel. The great body stiffened, its muscles forming ridges under the sleek coat. Monette raised his hand and made a soft karate chop in the air. The Doberman lay down.

"Don't pay any attention to him," Monette told her. "All he cares about is sport."

"If you call that sport," Rachel said. He gave no sign that he heard her as they walked slowly along the rust-colored gravel lane to the house. "What do you call the gentle creature in case I should ever meet him in a dark alley?"

Monette laughed. "You are witty," he said as if he had just been converted to an idea that was already generally accepted. "But if you meet in a dark alley there is not much you can do. He has no name."

Beyond the peach trees a thick-set woman wearing an apron was walking from the house toward the Greek temple. She carried an enormous aluminum washtub piled high with linen and plainly very heavy. She disappeared behind the temple. Monette followed the direction of Rachel's gaze.

"The previous owner was a Greek," he explained. "I believe he made a lot of money selling cheap olive oil in counterfeit Italian containers. Enough money to be able to keep his mistress here. Unfortunately she pined for her homeland, so he had this temple shipped here stone by stone from her native island. He told me it was dedicated to Venus. Now we use it for storage and laundry."

The walls of the temple had no windows. A brass

padlock hung from the heavy wooden front door half-hidden behind the columns. "Those columns aren't Greek," Rachel said.

"You are absolutely right. That was one of my strongest arguments when we negotiated the selling price." He laughed.

"It must have cost a lot."

"Not really. The Italians had uncovered his little game and were pressuring him through the Common Market. He needed the money."

"When did you buy it?"

"A few years ago."

They walked among the peach trees. Fresh green leaves shaped like little lances sprouted through the rough skin of the branches. As they went by the temple Rachel turned and saw the woman in the apron emerging empty-handed from the small door at the rear of the temple. She locked it and ran with short heavy strides to the side of the house, entering by a screen door.

"It is a shame you didn't delay your visit by a few weeks," Monette said. "The blossoms will be out."

"It had to be now."

Monette led her down a terra-cotta hall which went from the front of the house to the back. All the doors along the hallway were closed except one. Rachel glanced inside as she went by. It was the kitchen. With her back to the door the woman in the apron was reaching up to a spice rack above the sink. She tilted her head up to read the labels. In that position her short blond hair covered most of the thick neck.

Coffee awaited them on the terrace behind the house. They overlooked a narrow strip of vines, perhaps seven or eight rows, an olive orchard, and fields which rose gradually into treeless round hills, pale green in the distance. Rachel and her father-in-law sat under the same rich luminous blue sky that had long ago put the troubadors in a singing mood. A brown hawk circled lazily as if he owned it.

Monette sipped his coffee and watched the bird fly. After a while he placed the mug carefully on the glass table and looked closely at Rachel's profile. "Have you begun to accept it?" he asked her gently.

She swung around and stared at him in disbelief. "On what basis?" she said sharply.

"Perhaps a religious one?" His musical voice was very soft. "Forgive me if I am wrong, but doesn't your Bible frequently call on you to make sacrifices? The story of Abraham and Isaac, for example. God demands the sacrifice of Abraham's firstborn son."

"What kind of God is that?"

"The Jewish God," he replied quietly. "Perhaps you don't appreciate the significance of the story. It is really quite beautiful. In return for his willingness to take the life of his son, Abraham was given a land for his people." His eyes went to the hawk, endlessly circling, and he spoke almost to himself. "Unfortunately the next step, the next moral step, was too much for them. They will lose it. It is inevitable as the crucifixion."

"I don't understand what you're talking about."

"One day you will. Some people require more time than others. In the end everyone accepts."

She got up quickly and stood in front of him. "Let's get this straight," she said, clenching her teeth to hold back the fury: "I will never accept what has happened to me. Never. There is nothing I can do about Dan except find out who killed him and why. At first that didn't matter to me very much; now it does, and I'm going to do it. As for Adam, he is alive and I will find him no matter what it takes. They've drawn first blood, whoever they are, but I won't let them make a sacrifice of my son."

She looked at Monette's face, lifted up to watch hers, and she saw the face of a sunburned old gentleman who was a little afraid of her. "Please don't be angry with me," he said. "I was only trying to help you. It hasn't been easy for me either."

She remembered the expression on his face when she

found him in Dan's study, trying to bring to life an image of his son from a dust jacket photograph. "I'm sorry." She sat down and picked up her coffee mug. Her hand was shaking too much to be reliable. She lowered it to the table.

Monette cleared his throat. "What do the police say?"

"They are idiots."

The sun rose higher, warming their faces as they sat in silence. Beyond the olive trees a boy drove a flock of sheep slowly across the fields. They stopped and started randomly, stubborn balls of wool.

"Have you thought of a way to begin?" Monette asked after a few minutes.

Rachel opened her eyes and looked at him. The breeze had pushed his fine white hair over his forehead, like Robert Frost's. "I found a document. There's no doubt that he was killed because he had it." She took the English version from her handbag and gave it to him. "I think Dan considered sending a copy of it to you, but he never mailed it." She got up and stood behind him as he read. "This place Mhamid is in the Moroccan desert. He must have thought you might know something about it, since you fought in North Africa. I'm hoping the same thing. That's why I'm here."

Monette laid the sheet of paper on the table. "I'm sorry. I know it only on the map. I spent the war far to the east."

"Have you ever heard of Camp Siegfried?"

"No."

"Were there atrocities in the desert?"

"Of course there were atrocities," he said with an edge to his voice. "It was war."

Rachel walked across the terrace and gazed at the shepherd. He sat in the field with his back resting against a rock and his cap pulled over his face. The sheep grazed around him. It was peace on earth, goodwill to man, as far as the eye could see. She turned her back on it.

"What about civilian atrocities?"

"Civilian atrocities?"

"Yes. Like the Nazi death camps, on a smaller scale."

The tanned face wrinkled in puzzlement. "I never heard of anything like that. The only death camps were in Germany and Poland."

"What would happen if someone discovered that there was another death camp, not on German soil? A death camp run by the Nazis but with the co-operation of a foreign government."

"What foreign government?"

"Yours."

"Mine?"

"Vichy."

His skin reddened beneath the tan. "That was not my government," he said bitterly.

"Never mind that. Don't you see? It would be an incredible scandal. There would be an investigation. People would lose their jobs. French prestige would sink. Some people have a lot to lose, and they are fighting to keep the facts from coming out."

Monette picked up the sheet of paper from the table and turned it over in his hands as if there were something there he wasn't seeing. "You know all that from this note?"

"And other things."

"What other things?"

"Things people have done to me when they thought I knew."

Monette reread the copy of the document. "Where is the original?"

"Where no one can get his hands on it."

"But you will need it to make your case, won't you?"

"If I need it I can get it."

"And, forgive me, what if something should happen to you? If what you say is true, then you are in danger. Is there anyone else to carry on, anyone else who knows where this document is?" The walnut eyes watched her face.

"Yes."

"Someone reliable?"

"Of course." Ed Joyce was reliable, in his way. "I'm not doing this all by myself."

Monette's hand went to the coffee mug, but the mug was empty. He sighed. "Your evidence seems very tenuous," he said. "How do you think Daniel got this document?"

"It probably came from someone who had read his book. It fits. The book was about French behavior during the war."

"I've read it," he said mildly. "Was there a letter with the document?"

"Not that I know of."

"What about the envelope? Did it have a postmark?"

Rachel thought. "Yes. It did."

"Where?"

"Nice."

Monette closed his eyes and raised his face to the sun. "Nice is a big city." He folded his hands across his flat stomach. After a minute or two his chest rose and fell in deep regular rhythm.

Not far away a car honked its horn. "My taxi," Rachel said. She rose and turned toward the door.

"If I may say so I think you should forget all this and go home." His eyes remained closed.

Rachel thought of the charred ruins of home. "No. I'm closing in. I can feel it." She entered the long hallway. "Goodbye," she said.

"Be careful."

Rachel walked along the hall. Now the kitchen door was closed like the others. As she left the house Rachel looked back. Framed in the rear doorway the stocky maid was clearing the coffee mugs from the glass table. She dropped one of them into a wastebasket under the table, and carried the other toward the house.

Rachel walked through the peach orchard. A few blossoms were already showing, like pink chips of mother-of-pearl against the bark. Above her the brown hawk glided silently in the blue sky. The Doberman with no name still lay exactly where his master had told him. He was watching the hawk. When Rachel emerged from the orchard he fixed his eyes on her. He didn't like her but he had his orders.

23

As Rachel walked into the station the train to the Côte
d'Azur pulled out. The baggage clerk told her that there
would not be another until the next morning. He also told
her where she could rent a car.

None of the big agencies considered Orange worthy of
their presence. That suited the hefty woman who rented
sprung and rusted Deux Chevaux from her gas station on
the southern edge of town. Credit cards were not part of
the world as she knew it; fixed prices were the devil's
work. Rachel brought both ideas into the conversation,
causing the fat lips to purse and make bird noises. Only a
hefty deposit had the power to bring her out of it. Rachel
paid without much complaint: her record for returning
rented cars had not lately been good.

She avoided the main route to the coast, via Aix-en-
Provence, taking the more northerly back roads which
cut across the departments of Vaucluse and Var. It looked
shorter on the road map. There was almost no traffic at all
and she drove very fast, but not fast enough to escape the
feeling that time was running out.

A tangible hypnotic silence began to close around her,

separating the world of the car from the world outside. The little villages she passed through seemed to have been deserted moments before her arrival. Even when she saw movement, a cow drinking from a pond by the road or an old man in a black beret raising a pipe to his lips, it appeared to be part of a painting. There was something immutable about the rust-colored furrows, the stone bridges over the little streams, the high pine forests, the rounded green hills, the rounded Romanesque churches in the valleys. She was the only mutable flaw in never-never land and it made her feel lonely. More lonely than she had felt even in the desert, more lonely than she had felt in her life. She tried to rehearse in her mind all she had found out, but she couldn't even remember the German names in the document. All she could remember clearly was Adam's face, the silky hair against her lips.

And suddenly she found herself remembering the feeling on her lips of Dan's hair, too—the hair on his head, and on his chest. It made her think of a picnic long ago in Vermont, just she and Dan. The countryside had looked like this, but it hadn't made her feel lonely at all. She remembered the hot sun and the wine and the prickling grass against the backs of her thighs as they made love under a blue sky. It came back vividly, physically, in a way that made her swallow several times and take her eyes off the road.

Descending the southern slopes of the Côtes du Luberon, Rachel missed a turn. The small car bounced across a ditch and spun around several times in a grassy meadow. She got out and walked away, breathing deeply and rapidly.

The sun had lost its warmth. It was pushing the shadows of the cypress trees at her from across the meadow. She drove the Deux Chevaux back onto the road and stopped in the next village in front of a small café. She couldn't get her mind off the picnic. Her thighs prickled at the memory.

How do you pick up men? Women have tried batting their eyelids, dropping handkerchiefs, pretending to be interested in football. Rachel went in the café.

There was no one inside. Three small round tables, tin ashtrays supplied by Pernod, a plywood bar, a few bottles on the shelves. Rachel sat at one of the tables. After a few moments the plastic strips that hung in the doorway behind the bar were parted and a man entered.

He had lived long enough for the sun to cut a few deep lines in his face and for life in the village to make his eyes sad. He was used to hard work: the veins in his big hands stood out and the legs under his blue overalls looked solid. Glints of gray were scattered in his thick black hair like iron filings; there were more in his day-old stubble.

"Yes?" he said from behind the bar.

"A glass of wine, please." She had not been certain the words would come. Her scruples were blocking her throat. But she needed him, or someone like him. Her scruples would have to be reexamined anyway—she had killed two men.

"Red or white?"

"Red."

He took a thick cheap glass from a shelf, held it up to the light, wiped it with a fairly clean-looking rag and filled it to the brim with red wine from a large stone jar. "And one for yourself," Rachel said. He filled the second glass without bothering to go through the rag business. Picking up both glasses he came to the table. He set one in front of her.

"Sit down," she said.

He sat opposite her and placed his wine in front of him. The sad eyes were alert, and far more intelligent than she had suspected. She raised the glass to her mouth, spilling some of the wine on her chin and neck. She felt a trickle between her breasts. The wine tasted rough and strong. The man drained his glass at a gulp and stared at the wine on her neck. He turned the empty glass in his brown hand.

Rachel didn't bat her eyelids or drop a handkerchief or

pretend to be interested in football. "Have you got a room?" she said.

He rose and walked behind the bar and through the curtain. Rachel followed him. The closed shutters outside the only window kept the room dark. There was a sink in the corner and a double bed against the far wall. They lay on it.

He moved with an intensity that shocked her. It was more than anything she had felt with Dan, or the men before him. The realization brought a pang of disloyalty, but it was true. She made herself stop thinking and gradually an intensity of her own arose within her, an intensity that matched the man's, then after a while began to feed it, and finally consumed it.

Afterward the prickling was gone.

The man rolled over. He sighed very deeply. Rachel found her clothes in the dim light, dressed and went through the doorway. Behind the bar she saw a bottle of cheap brandy, with a silhouette of a Spanish dancer on the label. She took it with her, leaving what she thought was fair payment on the counter. As Rachel opened the front door she almost bumped into a woman entering. The woman, dressed in rural black, was leading a little boy by the hand and carrying a heavy sack of onions. They both looked at Rachel with curiosity. Rachel got into the car. She heard an argument start in the café.

She drove through the afternoon and early evening, drinking now and then from the bottle. There was still an immutability about the peaceful countryside but it no longer had the power to scare her. She had fooled herself into thinking she was part of it. She knew she was fooling herself but it worked anyway. By the time she reached Nice the bottle was empty.

Rachel checked into a hotel which stood in the middle of the line of hotels facing the sea. Her room had a shower, a bidet, a comfortable bed, a window looking onto the harbor and a porter who didn't think much of her tip. Nice was a big town. It had a big phone book to prove it. It listed no Reinhardts, three Shreyers but only one had the initial J., two Feldbrills, neither one an M., and one Kopple, H.

She dialed the number that gave her an outside line and followed it with the seven digits the book had printed beside Shreyer, J. Her call was answered on the fourth ring.

"Hello," a male voice said in English. It was an American voice with a southwestern twang like Tom Dawkins's.

"May I speak to Joachim Shreyer?"

"Sorry, lady, ain't no Joachim Shreyer at this number. You're the second one today. This here's Jim Shreyer."

"I'm sorry to bother you."

"'S okay." He hung up.

She tried Kopple, H. She let it ring twenty times, counting the rings to herself. Then she dialed it again in case she had misdialed the first time, and listened to twenty more.

She sat by the telephone table looking out the window. Under the clear night sky she saw a few people walking along the rocky beach, and the lights of the yachts rising and dipping gently in the harbor. A liner lit like Times Square was just about to drop off the horizon. Rachel fell asleep in the chair before it happened.

When she awoke she found herself in bed but she didn't remember how she got there. The man in charge of the gong for J. Arthur Rank was practicing conscientiously somewhere behind her forehead. Cheerful sunshine filled the room, illuminating the pleasant floral pattern of the wallpaper and hurting her eyes. She reached for the telephone and tried H. Kopple's number.

"Hello," said a woman in French.

"Is Hans Kopple there please?"

"You just missed him. They've gone to the beach."

Rachel felt her pulse quicken. "Can you tell me what beach? It's very importa' ."

"I don't know. I'm only the maid." Rachel waited. "Are you a friend of theirs?"

"Yes," said Rachel. "An old friend from Germany. I'm only here for the day."

"Then it should be all right," the maid said. "They always go to La Napoule. It's on the Esterel."

And what do they look like, these old friends, Rachel thought as she hung up.

It didn't matter because they were the only people she saw on the little beach. From the top of the stairs that led from the road to the sheltered cove far below they looked like two pink walruses sleeping in the sun. Their naked bodies glistened with suntan oil. A cool breeze blew in off the sea. It wasn't really a beach day unless you were supplied with abundant subcutaneous fat. Walruses are.

They lay on their backs less than an arm's length apart sharing a faded blue blanket. By their feet was a Lufthansa bag with a white brassiere poking out the zippered opening. Each wore opaque plastic goggles over the eyes to protect them from the sun. They were not aware of Rachel approaching across the sand. When she drew near she saw that their excess flesh seemed to fit them well. They were fat, but in proportion. The man's plump penis was tucked safely under his belly. His mate had a plump vagina to go with it. Rachel stood over them, throwing her shadow across their bodies.

"Hans Kopple," she said. "I want to talk to you about the orders you received on January 18, 1942."

Their heads came off the blanket with a start, tossing the goggles onto the sand. Each raised a hand and squinted at Rachel through spread fingers, trying to see her against the sun.

"What do you want?" the man said in a frightened voice.

"I just told you. I want to hear about a camp called Siegfried."

The woman's other hand touched the man's leg. "Oh, Hans."

"I don't know what you are talking about," the man said to Rachel.

"You two should get your stories straight. You've had plenty of time." Something in her tone made them draw up their knees as if to render themselves less vulnerable. Rachel picked up the Lufthansa bag with their clothes inside. "But I don't," Rachel went on. "I don't have much time at all. So talk."

"You have no right to disturb us like this," the man said. He was trying to inject more force in his voice but the added energy only affected the upper registers, making him sound querulous. "I have done nothing illegal."

"Then you must have another reason for not wanting to talk about it."

"People have a right to some privacy."

"They do, Lieutenant Kopple," Rachel said. "But they give it up when they start sending unsolicited documents through the mail."

"But I never intended—" Too late he checked himself.

"What? What didn't you intend?"

He kept silent. The woman sat up fully, her heavy breasts falling toward her stomach. "Who are you?"

"Don't ask stupid questions, Marthe," the man said angrily. "She's obviously an Israeli agent."

"You're wrong, Lieutenant Kopple. Maybe you should let her talk more often."

"Please don't speak to my husband like that. You don't know him." The strength in the woman's voice surprised Rachel.

"Then persuade him to talk."

"He will talk more easily if he knows who he is talking to. And if you allow us to dress."

Rachel looked closely at the woman's face. Except for the mouth which was a little too sensual it was the kind of face a smart advertising man might have put on packages of precooked pastries: Auntie Marthe's Frozen Pies. Rachel sighed.

"My name is Monette. My husband wrote a book called *The Dreyfus Disease*. Your husband sent him a German army document." The Kopples turned and gazed up at the road that ran along the top of the cliff, but there was no one to see. "It got him killed." Rachel dropped the Lufthansa bag on the blanket.

"Oh, God," the woman said softly. Her hand gripped her husband's forearm. His pink face had gone very pale. "How could you have known, Hans?" she asked him gently. He pulled his arm free, reached for the flight bag and awkwardly got to his feet.

"I'll talk," he said. He began removing clothing from the bag: cotton briefs, green polyester trousers, a red and blue striped shirt. Rachel watched him dress.

"My husband never meant for anything like that to happen," the woman said to Rachel. Rachel didn't answer. "He tried to do the right thing."

"I'll talk," Kopple repeated, almost to himself. "I should have talked long ago."

"Do you want me to go?" his wife asked him.

"No. Please stay." He turned to Rachel and added, "If you don't mind."

"I don't mind." The woman put on her brassiere, panties, a shapeless floral sundress. The Kopples sat on the blanket with their backs to the sea. Rachel sat on the sand facing them.

"Where do you want me to begin?" Kopple asked.

"I'm not sure. Why don't you start with the orders."

"The orders." He focused his eyes on nothing, far away. "On January 18, 1942, I was twenty-one years old. I had been a Lieutenant for three weeks, and in Africa for two. I was assigned to the Afrika Corps, 90th Light Infantry. It was considered an honor. I felt proud. I was not a Nazi. I loathed them. But I was proud to serve under Rommel." His eyes moved to Rachel. "Do you understand that?"

"No."

Kopple leaned forward and raised his voice slightly, not in anger but in the hope of making himself clearer. His German accent made his highly grammatical French come from too far back in the mouth, giving it a hybrid unmusical sound that reminded Rachel of something mechanical, like a player piano.

"Rommel was an honorable man. He was not a Nazi thug. He fought hard, yes, but by the rules of war. Because he was not a thug and he commanded us, we could not be thugs either. There was no S.S. in Africa." He paused and again his eyes looked into the distance. "So I thought at the time," he added in a quieter voice.

He lifted a handful of sand and sifted it through his fingers. "I was content to be in Africa. The alternative was the Russian front. In the middle of January we were camped at El Agheila, west of Benghazi. And then we received those very strange orders. They commanded me to lead three men, a corporal named Shreyer and two privates, Reinhardt and Feldbrill, over three thousand kilometers to the west, in the opposite direction to the fighting. The orders were top secret, seen only by me and my commanding officer. They made no sense. Neither of us had heard of this Camp Siegfried or of a place called Mhamid. We had to find it on the map. My commanding officer made an attempt to appeal the orders, but he could do nothing. They came from Berlin.

"We were supplied with equipment that was badly needed elsewhere: two jeeps, petrol, food, water. And civilian clothing. Under the Vichy armistice German soldiers were not allowed in French North Africa. There were a few hundred of them anyway, but they did not wear uniforms. We were given a more elaborate cover in a second set of orders which arrived the following day. They told us to pose as Austrian scientists in search of minerals in the desert. These orders accompanied appropriate passports and other documents. We left on the twentieth, the same day that the rest of the Corps began the thrust toward Gazala. They were told we had been reassigned to Germany.

"I was very frightened. Our cover story was thin. None of us knew anything about minerals. Of the four only I had even set foot in Austria. But we passed through Tunisia and Algeria and into Morocco with no difficulty. It helped that the whole region was under the control of Vichy.

"In ten days we reached Camp Siegfried. It was not impressive. There were only two structures—a barracks and a much larger building with no windows. I reported to an army captain. He commanded a unit of guards made up of two other officers and eight men. We were to supplement the unit. He did not explain what we were guarding, or from whom. He gave us new uniforms. And he told us that the big building was out of bounds. The laboratory he called it. It was the private territory of the S.S. There they were on the African continent, contrary to everything we had been told. But we knew enough to keep our mouths shut.

"We rarely saw them. They did not stay in the barracks with us; they hardly ever emerged from the laboratory. No supplies went in or out, not even water. The guard commander said there was a well dug within the walls. Occasionally a man in a white coat came out of the building for a few minutes and stood in the sun.

"Once or twice a month two Frenchmen came in a jeep from the direction of Mhamid. We were told they were our liaison with Vichy, but none of us believed that. Vichy could not possibly have known about the camp, at least not officially. It was in direct contravention of the armistice. These two Frenchmen wore civilian clothes, but they had képis on their heads. They were obviously demobilized French soldiers."

"What were their names?"

Kopple made a little snickering sound. "Names? We didn't know anyone's name, except those of the other guards."

"Can you describe them?"

Kopple thought. "I never had a close look," he said. "Usually I would be riding around the perimeter of the camp in a jeep, or watching the desert from the top of the rock. All I can really say is that one was taller than the other." He thought again. "The tall one always went into the laboratory and stayed for about an hour. The other one waited outside. Then they drove away."

"What happened in the laboratory?"

Kopple looked over Rachel's shoulder. "We never really knew." He inhaled very deeply. "Sometimes we thought we heard screams in the night. They were very faint. It could have been the wind in the desert." His wife shifted her weight on the blanket, moving closer to him.

"But eventually you found out," Rachel suggested. He nodded grimly. "What was it? The airplane?"

Kopple's eyes opened wider in surprise. "You know about the airplanes?"

"A little. Tell me more."

"How do you know?"

"I haven't got time to explain right now. Get on with it."

Kopple stroked his fleshy jaw. The suntan oil smeared across his palm. He regarded it with distaste and tried to wipe it off on the blanket. "The airplanes," he said. "I saw two of them while I was there, but both times from a distance. As soon as the airplanes appeared the guards were ordered into the barracks. There was one small window which gave a partial view. The airplanes had French markings. They were small transports of a type I didn't know. When they landed, the S.S. men came out of the laboratory, armed with rifles. Each airplane brought about fifteen women. They were dressed in Arab robes, but they were European women. That became obvious when the man in the white coat . . . inspected them. After that they were led into the laboratory, and the airplane flew away to the north. The second time the two Frenchmen were at the camp, and they left on the airplane."

"Did you see the women again?"

"Not alive." Almost imperceptibly Kopple began to rock back and forth. His wife placed her hand on his knee.

"So we stayed in the desert. It was very boring. We were promised leave at Christmas. That was all we had to look forward to. But Christmas never came. Early in the morning of November eighth the British and Americans landed at Casablanca and Algiers and Oran. An S.S. major came into the barracks and woke us with the news. It meant we were cut off. Our only hope was to somehow get to the sea and find a boat to take us to the Canary Islands. We wanted to leave immediately, but the S.S. major forbade any such plan. We were confined to barracks for the whole day and the following night. By then it was clear from the radio reports that the whole of French North Africa was in enemy hands. We were desperate to leave.

"At noon on the ninth of November the S.S. major returned to the barracks and summoned us to the laboratory. He ordered us to leave our weapons behind. We had no choice. He was the highest-ranking officer. We went into the big building. Inside it resembled a hospital. There was a long corridor down the center with rooms off it on either side. The corridor was filled with armed S.S. men. There must have been thirty of them. We had no idea there were so many. The man in the white coat was there also. He stood on a chair at the far end. He told us that we had been called into the laboratory because there remained a lot of work to be done before we could leave, and time was running out. The buildings had to be demolished, he said. And there were also bodies to be buried. But before we got to that he told us that we had made a great contribution to science by guarding the laboratory. Germany had been engaged in a great experiment, an experiment designed to investigate the nature of the bond between mother and child. To investigate its nature and to test its limits. And now it was over, he said. It was a total success."

Kopple laughed bitterly.

"They took us into the rooms, two S.S. to each guard. There were pallets on the floor, four to a room, and on the pallets lay women. Some of them were pregnant. The others had babies in their arms. They were all dead. They hadn't been shot or clubbed: it was probably poison or gas. But their deadness was not what you saw at first. It was the alterations that had been done to them. And to some of the children too." His voice became very thick.

"What do you mean alterations?" Rachel asked quietly.

"They were mutilated, medically mutilated. Before they were killed. You could see the stitches in some of them." Tears began to roll down Kopple's cheeks. "Some of the babies were mutilated. And many of them were blond, blond like the S.S." Kopple began to sob. His wife put her arms around him. She was crying too. In a little while they grew quieter.

"When I saw that I went a little crazy, I suppose. I started yelling at the S.S. men; I don't know what. 'What are you doing?' one of them asked me. 'They are only Jews.' I took a step toward him. I doubt I would have had the nerve to do anything, but I never found out. Something struck me from behind.

"When I woke up it was night. There was a heavy weight on top of me. I felt hair on my face, and suddenly realized I was lying in a pile of bodies. I managed to claw my way out, but before I could leave I heard footsteps approaching. I lay very still on the floor. A door opened and I could see by the light in the corridor. Two S.S. men entered. They went to a corner and lifted a round cover off the floor. Then they began to drag the bodies from the pile and push them into the hole. They were the bodies of the women and the babies. And of the guards.

"I waited until one of the bodies got stuck in the hole. While the S.S. men struggled with it I crawled out of the room. There was no one in the corridor. I ran outside. The night was very dark, but I could see the S.S. They were working like madmen around the barracks, demolishing it with sledgehammers. I ran away into the desert.

"I knew they would be going west when they finished, so I went the other way. I walked through the night, and all of the following day and night. The next morning I stumbled on a caravan of desert traders moving east. I persuaded them to allow me to travel with them. I had a vague idea of rejoining my unit, which I managed to do in January of 1943. I was just in time to be captured by the British. I spent the rest of the war as a prisoner in England."

Kopple stopped rocking. His face was slack, his body drained. He was an old, fat, sunburned man sitting on a faded blanket. The beaches of the Mediterranean were crowded with men just like him.

"And the others?" Rachel asked. "The man in white? The S.S.?"

Kopple shrugged.

"Why did you pick my husband?"

He sighed. "I didn't have the courage to speak up. And who would believe me if I had? But I knew from his book that he was a clever and resourceful man. I thought perhaps there might be some written records left somewhere that referred to the camp. And if so he was in a better position than anyone I knew of to track them down." He shook his head. "I am very sorry. I hope you believe me."

"That's not important," Rachel said. "There are a few things I still don't understand. Why did you wait all these years before doing something? What was the point of opening this up now?"

"That's just it," Kopple said. "I found out it was still open."

"How?"

"I left one incident out of the story. There was an escape attempt that summer. It happened at the beginning of August, in the worst heat. The *chergui* was blowing. It is a hot wind they have there, like the *khamseen*. We were awakened one morning before dawn. Outside our commanding officer was talking to the S.S. major and the tall French liaison officer. After a while the major and the Frenchman went into the laboratory. Our commander informed us that a woman had escaped during the night. He explained that the Frenchman was an expert on the desert and had drawn up a search pattern for us. Most of us were sent north, northeast or northwest. It was far less likely she would go south. To the south lay nothing but desert. Only one man was sent in that direction. He was Private Victor Reinhardt, who had been under my command in the 90th Light Infantry.

"We searched for a week, but we never found the woman. And we never saw Private Reinhardt again either. We found his jeep in the desert, filled with sand, but there was no sign of him. We assumed he had been lost in a sandstorm, and died.

"I forgot all about him until last October, when I saw his picture in the newspaper. At first I wasn't sure it was he, but in December I saw him on several newscasts. I had no more doubt. He has aged, but not very much. Even if he had I would probably have recognized him anyway. He was a very distinctive-looking man, even as a young soldier. He is now an Israeli politician. He calls himself Simon Calvi."

Rachel thought she had seen the name in print, but she wasn't sure. "I don't know anything about him."

"Neither did I," Kopple said. "But I've been doing some research. I have a file at home you can look at if you like. Some people think he is a very dangerous man."

"In what way?"

"He is the leader of a movement seeking equality for non-European Jews. He has passed himself off as a Jew of Moroccan origin. At first his movement confined itself to specific social goals—better housing, higher pay, that sort of thing. But in the past year or two he has grown much more radical. He talks of the special bond between Arabs and Oriental Jews.

"That's why I had to do something. He was a soldier in Hitler's army. I didn't want the whole thing to happen again." His wife squeezed his hand.

"Have you told this to anyone else?"

"No. Only Marthe."

Rachel got to her feet. "I'd better see your file."

"Of course. Come to our apartment. We'll be there in an hour or a little more."

He gave her directions. Then he and his wife folded the blanket and walked slowly across the beach, hand in hand.

24

In the late afternoon Rachel left the hotel and walked to the Kopples' apartment building. It was less than a mile away, on a street which ran parallel to the shore several blocks inland. For part of its length the street, rue de Lyautey, was closed to traffic. Restaurants spilled onto the cobblestones from dark cubbyholes in the walls. Rachel smelled garlic and onions and cheese on the warm kitchen breezes mingling in the air. Like the smells, the tables of one restaurant seemed to merge without demarcation into the next. Only the waiters, clad in brightly colored outfits like soldiers of a bygone century, knew the borders. They resembled each other closely, as if drawn from a race of waiters: short dark men who worked silently, spreading red tablecloths, folding napkins into cones which they stuck in the wine glasses, arming each place with steel cutlery. One poured wine for an early customer; in the sunlight of late afternoon it glowed in the glass like rubies.

Rachel felt the trail going cold in front of her. She walked faster as though the increased energy could warm it. How could she rely on an old man's guilt-ridden memories? She imagined him squinting at the flickering light of the television as he had squinted at her against the

sun, or holding the newspaper close to his eyes while he
shaped the tiny dots of a photograph into the face of
someone from long ago.

The Kopples lived in a large townhouse which had been
converted into apartments. A burgundy carpet covering
the stone steps told the neighbors it was an elegant
address. Two stone gargoyles cackled over the heavy
wooden door. They had evil little eyes.

A waiter across the street noticed Rachel looking at
them. "Monsters," he called to her, and with his hand
made a twisting gesture that she didn't understand. She
opened the door and went inside.

The burgundy carpet led up a broad staircase bounded
on one side by a delicate wrought-iron railing. Still lifes
hung on the wall, three to a flight. Most showed fleshy
flowers, a few overripe fruit. The Kopples' apartment was
on the third floor. Number six. A brass mailbox was
screwed to the doorjamb. In it was a rolled copy of *Die
Welt*. Rachel took it out and knocked on the door. No one
came. After thirty seconds she knocked again, harder.
The door swung open.

She stepped across the threshold and saw herself in a
gilt-framed mirror, with an alert look on her face and a
newspaper in her hand. She was in a small foyer. The
faded blue blanket lay folded on a small writing table
beneath the mirror.

"Hello," Rachel called. "Is anyone home?" She listened. A clock ticked, a refrigerator hummed. "Hello."
Thinking she would leave a note, Rachel went to the
writing desk and bent to open the drawer. Inside she
found writing paper and a pen. As she straightened
something caught her eye through the doorway of an
adjoining room. A sandal strapped to a bare foot, a few
inches of a green polyester trouser leg. The foot hung in
the air as if someone was sitting just out of sight with his
legs crossed.

But he wasn't. Hans Kopple was lying on a brown
leather couch with one leg extended over the end. His

head rested on a small embroidered pillow. The pinkness had faded from his skin. It was all gray, except for the little red hole in the middle of his forehead.

His wife lay on the floor beside him, her face in the deep pile of the beige rug. It hadn't been so tidy with her. Her right hand still clutched a bronze table lamp. The frame of the shade was twisted and the flimsy cloth rent. Blood had soaked into the carpet around her head and chest. Her floral sun dress was drawn up high on her big legs. Rachel pulled it down. Then she remembered to feel the woman's wrist. The skin was neither hot nor cold. It could have been a modern fabric. Nothing moved underneath.

Rachel looked at her watch. Five forty-two. She gave herself five minutes to find the file. She began in the obvious places: the desk, the bookshelves, the bedside tables. After that she tried the clothes closets, the kitchen drawers. In the oven she found a duck roasting in peach sauce. It needed basting but was almost done. She closed the door and left the oven on. She searched under the mattress on the bed and under the pillows of the furniture. To look under the pillows of the brown couch she had to lift Kopple's legs. Her watch said five forty-eight. But before she left she recalled that some people liked to hide things in the toilet cistern, and she went into the bathroom.

A young woman wearing a black dress and a white apron lay in the bathtub. She faced the wrong way; her head was wedged between the taps at an awkward angle. But comfort no longer mattered: she had a red hole in her forehead too.

Rachel lifted the cover off the cistern, knocking a gold lipstick into the toilet bowl. There was nothing in the cistern but rusty water and a floating brass ball. She turned to leave and saw a ragged piece of blue silk in the maid's hand. She pried back the cold fingers one by one. It appeared to have been ripped from the back of a shirt or a blouse. There was no label, but she could see the stitching where it had been. Under the bottom row of stitches someone had sewn a black name tag with a name printed in gold thread. Rachel Monette, it said.

Rachel put the piece of silk in her pocket. Then she picked the lipstick out of the toilet, dried it on a hand towel and set it on the cover of the cistern, handling it with the towel. She dampened the towel under one of the taps in the sink and retraced her steps through the apartment, wiping anything she thought she had touched. When she finished she folded the towel and hung it on the rack. On her way out the door, she dropped *Die Welt* into the brass mailbox.

Rachel went down the stairs to the ground floor. She was about to open the front door when she heard heavy footsteps approaching outside. She ran to the rear of the hall and started down the stairs that led to the basement. The stairs were unlit and she had to feel her way. Halfway down she paused, her eyes at the level of the hall floor. She could see the front door through the balusters. It opened. Two policemen entered, revolvers in their hands. They went quietly up the stairs.

Rachel continued down to the basement. The only light in the large damp room filtered through a small dirty window set high on the street-side wall. Planted outside the window were two highly polished black shoes, which grew into blue trouser legs with navy stripes along the seams. On the opposite wall was a narrow steel door. Rachel put her ear against it. She heard a faint rustling. She turned and looked through the window. The black shoes hadn't moved. Above her the floor creaked. Again she put her ear to the cold metal, and again heard a rustling sound. She opened the door very slightly.

On the other side was a quiet alley where people left their cars and their garbage. A few inches from the door a big brown rat was gnawing through a plastic garbage bag. Seeing Rachel it stopped gnawing, but it didn't leave. It kept its snout in the garbage and one little red eye on her.

Rachel walked along the alley until she came to a busy cross street. She turned into it and tried to look like everybody else.

She went into the lobby of the hotel. The desk clerk didn't look at her in any special way as he handed her the room key. Her room seemed the same as she had left it. Her white cotton slacks lay in a heap on the floor and her underpants were drying on the bathroom doorknob. She threw everything in her suitcase and returned to the lobby to check out.

"I'm sorry, madame," the clerk said. "I have to charge you for the full day."

Rachel didn't make a fuss. She paid him and drove the rented Deux Chevaux to the airport. She parked near the terminal and got out, leaving the keys in the ignition.

"You there," a voice called behind her in French. A policeman leaned against a pillar near the entrance to the terminal. He was tapping his nightstick lightly against his palm. "Can't you read?"

"I beg your pardon?" Rachel said in English. She thought her voice sounded high, and very thin.

He raised the nightstick and pointed at a blue metal disc with a red diagonal line through it. "No parking," he said in English. He had an accent like Maurice Chevalier's.

Rachel held up her index finger. "One minute. I'll only be one minute." The policeman raised his eyes to heaven like a Guido Reni martyr. It is a look policemen everywhere enjoy using on silly women. Rachel lugged her suitcase into the terminal and caught a flight to Tel Aviv.

25

"We've got to get up," Simon Calvi said. "You'll miss the flight."

Gisela clung to him. "I don't care."

"I do."

"Five more minutes," Gisela said, holding him tighter. He worked his arm free from under her shoulder and looked at his watch. Eight thirty-two, it told him, Wednesday the thirty-first of March.

"We haven't got five minutes. It takes almost an hour to get to Lod and you're not even packed yet." In answer she moved her hip against him. He pushed her away and got out of bed. Gisela turned her face to the pillow. She didn't move or make a sound but he knew she was crying. "Gisela, for God's sake. You're behaving like a schoolgirl. It's only for a few days. What is the matter with you?"

She lay on the bed, prone and silent. He watched her while he dressed. Perhaps something had frightened her: urgency in his tone or trouble in his eyes. Or could she sense that he was following a schedule known only to himself? Did it make her jealous in some way, jealous enough to be disruptive?

"Listen, Gisela, if it will make you feel better I'll cancel the taxi and drive you myself."

Gisela rolled over quickly. "Oh no, that's not necessary." She had stopped crying: her eyes were dry. Had she been crying at all?

"I know it's not necessary, but I would prefer it. I should have offered in the first place."

"Please don't, Simon, I promise to hurry." She threw off the sheets and got out of bed as energetically as her heavy body would allow.

"It's no trouble." Calvi went downstairs to make coffee. He chose a decaffeinated blend. Enough anxiety was percolating inside both of them already. There was no need to add an oral dose.

Calvi opened the front door and stepped outside. For the first time in months there was a biting strength in the sun's heat. In the lime green Fiat parked under the carob tree sat Sergeant Levy with his sleeves rolled up. Calvi walked across the street. The car seemed to shrink and Sergeant Levy grow bigger as he approached.

"It must be hot, cooped up in the car like that," Calvi said through the open window. Being angry with him was pointless.

"That's the price of eternal vigilance," Sergeant Levy replied amiably.

Calvi went into his garage and started his own car, a compact American model. He backed it into the driveway and waited. After a few minutes Gisela came out of the house carrying two suitcases. She was dressed for a northern climate: tweed skirt, a sweater, a raincoat over her shoulders. The bulky material hid the definition of her full figure, making her appear thick and shapeless and unfamiliar. Her face wore the forlorn expression of a one- or two-night lover who had hoped for more.

Calvi got out of the car and took the suitcases. After he loaded them in the trunk he put his arms around her and kissed her mouth. She responded passively. "I wish you would be more cheerful. Is this the way to start a holiday?" Her pale blue eyes gazed up at his face: he saw a profound resignation.

"You'll never come."

"Don't be ridiculous," Calvi said lightly. "I've got a charter fare ticket and there are no refunds." Gisela looked blankly at him. He felt Sergeant Levy's eyes on his back. "Let's go."

Calvi drove to Jaffa Road and began the descent to the west. Overhead the sun followed, rising slowly in the sky. The green Fiat followed more closely. Calvi could see Sergeant Levy's face in the rearview mirror. His lips were moving as though he were talking to himself, but his huge fingers tapping on the steering wheel made Calvi think he was singing. He sang all the way to the airport. Calvi and Gisela rode in silence.

He walked her to the security gate. "Don't forget to call for the package," he said.

"You've told me a thousand times, Simon."

"It's important. Remember to rent a van."

"Yes, yes."

"And where will you open it?"

"Please, Simon: not again."

"Where?"

Gisela sighed. "On a back road outside the city."

"Good," he said. "I know I'm being difficult, but I don't want to spoil the surprise."

The airport loudspeakers broadcast the final announcement of the flight to Munich. Simon and Gisela embraced. She buried her face in his chest. He watched Sergeant Levy standing by a newsstand on the far side of the concourse. "I wish you'd tell me more about this surprise," Gisela said.

"And ruin all the fun? Never."

"But I'm worried, Simon. I'm worried that you're sending some kind of present to make up for not coming yourself."

"No, Gisela." He kissed her forehead. "It's something to make our holiday more worthwhile, yours and mine."

She lifted her face for a longer, deeper kiss. "I hope so, Simon." Gisela turned and walked through the surveillance tunnel. The security guard ran a metal detector over her body before allowing her to go on.

"See you in a few days," Calvi called after her, but she was gone. The little convoy returned to Jerusalem.

On the way Calvi found himself thinking of the night he and Gisela had eaten dinner on the Mount of Olives. He recalled her anger when he sent her home alone in the taxi. Perhaps she really did feel so strongly about even short separations. Did she love him after all? Then he began remembering other incidents that had happened the same night. The man in the broad-brimmed hat who had made no attempt to follow him when he left the villa with Gisela. Why not?

Calvi switched on the radio. A man and a woman were talking about him. They were trying to explain to the audience why he had become more radical during the last few years. The man thought it had something to do with the possibility of increased immigration from Russia. The woman tied it to the growth of ethnic consciousness outside Israel. The announcer cut in to tell them thirty seconds remained. In that time could they make a quick prediction about his speech on Friday? The man couldn't say but he thought there would be a big crowd; the woman said everyone would have to wait and see. The announcer thanked them very much. Calvi turned off the radio and glanced in the rearview mirror. Sergeant Levy's head was thrown back and his mouth opened wide: he was reaching for a high note.

Calvi drove directly to the office and parked in his reserved space. Sergeant Levy parked behind him.

"It won't matter that I'm blocking you," he said to Calvi as he squeezed his enormous body out of the front seat. "We'll be leaving together anyway." He laughed at his joke and clapped Calvi on the back with bone-crushing force.

"You're a funny fellow," Calvi said, "especially for one of Grunberg's men."

"It's an asset in any line of work." Sergeant Levy accompanied him to the office and sat on the couch in the reception room.

"This is Sergeant Levy," Calvi announced to Sarah, who was typing a letter. "Major Grunberg has assigned him to protect me from myself until the rally."

Sarah nodded at the sergeant and held out a sheaf of messages. As Calvi took them she said: "Moses is in his office. He wants to talk to you." Something in her tone made him look at her closely. She wouldn't meet his eye.

Calvi went through the door which led to the two inner offices. The smaller one was Cohn's. He was standing with his back to the door, looking out the window.

"You wanted to see me?"

Cohn turned slowly to face him. His wiry red hair was uncombed. It stuck out in spikes from his skull. The effect should have been comical, but there was a fierce glare in his eyes which made the hair seem right.

"What's wrong with you, Moses?"

"What's wrong with me?" Cohn's voice rose to a shout.

"Quiet," Calvi hissed. "I've got one of Grunberg's thugs in the outer office."

"So you should," Cohn said almost as loudly as before.

"What is that supposed to mean?"

"A lot of things."

"Like what? And keep your God-damned voice down."

Cohn took a step toward Calvi. He was so tense his skin could barely contain him: the cords on his neck stood out and the veins in his temple rose in trembling ridges. "We're through, Simon," he said through gritted teeth. "Finished. There's no more trust between us."

"Speak for yourself."

"That's what I'm doing. You've been lying to me and hiding things from me and I'm not going to accept it anymore. It's as simple as that."

"I don't know what you are talking about," Calvi said in a tone that was more puzzled than cold.

"Don't you? I'll give an example to help you understand. Sunday night."

"Sunday night?"

"Yes. Why don't you tell me what you did on Sunday night."

"That's no secret," Calvi said. "I took Gisela to dinner. We tried Rubin's, the tourist trap on the Mount of Olives." Calvi reached into his pocket for a cigar and sat on the edge of Cohn's desk. "The food was not bad," he went on, lighting his cigar, "but the service was lousy."

"And what happened after?" Cohn pressed.

"After? We went home to bed. It was late."

"What time was that?"

Calvi waved his cigar impatiently. "Hell, Moses, I don't punch a clock every time I go in the house."

"Approximately what time then?"

Calvi puffed on the cigar and thought. Cohn stood on the other side of the desk rigid as granite. "I would say about eleven-thirty," Calvi finally replied.

"You are a liar," Cohn said in a clear and savage voice. "I know you're a liar, Simon, because I saw you coming out of an apartment block on Givat Shaul at one-fifteen." Cohn's angry eyes probed into his own. Calvi waited. "Do you deny it?"

"No." He smoked the cigar. He thought about the man in the broad-brimmed hat who had not bothered to follow him that night. "Tell me one thing, Moses, just out of interest: when did you start working for Grunberg?"

Red spots appeared on Cohn's face like instant measles. "You are talking shit," he said hotly. "I would never work for Grunberg."

"Then why were you following me?"

"I was not following you. I happened to be at a tenants' meeting in the building beside the one you came out of."

Calvi's eyebrows rose. "A tenants' meeting at one-fifteen?" he asked sarcastically.

"I stayed after for coffee. Don't try to put me on the defensive, Simon. You're the one who has the explaining to do, not me. Try telling me, for example, why anyone would leave an apartment on Givat Shaul at one-fifteen in the morning and take a taxi to a dirty little shop in the Old City, a dirty little shop that turns out to be an under—"

In one quick movement Calvi whirled around the desk and clapped his hand over Cohn's mouth. He lowered his mouth to Cohn's ear and whispered: "Don't be a fool. The whole office is probably bugged."

With surprising strength Cohn wriggled his wiry body free and darted to the other side of the desk. "I've got nothing to hide," he said defiantly. "You can't say that, can you?"

"No one over the age of five can say it, Moses."

Cohn shook his head furiously. "Stop feeding me generalities. Let's talk about you."

"Very well," Calvi said. He sat at the desk and took a pencil and a sheet of paper from the drawer. He wrote: "Not here. I have something at home to show you. It explains everything you want to know." He turned the paper so Cohn could read it. Cohn read it. His face remained hard but he raised and lowered his head in one affirmative nod. Calvi held the sheet in his hand and touched it with the glowing tip of the cigar. As it caught fire he dropped it in an empty metal wastebasket. Then he and Cohn went into the outer office.

Sergeant Levy was reading a day-old newspaper. Sarah was pasting stamps on envelopes. They were doing these things with an unnatural intensity.

"We're going to the house to work on the speech," Calvi said to Sarah. With an annoyed glance at Cohn he added, "Apparently it's not quite right."

Sarah looked closely at her husband. "Will you be home for dinner?"

"What do you think?" he asked Calvi.

"Oh, sure."

They went out the door, Cohn, the smallest man, first,

trailed by Calvi and Sergeant Levy. Between them, Calvi thought of cartoons he had seen of fish with their mouths open wide, about to gobble up a smaller fish in front and be gobbled from behind.

Sergeant Levy backed the green Fiat, giving Calvi room to turn around. He made a few hand signals to help Calvi get his car out of the space.

"That's far enough," he yelled. "Straighten the wheel." Calvi drove off with the Fiat close behind.

Moses Cohn switched on the radio and turned the volume up high.

"Loud enough?" he asked over the noise.

"Yes."

"Then suppose you tell me who the coffin is for?"

Calvi's eyes went to the rearview mirror. Sergeant Levy was trying something up-tempo. "You're not making sense, Moses."

Cohn banged his hand on the dashboard. "That's not good enough. Don't you understand? I went in there the next day. I asked them, those pretty friends of yours. 'I'm an inspector with the Mishtara,' I said. 'What was Mr. Simon Calvi doing here at three o'clock this morning?' The greasy, bald one treated me much the way you are now: 'You're not making sense, I don't know what you're talking about.' So I asked to see the boy's identity papers, just on the chance he was a Jordanian. It's not impossible in the Old City, as you know. It seems his papers are lost. 'Then I have to take him in,' I said. That's when the bald one remembered your visit."

A voice on the radio was shrieking a song about love that lasts forever and a day. Looking in the rearview mirror Calvi realized that Sergeant Levy was singing along with it. Cohn's words cut through the din: "So tell me about the coffin, Simon."

"I intend to. When we get to my place. I have something there that will explain everything."

"Why not start now?"

"It is a very long story," Calvi replied. And he felt a

strong desire to tell Cohn everything. He had locked a whole life away, hidden from wife, sons, lovers, friends, colleagues; now it wanted to be free: free of the Captain's orders, or Grunberg's dark gaze. But it was too soon.

Calvi turned the car into the driveway. Sergeant Levy parked the Fiat in the shade of the carob tree. From under the dash he took a radio phone and said something into it. Calvi led Cohn into the house.

"Upstairs," Calvi said. "In the bathroom."

"What makes you sure your house isn't bugged?" Cohn asked.

"I'm not. When we get what we need from the bathroom we'll go outside and sit in the garden."

They walked along the dark hall toward the bathroom. A dead quiet filled the house. Calvi felt Gisela's absence keenly, yet it had been only a few hours since she got on the plane.

"In here," Calvi said. He held the door open for Cohn. Cohn went in and turned to Calvi, an expectant look on his face. Calvi leaned in the doorway. "In the closet," he said, pointing to a door on the opposite side of the bathroom. "On the second shelf from the bottom."

Cohn opened the closet door and bent forward. He felt along the shelf with one hand. "It's at the back," Calvi said. Cohn knelt on the floor and reached deep into the closet.

"There's nothing on the shelf."

"Here." In two strides Calvi crossed the bathroom floor. Cohn heard him coming but before he could move Calvi had thrown a powerful six-inch punch down at his lower head. It caught him behind the right ear. In the cramped space there was no room to fall. Cohn let his body slide to the tile floor. Calvi stepped back to give him room. As he did he saw Cohn's hand move to his coat pocket. Calvi fell on top of him and grabbed his wrist with both hands. Even stunned by the blow to his head Cohn was very strong. The nose of the revolver in his hand turned slowly toward Calvi. He drove an elbow into

Cohn's stomach. As the smaller man gasped Calvi cracked his wrist against the corner of the tub. The gun fell to the floor. Calvi grabbed it and struck it, not too hard, against Cohn's temple. Cohn went limp.

Calvi touched Cohn's neck with the tip of his index finger. The pulse was strong. He lifted Cohn into the bathtub and laid him there face down. Before going downstairs he looked out the window. Sergeant Levy was talking to a little boy who stood beside the car.

In the kitchen Calvi found some electrical wire. He bound Cohn's hands and feet together so that his arms and legs formed an inverted vee over the bent rocker of his torso. He wound one end of the wire around the shower curtain rod and tied it tightly. Then, stretching its long extension cord to the limit, he brought the telephone from the study into the bathroom. He lowered the cover over the toilet and sat down to wait.

After a few minutes he heard a low moan from the bathtub. He turned on the tap at the sink and drew a glass of water, which he held to Cohn's lips. "Are you all right, Moses?" Cohn remained silent, but he swallowed some of the water. "Listen. I am going to call Sarah. I want you to speak to her. Tell her there is a lot to be done on the speech and you probably won't be home tonight."

"The speech," Cohn said. His voice was thick and bitter. "It was much too easy. You would have let me write anything I wanted. You never had any intention of using it anyway. Did you?" Calvi saw the revolver lying beside the sink and put it in his pocket. "What is the real text, Simon? Rise and slay your fellow Jew?"

"Don't be ludicrous."

"And who shares this little secret?" Cohn continued, ignoring him. "The Syrians? The Lebanese? The P.L.O.? All of them? Is that what Grunberg's worrying about? Is it? Answer me!"

"Don't make me kill you, Moses," Calvi said quietly. He heard Cohn breathing heavily in the tub.

"Why, Simon? Why?"

Calvi answered with a short barking laugh that was scarcely human.

"That's not good enough, Simon. There has to be a better reason for starting a war."

"No one is starting a war," Calvi said angrily. He picked up the telephone. "Now talk to Sarah."

"Never. You will have to kill me after all."

"That's very brave, Moses. But is it fair to Sarah, or the three kids?" Cohn was silent. "It's only two days until the speech, Moses. Then you'll see them again."

"You'd let me go after this?"

"You will be freed after the speech, I promise you."

"But you told me to say I'd be here only for tonight. What about tomorrow and tomorrow night?"

"We'll think of something later."

Cohn sighed. "All right." He gave in much too quickly, Calvi thought as he dialed the telephone. He knelt by the tub, leaning over the rim and holding the receiver so that each could hear. His other hand held the gun, pointing to Cohn's neck. Sarah answered.

"Mr. Calvi's office," she said.

"Hello, dear." Cohn lifted his head to speak into the mouthpiece. "It's me. Listen, I'm very sorry, but I think we're going to be at this thing all night."

"You sound funny, Moses. Is anything wrong?"

"No, no. We've just been arguing, that's all."

"What's he up to?"

"Nothing."

There was a long pause. "You can't talk right now, is that it?"

"No. I can talk. I don't think he's up to anything, that's all."

"You certainly change your mind in a hurry," she said, slightly irritated. "So, you probably won't be home tonight, is that it?"

"I'm sorry. Kiss the kids for me."

"Sure. Goodbye." Calvi heard a click, followed by the single note of an unchanging hum. He hung up. Cohn turned his head away. They had nothing more to talk about. Before he left the bathroom Calvi stuck a strip of adhesive tape over Cohn's mouth.

He needed a drink. He found nothing in the house but a bottle of vodka. He hated the stuff, but poured a glassful anyway. As he took the first sip the door bell rang. His hand shook as he set the glass on the liquor cabinet. He went to the door.

Sergeant Levy stood outside, with a thin old woman beside him. Aziza. She carried a large paper bag in both hands.

"Yes?" Calvi said, opening the door. He heard the tremor in his voice.

"Sorry to bother you," Sergeant Levy said. "This woman says she has melons for you."

"That's right. She grows the best melons in Israel. Do you want to examine them first?"

"I already have," Sergeant Levy replied, smiling. "No bombs. I just wanted to check with you about it."

"I appreciate it." To Aziza he added, "Step inside for a minute. I haven't got my wallet with me."

He led her into the kitchen. "What the hell are you doing here?"

She looked small and out of place in the fancy kitchen. Calvi saw she was afraid. "I came to warn you, Simon. It was the only way I could think of."

"Warn me?"

"Yes." She had received a letter from an old friend who had hung on in the mellah of Taroudant with the few remaining Jews. Her friend reported that a man had come to the mellah a few weeks before, asking questions about Calvi. No one knew his name; all she could say about him was that he had heavy black eyebrows.

"What kind of questions?"

"How well she knew you. How you lived in the mellah. Where your family came from."

"And what did she tell him?"

"Nothing. She thought he was working for the Arabs."

"Good." He was afraid of those questions. Long ago he had left Aziza because she knew some of the answers, left Taroudant and tried to start again in Fez where no one knew him. In this he was successful for a year or two. Later she had followed him to Israel, and demanded not her own rights but those of the boys. Now Grunberg was working back along the trail.

"Is everything going to be all right, Simon?"

"Of course." He took the bag of melons. "Here's the money for the fruit."

"I don't want it."

"Take it. It has to look right." He showed her to the door. She opened her mouth as if to speak, but whatever it was stayed inside. Through the window he watched Sergeant Levy watching her walk away. He had forgotten to thank her.

Calvi finished the glass of vodka and went to bed early. Sleep would not come. In the night he got up and looked in the bathroom. Cohn's face was turned away but Calvi knew he was awake. He drank another glass of vodka and returned to bed.

Just after dawn the telephone rang. The caller asked for Simon Calvi. It was a woman, and she spoke English. With an American accent.

26

In Israel, Rachel's father liked to say, Jews are not only doctors and lawyers, but garbagemen, cops, and brick-layers as well. His eyes filled with pride whenever he made the observation, as if he were boasting of a favorite nephew who was doing well. He visited Israel at least once a year, and always returned with glowing reports. "The first time I went I saw three cars the whole week. Now you can't find a parking space." What infuriated him at home—taxes, government, inflation—he didn't even no-tice in Israel. They were beside the point. Israel was special.

To Rachel it had never been much more than just another country. She hoped for it in war, but with a hope not much stronger than her hope for the Red Sox in a pennant drive. In one of his infrequent moments of insight her father had told her that the cause of this lack of feeling was a lack of thinking. He was right. She knew it when the Jewish immigration officer at Lod Airport stamped her passport. If someone had been doing the same job forty years before there would have been no cattle cars, no tattoos, no gas chambers. No well of bones. The thought began to divide Israel from other countries and bring it closer to her, to Adam. It put the Red Sox in perspective.

In front of the terminal waited a long line of taxis. Most of them, Rachel noticed, were made by Mercedes Benz. She rode in the back of one toward Jerusalem.

"First visit?" the driver asked her in English after they had gone a few miles.

"How did you know?"

He laughed. "By the way you're looking out the window." The darkening sky was draining the color out of the old and gentle countryside. The land of milk and honey. It did not seem so fertile as that, but perhaps it was just the light.

The driver was watching her in the rearview mirror. He had a dark alert face with thick curling hair and a black moustache. Their eyes met. His had a knowing expression, reinforced by his correct guess, she supposed. But it was not just Israel: she always looked that way at things she was seeing for the first time.

She imagined a conversation with the driver: "All Jews should live in Israel," he would say. "One day America may not be such a hospitable place for Jews."

And she would reply: "If that happens why would I be better off here?" She was prepared for a verbal attack that never came. Although he kept glancing at her in the mirror she could see his interest was not political. It struck her that her interest in the driver was totally political. She wondered what he thought of Simon Calvi, but she didn't risk asking: Israel was a small place.

He drove her to a large television and radio store in west Jerusalem and waited while she bought a bulky reel-to-reel tape recorder and a very expensive and very small cassette recorder. Then he took her to a little hotel he recommended on Jaffa Road. After she paid the fare he opened the trunk and removed her suitcase. He filled his brown eyes with sex: "Israelis are very direct. I would like to go to your room with you."

"No." When in Rome, she thought.

He shrugged. No big investment had been blown. He was probably one of those gamblers who had learned never to wager more than he could afford to lose.

But she liked his taste in hotels. The one he had chosen for her was decaying gracefully in its middle age, like a face with good bones. The good bones showed in the wrought-iron front doors, the marble floor of the lobby, the high ceilings. The decay was harder to trace: she saw it in the thirsty posture of the potted palms, the sagging furniture, the unshaven face of the desk clerk.

He gave her a room key and sold her a clothbound guide to the city. The room had shower, toilet, bed, chair. And a bus stop outside the window. She was sick of hotel rooms, sicker when she recalled they were all she had. She found herself thinking of the room behind the bar on the slopes of Luberon. Enough, she told herself. She saw a future in little rooms like that.

Rachel lay on the bed reading the guidebook. The author, an American, had a breezy flippant style and an ethnocentric outlook: he made the reader want to stay home. He advised Rachel where to stay (her hotel wasn't mentioned) and where to eat (suggesting the use of the code phrase white steak when ordering pork). He called Jerusalem the holiest chunk of real estate on earth and devoted twenty pages to its best shopping bargains.

The book contained four sequential pages of color photographs so it could be advertised as the all new, color photoguide to Israel. One of the pictures caught her eye: an exhausted soldier resting his head against the Wailing Wall, cheeks damp with tears that glistened in the night. The editor had added a caption taken from Jeremiah. "Thy children shall come again to their own border."

Rachel turned the little screw that opened the twin roofs of her safety razor and took out the blade. She laid the guidebook on the floor and knelt in front of it. Carefully she began cutting a rectangle out of each page, leaving a one-inch margin on all sides. When she finished she unwrapped the cassette recorder, set it in the cavity she had made, and closed the cover. It looked like any other guidebook. Rachel pressed the record button, turned up the volume and reclosed the book. She put it on the bed and stood three feet away.

"To be or not to be. That is da da dada da da dada." She rewound and listened. The machine said it back to her in a slightly muffled voice.

Before she went to bed she checked the telephone directory. Simon Calvi had listed his home and office numbers. The sight of his name excited her, and kept sleep away. She rehearsed her plan, and her fall-back plan.

After a while the buses stopped running. The street became quiet. Rachel rolled onto her stomach, slipping her hands under the pillow, her favorite sleeping position. Hours later, when sleep still would not come, she allowed herself to think of Adam, and the things they would do when they were together again. But first she would have to tell him that he had no father, no house, no dog. She tried to think how she would do that. The effort left her mind dark and empty. She slept.

The squeak of brakes woke her. She sat up with a start. Pale silver light entered from the window. Rachel got out of bed and looked down on the street. Two little boys with side curls on their faces were boarding a bus. On the sidewalk a gaunt man struggled under the weight of a large block of ice balanced on his head. Slowly it melted under the rising sun, drenching him in a private rain.

Rachel watched him until he was out of sight. Then she took a deep breath and picked up the telephone. She dialed Simon Calvi's home number. It was answered immediately.

"Shalom," said a deep male voice.

Rachel squeezed the telephone in her hand. "May I speak to Simon Calvi?"

"This is Simon Calvi." Something in the way he pronounced his vowels suggested he knew English but seldom spoke it.

"I'm sorry to call so early, Mr. Calvi, but I wanted to

reach you before you went out. My name is Rachel Bernstein and I work for a public radio network in the United States. I'm making a documentary on societies where different ethnic groups co-exist in the same state, and I would like to interview you very briefly."

"Go ahead."

"I'm afraid I can't do it on the telephone, Mr. Calvi. The sound quality isn't good enough. Perhaps I could meet you at your office."

"No," he replied firmly. "I haven't got time. Call me in a few days."

"Oh, dear," Rachel said. "I have to leave the country tomorrow morning. I promise not to take more than ten minutes of your time."

"Why didn't you call me earlier?"

He was quick and smart. Because I just got here. "Because I hadn't done enough research," Rachel said. "But from what I've found out in the past few days I know that the documentary will be incomplete without this interview. I think it's important, Mr. Calvi." She was talking fast like dogged reporters everywhere. "The documentary will be heard in major cities all over the United States. And quite frankly I should tell you that our outlook will be quite positive when it comes to your movement."

"You know that before speaking to me?" His tone was wry, superior. He was used to handling reporters. She knew she had him.

"Yes. It doesn't mean I'm not objective. I told you I've done some research. Besides, I'm a member of a minority group myself."

"What one is that?"

"I'm Jewish," she answered in surprise.

"So am I," Calvi said drily.

"I know. But in America it's a minority group."

He laughed. "You win," he said. "But you had better do some more research. In Israel the Sephardim are the majority."

"If you include the Oriental Jews," Rachel said before she could stop herself.

There was a pause. "That is true." Calvi's tone was cooler.

"And of course it makes sense to do so," Rachel went on quickly. "The two have a lot in common, from what I've read. You yourself are a mixture of both, I would guess. As a Moroccan you fall into the Oriental group, but the name Calvi suggests that your ancestors came from Spain, and were thus Sephardic. Am I right?"

"You are," he said, in a friendlier voice.

Rachel had interviewed enough of them to know that politicians everywhere loved a good sucking up. You just had to find the right place to suck, and then keep on sucking until they were dead. "Well, that makes you the ideal leader for your movement, doesn't it?"

"You're very charming," he said with a chuckle. "I had never thought of it like that before. All right, Miss Bernstein, ten minutes. Come to my house at noon."

How about a dark alley? "Thank you very much, Mr. Calvi. But there's one little problem. For national network documentaries like this we like to have a lot of live sound. Background noises—cars, shoes walking on the pavement, that sort of thing." And lots of people, she thought. "It gives the listener a sense of the flavor of the place. Anyway, I've found a terrific spot."

"Where?" Calvi asked, growing annoyed.

"The square in front of the Wailing Wall. It's ideal."

"Really, Miss Bernstein, I—"

"Call me Rachel," she said. "The Wailing Wall is perfect, and I take pride in my work. Naturally I want to take care of any transportation expenses you incur, a taxi or—"

"That will not be necessary."

"Then I'll take you to lunch after, if you have time."

"We'll see."

"Good," Rachel said. "At noon then?"

"Noon. Goodbye, Miss Bernstein."

"Wait. How will I know you?"

"From your research, Miss Bernstein."

Rachel hung up the telephone. She paced about the small room until her heart stopped racing. It had gone well, better than she had hoped. She wondered what would have happened if she had used her married name.

27

Simon Calvi yanked on the drawstring and pulled his bedroom curtains open wide like a man who has nothing to conceal from his neighbors. Outside a small black car, wearing a coat of glistening dew, was parked beneath the carob tree. As he watched, the green Fiat rolled into view and stopped behind the black car. Sergeant Levy got out, stretched, and approached the other car on the driver's side. He bent forward to speak to the person inside, resting his hands on the roof: the car rocked under his weight. Sergeant Levy talked, listened, shook his head. Calvi heard the high-pitched whirr of the black car's ignition, and the catching of the engine.

The car drove away. Sergeant Levy turned and looked up at the villa. Seeing Calvi at the window he smiled with delight as though it were the happiest surprise imaginable, and gave him the thumbs-up sign. Calvi raised his hand in reply and stepped back into the room.

In robe and slippers he walked along the quiet hall to the bathroom. Moses Cohn lay on his stomach in the bathtub, hands and feet wired together above the small of his back. His hands were bloated and purple with engorged blood, and a trail of dried mucus ran from his nostrils to the adhesive tape which covered his mouth. His eyes were closed, his breathing shallow. Quickly Calvi knelt and ripped away the adhesive. He began untying the knotted wire. Cohn moaned softly. His eyes opened. Slowly he turned his head as far as he could and gazed up at Calvi. He parted his lips and said something, but his voice was so low, so thick and raspy that Calvi could not understand.

"What is it, Moses?"

Cohn ran his dry yellow tongue over his lips in a futile attempt to moisten them. He took a breath and tried again. "Water," he said in a faint voice.

Calvi turned the tap and cupped his hands under the faucet. He held the water to Cohn's mouth and felt the lapping of his lips and tongue as he drank. When he had drunk enough he lowered his head to the porcelain, facing away from Calvi. Calvi finished untying him. Cohn's arms fell to his sides. His legs remained bent as they were. Calvi pushed on the ankles to straighten them but they were cramped rigid. He felt Cohn's hamstring muscles: hard as fists.

With an easy motion Calvi lifted him out of the tub and carried him down the hall to the guest bedroom, which faced the garden in the backyard. He laid Cohn on the old four-poster bed. Taking one heel in both hands he pushed with all his strength. Slowly the muscle yielded and he forced Cohn's foot to the bedspread. As Calvi began on the other leg the straight one suddenly sprang back into the cramped position. Cohn cried out in pain. Furiously Calvi grabbed both feet and jerked them down onto the bed. Then he sat across Cohn's calves to hold the legs still and beat on the hamstrings with the edges of his hands until they unclenched.

"Is that better, Moses?" he asked. Cohn said nothing. His eyes were closed, his breathing still very shallow. "I'll get you something to eat."

Calvi left him on the bed and went downstairs to the kitchen. He made soft-boiled eggs, toast, and coffee.

Through the window he kept his eye on Sergeant Levy, sitting on the Fiat's bumper and reading a newspaper. He put the food on a tray and carried it up the stairs.

No one lay on the bed in the guest bedroom. No one was in the room at all. Calvi dropped the tray and ran down the hall. He burst into his bedroom. Cohn was crawling across the floor, toward the window. Calvi pounced on him.

"Help." Cohn tried to raise his voice but the sound was no more than a soft croak. Calvi slapped his hand over Cohn's mouth and looked cautiously over the window sill. Sergeant Levy was still reading the paper.

With his hand on Cohn's mouth Calvi lifted him awkwardly and dragged him across the hall to the bathroom. He tore off a long strip of adhesive tape and wrapped it around Cohn's head several times, covering his face from upper lip to chin. Then he carried Cohn back to the guest bedroom, laid him on his back on the bed and with the electrical wire tied him spreadeagled to the bedposts. He had not intended to wind the wire so tightly around the wrists and ankles this time, but he felt Cohn trying to expand his tendons to give himself more room later on. Perhaps enough room to wriggle free. He bound him as tightly as before.

"Now you will be sore," Calvi said. "It's your own fault." Cohn's blue eyes glared at him, and a blue vein throbbed in his temple. Calvi sat on the edge of the bed. The two men watched each other. Outside they heard a mother calling her children. At first her voice was pleasant. When they didn't come it became angry. After a while she gave up. A door slammed.

"In a way, Moses, you brought this on yourself," Calvi began in a thoughtful tone. "I don't mean being tied up on the bed. I'm talking about this whole situation. If you hadn't got me interested in politics none of this would have happened." Calvi sighed. "But I suppose you couldn't stop yourself, could you? You were an idealist. You still are. And I was the perfect vehicle for your ideals.

In that way you used me, Moses. I don't blame you: I was well suited. I was good at it. I enjoyed it, loved it at times. You weren't the only one using me, that's all." Cohn stared at the ceiling. Almost to himself Calvi added, "I wish to God you had been the only one, Moses, I really do. At least with you I was willing." Cohn kept his eyes on the ceiling. "I'm a Jew, Moses, after all." But the blue gaze stayed where it was. Suddenly Calvi sprang up, grabbed Cohn by the front of his shirt and shouted:

"I had no choice, God damn you. Can't you see that?" Their faces were as close as lovers' faces before a kiss. Cohn closed his eyes. "Listen to me, you bastard." His voice began to rise out of control. The telephone rang in his bedroom. Now the blue eyes moved to meet his. They seemed to reflect the fear they saw, but it might have been a fear of their own. Calvi ran down the hall and answered it.

"Hello, Simon," Sarah said to him coldly. "Would you put Moses on, please."

Calvi was on the point of saying that Cohn had gone out for food, for anything, but he remembered that Grunberg almost surely had a tap on the phone and could check anything he said with Sergeant Levy across the street.

"Simon. Did you hear me?"

"Of course," Calvi said. "I was just listening for him. I think he's in the shower."

"Could you check, please?"

"Very well." Calvi put down the receiver and walked along the hall. He looked into the guest bedroom. Cohn lay bound on the bed. His eyes searched Calvi's face. Calvi returned to his bedroom and picked up the telephone.

"Still in the shower."

After a short pause Sarah said, "Have him call me. I'm at home."

"Is there a message I can give him?"

"That is the message," she said. "Call me at home."

"I'll try."

"What do you mean?" He felt the anger she was barely holding back, and something else, too. Suspicion, he thought.

"Nothing. We're working very hard, that's all. And we still have to go out to the university and see that they haven't messed up the preparations."

"If he has time to shower he has time to call his wife."

"I'll give him the message, Sarah. What more can I do? But I'm very surprised by your attitude. Surely you realize how important this speech is?" She was silent. "Don't you?"

"Yes," she answered finally in a flat, sullen voice. He paid her wages.

"Good. He'll call you as soon as he can." She hung up without saying goodbye.

Calvi went into the guest bedroom. He picked up the eggs and toast and the broken dishes and put them on the tray. With a paper napkin he wiped up the spilled coffee as well as he could. Lifting the tray he turned to leave the room. Cohn's eyes were again fixed on the ceiling.

"Moses. I know you are hungry. I'll bring you more food if you promise me you won't shout when I remove the tape." Cohn lay very still on the bed. "Nod your head if you promise." Cohn did not move a muscle. "Have it your way," Calvi said. He left the room.

Although he knew Cohn was securely bound, Calvi was afraid to leave the villa. Yet he had agreed to meet the American journalist by the Wailing Wall. He thought simply of not going, but journalists were persistent, and this one, he thought, particularly so: she might even come to the villa to look for him if he didn't appear.

Calvi went into the bathroom and broke open four strong sleeping capsules. He poured the white grains into an empty glass in the kitchen and filled the glass with milk. Then he climbed the stairs to the guest bedroom. Cohn's eyes followed him as he entered the room.

"Stop looking at me as if I had fangs." Calvi sat on the bed. He felt Cohn trying to shrink away. He sighed.

"You've got to have something nourishing, Moses," he said gently. "I'm going to take off the tape and let you drink this milk. You can scream all you want, but Levy won't hear you. He's got the windows of the car rolled up and he's singing his head off."

Calvi unwrapped the tape and helped Cohn lift his head. He put the glass to his lips. Slowly he drank, his thyroid cartilage bobbing in the thin neck. Calvi lowered Cohn's head to the mattress; it looked like a child's in his big hand. Cohn opened his mouth and spoke in a strained and weary voice.

"How did the Arabs get to you?"

Calvi stood up. "The Arabs didn't get to me," he said coldly. He rewound the adhesive tape over Cohn's mouth, but it didn't stop Cohn from calling him a liar. He did it with his blue eyes.

Calvi dressed and went outside. He crossed the street to the green Fiat and opened the door on the passenger side.

"Why waste gasoline?" he said.

Sergeant Levy laughed. "You're right. Get in." And he drove Calvi to the Old City.

Sergeant Levy parked the car near the Dung Gate. Side by side they walked along the narrow street which led to the square of the Wailing Wall. Sergeant Levy made Calvi feel small, a feeling he had seldom had in his adult life.

In a doorway lurked a young Arab with a cigarette dangling from his lips, ready to prey on tourists. He had a dozen gaudy watches on his skinny arm. When he saw Sergeant Levy approaching he rolled down his sleeve.

From the cramped and fetid alley they stepped into the broad square which faced the Wailing Wall. The midday sun gilded the worn stones under their feet, and the old venerated stones of the wall. It warmed the scrawny necks of the Orthodox Jews who rocked back and forth within touching distance of the wall, mumbling their prayers.

"I was here that night," Sergeant Levy said quietly. Calvi knew he was talking about the night of June seventh 1967 when Israeli troops took the Old City and afterwards gathered by the Wall. "That's something to tell my grandchildren."

"Yes," Calvi agreed. He looked around for the woman.

"If there is still an Israel by the time I have grandchildren," Sergeant Levy added.

Calvi did not reply. On the far side of the square he saw a tall big-boned woman with a large tape recorder over one shoulder. He started walking toward her, Sergeant Levy following. The woman was gazing at the Wall and didn't become aware of them until they were very close. Calvi had seen many American Jews mesmerized that way by the Wall.

The Wailing Wall, Rachel noticed, was divided by a screen into two unequal sections. The bigger part, about two thirds of the whole, was reserved for men; the rest was for women. Since the destruction of the Second Temple it had helped keep Jewish hopes alive; now Jewish men and women were united with their ancestors, but not with each other. In the guidebook she had read that the divine presence is said to rest eternally on the Wall: she wondered which section the presence chose.

A group of Americans went by, the men in prayer shawls and skull caps, the women in Saks Fifth Avenue. They walked purposefully toward the Wall, all except a boy at the rear who dragged his feet. He had blackheads, pimples, and a voice which kept breaking; he whined in both man and boy registers. "I don't care where it is," he was saying. "I don't want a Bar Mitzvah."

"Sh," a plump woman said to him. "What if Uncle Hy hears you?"

"So what?"

"So maybe he won't give you the stereo you asked him for," a short man told him through gritted teeth. "Don't you want the stereo?"

"Yes."

"Then stop bitching. It will be over in ten minutes. Jewish boys have Bar Mitzvahs and that's that."

"But, Dad, I'm not religious."

"Don't be silly," the plump woman said. "How can you know you're not religious when you're thirteen years old?"

"Then how can I know I am religious either?"

"And don't be a smart ass," the short man hissed.

A tall man at the head of the group turned and said: "Imagine. A Bar Mitzvah at the Wailing Wall. What a lucky young fellow."

"He sure is, Hy," the short man nodded vigorously.

The lucky young fellow and his family made their way to the Wall. The man named Hy gave it a chaste little peck with his lips. It was a signal for the others to do the same. All did, except the boy. Finally the short man took his hand and led him to the Wall. He wasn't far from kicking and screaming. Rachel watched as the short man and his son stood before the Wall. The short man began to wave his hands in the air. The boy kept shaking his head. The short man put a hand on the boy's back and pressed him without much force toward the Wall. With the whole group watching the boy gave in and quickly brushed his lips to the old stones. Then he stepped back and wiped his mouth with the back of his hand, as if he had just been made to kiss a relative he didn't like. The family began to applaud. One of the Orthodox Jews at the Wall interrupted his prayers to shout something angrily at them. Rachel could not suppress a laugh.

"It is a happy sight, isn't it?" said a deep voice right behind her.

She whirled and faced a tall, broad-shouldered man with dark gray eyes that looked right into hers. And behind him a giant. The surprise, their dimensions, sent a sharp tremor of fear through her body.

"You scared me," she said.

"I'm sorry," the man replied with a smile. "I was just talking about the Wall. It means the end of wandering for the wandering Jew." The giant nodded. "You are Miss Bernstein?"

"Yes."

"I am Simon Calvi." He held out his hand. Rachel took it in her own. It was a big strong hand, very slightly damp, which knew how to execute perfect handshakes. Not too strong or weak, long or short, warm or cold. "And this is a gentleman the state has kindly sent to protect me from all evil: Sergeant Levy." She heard ironies in his voice that must have meant something to somebody, perhaps the Sergeant, perhaps only himself.

"Hello," Rachel said. The giant smiled a big warm smile.

"Now, Miss Bernstein," Calvi said, "shall we get down to business? I believe you asked for ten minutes. Since you turn out to be such an attractive woman I think we can stretch it to fifteen."

"And had I been a hag what would you have done? Cut it to five?"

Calvi laughed, a deep rich laugh which promised to last for a long time, but didn't. "Zero, Miss Bernstein. Zero."

Rachel led him to a small stone bench on the edge of the square. An Arab boy carrying a large straw basket intercepted them. Blocking their path he plunked the basket at their feet and fished out a silver star of David. He put it in Rachel's hand.

"You like, madame?" he asked. "Five hundred years old silver. I make you good price." Rachel tried to hand it back but the boy wouldn't take it. He was smaller than the Bar Mitzvah boy, and younger too, in everything but the look in his eyes: a look Rachel associated with men who had spent their lives selling door to door. She dropped the trinket into the basket.

"Oh, sorry, sorry, sorry," the boy said, and reached into the basket for an olivewood crucifix. "You no Jew? You like this cross? Olivewood. From a tree that Jesus sat by on the olive mountain."

"No, thank you."

"Wait, madame." The boy placed a restraining hand on her arm and felt again in the basket. "This you like." He brandished an olivewood plaque which said God Bless This House. Rachel pulled her arm free. Calvi spoke sharply to the boy in a language Rachel didn't know. His face impassive he picked up the basket and walked away to try someone else. Scratching a living out of tourist attractions was the same at the Wailing Wall as at Niagara Falls.

They sat on the bench, Calvi on one end and Rachel in the center, with the tape recorder between them. Rachel laid her guidebook to Jerusalem beside the tape recorder. Calvi picked it up and read the cover. "I don't know this one. Is it good?"

"Mediocre." Calvi put it back on the bench. As Rachel was about to press the recording button, Sergeant Levy sat down beside her. She turned to him.

"Please don't think I'm being rude, Sergeant, but I've found that the presence of another person often makes the interview subject self-conscious."

Sergeant Levy smiled his big smile, but he didn't move. "I don't think Mr. Calvi minds."

"Not at all. I'm used to interviews."

"I'd still prefer it, Mr. Calvi," Rachel said.

"Very well." Calvi looked at Sergeant Levy and shrugged. Sergeant Levy lifted his bulk off the bench and walked to the middle of the square. He moved very lightly for such a big man.

"Thank you," Rachel said. She turned on the tape recorder. The reels began rotating soundlessly, passing the shiny brown tape between them. Calvi took a fat cigar from his pocket and lit it with a match he struck on the stone arm of the bench. He expelled a mouthful of smoke, and a little sigh.

"Testing, testing," Rachel said into the microphone. "One two three four." She looked up and saw the amused expression in Calvi's eyes. "What's so funny?"

"Don't you think testing testing one two three four sounds funny?" he asked.

"I suppose." Rachel pressed the stop button, rewound

the tape and played it back. They listened to her say it again. She stopped the tape and touched the record button.

"All ready?" Calvi asked.

"Yes, Mr. Victor Reinhardt, I'm ready," Rachel said. "I want my son." She pointed the microphone at his face.

28

Rachel watched the color drain from Calvi's face. His skin turned gray before her eyes, gray and damp. But he did not faint, or try to run away, or even drop his cigar: she felt the strength of will which kept him from doing any of those things. Slowly and deliberately he extended his right arm and pressed the stop button of the tape recorder with his index finger.

It was very quiet. Faintly Rachel heard a man chanting by the Wailing Wall. Sergeant Levy stood in the center of the square, his feet planted wide apart, his face lifted up to the sun. Rachel lowered the microphone to her lap.

"Who are you?" Calvi asked softly.

She watched the gray eyes. "Adam's mother." She saw no fear, no surprise, no comprehension. "It won't work. I know all about Siegfried and what happened to the women there. What you helped make happen to them." She thought she saw his pupils wince, but it was over very fast.

"You work for Grunberg?" Calvi looked around as if he expected to find someone standing over his shoulder.

"Who is Grunberg?"

Calvi regarded her carefully. "You don't know Grunberg?"

"No. Let's not play games, Mr. Reinhardt—"

"Don't call me that," he said angrily. He glanced quickly into the square—Sergeant Levy was watching them. "It's not my name," he added more quietly.

"It was. You've gone to a lot of trouble to cover it up, you've killed a lot of people, but I know the truth."

"What are you saying? I've never killed anyone in my life."

Rachel thought of Dan, and Andy, the Kopples, their maid. "You had them killed then, if you prefer to put it that way. And for some reason your man kidnapped my boy. Maybe he did it on his own: I don't even want to think why. I just want him back."

Calvi's eyes seemed puzzled. It was useless to watch them. He had them under control, like marionettes.

"You are not making sense to me, Miss Bernstein," he said, almost as if he wanted to help.

"Bernstein is my unmarried name. My husband's name was Monette." He knew the name; for less than a second his guard went down, long enough. "Daniel Monette. He was stabbed to death."

"I didn't kill him, Miss Bernstein, or have anyone kill him. I never heard of him until this moment."

"I suppose the name Hans Kopple means nothing to you either."

Calvi waited a long time before he replied. "The name Hans Kopple I know," he said at last. "I knew him during the war."

"When was the last time you saw him?"

He thought. "August of 1942," he said quietly.

"And you haven't seen him since?"

"No."

"Have you ever been to Nice, Mr. Calvi?"

"Several times."

"When was the most recent?"

"Really, Miss Bernstein, I don't understand what you are leading to."

"Just answer the question," Rachel said fiercely.

"Keep your voice down." Calvi looked across the square. Sergeant Levy had stopped watching them and again had his face tilted up to the sun.

"Answer me," Rachel repeated more quietly.

"It must have been three years ago this summer. I went to a congress of parliamentarians."

"You weren't there yesterday by any chance?"

"Of course not."

"Can you prove it?"

"Easily. Why do you ask?"

"Hans Kopple was murdered in Nice yesterday afternoon."

Calvi's eyes narrowed very slightly. "Do you know who killed him?"

"Someone who didn't want him to tell me who you really are. But he was too late. I already knew. Hans Kopple was killed for nothing." She paused. "Have you any idea who might have done that?" she added coldly.

He shook his head. "Do you?"

"Yes. A tall man, tall as you. Who likes to dress up as an Orthodox rabbi."

"Why do you say that?" Calvi asked quickly.

"Because the man who took my boy was wearing rabbinical dress." Now for the first time since she had called him by his real name she saw fear in his eyes. "Would I find rabbi's clothing hanging in one of your closets, Mr. Calvi?"

"No," he answered in a low voice.

"That's not good enough. You are a convincing liar, but a liar all the same. Understand me, Mr. Calvi: I don't accuse you of killing my husband. The blond man did that. But you took my boy, didn't you?"

"The blond man?"

"The one who does your murdering for you."

"No one does any murdering for me," Calvi said furiously.

"Or should I say did. He's dead. I killed him." With astonishment, and disgust, she heard the pride in her voice.

Calvi's eyes flickered; his jaw dropped a fraction of an inch. He didn't say a word.

"How can you keep denying it? It's written all over your face—you know what I'm talking about."

"I'm glad the blond man is dead," Calvi said slowly. "But you are mistaken, Miss Bernstein. He did not work for me. I don't know exactly what is happening, but I think I am as much a victim as you are. Please believe me. I know nothing about your son. Or your husband."

Something in his eyes, or in his tone, or perhaps in her mind at that moment made her realize that despite all her reasoning and all her hopes he was telling her the truth. She had dug and dug, dug down as far as Simon Calvi, but she had not dug deep enough. He was digging too, she thought, but in a different direction. Perhaps he was digging up while she dug down: like moles underground they had touched in the blackness. She shot one final round.

"Listen to me. You must be aware what would happen to your career if what I know about you became public knowledge. An Israeli politician, a leader of the Oriental Jews—who is not an Oriental Jew, not even a Jew, but who spent the war as a Nazi guard at a concentration camp where medical experiments were performed on Jewish women."

"I was not a Nazi," he said hotly.

"A soldier in Hitler's army, then. It won't make any difference."

They stared at each other. Drops of sweat hung on Calvi's upper lip. Rachel felt her own sweat in her armpits and the small of her back. "And babies," she continued quietly. "I forgot to mention that it is almost a certainty that medical experiments were performed on babies at Siegfried."

"I didn't know." His voice was hoarse.

"No, you had gone before that became apparent. At least to Kopple. You can explain that to the press. Or the courts." She leaned across the tape recorder and placed her hand on his: "Or you could tell me how to find my son. Maybe you didn't take him—but you have information you're holding back that will lead me to him. I'm not a fool, Mr. Calvi. I can see that. Tell me what it is and I won't breathe a word of what I know. I will let you live out this fraud for as long as you want." Rachel heard herself pleading with him, but she made no attempt to change her tone. She kept her hand on his.

He looked up, across the square. She followed his gaze. The Bar Mitzvah was over. The boy and his family were returning in high spirits. Even the boy seemed delighted: he would never have to go through that again, and he had his stereo. He yanked off his skull cap and stuffed it into his pocket. They flowed around Sergeant Levy like a river around an island. Sergeant Levy reached down and patted the boy on the head. The family grinned nervously, perhaps only because of Sergeant Levy's size, but the boy didn't seem to mind.

Calvi noticed the cold cigar between his fingers and let it fall to the stones. He watched the American family trail across the square in the direction of the Jaffa Gate and a late lunch. "It's not the fraud you think it is," he said to Rachel. He drew his hand away and twisted on the bench to face her:

"You are right. I am not a Moroccan Jew. But I am a Jew. A Jew and a German." Rachel watched the gray eyes closely but they were opaque and far away, in space and time. "If real name means the one you are born with, then Reinhardt is no more my real name than Calvi. Even less." His voice rose: "I made Simon Calvi real, far more real than Victor Reinhardt ever was."

"What name were you born with?" Rachel asked softly.

For a long time Calvi said nothing. The bearded old men rocked back and forth, each one alone with the pitted stones. The wall answered all their prayers just by being there.

Calvi raised his eyes up, over her head, toward the horizon. "Victor Mendel," he said at last, as if he had gone to the edge of memory to find his name.

He laughed a short laugh. An embarrassed laugh. "Victor Mendel. Who the hell was he?" And suddenly he looked at Rachel as if they were old friends sharing a joke from long ago. The surprise made her inhale sharply, the surprise of his familiarity and her reaction to it: she wanted more knowledge of this man for its own sake. Wild thoughts darted through her brain. I'll sleep with you if you tell me where Adam is. He probably has no idea where Adam is, and if he does he probably doesn't know he knows. I'll sleep with you anyway. Rachel bit hard on the inside of her mouth, to bring her mind to order. She tasted blood on her tongue.

"Who was Victor Mendel?"

But he chose to start somewhere else. Old friends have time to digress. "Names. They can be as dangerous as wearing the wrong uniform in a battle. What is wrong with giving them up if they become unsafe?"

Rachel was not sure whether the question was rhetorical, but she had an answer: "Because whenever you do you give up a little of yourself."

The gray eyes fastened on her own; there was a gentleness she had not expected. "I suppose all women must learn that when they marry," he said.

At that moment Rachel remembered the guidebook lying on the bench between them. It occurred to her that she was invading her own privacy as much as his.

Calvi patted his pockets, but he had no more cigars. His last one lay at his feet. He left it there. "Statistically," he said, "Victor Mendel was a very lucky boy. He exists. He

still exists. How many Jews who were living in Munich in
1938 can say the same?"

"I don't know."

"Very few. Ninety percent of the Jews alive in Germany
before the war were dead by the end. And the war ended a
long time ago. That war. So I am a survivor. I don't make
a cult of it the way some others do, but I am a survivor
with my dues paid in full."

As he spoke his eyes grew less watchful, the muscles in
his face relaxed. Rachel knew there would be more and
waited while he thought.

"Innocence is the currency. Survival is bought with
innocence. You are born with an abundance of innocence
and no knowledge of how to survive: you spend your life
trading one for the other. But it only works one way. You
can't buy back your innocence." Calvi rubbed his hands
together as though they were suddenly cold, despite the
afternoon sun. "My account has been overdrawn for
years." His tone was light, and had nothing to do with the
look in his eyes. They were sad and lonely.

"Tell me about Munich in 1938."

"Everyone knows about Munich in 1938. There is
nothing to tell."

"I meant how did you go from Munich into Rommel's
army?"

The sadness and loneliness sank out of sight as quickly
as lead in water. Calvi glanced at Sergeant Levy, who had
begun pacing slowly back and forth. "You know so much
about me, Miss Bernstein. It's very disquieting."

"I haven't heard what I need to know."

"I'm sorry, I don't know anything about your son. No
amount of pressure will force me to reveal something I
don't know. You are making a mistake."

"No."

Calvi sighed. "What do the police say?"

Rachel answered with a sarcastic grunt. For a minute
or two they both watched Sergeant Levy walk. There was
nothing lumbering about the way he did it—he had the

quick sure stride of a gymnast or fencer. His size made it look dainty.

"Munich. 1938." Calvi's hand moved from his thigh to his pocket, stopped, and returned to the thigh. "How old are you, Miss Bernstein?"

"Thirty-one."

"So the war was finished before you were even born?"

"Yes."

"Have you ever heard of Kristallnacht?" The German was music on his lips.

"Of course."

"Not of course, Miss Bernstein. People forget. Soon it will be just a footnote in a textbook. Kristallnacht. November the tenth. It was the night that the Jewish community in Germany was shattered like a pane of glass. Did you know that for months after Kristallnacht over half the Jews who died in Germany were suicides?"

"No."

"From that night on everyone knew. We knew, even if we did nothing about it. What message could be clearer? We were finished. Many heard the message but did not believe it. My father was one of those. I suppose he had a lot to lose, my father. He was a doctor. We had a big house, a maid, a cook. I was the only child. I went to a good school. On weekends I rode through the countryside with my Aryan friends, on my own horse. Mozart, I named him." He shook off the memory. "I've never told this to anyone. Why you?"

"I asked."

Calvi smiled, and continued. As he spoke the smile faded like a last firework against the night sky. "My father was already a doctor in the past tense by November the tenth. Jews had been forbidden to practice medicine a few months before. He was not even permitted to treat Jewish patients, except as an orderly. But through all this he was convinced that the persecution was temporary. He was a cultured man. The Nazis were common hoodlums, drawn from the lowest elements of society. He made that point many times to my mother when she tried to persuade him to take us out of the country while we still had a chance. 'The natural order will reassert itself,' he would say. He didn't understand that was exactly what was happening.

"On Kristallnacht a band of thugs came to the front of our house. My father went to the door. I wanted to go with him but my mother made me hide with her upstairs. I was sixteen years old and could have insisted that I stay with my father, but I was afraid and yielded to her. We watched from a window on the third floor. My father was a big man, as big as I am. He opened the door. No one hit him. No one tried to force his way into the house. Their leader, a man half my father's size, simply stepped up to him and spat in his face. The saliva slid down his chin, onto his silk cravat. They laughed and went away. We were lucky.

"Even then my father was unable to understand that German society would never make a move to stop the hoodlums. He couldn't see they were the same people. My mother pleaded with him. He told her to be patient. But he allowed her to send me away, to stay with a Christian family she knew living in a little village near Balderschwang on the Austrian border. I never saw my parents again.

"This family hated the Nazis. When I arrived in the village they let it be known that I was a cousin whose parents had died in an automobile accident. They adopted me legally as their son. I took their name. Reinhardt.

"As a German with full citizenship I was naturally obligated to serve in the army. In 1940 I was taken into the Afrika Corps and sent to North Africa." Calvi looked up over the Wailing Wall at the golden dome of the great mosque. "Kopple must have told you the rest."

"Some of it. I don't know exactly what happened the day the woman escaped."

Calvi shrugged. "Nothing happened. I used the opportunity to escape myself."

"Why then?"

"I didn't know if there would be a better chance."

"Had you intended to desert for a long time?"

"Not consciously." Rachel thought that Calvi's face seemed older than when they had first sat on the bench, as if talking about years gone by had given them another go at aging him. But it did not make him weak or pathetic or diminish the feeling his physical presence gave her.

"What became of the woman?"

"I have no idea." They both thought about that.

"Why don't you ask if Kopple told me the woman was found?" Rachel asked.

"It wasn't even important to me at the time. It is less important now. I never had any intention of looking for her."

"What if she survived to tell the whole story?"

"Then I would have heard it."

"Doesn't it bother you—what they did to the women at Siegfried?"

"Of course."

"Not of course," Rachel said quietly. She looked again for the wince in the gray eyes, and saw it. "How can the man who wants everyone to remember Kristallnacht keep his mouth shut about something like that?"

"Don't be ridiculous. You know the answer. It is not merely a question of my career. I am in a position to help a lot of poor people. Not a little of the social reform enacted in this country in the last ten years has been due to me personally. Is dredging up the past more important than that?"

"You put yourself in a flattering light. I've heard that you've been splitting Israel down the middle so the Arabs won't have to work up a sweat when they march in."

Calvi jumped up and faced her. "My movement is completely legitimate," he shouted. "Completely."

"But you're not." Was he a man who believed his own lies? In the square, Sergeant Levy was watching them carefully. "That is a fact. I know it. Maybe someone else knows it too. Someone else must at least be suspicious. Does that explain Sergeant Levy? I thought bodyguards kept their eyes peeled for potential attackers. He keeps his eyes on you."

She saw Calvi stop himself from turning around to look. He sat down. Only after a few seconds did he glance across the square. Sergeant Levy had resumed his pacing. "You don't know what you're talking about," he said to Rachel coldly.

"Perhaps not, but I'm making good guesses."

"You delude yourself."

"Then help me. Explain how you passed as a Moroccan Jew, for example."

"I am not obliged to explain anything to you."

Rachel laughed in his face. "That's true. And I'm not obliged to stop myself from calling Sergeant Levy over here and telling him all about Victor Reinhardt."

The gray eyes showed anger, fear, nothing. Calvi made a gesture of acquiescence with his hand. "There is very little to tell. I found my way to Taroudant, in the Atlas. There was a large mellah there, very ancient, very crowded, very poor. I went to the chief rabbi and told him I was a Jew on the run from the Nazis. He gave me protection. I stayed there for three years. I learned the jewelry trade. I learned to speak Arabic. And Hebrew. The rabbi was surprised I knew so little Hebrew. Assimilation was a foreign concept to him. Later I went to Fez and lived among the Jews there as a Moroccan Jew. Any oddness about my mannerisms they attributed to my origin in the backward south. In 1948 I came to Israel and after a while got interested in politics." He leaned back on the bench. "Now you know all there is to know about me. I am at your mercy." He was very calm about it.

"Are you married?" Rachel heard herself asking.

"No."

"You didn't marry during all those years in Morocco?"

"No."

Rachel suddenly felt a tremendous fatigue, a tremendous sense of futility, as though a much thicker atmosphere than she was used to was pressing on her body. Simon Calvi was adapted to that pressure; perhaps he thrived under it; perhaps he was its source. She remembered the twelve-month pregnancy of her dream. A thousand clues had led her to a puzzle that had nothing to do with Adam. Rachel tried again. She spoke quietly, without passion:

"Simon. I don't agree with you. I think you can make deposits in the innocence account. That is what doing good is about. I want my son back."

"I told you—"

She held up her hand. "I know. I accept your word that you didn't take Adam, didn't have him taken or have anyone killed. But there is a connection between us and if we examine it carefully I'm sure we will find someone or something else connected to us both. I'm asking you to help me."

Calvi put his hand on her knee. "How can I, Miss Bernstein?"

"Rachel."

"Rachel." He used the Hebraic pronunciation. "How can I?"

"I don't know. We can start by going over our stories together, line by line. Something you know that seems trivial or irrelevant may mean everything to me. You see that by now, don't you?"

"Yes." He removed his hand, leaving her knee warm where it had rested. "I will do what I can to help you. But you must wait."

"Why? There may not be much time."

"Only until tomorrow. Tomorrow morning I am giving a speech at the university."

"I saw a poster."

"It's an important policy speech, one we've been planning for a long time." He looked at his watch. "I'm now two hours late for the final preparatory meeting. But tomorrow after the speech I can see you for as long as you like. Does that seem reasonable?"

"I don't have much choice."

"Don't talk like that, Rachel. It's less than twenty-four hours." He rose. "Why not come to the university tomorrow morning? My speeches are said to be entertaining, if nothing else. We can meet after and go somewhere from there."

"All right."

"Until then I don't have to tell you to be very careful. The boy's life may depend on our discretion."

He leaned forward and kissed her on the forehead. Then he turned and walked toward Sergeant Levy. Together they crossed the square toward the southern wall of the Old City.

Rachel felt the hot circle of his lips on her skin. She pulled the strap of the tape recorder over her shoulder, took the guidebook in her hand and stood up. Immediately a dizziness flowed through her body: white mist rose on the edge of her vision, obscuring the mosque, the wall, the stones of the old square. Rachel lowered her chin to her chest and it slowly dissipated.

She left in the opposite direction to that taken by the two men. Behind her a little boy ran to the bench, picked up Simon Calvi's cold cigar and stuck it in his mouth.

29

"Was she a good interviewer?" Sergeant Levy asked as a way of making conversation. In his hands the Fiat's steering wheel was a baby's toy, easily crumpled.

"Not bad," said Simon Calvi. He had endured enough conversation. As they drove toward Rehavia he was thinking about it. In his whole life he had never once loved a woman, but it hadn't troubled him at all until today, until a few minutes ago. It was too late. Of course he didn't love the woman—he knew that without a doubt. And yet he had fought a strong desire to tell her what he supposed she wanted to know. He had even tried to convince himself that it was a sensible idea: he could set her on the Captain. But the Captain was far too smart for her; so was he, for that matter. Perhaps later, he told himself, he could find a way to send her a message. It was possible.

"She was Jewish, wasn't she?" Sergeant Levy said.

"Nominally."

"It's so hard to tell with some of the Americans. They don't speak Hebrew, they don't speak Yiddish, they have their faces reshaped by plastic surgeons."

288

"This one kept her real face," Calvi said. Something in the way he spoke made Sergeant Levy glance at him from the corner of his eye.

"What was the interview about?"

"The usual subjects. The survival of ethnic cultures, the Arab threat, the peace talks."

"You must get bored answering those questions all the time."

"It's part of the job," Calvi replied. "You must get bored watching me all day."

Sergeant Levy turned and gave him a big smile. "I enjoy every minute of it." A battered pickup truck, crammed with passengers, cut sharply in front of them. Out of the back popped an iron washtub. It bounced on the road, scattering dozens of dried salt fish on the pavement. Sergeant Levy swerved smoothly around the tub. The pickup pulled over to the side of the road. Women began yelling angrily in Arabic.

Sergeant Levy parked in the shade of the carob tree. From one of its lower branches a long seed pod dropped, falling on the hood of the car with a soft thud. Calvi started involuntarily at the sound. He noticed that Sergeant Levy did, too.

"They make good cattle fodder," Calvi said opening the door.

"I didn't know that." Sergeant Levy watched it carefully through the windshield.

Calvi entered the villa and went into the kitchen. In a cupboard above the sink he found a box of cigars. He lit one and drew the smoke to the back of his throat, let it linger there, and slowly breathed it out through his nose and mouth. He felt his body begin to relax. As he was about to bring the cigar to his lips again, he heard a muffled squeak somewhere above his head. It was the kind of sound bedsprings might make.

Very quietly, taking his weight on the balls of his feet, he walked to the stairs. Slowly he went up, keeping to the outside of the steps where they were less likely to creak, up the staircase and along the carpeted hall to the guest bedroom.

The door was open. Sarah stood by the bed, her back to the door. She was supporting Cohn in a sitting position. She had removed the adhesive tape from his mouth, untied the electrical wire from his wrists and ankles, but she was having trouble rousing him from his drugged sleep. His eyelids, thick and puffy, drooped like heavy curtains.

"You shouldn't have come, Sarah," Calvi said.

Letting go of her husband she spun around to face him. Cohn sank limply back on the bed. "What's going on, Simon?" Fear pitched her voice much higher than normal.

From the doorway Calvi watched her but didn't say a word. He thought of several alternatives, none good. She was afraid of him, almost hysterically afraid: her eyes were opened so widely he could see the rim of white all around her pupils; her hands trembled. There was nothing to stop her from screaming, once.

"What have you done to Moses?"

"I gave him a few sleeping pills, that's all. He will be fine." Calvi spoke in a tone he would use to soothe a frightened child. "I don't want to hurt him." Or you, he thought. "You know that."

From the bed came a groan and an indistinct mutter. "You lured him here yesterday to kill him," Sarah said. The panicky edge in her voice had become sharper. "He knows something about you, doesn't he? Something about you and the Arabs. They got to you in the past few years, didn't they, Simon? How did they do that? Money? How much are they paying you?"

"Don't be silly."

"Silly? If I'm so silly why was my husband drugged, bound and gagged on your bed?"

"It's not what you think, Sarah. Trust me. We've known each other for a long time."

She laughed a nervous laugh which cut off abruptly. "We can never trust you again." She turned to Moses and lifted one of his arms onto her shoulder. "I'm taking him home now."

"I'm afraid I can't let you do that." Calvi took one step into the room. "Neither of you will come to any harm, but I have to keep you here until tomorrow." He advanced another step.

"No," she said, in a small, strangled voice. He didn't like it at all.

He shook his head sadly. "You shouldn't have come," he repeated.

"But I did." Gently she lowered Cohn's head to the mattress. It should have been a signal to him, but it wasn't. He was watching the tender way her hands held his head. He should have been reminding himself that she was a very fit woman, and twenty years younger than he. He should have, but he didn't.

With a quickness that caught him by surprise she darted across the room and dodged around him, weaving low to the ground like a soldier under enemy fire. Off balance Calvi reached out and grabbed her arm. He heard a ripping noise and her blouse came away in his hand. She raced down the hall.

Calvi charged after her. She was making a quiet whimpering sound in the back of her throat, like a child chased by a dog. She started running down the stairs, taking them two at a time as she made for the front door. She was almost at the bottom by the time he reached the top step. With a long stride he launched his body, aiming to land somewhere in the middle of the staircase, but one heel caught on the way, sending him head first down the stairs like a projectile. Just before he crashed into Sarah he saw a pattern of little freckles on her naked back. Then he saw white, black, and nothing at all.

Munich. He knew the buildings, the streets. He was a little boy, in white short pants, a sailor shirt and shiny black shoes. Very pretty shoes, but no good for running.

And he was running. As fast as he could he was running on a sunny, deserted street. He was being chased. He glanced back over his shoulder. No one. He did not have to see them: he heard them coming closer and closer. They made the sound of shattering glass. He ran. The sun was unbearably hot. The streets were filling with sand. Ahead walked a woman wearing a robe. She walked very slowly but he could not gain on her at all. He knew she would save him. He ran. "Mother," he cried. "Mother." But she didn't hear. Glass shattered at his heels.

Calvi awoke drenched in his own sweat. The house was dark. Through a window he looked up at the black sky, the cold white stars. The back of his head ached. Carefully he reached around and touched it with his fingers. It felt sticky and wet. He lowered his hands to brace himself for standing up. His right hand rested on something soft and cool. The coolness passed through the skin of his hand and spread through his body: it turned him ice cold.

He got to his feet. Waves passed over him: dizziness, nausea, pain. He found himself clinging to the wall, quivering. He felt a light switch against his palm, and pressed it.

Sarah lay on her back on the marble floor. She looked fine. No blood. No bruises. Her little round breasts looked fine. Everything was fine except the angle her head was forming with her body. It was wrong.

Calvi knelt and laid his thumb gently on the side of her neck. He felt his own blood pulsing under the skin of the thumb pad. Nothing more. He stayed there for a long time, kneeling on the floor with his hand touching Sarah's neck. "But I did," he heard her say, over and over. The stars moved across the sky. After an hour, two, three, he didn't know, he made himself stand up and peer through the window in the top of the front door. A small car was parked in the dappled light of the street lamp filtering through the branches of the carob tree. He thought of opening the door and calling, "Sergeant Levy, come here."

But he turned back instead. He looked at his watch: in

less than nine hours the speech; in sixteen, seventeen perhaps if Gisela was slow—freedom.

Freedom, he thought. It means a new identity. He laughed aloud at himself, a short, bitter laugh. It echoed through the quiet villa and came back to him so he could hear the bitterness in it. Was that the laugh of the little boy in the sailor shirt and shiny black shoes? He bent down and dragged Sarah's body into the kitchen.

Calvi opened the broom closet. He pushed mops, buckets, dustpans, detergents to the back. Then he put his hands in Sarah's cold unshaven armpits and lifted her inside so that she stood, facing the back of the closet. Before she could fall back into the room he closed the door and leaned against it. Inside the closet he heard a thud, and then a softer one. He let go of the door and stepped away from it. Slowly it opened, and Sarah Cohn fell stiffly onto the kitchen floor.

Calvi bolted to the dining room. He found the bottle of vodka, tilted it to his mouth and drank it like water. Then moving quickly he returned to the kitchen, stepped over Sarah, yanked everything out of the broom closet, the mops, buckets, dustpans, detergents, pushed Sarah inside, forced the body into a squatting position, threw everything back into the closet and shut the door. It stayed shut.

He returned to the dining room for more alcohol. His hand closed around the bottle. He stopped himself. Nine hours. Timing was important. Self-control was important. They were all he had.

Slowly he climbed the stairs. In the darkness of the guest bedroom he heard the deep regular breathing of Moses Cohn. He switched on the bedside lamp. Cohn lay on his side, knees drawn up to his chin, one hand tucked between his thighs. Calvi rolled him on his back. Cohn sighed a deep sigh.

On the floor beside the bed Calvi found the lengths of electrical wire. He wound one of them tightly around Cohn's ankle three times, and tied a tight reef knot. He drew the free end tautly to the bedpost, wound it around three times and tied another knot. Then he did the same to Cohn's left ankle. The activity quieted his mind. Working methodically he bound Cohn's wrists to the other bedposts. Then he went down the hall to the bathroom for more adhesive tape.

When he returned nothing had changed except Cohn's eyes. They were open. They turned a poorly focused blue gaze on Calvi.

"Where is Sarah?" Cohn asked thickly.

"How should I know?" Calvi replied. "I suppose she's at home."

"You're lying." Cohn's voice was very feeble. Calvi could barely distinguish the words. "You're lying. You always lie."

"Stop raving."

Cohn opened his mouth, closed it, opened it again. "She was here," he said weakly. "When it was light. She was here." The blue eyes sought out his own and clung to them like a terrier. "What have you done with her?"

"Yes, yes, she was here, for God's sake. Stop nagging at me. She had to come here, had to make sure her little husband was safe with the big bad man. She treats you like a God-damned baby."

"Where is she?" Cohn said hoarsely.

Calvi waved casually over his shoulder. "What was I supposed to do?" he asked. "I had to tie her up, too." Cohn's face twisted into a shape Calvi had never seen before. "Don't worry, she's completely unharmed. She's in the living room. The knots are so loose she could go dancing."

"You son of a bitch. Sarah is three months pregnant. If she loses the baby because of this I'll kill you. I swear I'll kill you if I never do another thing in my life."

Calvi felt his stomach rising. "Stop fretting. She's fine." But he heard the sickness in his voice, and knew that Cohn had heard it, too. Cohn's chest rose. He filled his lungs. He opened his mouth and screamed as loudly as he could scream. But it was no more than an ugly gurgling. Calvi strode across the room and punched him very hard in the mouth with his closed fist. It was enough to stun him. Calvi cut a long strip of adhesive tape and stuck it firmly over Cohn's mouth.

The door bell rang. Calvi's body jerked as if he were wired to it. Feverishly he untied the four pieces of electrical wire and threw them under the bed. He ripped the adhesive tape off Cohn's face and stuffed it in his pocket. In the closet he found a blanket. He spread it over Cohn and tucked a pillow under his head. Then, with all his strength, he struck him on the point of the chin. Once. Twice. The door bell rang again. He switched off the bedside lamp, took off all of his clothes, tossed them into his bedroom and went downstairs.

"Who is it?" Calvi called through the door.

"Open up." There was a hardness in Sergeant Levy's voice that he had not heard before. But it didn't surprise him.

"What do you want?"

"Open it or I'll break it down."

Calvi opened the door. Sergeant Levy swept in, barely glanced at him and started up the stairs.

"Would you mind explaining what this is all about?"

Sergeant Levy gave no sign of hearing. He disappeared down the hall. Without haste Calvi followed. He watched Sergeant Levy snap on the lights of the rooms off the hall and looked quickly into each one. He came to the guest bedroom, felt on the wall inside.

"Where is the switch?" he demanded.

"Please keep your voice down," Calvi said. "There is no switch. There's a lamp by the bed."

"Show me."

Calvi pushed past him. There wasn't room for the two of them in the hall. He turned on the light. Cohn lay under the blanket, his mouth slightly open and his eyes shut, like a dreamer of sweet dreams. A red blotch marred his chin, but it was very faint by the light of the bedside lamp. They watched Cohn breathe for a while.

"Where is your bedroom?" Sergeant Levy asked.

"Down the hall on your right."

Sergeant Levy poked his head into Calvi's bedroom. "Your bed hasn't been slept in," he said, turning to Calvi. Calvi looked at his toes. Bashfully. "My God." Sergeant Levy's voice was very low.

"So you've found us out, Sergeant. I hope you're not shocked by our little secret." Sergeant Levy didn't answer. "Or are you already pondering the blackmail possibilities? That would fit with this sort of storm trooper behavior."

Sergeant Levy moved very fast. Calvi felt Sergeant Levy's hands squeeze his biceps, he felt Sergeant Levy lift him in the air as though he were a bag of feathers. "Don't ever say that again," Sergeant Levy said through gritted teeth. Very slowly he lowered Calvi to the floor. A numbness spread through his arms to the tips of his fingers.

Sergeant Levy's great chest heaved: for a few moments his breathing seemed to fill the house. Then he walked down the stairs, across the hall and out the door. He slammed it shut as he left. The whole house shook.

Calvi stood naked in the hall, rubbing his arms. He heard a car door close. After a few minutes he went into the bathroom and found the vial of sleeping capsules. He brought them into the guest bedroom. On his hands and knees he reached for the electrical wire. Again he bound Cohn to the bedposts, as tightly as he had before. He removed the cap from the vial, dropped three capsules onto his palm, pried open Cohn's mouth and shoved the capsules down his throat. Cohn gagged, and then resumed his regular breathing. Calvi tore off a fresh strip of adhesive tape and wrapped it around the lower half of Cohn's head. He switched off the bedside lamp.

In his own bedroom he picked up the telephone and

dialed Cohn's home number. A woman answered. "Sarah?" she said in an anxious voice.

"No. This is Simon Calvi. With whom am I speaking?"

"Sarah's mother, Mr. Calvi. Mrs. Perlman."

"Of course, Mrs. Perlman. We've met. I'm very sorry to call so late, but we completely lost track of the time. I just went down to the living room and saw that Sarah and Moses had fallen asleep on the couch. I didn't have the heart to wake them. I thought I'd call you and see if you could manage till morning."

"I can," she said. There was a pause. "But this is very unlike Sarah."

"She's been working hard lately, because of the speech," Calvi explained. "They both have."

"She shouldn't be working so hard." A fresh wave of anxiety rose in her voice. "Especially now," she added, more to herself than Calvi.

"Well, Mrs. Perlman, it's time for me to go to bed, too. I hope I didn't disturb you."

"Will you put a blanket over them?"

"I already have."

As he hung up the telephone Calvi felt an ache in his biceps. Blue bruises were already showing on both arms. Sleep. He needed it but knew it was hopeless. His eyelids were wired open.

On a wicker chest of drawers was a blue-green vase full of dying red lilies. The vase appeared to be a hard metallic stone like malachite, but was in fact made from clay taken from Solomon's copper mines near Timna. It broke easily when he dropped it on the floor. Squatting, Calvi poked through the ceramic pieces. He found a large cut diamond, and then another, slightly smaller.

He went into the bathroom and took a condom out of the medicine cabinet. He inserted the diamonds into the condom, tied the open end, and forced it into his anus until it was entirely inside his body. He washed his hands.

In the bedroom Calvi gazed at the broken vase and the flowers strewn on the floor. He thought of sweeping up the mess, and of the broom closet in the kitchen. He left it the way it was: a broken vase was nothing to worry about. He kept looking at it all the same.

After a while he returned to the bedroom and opened the towel closet. Standing on the tips of his toes he reached to the back of the top shelf for the small round hot water bottle. He removed the rubber stopper with the string dangling from the hole cut in the center. From the drawer beside the sink he took a packet of coloring dye. He tore off one corner and poured the red powder into the hot water bottle. Then he filled it with warm water from the tap.

Simon Calvi strapped the hot water bottle to his chest. He dressed himself in socks, undershorts, his silk shirt, his navy blue tie, his new suit, his best shoes. He tied the string that dangled from the rubber stopper to the inside flap of his trousers. In the full length mirror behind the door he saw a big well-dressed man in late middle age who looked something like him. But his eyes were the eyes of a stranger. He sat on the bed and waited for morning.

30

Slowly Rachel walked through the Old City. There was nothing she could do until the morning but wait. A long wait, her thoughts and she alone. She felt her memory begin to open: Adam on the playroom floor, kneeling over his puzzles. He liked to hum while he fitted the pieces together. The farmer in the dell, the farmer in the dell, hi ho the derry-o, the farmer in the dell. Simple puzzles. No piece would fit in more than one of them.

She came to a narrow cobbled street. Medieval arches overhead linked the decrepit buildings on either side; their shadows fell in stripes across the cobbles. In her path stood three fat men, alike in their fatness, business suits, carefully barbered silver hair and clerical collars.

"I can't figure this out for the life of me," said one, leafing through a copy of the same guidebook Rachel had in her hand. "It should be number four. But I don't see a sign."

"Five," the second one corrected. "Four is back where you stepped in the donkey mess."

"Not according to this."

"Hurry up, you guys," said the third. "My goldarn arches are killing me."

The man with the guidebook waved to a pimply Arab youth leaning against a wall. "Hey there, is this number four or number five?"

The boy came forward with a big smile, eager to please. "Yes," he said with a thick accent.

"Four?"

"Yes."

"Or five?"

"Yes."

"Let me handle this," said the second man. "Numbers probably don't mean anything to him." He turned to the boy and spoke in a loud voice, so slowly and with such exaggerated diction that it scarcely sounded like English at all. "Listen carefully, sonny: is this where Jesus met his mother?"

"Yes."

"Or where Simon the Cyrene took the Cross?"

"Yes."

"Come on, you guys. He doesn't know his butt from his elbow."

"Wait a second," the second man said, using the same loud careful voice on his colleague. He placed a hand on the boy's shoulder. "Sonny, are you a Christian?"

"Yes, yes," the boy answered happily, and pulled an olivewood cross from his back pocket. "You like?"

The second man looked at it closely. "It's real beautiful."

"Ten dollar," the boy said.

The man whose feet hurt began to laugh.

"What a shame," the second man said. "Right here where He lived and breathed. All forgotten."

"It's not fair to judge them by our standards," remarked the first one as they turned to go.

"Seven."

Not a bad price, Rachel thought, for wood from a tree Christ leaned on. Via Dolorosa read a grimy sign beneath an arch. And below it a number, four. Jesus meets his mother. The Virgin Mary. One of the many biblical figures Rachel found completely alien. Abraham headed the list, for what he had been willing to do to Isaac. Or perhaps God did, for asking him to in the first place.

She shifted the weight of the tape recorder on her shoulder and crossed the street. Something made her look back. Two men were watching her, a short one and a tall one. They both had wrestler's bodies. All over the world men find time to give unaccompanied women the eye. Rachel continued on her way. But not eyes like those, she thought: hard narrow eyes staring so coolly, with no heat of lust in their gaze. She walked a little faster, and heard the leather heels of their shoes clicking on the stones behind her.

Rachel entered a crowded bazaar. Little shops lined an alley barely wide enough for two people to walk abreast. Butcher shops. Carcasses hung on hooks from the roofs. Bloody sides of beef swarming with brown flies, sheep by the dozen, by the hundred, chickens, rabbits, pigs skinned whole, their eyes sightless in their naked faces. Ask for white steak. Rachel walked still faster. She pushed past a plump specter—a veiled woman in a white robe that dragged on the ground. Through the veil came an angry protest, briefly joining the other noises that filled the stinking air: haggling of shopkeepers, cries of butchers, the snuffling oink of a pig, thudding of sharp knives on blocks of wood, the click of hard heels on stone. Rachel turned a corner, dropped the tape recorder and ran, clutching the guidebook in her right hand.

She raced down another narrow alley. It branched into three more that looked the same. She took the middle one, which quickly degenerated into little more than a cleft between two buildings. She felt beyond the bounds of civilization, trapped in the Dark Ages.

A man with his hands full of orange curry powder leaned aside to let her go by. Behind she heard two runners. One seemed to gain with every quick stride. The short one. The other was farther back, not gaining, not falling behind. Rachel ran faster.

Suddenly she emerged in a small square packed with Japanese tourists. Ahead rose one of the massive gates in the Old City wall. The short man was very close. She heard him panting. Rachel ran directly at the Japanese tourists. Almost in one motion they parted like a pair of cymbals. Through the gap she went, through the gate, and into a busy modern street, sucking in air and straining with every muscle.

But she wasn't fast enough. He was right behind her, his footsteps and his panting as loud in her ears as her own. She heard him leave the ground, felt his hands around her waist, his shoulder in her back. They tumbled, rolling on the pavement.

Even as they rolled he began to close her in an iron grip. She tried to jab an elbow into his stomach. He grunted. For an instant the power in his muscles ebbed. Rachel twisted free, jumped up and began running again. Her skirt came off in his hands.

Without it she was faster. She lengthened her stride. People turned to watch her but she didn't think of stopping. She was looking for a policeman, a soldier, someone with a gun.

She ran. Down one street. Into another. And behind her two sets of footsteps she couldn't shake. She found herself in a street where all the inhabitants seemed to have come intact from a nineteenth-century European ghetto. She ran by men in long black coats and fur hats, and skinny boys with side curls on their faces. Some yelled at her. They were angry, she made them angry. Why? A bearded old man rode by on a bicycle. He spat in her face. The yelling grew louder. She ran for her life.

At the corner. A policeman, directing traffic. No. A policewoman. Rachel ran to her, threw her arms around her.

"Help me." She looked back. The two men were coming fast.

The policewoman pushed her away to arm's length. She

was almost as tall as Rachel, but broader and more muscular. "You should not come here dressed like this," she said in very good English. "This is a very pious district. They demand modesty."

"For God's sake. Those men are trying to kill me." She pointed down the street. The policewoman's eyes followed her finger. They were less than half a block away.

"Those men?"

"Yes yes. Get out your gun."

The tall man opened his mouth and shouted something. Rachel did not understand the words, but she heard the commanding tone.

The policewoman smiled at her. She had big white teeth. "Not those men," she said.

"Yes," Rachel screamed at the top of her voice. The policewoman reached to her belt and unhooked her nightstick. With one fluid motion she brought it down hard on Rachel's head.

Yellow trucks in the playroom. A big fleet. They had CB handles. Adam was Mudslinger, she Coyote. "Mudslinger to Coyote, Mudslinger to Coyote. Come in, Coyote."

"I hear you, Mudslinger."

"Say Coyote here first."

"Coyote here. You're coming in loud and clear, Mudslinger."

"Good. I just wanted to tell you that Smokey's up the road."

"Much obliged, Mudslinger. Ten-four."

"Ten-four." Adam drove a yellow truck into a garage. He had to stand on the seat to see where he was going.

"Careful."

The door closed. She waited outside. She waited for a long time. He didn't come out. "Adam." She opened the garage door. There was nothing inside but concrete blocks.

Her job was to remove the blocks from the garage and

pile them inside a Greek temple. Ten blocks to a pile, they said at first. Then they changed it to seven. She had to lift three blocks from every pile she had finished and stack them again. Three three and one made a pile. Two three and two. One three and three. Three three and one. She carried the blocks on her head like an African. After a while her head began to hurt. It began to hurt badly.

Click.

"Testing testing one two three four. What's so funny?"

"Don't you think testing testing one two three four sounds funny?"

"I suppose."

"All ready?"

"Yes, Mr. Victor Reinhardt, I'm ready. I want my son."

Click.

"That's all?" A midwestern accent.

"That's all." Slightly guttural. Israeli.

"So what do we do now?"

"Wait. Unless you know a way to bring her out of it."

"We don't have much time."

"You don't need to tell me that."

"Sorry. Why did that Amazon have to bop her so hard?"

Sigh. "She is a mean one."

"Or else it's her period." Laugh.

Rachel opened her eyes. She looked through a small hole in a gray fog. She seemed to be in a small bare office. She was sitting in a steel chair. A strange chair she noticed: it had leather straps on the arms. They were tied tightly around her wrists. And her head was bound somehow to the back of the chair. She couldn't move her head at all. In front of her was a long wooden table. On it she saw her reel-to-reel tape recorder, her open suitcase, her handbag, her skirt. She felt the air on her bare legs.

Two men stood on the far side of the table. One had sandy thinning hair, horn-rimmed glasses and a tan suit.

The other man, a tall very broad man, wore a beige uniform. He had thick black eyebrows. Neither of them was looking at her.

"What would you know about a woman's period?" Rachel said. She tried to make her tone nice and nasty. It brought them on the run.

"I think she's coming to," the sandy-haired one said.

"Did you understand her?"

"No." He leaned close to her. "Did you say something?" She vomited in his face. "The God-damned bitch," he said incredulously. "She puked all over me."

The fog rolled in.

She went back to work, carrying blocks from the garage to the temple and arranging them in piles of seven. They were heavy and there were so many of them. She worked until her head was pounding, but she wasn't getting anywhere.

"Enough," she said. She braced herself for a big effort, and lifted her eyelids. She was looking into a pair of dark sunken eyes, older than any eyes she had ever seen. But they were not the eyes of an old man: the eyebrows which hung over them sprouted with luxuriant vigor. "You're not so old."

"I'm glad to hear that," the man said in a soft Israeli accent. "Who are you?"

"Everyone keeps asking me that. It's making me self-conscious."

"Who are you?" he repeated. His tone wasn't as soft the second time.

The sandy-haired man stepped out of the fog. "There's no time to play games with her." He was the same sandy-haired man, but he had changed from his tan suit into a pair of jeans and a sweat shirt. He seemed very uncomfortable in the new outfit.

"That just isn't you," Rachel told him. She listened to what she had said. Perhaps it was rude. "But what do clothes matter? Take me for example. I'm very informal."

She laughed. She would have slapped her bare thigh, but her arm appeared to be strapped to the chair.

"How much hop did they shoot into her, for Christ's sake?" the American asked.

"Nothing excessive," the Israeli said sharply. "She is a big woman."

The American seemed to be taking her side. That was very courteous considering that she had once done something bad to him. She tried to remember what it was.

"You're an American, aren't you?" He didn't answer. "Don't tell me, let me guess. I'm a whiz at accents." She closed her eyes. "Minnesota," she said finally. "I'd say you're from Minnesota." Her eyes stayed closed. It was good to talk to another American. She hadn't seen another American, not to talk to, for a long time. It was a hopelessly provincial reaction, she realized, but what was wrong with wanting to be with people who spoke one's own language?

"Perhaps we should try walking her," the Israeli suggested.

"Can't hurt."

The straps on her wrists and neck were loosened. Her head was free to loll wherever it wanted. She let it.

"Jesus Christ," the American said. She felt strong hands in her armpits, heard a grunt of effort, rose out of the chair. "She's one solid piece of meat."

She went for a walk. It was very pleasant. For a while she bent her knees and kept both feet off the floor at once; when that grew boring she dragged them behind.

"Mother, may I take three baby steps?" she asked.

"Do whatever you want," the American said. "Just keep walking."

She took them one, two, three, and got away with it. That was very funny. Two such alert-looking men and neither one had noticed that she hadn't said may I again before taking the steps. She should have been sent back to the start. She began laughing. Laughing and laughing.

She didn't stop until something cool and sharp reached in her nostrils, right up to the back, and into her brain. It didn't fool her for a second. She was just as good at smells as she was at accents. Mr. Clean. Mr. Clean was poking around inside her nose. The bald little devil. No. Wrong. It wasn't Mr. Clean. Just ammonia. Pure. Her eyes opened fast.

She was looking again into the dark sunken eyes. "Is she coming around?" she heard the American ask nearby.

The eyes moved a fraction in their deep sockets. "I think so." The breath that carried his words brushed her cheek. He stepped back, putting a stopper into a small glass bottle. The American came forward, stooped, stared into her eyes. Suddenly everything came sharply into focus: the red flecks in the American's green irises, two in the left, one in the right, the simple office, two steel desks, a rectangular wooden table with her things on it, two fluorescent tubes which ran the length of the ceiling, the steel chair in which she sat, bound; and through the single window the night sky, yellow lights winking on a distant hill.

"My head hurts."

The American smiled, or rather the corners of his mouth rose. The green irises with the red flecks remained the way they were. "It could have been worse," he said unsympathetically. "You've got a skull like a rock."

"I don't."

The two men pulled up chairs and sat opposite each other. The dark man opened the flap of his shirt pocket and took out a passport. Her passport. He thumbed through the pages. "Rachel Monette," he said in a matter-of-fact tone.

"Yes."

"Have you ever been in prison?"

"No. Of course not." Could he know about Mhamid?

"Then at least it will be a new experience. You are going to prison for a long time."

"What the hell are you talking about?"

"Terrorism," he said coldly. "Against the state of Israel."

"That is an absurd suggestion. For one thing I'm Jewish."

"Are you, Rachel Monette?" he asked softly. "Say something to me in Hebrew. Or Yiddish, if you prefer."

She knew not much more than shalom in one, oy vay in the other. "I'm not the only Jew who can't speak Hebrew or Yiddish. It's quite common at home."

"I am sure it is." The dark head leaned toward her, not much, no more than two inches, but she somehow felt she was in the presence of tremendous aggression. "And you are not the only Jew who is also an anti-Semite," he added in the same quiet tone.

"Garbage."

"Shut your dirty mouth." The American was on his feet. Without turning the dark man placed a restraining hand on his arm. The American sat down.

"Or the first American adventuress attracted to the Arab left. They love sending pretty western women on errands." The Israeli continued as if there had been no unpleasantness. "Who are you working for? The P.L.O.? The P.F.L.P.?"

"I won't say another word until I know who you are and why you are holding me here."

Rachel saw blood rush to the American's cheeks, as if she had slapped them. The Israeli held up his hand before he could jump to his feet again. "My name is Grunberg," he told her calmly. "I am a major in Israeli army intelligence. This gentleman is Mr. Dorschug. He is a representative of the United States government. You are here because you are one of the team that has been running Simon Calvi for God knows how long as an enemy agent inside this country. Naturally, now that we have you, we want to find out more about what has been going on. We would like you to tell us soon. Before Mr.

Calvi's speech at the university, in fact." He looked at his watch. "That gives you a little more than six hours."

"So talk," Dorschug prodded her.

She faced him angrily: "If you're with the U.S. government you should be doing something to help me."

"You stupid bitch. Don't you understand? You're going to rot in jail. If you start talking now there's a chance you won't rot quite so long. It's as simple as that."

"There's no sense trying to protect Mr. Calvi," Grunberg said. "We know all about him. We even know that he is planning to say something dramatic in his speech. Something that at this very moment has the Lebanese and Syrian armies on full and secret alert. We even got a report in the last hour of troop movements in Jordan. So we are far ahead of you, Rachel Monette. What we would like to hear from you are the details of the speech. How does he propose to start a war?"

"I don't know anything about it." Rachel needed five minutes alone. Calvi was her only hope. Without his help she would never see Adam again. These men thought Calvi was working for the Arabs. They said they knew all about him, but they couldn't know what she knew: if they did Calvi wouldn't still be in business. And Munich. If Munich was true, and she believed it was, then Calvi could not be an enemy of Israel. Not willingly, she thought suddenly. Not willingly. Who else knows?

She became aware that they were watching her closely. "I need to use the toilet," she said.

Dorschug snickered. "First you must talk," Grunberg said. It was not a threat; more a reminder of the natural order, like you have to learn how to walk before you can run.

"All I can tell you is that you're making a big mistake. I am a freelance journalist. I make documentaries for radio. This afternoon, yesterday afternoon, I suppose by now, I saw Mr. Calvi for the first time in my life. We did nothing illegal. I interviewed him for a documentary I am making on multi-ethnic cultures. That's the whole story."

"Very good. That should be easy to prove. We have only to listen to the interview." He turned to the tape recorder and switched it on.

"Testing testing. One two three four," she heard herself say. Pause. "What's so funny?" She sounded frightened and suspicious. How could he not have heard?

Calvi's deep voice, amused, wordly. "Don't you think testing testing one two three four sounds funny?"

"I suppose."

"All ready?"

Her voice shook. "Yes, Mr. Victor Reinhardt, I'm ready. I want my son."

They watched the reels go round and round. "There is no more on the tape. As an interview about ethnic cultures I find it rather brief and unsatisfying." The opaque black eyes bored into hers. "As what it is, I find it too baroque."

"I don't understand you."

"Yes, you do. You see, I believe you when you say you never met Mr. Calvi before yesterday. It follows that you must have a method for identifying each other. Passwords, Rachel Monette. I am talking about passwords. This one is sillier than most of them, that's all."

"Surely you can't believe what you're saying. Why would anyone put something like that on tape?"

"I asked myself the same thing. It is not really as difficult a question as it seems. There are amateurs in every profession, including this one. I hope you won't be too insulted if I tell you Sergeant Levy reported that you were one of the most amateurish he had ever seen. Sergeant Levy works for me," Grunberg added in the tone he used for explaining the natural order. "Apparently you didn't even hold up the microphone to make it appear as though you were recording an interview. And the excuse you used to get rid of him was laughable."

"It's only laughable if you don't believe I am who I say I am."

"How can I believe you?" He allowed his voice to rise very slightly. "You are clearly not a journalist: a journalist would have recorded an interview."

"Jesus Christ," Dorschug said. "We don't have time for all this pussyfooting, Major. With all due respect. We've got to start knocking heads."

"You fool!" Rachel shouted. "You could knock my head right off my shoulders and it wouldn't make any difference. I can't tell you what you want because I don't know. You've made a mistake."

Dorschug cracked her across the face with the back of his hand. He cocked it for a second blow but Grunberg said, "No," in a tone that stopped him. He should have spoken sooner. The damage was done. Her whole head throbbed in pain with each beat of her heart. She could barely keep from crying out. The two men watched her, waiting.

"Do you think she's going to puke again?" Dorschug asked. Grunberg ignored him.

Rachel tried to think. She had a tired aching brain but it was still willing. The trouble was she had nothing to work with. It probably would not have mattered even if she had. All she wanted was to talk to Calvi.

"I'll make a deal."

"No deals," Dorschug said.

"Go ahead," Grunberg told her. "We'll listen."

Dorschug stood up and faced Grunberg. "Absolutely not. No deals with terrorists."

Grunberg sat very still, looking up at him from under his heavy, hanging eyebrows. He spoke mildly. "In the end it is we whose lives are at stake, not you. We will deal." Dorschug strode out of the room and slammed the door. "He won't go far," Grunberg said, more to himself than to Rachel: "His job is to spy on me." He sighed. "All right. Talk."

312 THE FURY OF RACHEL MONETTE

"I want to put my skirt on."

"After. Talk." He didn't seem interested in her legs anyway. Only her eyes.

"I'll tell you everything I know on one condition: that I get one hour alone with Calvi tomorrow. No matter what happens."

"Agreed."

"How do I know you'll keep your word?"

"How do I know you will tell me everything?"

"Because you can keep beating me on the head until I do. I haven't got the same privilege."

"Then you will have to trust me." He said it without irony.

"All right. But it's not going to help you at all."

"We shall see."

And she told him a story that began one afternoon when she found her husband in his study with a letter opener in his chest. A story about a blond man in her basement, a well in the desert, and a man named Victor Mendel. By the time she finished darkness was beginning to lift. The first silvery fingers of dawn had slipped under the dome of the sky on the eastern horizon. Not once did Grunberg take his eyes off her face. He seemed to be drinking in every word.

Silence. He leaned back in his chair. "I take it back," he said coldly. "You are very good. Far from an amateur."

"What do you mean?"

"Very good," Grunberg repeated. "That is easily the most inventive cover story I have ever heard. Lovely detail. The difficulty is, it would take days to discover if any of it is true. And we don't have days. We have a few hours." He stood up. "You stall very cleverly, Rachel Monette. I suppose you can be proud that you've done your job well." He turned to the door.

"Where are you going?"

"There is nothing more I can do here."

"And what about me?"

"I told you that at the beginning." He opened the door.

"What about my hour with Calvi?"

Grunberg opened his mouth. A harsh ragged sound seemed to tear itself from his throat. His laugh, she realized.

"But I told you the truth, you God-damned bastard. I want that hour."

"Prove it's the truth." His voice was almost a whisper. He closed the door. She heard his footsteps in the hall. She looked at the door. It stayed closed. Her eyes went to the table, the tape recorder, her skirt.

"Grunberg," she shouted. "Come back. Grunberg. Grunberg."

The door opened. The dark eyes looked in. "Grunberg," she said, trying to control the excitement in her tone: "Where is the guidebook?"

"Guidebook?"

"Yes. I can prove everything with the guidebook. I had a cassette recorder inside. I taped the whole conversation with Calvi."

Grunberg crossed the floor in a moment. His hands darted through the things on the table. No guidebook. He picked up a telephone, dialed, spoke rapidly in Hebrew, listened. Whatever he was told made him angry. His back stiffened and his tone turned to ice. He hung up.

"Well?"

"We wait. At least someone remembers seeing it." He spoke with contempt.

"Do I have to be strapped into the chair?"

"Yes."

Without speaking a word to each other, they waited. Rachel's head hurt. She felt the sweat in her armpits, between her legs. She could smell it. And his sweat. She smelled that too.

A knock at the door. A thick-set woman entered, hair rumpled, eyes puffy from sleep. She wore faded jeans and a T-shirt; in her hand she had the guidebook. At first Rachel did not recognize her. Then she did: hours before the same hand had swung a nightstick.

Grunberg did not take it from her at once. He stared at her instead, until she lowered her eyes and mumbled something faint and apologetic in Hebrew. Grunberg opened the book so she could see the cassette recorder inside.

"Speaking of amateurs," Rachel said. She couldn't help herself. The policewoman went out. Dorschug came in.

"Got something?"

"Perhaps," Grunberg said. He pressed the play button. They listened. Rachel talked. Calvi talked. Rachel talked. Grunberg touched a button. He talked. Dorschug talked. If she closed her eyes the pain in her head wasn't as bad. She closed them. They all talked. Calvi had the best voice. Then she. Grunberg. And Dorschug.

Somewhere a man began to chant. Other men joined him, some nearer, some farther, singing the same chant. They sounded peevish and bored, all except one who sang beautifully. Then it was over. Calvi talked. Grunberg talked. The other man talked. She talked.

Someone untied the straps. She felt a bite on her arm, near the triceps. A deep bite, but nothing at all compared to what she felt in her head. Up in the air, sagging in someone's arms. Lying full length on her back.

Full length. On her back on the playroom floor, the baby Adam an airplane high above. Coming in for a landing. Kiss. Take off. Kiss.

"Okay. Now what? Pull him in? Stop the speech?"

"And turn him into a political martyr? No. He makes a speech. A different one."

"Yeah?"

"Certainly. Now we know what they know. Why not play the same game?"

"So who took hubby out? Them?"

"Or him. It doesn't make much difference."

"And the kid?"

And the kid? And the kid? But there was no answer. Kiss. Take off into the night.

31

First the sun touched her feet. Slowly it spread its warmth up her legs to her body and finally her face, until she lay wrapped in a cocoon of golden down. A man was speaking. His words were incomprehensible but she knew the voice. She had heard it before, one afternoon sitting on a bench. A stone bench in Jerusalem.

Rachel opened her eyes. She was lying on a couch beneath the only window in a small plain office. The rich sunlight pouring through the window made the office look as mean as it was. Like many offices it was more easily endured on rainy days. In the center of the floor two straight-back wooden chairs facing a steel one formed an awkward little group: makeshift stage props of a third-rate theatrical company. The man kept speaking.

Rachel stood. The action set off a banging in her head that made her gasp aloud. After a few moments it became less intense: sure that his presence was felt right from the beginning the banger withdrew to the background. Rachel stripped off her underpants, shirt and brassiere and found fresh clothing in her suitcase, open on the rectangular table. She put on clean white corduroy slacks and a navy blue silk shirt, but she didn't feel any fresher. She opened the door and went into the hall.

Sergeant Levy was waiting for her, seated on a wobbly cardtable chair. A transistor radio lay in his hand like a black egg lost in a nest that was far too big. The voice came from the radio. Simon Calvi. He was speaking in Hebrew.

"What is he saying?" Rachel's tongue felt thick and clumsy; she tasted vomit. A confusion of wispy memories of the night gone by floated through her mind.

With old-fashioned courtesy Sergeant Levy got to his feet. The chair squeaked and stood a little taller. "Do you feel better, I hope?"

Better than when—after the hit on the head but before the slap on the face? After the drugging but before the rotting in jail? "Tell me what he is saying."

Sergeant Levy looked disappointed at the tone she was taking, but he put the radio close to his ear. Rachel sensed a large crowd, listening quietly. Very quietly. "He says that all Jews must stand together in a dangerous world." She listened to Calvi's voice. He may have been saying it, but he wasn't backing it up with any enthusiasm. She said so.

Sergeant Levy beamed down at her, delighted that she was catching on. Perhaps they could still be friends. "No, he is not very happy. He is saying what the Major told him to say. He is a clever fellow. The Major," he added, in case there was any ambiguity.

The almost bovine self-satisfaction in his tone gave Rachel a jolt: she realized then that her hand was being taken away; others were playing the cards she had gathered, and they would play them toward ends of their own. Calvi was slipping away. "I want you to take me to the rally," she said.

The expression on Sergeant Levy's face spoke of the limits to friendship. "I don't think it is possible."

"Why not? Am I still being held here?"

"No, no, no." The idea shocked him. "The Major says

that you are a great friend of the state of Israel. He thinks you will be given a medal."

"Good. This friend of Israel wants to go to the rally."

Sergeant Levy bit his lower lip. "The Major thought you would prefer to rest here until he returned." To keep her out of the way, to have the field to himself. But she had an hour coming to her. An hour alone with Calvi.

"That just shows how little he knows me. Where is he?"

"At the rally," Sergeant Levy said resignedly.

"Let's go."

Sergeant Levy drove her to the university in a green Fiat which seemed to constrict his movements like a too-tight suit. Rachel saw soldiers everywhere—in twos and threes on street corners, parked in jeeps by the roadside, standing beside a tank in a green park. They had grenades hanging from their belts, rifles or submachine guns slung over their shoulders, steel helmets on their heads.

"All that for a public speech?" she asked.

"For war," Sergeant Levy said.

He turned on the radio. An operatic tenor was singing a dramatic aria. Sergeant Levy slapped the steering wheel in sheer delight: "'Nessun Dorma.' My favorite, favorite aria." He listened carefully. "And that is Pavarotti, of course. I love him." The song ended on a passionate crescendo with the singer crying something that sounded to Rachel like "finch adore." He repeated it three times to get the idea across, throwing at least five ringing notes into the last "adore" alone. Completely forgetting the traffic Sergeant Levy closed his eyes in ecstasy. Then he shook his head like a man emerging from a trance, breathed deeply, and turned the dial.

Simon Calvi's voice came through the little speaker, subdued and weary. And something else: tense? afraid? The shoddiness of the speaker, or Calvi's self-control prevented her from knowing what it was. The crowd, she noticed, had grown noisier. She could hear pockets of grumbling, muted more by their distance from the microphone than by any reticence of the grumblers.

Rachel had trained her ear for detail like that. None of it interested Sergeant Levy. Under his breath he was singing "finch adore" over and over. He didn't hit a note.

They drove up a long winding hill. At the top a line of soldiers stood across the road. They had stopped an emaciated little man who was sitting on a donkey even less well nourished than he. The man pulled some tattered papers from inside his stained shirt and handed them to the officer in command. Sergeant Levy honked the horn. The officer whirled around, his features turning angry. Then he saw Sergeant Levy in the driver's seat and his features in ragged order assumed a respectful expression. The soldiers parted and Sergeant Levy drove through. He didn't need to show any papers. They all knew who he was.

Rachel glanced back. The officer had recovered his angry look before it faded entirely. He made an imperious gesture and the skinny man slid down off the donkey's back. He turned his gaze inward where there was no one to take offense.

Ahead lay the rolling lawns of a broad campus. The modern white buildings were arranged in the simple geometric patterns of someone's master plan. They caught the sun's glare and bounced it right back. Rachel liked her universities old and musty. If, she thought suddenly, she liked them at all. She peered for a moment into a muddy future.

Sergeant Levy parked behind a large L-shaped building which, with another L-shaped building, bracketed a row of I-shaped ones in between. He led Rachel across the lot toward the entrance. Two soldiers stood by the door, submachine guns in their hands. An officer sat in a chair nearby, tanning his face and smoking a pipe.

"Hello, Pinchas," he said to Sergeant Levy. Sergeant Levy nodded. One of the soldiers held the door open for them. They climbed three flights of stairs. Rachel heard Calvi's voice, like an echo across a canyon. It seemed to come at her through the walls, growing louder as they went up.

When they came to the third floor they walked down an airy well-lit corridor. Two more soldiers stood in front of a heavy dark paneled door. A highly polished brass plaque on the door had writing on it, in Hebrew and English. President of the University, it said in English. The soldiers stepped aside. Very gently Sergeant Levy turned the knob and pushed the door open. Rachel followed him in. A soldier closed the door behind her.

They were in a large bright room, furnished mainly with books which packed the shelves from floor to ceiling. The furniture, a big desk, a couch, a few swivel chairs, had been pushed against the walls. A soldier stood in a corner by the door. His fingers moved restlessly on the stock of his rifle, but his face was inert. On the couch sat a man wearing jeans and a sweat shirt that seemed too big for him. He was the kind of man who usually would take care to comb his thin sandy hair over his bald spot, but not today. He turned as he heard them enter. He lifted a ginger-colored eyebrow at Sergeant Levy, but there was nothing in Dorschug's expression to show that he had ever laid eyes on Rachel before.

On the far side of the room two tall glass doors opened onto a narrow balcony. Seated on the thick red Persian carpet, out of line of sight of anyone on the ground outside, was Major Grunberg. He sat cross-legged, his back to the room. On the floor beside him lay Rachel's cassette recorder and a long black pistol. He held a dozen or more typewritten sheets of paper in his hands, and his eyes followed the text line by line.

On the balcony, a few feet in front of Grunberg, and also with his back to the room, stood Simon Calvi. He wore a very expensive-looking suit which fit his broad shoulders perfectly. It was a fine charcoal worsted; as Rachel came slowly forward she could see in the bright sunlight the thin red stripe running through it.

Calvi was speaking into a battery of microphones, some attached to the wrought-iron guardrail, others on floor stands. Two voices, one electronic, the other unaided, filled the room. They were not quite in unison. Rachel thought of the mighty Oz, hiding behind a curtain while he operated the machinery that made him a wizard.

Simon Calvi had no curtain. All he had was a sheaf of papers in his right hand. He and Grunberg seemed to be turning the pages at the same time. As he spoke Calvi seldom lifted his eyes from the text.

Rachel stopped just behind Grunberg. Over his shoulder she saw that the pages bore the sword and olive-branch symbol of the Israeli army. She raised her eyes and looked beyond Calvi at the crowd below: a field of dark faces stretching to the other L-shaped building a few hundred yards away. Those nearby were sitting; farther back they stood. She heard muttering, some of it puzzled, some irritated, some angry. His head bowed, Calvi did not appear to notice.

Suddenly Grunberg became aware of someone standing over him. He twisted his head, saw Rachel and impatiently waved her back. Although it was the kind of gesture Rachel hated, she complied.

But before she did she looked down, right into his sunken eyes, and said, "I want my hour," in a quiet, but very clear voice.

32

The crowd. Second-class Jews from dark-skin back-waters: Yemen, Syria, Kurdistan, Algeria, Morocco. They arrived in Israel timid but hopeful; grew dissatisfied; died angry. To ease their dissatisfaction he tried to give them better jobs, better housing. To soothe their anger he gave them pride.

Sometimes it was simple. He could call them to a rally on the grounds of the university. Here at the seat of learning was the unspoken message, you belong as much as your Ashkenazi bosses. So they came, to feel for a few hours the pride in their veins, to demonstrate their strength. And more and more to hear him say that the future lay in the east, and in eastern ways.

But Simon Calvi wasn't saying it today. Instead, in a soft, almost diffident voice he murmured of patience and common enemies and long-term solutions. They did not want to hear it; he had never disappointed them before. Why now? He felt their frustration grow as he spoke. It rose up from the campus with their body heat, up to the balcony where he stood.

You don't like this speech? he thought. It's not mine. It's the unaided effort of Major Grunberg, typed with his own two hands. You find it bland? So do I. But the major sold it to me with the help of a short audio presentation. He's a very persuasive fellow.

I had another one, somewhat stronger. My friend Moses Cohn, who couldn't be with us today, wrote that one for me. He writes very good speeches, but the one he prepared for today was just part of a little joke I was playing on him.

I even had a third, so hard do I labor in your behalf. You won't know the author of this one, a certain Captain I knew in my early years, but he is a true friend of yours. In the past decade he more than anyone else, far more, has been responsible for making me the tough uncompromising champion of the Sephardim you came to see today. I have a notion it was just the sort of thing you wanted: it called for action. Nothing irresponsible. Merely a two-hour nationwide strike of all Oriental and Sephardic Jewish workers, to begin today at one P.M. Tough, yes—it wouldn't have left the government much time to react. But hardly an act of revolution these days. No, nothing wrong with it at all, except that you needed the right copy of *Crime and Punishment* to decode the text, and the Captain was keeping company with a few friends who may have come from the wrong side of an obsolete canal.

Calvi paused at the end of one of Grunberg's tedious phrases and raised his eyes from the pages in his hand. He looked over the heads of the crowd, scanning the top-floor windows of the L-shaped library on the far side of the quadrangle. He didn't see the boy.

He returned to the text and read a sentence about the need for cooperation. An analogy was drawn to the story of the Tower of Babel. In no way could he find it apposite. He mumbled quickly through it, deleting what repetitious parts he could. He hoped that nothing was keeping the boy, that nothing had gone wrong.

One step at a time. In a few minutes if all went well, it would be out of his hands, and he would be beyond the reach of Grunberg's power. Or the Captain's. Then it would depend on the undertaker's boy, his sons, the undertaker, and, by the following dawn, Gisela. By the following dawn. If all goes well.

Perhaps she loved him after all. Perhaps he could even learn to love her.

In a way he knew he was relieved that Grunberg had forced this abject little speech on him. How often had he asked himself what would happen in those two hours from one to three? Nothing, he had answered every time, but the question never went away. Now he would never know. To comply with the Captain and get out, or not to comply and get out. He preferred the latter. But the important thing was getting out.

Where was the boy?

He sensed the crowd growing more restless. Did someone jeer, there, by the economics building? Let them jeer: how they will regret it very soon.

Behind him he heard a door softly open and close. He felt eyes on his back, could almost hear Grunberg breathing. A woman said, "I want my hour." There was such menace in her tone that he almost turned around. Then he recognized the voice. The American woman. She was far more clever than he had thought. Had she been working for Grunberg from the beginning? No. Still, in only a few hours she had been able to find him and set him into action. She was very impressive. But it wasn't going to be enough.

As he turned a page he saw an ambulance approaching on Magnes Boulevard. It pulled to the curb and parked nearby. No one would have looked at it twice. At any moment in a crowd this size someone could have a stroke, or a baby.

And then like a fish about to break the surface a shadow flitted behind one of the windows on the top floor of the library. Calvi's pores opened wide. He felt the sweat streaming over his body, soaking his silk shirt and his worsted trousers, making the hot water bottle slippery on his chest. The words crawled over the page like bacteria under a microscope. He stumbled over them, skipped two lines so that the beginning of one sentence married the end of another, plunged on. His throat felt dry as ashes.

The window opened. His heart beat so violently that his whole body pulsed to its rhythm. Sweat ran off his face in torrents. Couldn't anyone see? Couldn't Grunberg, a few feet away? But no one moved behind him, and the sour mood of the crowd remained unchanged.

The boy leaned out the window. Calvi realized that he had almost forgotten to hook his thumbs over his belt. He found that his hands were glued to the speech. It required all of the power of his will to relax his fingers. The pages fluttered to the floor of the balcony. As slowly as a somnambulist he lowered his hands to his waist and felt for his belt. He stood there, thumbs hooked over the belt, the way men do when they are about to talk tough. But he wasn't talking tough; he wasn't talking at all. His text lay at his feet. A wild urge seized him suddenly, an urge to call for the strike after all. A crazy thought, and Grunberg right behind him. He fought it down.

Seeing him abandon his prepared speech and strike an aggressive pose, the crowd began to stir. Here was the old Simon Calvi at last. But he had nothing to say. He heard himself muttering again the idiotic analogy with the story of the Tower of Babel.

Why was he so slow, the boy? He seemed to be gazing out the window, watching the crowd. At last he poked his arm out. There was a small black object in his hand. He pointed it toward the ground. Calvi's thumbs were knotted around his belt, the muscles in his wrists and hands rigid.

Hurry. For God's sake. Hurry.

A quick movement caught Calvi's eye. A movement on the roof of the library, almost directly above the window where the boy was. A figure stepped out from behind a steam vent. A tall figure, his face almost covered in thick black beard. He wore a black hat with a round rim, and his body was cloaked in a long black robe, or coat. He

looked like an Orthodox rabbi. A rabbi. A rabbi who
knew that Simon Calvi was not going to call for a two-
hour general strike, that day or any other.

Oh God. Now. Pull the God-damned trigger. God
make him pull the trigger. The boy was very still. He
seemed to be watching Calvi. A hush swept over the
crowd. They were watching him too.

Pull it.

The figure on the roof withdrew something from the
folds of his long black garment. A rifle. In one economical
movement he brought it to his right shoulder. He handled
it the way a man handles a rifle when he knows what he is
doing. And something in the way he held it made Calvi
certain who he was. He swept the barrel in a short arc and
pointed it at Calvi's head.

The boy fired the starter's pistol at the ground. It
sounded no louder than a single genteel hand clap. But
Calvi heard it. He shoved his hands down on his belt, felt
the wetness, and reeled back in a falling pirouette that
would take him into the room and safety. Before he
landed he felt a hard hot finger poke at his chest. And
heard a loud crack, a crack like a whip. Perhaps the whip
preceded the finger; they were so close he couldn't tell.
The whip cracked only once. The hard hot finger stayed
where it was. He felt his chest grow wetter. For the first
time he found the hot water bottle constricting. It had
worked perfectly of course, but now it was terribly
constricting. He could not breathe at all. He had a
moment of panic. Then he found that he could get a bit of
air by breathing in shallow breaths. Sniffing, almost, like
a dog. It was very tricky and demanded all his concentration. Soon someone would remove the hot water bottle
and everything would be all right. He shitted diamonds.

"Stand back, please. I am a doctor." His son. Perfect.
The hot water bottle would be off in a moment. It was
going like clockwork. From outside he heard with
satisfaction the wail of a siren. Right on time.

A face lowered itself to his, like a lover maneuvering for

a kiss. A face like Victor Mendel's. His eldest son. How well he looked in his white doctor's coat. Was he a resident yet, or still an intern? It didn't matter. Young dark eyes like Victor Mendel's. Careful. Concerned. A little nervous. That was natural. This was the difficult part, getting him out of there, away from Grunberg.

And suddenly the eyes filled with horror. Buck up, for God's sake: don't go bad on me now. "The stretcher. Quick," his son cried. That's better. Don't give Grunberg a chance to take command.

"Can't you do something about the bleeding?" Grunberg. He couldn't stop interfering. Lifelong habit.

"I'm not sure." Oh come on. You've got to do better than that, or we're sunk.

"Try something," Grunberg shouted. "What kind of a doctor are you?" Someone make him stop shouting. Doesn't he know how much the finger is hurting me? His son's face again, tears in his eyes. That was going a little too far. Hands groped at his shirt. Good idea.

"Just loosen that hot water bottle a bit," he whispered. His son didn't seem to hear him, so he repeated it a little louder. He still didn't hear. Was he panicking completely?

He felt air on his chest, and heard a gasp from somewhere in the room. Gasp, gasp, gasp. Haven't you seen red dye before? A hand touched the hot water bottle. Wait. Grunberg might see. He looked his son in the eye and said urgently, "Get rid of Grunberg. Send him for bandages. Anything."

No reaction. Just those eyes full of horror. What kind of a son was this? At least he should be able to manage a simple task like removing the hot water bottle. "At least get the hot water bottle off me," he said with exasperation. He knew he shouldn't allow himself to show irritation with his son, but there is a limit. Then he saw him put the hot water bottle on a chair. It made no sense at all, because he still couldn't breathe. Perhaps the straps had left an imprint in the skin that continued to bind him. That must be it; he'd take a few deep breaths and be back to normal. He tried one, but the finger in his chest didn't like it. The finger was less hot now, but seemed to be pressing harder, and deeper. He must have broken a rib as he fell. Wouldn't that be his luck? He had never broken a bone in his life.

"What the hell is that thing?" Grunberg again. He never quit. "It's a hot water bottle," Grunberg said in surprise. He heard him shaking it, felt a drop strike his cheek. "It's got water in it. Red water. What the hell is going on?" God. He was so afraid of anyone knowing something he didn't.

Footsteps on the rug. He wished they would walk more lightly. "The shaking hurts. I don't like to make a fuss, but it hurts."

A stretcher was lowered beside him. His two other sons looked down at him. They had done a nice job getting the right sort of ambulance attendant uniforms, but he was beginning to lose confidence in the lot of them. The horror quickly spread to their eyes too, like a contagious disease. He and Grunberg were apparently the only people in the place with any presence of mind at all. That suited him: he could handle Grunberg.

Hands gripped his shoulders and ankles. Someone held his hips. "Careful. He's heavy." A son, he didn't know which. They lifted him onto the stretcher. They crushed his heart in a vise. He supposed he had cried out, because his eldest son kissed him on the forehead and said, "I'm sorry, I'm sorry, I'm sorry." This nonsense had to stop. He was going to miss his plane.

He closed his eyes and went to sleep. Breathing in the coffin was much more difficult than it had been during the test at the undertaker's. That pig. It surprised him because that was something he had checked very thoroughly. Perhaps he had forgotten to remove the wooden block which hid the air holes. He felt above him in the dark. No, the block wasn't there. It must be a factor of the air supply in these cargo planes. It was possible he had already breathed most of the available air. He had no idea how long the plane had been flying. It couldn't be much longer. Until then he would have to do his best to conserve air. He tried to imagine how a mouse would breathe, and breathed like that. It was all he could think of to do.

He listened to the roar of the big jets, pushing the plane through the cold black sky. They must be landing soon. The distance from Tel Aviv to Munich really wasn't great, although, he reflected, it had taken half of his life to make the trip the other way. The thought made him laugh; he would have laughed more, but it used too much air. He realized he was becoming excited, like a schoolboy going home for summer vacation. He tried to picture the look on Gisela's face when she opened the box. Surely he could learn to love her; was that so much to ask?

At last he felt the airplane begin its descent. A good thing too: there was almost no air left to breathe. Down it went, somewhat too steeply he thought. His back was pressed against the bottom of the box in a very uncomfortable way. In a few moments he felt a leveling out, and then the big wheels hit the runway, bouncing once, twice, three times. The bouncing was even more uncomfortable than the descent, but he could endure anything now. The plane taxied for a long time before finally coming to a stop. Then the engines were cut off. Silence. A welcome silence. A long silent wait, but he didn't mind. It was very peaceful. At last he heard Gisela's voice.

"Where is he?"

Careful, Gisela. You'll give the game away. That would be heartbreaking now. He stayed very quiet, very still. They were lucky. Despite her indiscretion no suspicion had been aroused. He felt the box being lifted, being carried, being slid across a metal floor. Then the floor began to move. They were alone in the van. It had worked.

After a while the floor stopped moving. He heard a car door slam, heard another door slide open.

"Oh God," Gisela said.

Of course. She's frightened by the coffin. He should

have expected that. "There's nothing to worry about Gisela," he called. "It's me."

He opened his eyes and there she was. She was so full of joy that tears were rolling down her cheeks. "There, there, Gisela. Stop crying. Everything is all right."

"He's trying to talk," she said. "Listen."

She seemed to be speaking to someone else. Has she hired a van with a driver? How foolish. He looked around, and saw that he was lying on the floor of the president's office at the Hebrew University in Jerusalem.

"Gisela. We're not in Munich?" Was it possible? "You're not in Munich." It must be one of Grunberg's tricks.

"He is. He's trying to say something." She was sobbing. He'd made a mistake. She wasn't happy at all. Grunberg appeared behind her and laid a hand on her shoulder in a comforting but impersonal way. And it was all very clear. She worked for Grunberg, had been working for him the whole time.

He gathered all his energy into this throat, and spoke as loudly as he could: "Go away." With a wail Gisela drew back and passed from his sight. He didn't care. He didn't feel anything for her, he never had. All he felt was the finger in his chest.

Another face. Would they never stop bothering him? But this one was different: he found its angles fascinating, its skin rich and full of life, the eyes as deep as the sea. The American woman. He tried to recall her name.

"Simon," she said. He found her voice soothing. It reminded him of his mother's voice. Long ago. "Please don't think I'm being cruel. This may be my last chance to find my son. It may be your last chance to buy back a piece of your innocence. Remember we talked about that?"

"You unfeeling bitch," he heard Grunberg say. He had had enough of Grunberg. He happened to enjoy listening to this woman.

"Please, Simon. Have you thought of any connection

that will lead me to my son? There must be one. Does it explain this, too?" She held her hand out to the room. At least he assumed she did: it left the range of his sight.

A connection. Wasn't it obvious? He remembered the day the Captain had walked into his office, about five years after he had gone into politics. How had he begun? Like the woman: "Victor Reinhardt." He had worn his rabbi outfit then too. And the only other time he had seen him since, in the desert south of Beersheba. It was his only joke.

He saw the rifle barrel turning in a short arc. He thought again of setting this woman on the Captain. But what was the point? He was past feeling, past caring. Not even the finger bothered him now.

The room became very cold. His mother was rocking him on her lap. She called him *shainer bocher* over and over again. In Yiddish it meant pretty little boy. He looked one last time into the deep, dark eyes. *Shainer bocher,* his mother called him.

"The Captain," he said as he rose to meet her.

33

Major Grunberg and Rachel sat in the back seat of the
green Fiat, waiting for Sergeant Levy. The campus was
deserted, except for the few remaining soldiers who
patrolled the green lawns, bobbing from time to time like
birds for scraps of paper left by the crowd. The late
afternoon breeze had made its way over the plain from the
Mediterranean: patiently it prodded the litter across the
grass, and swept the stale air out of the car.

Two red blots stained Grunberg's uniform, a small one
on the collar and a larger one on the right sleeve. "I think
it would be a good idea if you left the country as soon as
possible," he said without looking at her. "This evening
would make me very happy."

"Why?"

"Please don't take it personally." Grunberg turned to
face her. There was nothing in the sunken eyes to show
whether he cared how she took it. "My aim now is to
avoid any public indiscretions."

"And you find me indiscreet?"

"Very. I can't afford to have you poking around any
longer." His tone did not encourage discussion.

"I find you a very fickle man, Major Grunberg. A few

hours ago Sergeant Levy told me you were thinking of giving me a medal."

Grunberg was not a man who appreciated irony. He did not even notice it. "It's true. You will receive a medal. We will mail it to you if you leave us your home address."

Rachel laughed. There was no mail slot at home, no doorbell for the postman to ring. "Never mind the medal."

Grunberg shrugged. "It has nothing to do with me. A committee decides all questions relating to the awarding of medals."

In his tone and phrasing Rachel heard the bureaucrat, ceaselessly trying to draw a blanket of routine over anything abnormal. He wanted nothing more than to close the file. She could not prevent her voice from rising slightly: "Don't you want to find out why he did what he did? Whether he acted on his own or was forced?" Grunberg had his eyes on the soldiers picking up the litter. "Don't you even want to know who killed him, for Christ's sake? Isn't that your duty?"

His head whipped around. "Don't tell me my duty. My only duty is to Israel. It is best for Israel if none of this ever becomes public knowledge. That is not my decision: it was made at Cabinet level an hour ago."

"Was your pal Dorschug in on it?"

"Shut up." Grunberg glared at her. "This affair is finished, finished forever, and finished well. Remember that if you ever have any crazy ideas. We'll deny anything you say."

"Finished well?"

"From our point of view. Don't you understand? He was about to trigger a war." Grunberg paused. "No, we could not have hoped for better. The Lebanese and Syrian troops are no longer on alert. We have told a few reporters we trust that we suspect he was assassinated by Palestinian terrorists who had foreknowledge of the speech and would not accept his apparent move toward moderation. That should finally make it clear to some people that this whole Sephardic business has played right into the hands of the enemy. And we've also arrested a suspect. Not a very likely one, I admit: a boy with nothing more than a starter's pistol and a wild story. But he has no Israeli papers. He is probably Jordanian, and that is perfect for our morning newspapers. In the foreign press it will be nothing more than the murder of a minor politician, not a completely uncommon event these days."

Fine and dandy. "And what about from my point of view?"

"I hope you find your boy." Grunberg spoke in the tone people use for wishing friends a nice trip. "But we can do nothing more to help you."

"Nothing more? You haven't lifted a finger to help me."

"There is nothing we can do," he repeated implacably. "I hope you are not going to be difficult." There was a lot more emotion supporting his second hope than his first. Rachel got out of the car and slammed the door. Anyone might have thought they were having a lover's quarrel.

She saw Sergeant Levy come out of the administration building and walk toward them. An anxious-looking woman was at his side, forced into a brittle trot by the length of his stride. Sergeant Levy seemed anxious too. He talked rapidly to Grunberg in a voice so low Rachel could not be sure whether he was speaking English or Hebrew. The worried look was passed to Major Grunberg.

"What's going on?" Rachel asked.

The old woman turned to her with tears in her eyes. "Something has happened to them. I know it."

"Who?"

"Sarah and Moses. I haven't seen her since yesterday, and he's been gone for three days." Fear had a tight grip on her throat, squeezing her words to a high quavering pitch. She walked around to the front door on the passenger side, opened it, and stood holding the handle in indecision.

"Who are Sarah and Moses?"

"Oh God. There's no time for this," the woman said.

Sergeant Levy leaned over the roof of the car and quietly answered Rachel's question.

"I'm going with you."

Grunberg's hand darted through the open window and grabbed her wrist, very tightly. "No."

"Let go of me. There has been enough of that." His hand dropped away. Rachel opened the door and sat in the back seat. "I'll leave the country tonight," she said to Grunberg. "On any flight you like. But first I want a look inside that house."

Grunberg did not say a word. Sergeant Levy sat in the driver's seat and closed the door. "Get in, Mrs. Perlman," he said gently. The old woman sat down beside him and Sergeant Levy started the car.

They drove quickly through the shaded old streets of Rehavia. On its way west the late afternoon sun cast the shadows of the trees in long silhouettes across the road. A feeling of dread filled the car. It poisoned the air and made them all breathe faster.

Sergeant Levy parked the car beneath an evergreen of a type Rachel had never seen before. They crossed the street, climbed a few stone steps, and walked across a lawn in need of water. Rachel scanned the windows of the large stone villa. All the curtains were drawn.

Grunberg tried the door. It was locked. He took something shiny from his pocket, slid it into the lock, and pushed the door open. He led them into the house. In the front hall he called out a short phrase in Hebrew. It echoed through the house. He repeated it more loudly. The echo came back louder than before.

"Oh, God," Mrs. Perlman said. Sergeant Levy put his arm around her thin shoulders.

"Quiet," Grunberg hissed.

From the depths of the house, from the walls themselves it seemed, came a faint whining hum. It turned Rachel's spine to ice.

"What a fool I am," Sergeant Levy cried suddenly. He ran up the stairs, taking them three at a time. They followed him as fast as they could. A door opened violently and banged back on its hinges. Rachel heard Sergeant Levy yell something in Hebrew. She had never heard a man angrier.

Spreadeagled on a bed in a room upstairs lay a little man with russet hair. Sergeant Levy was bent over him, unwinding the adhesive tape from his face. His fingers moved very gently, but not gently enough to stop the little man from whimpering, deep in his throat. Rachel could see how painful it was: the man's jaw and cheeks were so swollen that the tape had gouged bloody lines in his skin. The lower half of his face was one purple bruise; the upper half had no color at all. When Sergeant Levy had stripped away the last of the tape the man's mouth slowly opened. His tongue emerged, yellow, hard and dry as a snake's skin, and touched his cracked lips.

"Sarah."

Twenty minutes went by before they found her. They had even begun to hope she had got away when Sergeant Levy opened the broom closet and she slumped out, driving a clutter of kitchen tools ahead of her.

Mrs. Perlman sank down beside her. "Sarah, my baby, my baby." Her tears fell on the blue-gray skin of the dead woman's face. "God help her, please help her."

But it was far too late. They all knew it from the odor that began to fill the room. Nature carried on with one of the distasteful jobs it had to do. Even Mrs. Perlman knew it. After not very long she allowed Sergeant Levy to help her to her feet.

They went outside. Sergeant Levy bore the little man in his arms because he had no feeling in his hands or feet.

After the ambulance left, Sergeant Levy remained to watch the house until Grunberg could send some people to go through it. Rachel stayed with him. Grunberg did not seem to notice her; if he did he was for once too tired to care.

With heavy footsteps Sergeant Levy entered the house and sat on the stairs in the hall, looking at nothing. Rachel closed the front door and began going from room to room, systematically searching through the contents of every drawer and cupboard. She remembered some of the places she had tried when hunting through the Kopples' apartment, but Calvi's house yielded nothing that could help her. At last she sat at his desk in the study, turning the pages of his leather telephone and address book. There were many names in it, all written in Hebrew.

She closed the book and stared at it for a while, her mind a void. She felt a nudging inside, like a baby bird struggling to break its shell. And suddenly she remembered the old woman with maroon circles under her eyes, scrubbing the dirty steps at 298 rue de Millet. And Lily Gris, and the friend of Dan's father who had married her in 1948. Quickly she reached into her handbag for her notebook and found the page. She had told the old woman she would call yesterday afternoon. What was the point of taking notes if she never read them, she thought, angry at herself. But then she recalled what she had been doing yesterday afternoon.

A black telephone sat on the desk. The phone company couldn't bill a dead man, not even for a call to Paris. Rachel lifted the receiver and gave the operator the Paris number she had written in her notebook.

It rang seventeen times before the operator said, "There is no answer at that number." She seemed happy about it.

"Please let it ring." The operator made a clicking noise of disapproval, but she did as Rachel asked. Someone answered on the twenty-ninth ring.

"Hello," a man said in French. He had a loud coarse voice. Guy. The forty-two-year-old boy who sat in his underwear with his legs apart and didn't make his bed.

"Hello. This is Rachel Monette. I bought a painting from you last week. Do you remember?"

"You didn't tell us your name then," he said suspiciously. The connection was very clear. He seemed to be in the next room. She could almost feel the anger in him, an anger, she remembered, which pressed hard against his surface.

"I'm telling you now. Let me speak to your mother, please."

He snickered. "You can't. She's in the hospital."

"Is anything wrong?" Of course there was: those faded eyes.

"Cancer. They give her a month more, maybe six weeks."

"I'm sorry."

"Don't be. She doesn't care. She's had enough, she says."

And you've had enough of her, haven't you, Guy? Rachel could think of nothing to say that would bring the conversation around to what she wanted to discuss. She heard his breathing in her ear.

"So. Is that all then?"

"No. I asked you to try to discover the name of Monsieur Monette's friend. The one who married Lily Gris. You thought the clerk at the post office might remember, when he returned from his vacation."

He didn't speak. He just kept breathing in her ear.

"I said I would give you two hundred francs if you found out."

"Two hundred and fifty."

She had already left fifty as a down payment. "Yes. Two hundred and fifty."

"That's right."

She couldn't believe that anyone could breathe so loudly. "Well? Have you got any information?"

"Yes. Monsieur Tremblay remembered."

"Good. What was the name?"

Guy breathed a few times before he answered. "Where are you?" His voice had grown fur on the edges.

"I'm out of France right now."

"Then how will I get the money?" There was a note of

triumph in his voice, as if he had just stumped Clarence Darrow.

"I will send you a postal money order as soon as I hang up the phone. I have your address. Two ninety-eight rue de Millet."

"How do I know you will send it?"

"Trust me. You don't know how important this is. That money will be on its way to you in ten minutes. I promise you. Two hundred and fifty francs."

He seemed to be considering. He breathed huskily. "I want more than that," he said finally.

"How much more?"

"Not money," he said thickly. "I want you. With your clothes off."

"What for? Two hundred and fifty francs will buy you any girl in rue Saint Denis. Young girls, much more satisfactory than I am."

She thought she could feel his breath. "I always pay for it. This time I want it for nothing."

"Then use the money to find some nice woman, take her out to dinner and see what happens."

Guy snickered again. They came from different planets. More breathing. "I want you. You're a Jew, aren't you? I've never given it to a Jew." He grunted softly. "I've got it out now. It's long and hard and ready for you."

Jesus. "I told you I'm not even in France."

"I can wait."

"I can't. I have to know that name now."

The snicker. Another soft grunt. "All right, but first talk to me."

"Talk to you?"

"Yes. Until I come."

So Rachel began stringing together sentences composed of all the dirty French words she knew. When she exhausted her supply she switched to English. It seemed to work just as well. She held the phone away from her ear so she wouldn't have to listen: it gave his rutting a tinny sound. His breathing grew to panting, his grunts turned to moans. A cry. Rachel stopped talking and heard his excitement subside.

When the silence became complete he said one word: "DePoe." The line went dead.

Rachel sat at the desk, struggling with a strange combination of exhilaration and stomach sickness, as if she had taken a street drug. A sudden disquieting thought came to her, and she jerked her head around to the door, half expecting to see Sergeant Levy watching her. The door was closed. It would not have been easy to explain.

Rachel found him still sitting on the stairs. He held his head in his huge hands: he was sobbing.

"What's wrong?" She went to him, reached out and stroked his shoulder. It felt like a block of mahogany, turned on a lathe.

He fought to control himself. "I am so stupid," he said at last. "If I had the Major's brains I might have saved that woman's life."

"Don't be ridiculous. You're ten times the man he is."

Sergeant Levy sat up straight and shook his head. Rachel went on stroking his shoulder. She liked the feeling. Then she recalled her telephone conversation and the feeling disintegrated. She lowered her hand. Sergeant Levy rose, drying his eyes on a wrinkled but clean handkerchief. He looked down at her with eyes she thought were tender. Something had passed between them, both knew it, but there was not time to find out what it was.

"Pinchas," she said, remembering what the officer with the pipe had called him. "Pinchas," she tried again, but it was a silly name no matter how she pronounced it.

"You don't like my name?"

"No. But I like you."

Outside she heard a car stop in front of the house. Grunberg's men. Sergeant Levy heard it too, and stepped back, increasing the distance between them.

"I must leave tonight, Pinchas."

"I know."

"But before I do I need your help."

"What kind of help?" Feet moved on the stone path leading to the door.

"I need a gun. A gun that can't be traced. I have to get on the plane without being searched. And—I need your advice."

"Advice?"

"On how to kill a man."

As the doorknob turned Sergeant Levy said simply, "I will help you." For a horrifying second Rachel feared he thought of her as a female Grunberg, someone cold and smart to be obeyed without question. She hoped it wasn't true because she knew she wanted to see him again. After.

34

The big jet glided through the night over a sea as dark as outer space. Steadily a distant cluster of lights drew nearer, glowing like an undiscovered galaxy. But from the moment the tires made their first shrieking contact with the runway it was only Marseilles.

The immigration officer found her passport in order and admitted her to France. A customs man allowed her baggage in with her. From years of habit and training they had both developed an iron discipline to guard against the temptation of behaving politely. But they were not rude enough to lift her skirt and find the gun taped to the inside of her thigh.

In front of a car-rental counter Rachel hesitated, remembering a jeep in the desert and a Deux Chevaux parked outside the airplane terminal in Nice.

"May I help you, madame?"

People in the rental business felt upset when their property dropped into limbo; they might even use their computers to keep track of those responsible.

"No, thanks." Rachel took a taxi to Aix-en-Provence, eighteen miles north on the autoroute of the sun.

April is too early to find massed ranks of tourists in

Aix. Even the Cours Mirabeau, the broad central avenue, was quiet. A few late coffee-drinkers lingered at outdoor tables. The waiters stayed inside, avoiding the night chill and waiting for the annual migration from the north and the money that came with it. Rachel spotted a telephone kiosk and asked the driver to stop.

The kiosk stood beneath one of the spreading plane trees which lined both sides of the Cours. High above the pavement the leafy boughs embraced, forming a shady bower that gave tourists trouble with their F-stops and made Rachel slightly claustrophobic. Eight DePoes were listed in the directory, but only one had two numbers: the first for the department of anthropology at the University of Aix, the second for the professor's residence. Rachel gave the address to the driver.

It was an old narrow house on a little street off the Cours. The two flanking buildings, bigger and newer, were squeezing the life out of it. And she had done her part too, Rachel thought, and might do more before the night was over.

She opened her suitcase on the seat and took out the painting of the bridge on the Seine. "Would you wait for me, please?" she asked the driver. "I won't be very long."

The driver looked at her in the rearview mirror. He was an old man with worn-out skin and a big runny nose. "I haven't seen any money." He spoke a coarse Mediterranean French which she understood with difficulty.

"How much to hire the cab for the night?"

He wiped his nose on his sleeve to give himself time to think. "One hundred and fifty francs."

Rachel gave it to him. "Wait here."

She got out of the car and rang the doorbell. The door opened immediately, as if she had been expected at any moment, but opened only as far as the brass chain permitted. The thin profile of a woman's face appeared.

"Excuse me for calling so late, but I need to have a painting authenticated. It's very urgent."

"Prehistoric?" the woman asked. She had the kind of

Parisian accent which made the word something Rachel
wanted to hear again. It turned the vowels to honey and
wrapped them in crystal consonants. "I am sorry. My
husband is away on a field trip."

"It's nothing as old as that," Rachel said. "I'm told it's
one of yours."

"Mine?"

Rachel held up the painting so the woman could see it.
"You are Lily Gris?"

"Lily DePoe. I was Lily Gris, a long time ago." Her
voice sounded distracted: all her attention was on the
painting.

"Is it yours?"

Lily DePoe did not answer at first. She could not lift
her gaze from the picture. By the poor light of the street
lamp Rachel thought she glimpsed a fascinated terror in
the woman's face, as might come over a rabbit encountering a rattlesnake. "Yes," Lily DePoe answered finally.
"Where did you get it?"

"From a collector. If you don't mind I'd like to ask you
a few questions about it."

"I don't know—"

"I'll take no more than three or four minutes. It's just
that I'm impressed by the painting and want to know
more."

"Very well." Lily DePoe unhooked the chain and
Rachel stepped into the hall. In better light she saw a
striking woman, almost as tall as she, and very thin; her
wrists were like test tubes. Despite her age she did not look
at all absurd in her almost Bohemian dress—black clogs,
dark brown leather trousers, black turtleneck sweater.
Her face allowed her to get away with it: white delicate
skin stretched tightly over fine angular bones, so tightly
that the lines of age did not penetrate the skin but seemed
to have been drawn on its surface. Her long hair was
collected in a bun on the crown of her head; it was a shiny
jet black that no hair could naturally be. The whole,
Rachel realized, clothes, skin, hair, was a dramatic setting

for her eyes, blue eyes without the least hint of green. The effect was almost shocking. It made her think of the painting in her hand.

Lily DePoe led her to a small sitting room off the hall. Evidently she had been there during the evening. A cigarette in a stone ashtray had burned to a long cylindrical ash; beside it a book lay open upside down. Huysman's *Au Rebours*. There was a faint smell to which Rachel could not quite give the name. Incense? Perhaps the whole house was a setting for those eyes.

They sat in matching velvet chairs. Now that she had seen the painting Lily DePoe seemed to have little more interest in it. "What do you want to know?" she asked.

Rachel was surprised. She had been prepared for a line of questions about how she had known Lily DePoe was Lily Gris, how she had found her in Aix. "Well," she said, off guard, "what's it about?" She knew as she spoke that she could not have chosen a more stupid question to ask an artist, but it didn't seem to bother Lily DePoe.

"Death," she answered.

"Death of anyone in particular?"

"Anyone in particular?"

"Yes. Someone you knew, for instance."

Too much. Lily DePoe leaned slowly back in the chair, her blue eyes very alert. She should have taken more care in moving her from metaphor to reality. Now Lily DePoe had landed in it with a jolt.

"Why should it be someone I knew? Artists live in the world of the imagination."

"But imagination can work with real events, surely?"

"I suppose." Lily DePoe was not interested in her esthetic theories.

"I only ask because I was told you had been inspired by something which really happened."

"Who told you that?" Lily DePoe asked warily.

"Pinchas Levy." It was the first name that came to mind. Lily DePoe made a very French gesture with her shoulders, a shrug which said that the name meant nothing. "I'm sure the painting has passed through several hands since you finished it."

Lily DePoe thought about that. It seemed to please her. Her eyes went again to the painting, which lay on a small table between them. "It was the last one I ever did. I was still a girl, really."

"But why did you stop? It's a very good painting. You must have known that." Rachel spoke with real feeling.

Lily DePoe heard it, too. "Thank you." Rachel was surprised by the intensity of the gratitude in her tone, and the sudden wetness in her eyes.

"Did it have to do with this painting?" she asked very quietly. "Did something upset you?"

Lily DePoe lowered her gaze to the floor. "I saw a man kill a woman. He pushed her off a bridge." Without looking she pointed to the painting. "That bridge."

Rachel tried to keep her voice quiet and casual. "Why did he do that?"

Lily DePoe seemed to speak from far away. "They were drunk. And they had been quarreling."

"Quarreling?"

"About the war." Her head came up quickly, as if someone had entered the house. "The Second World War," she explained. Her voice had lost its intimacy. She opened a little case that was studded with pieces of amber and took a cigarette. She lit it. "As I told you it was a long time ago." Rachel felt her slipping away.

"What did you do about it?"

"I beg your pardon?"

"The murder."

Rachel heard a sharp intake of breath. Lily DePoe looked away; her eyes rested on the cigarette, watched it burn for a few seconds, and returned their gaze to the floor. Rachel thought that as long as she kept her looking at the floor she would be all right. She realized that Lily DePoe was one of the most highly strung people she had ever seen, highly strung and possibly addicted to tranquilizers. She was certainly full of them now.

"Did you go to the police?" Rachel asked gently.

"No." The distant voice had returned.

"Why not?"

"I wasn't sure. It might have been an accident. She was walking on the balustrade. He went to help her down." Lily DePoe sat very still. The cigarette consumed itself in her fingers.

"But he pushed her instead."

"I don't know," Lily DePoe replied in a whisper. "I never knew."

You knew, Rachel thought: look again at that painting. "And the others? What did they think?"

"Others?"

"With you on the bridge."

"There were no others. Only my fiancé and I. And the little boy. I was carrying him. Daniel." The long cigarette ash curled at the tug of gravity and fell to the floor. "I never had a child of my own."

"And your fiancé?"

"No." Lily DePoe shook her head slowly. "It's me. The doctor says I'm barren."

"I meant what did your fiancé think happened that night?"

"He said it was all my imagination and never to mention it to him again. If I let my imagination control me it would drive people away."

"Did you tell him that you had heard them quarreling?"

"Yes. He said that married people do that. He was right."

"Did you see the man after that night?"

"Yes. A few times. He was a friend of my fiancé."

"Have you seen him recently?"

"No. Not for years." Lily DePoe seemed to become aware of the cigarette ash on the floor beside her foot. Time was running out.

"You said he was a military man." Rachel tried not to rush the words.

"Did I?"

"Yes. Do you remember what rank he held?"

Lily DePoe nudged the white ashes with the toe of her clog, watching them carefully. "Captain, I think."

"Does your husband still see him?"

Lily DePoe's fine head snapped up. "Why don't you ask him?" she said angrily. The anger did not hold her for more than a few seconds. "Forgive me. He's not even here right now, of course. He's still away on that field trip. He was due home yesterday." She raised the corners of her lips in a weak smile: "Men. They're so naughty when it comes to sticking to schedules."

Her words were as hollow as her smile. She had no talent for making ladies' chitchat. Her talent was for painting.

Rachel stood up. "I won't keep you any longer. You've been very generous with your time."

"It's easy to be generous with time. For me."

Rachel's eyes were drawn to the painting. "I'd like to leave the painting as a present."

"Oh, no," Lily DePoe said with horror.

Rachel picked it up and left the house. The driver lay across the front seat, asleep. He had locked all the doors. Rachel knocked on the window.

"Not now," he muttered in his sleep, loudly enough for Rachel to hear.

But it was now, and Rachel kept knocking until he sat up and let her in. "Orange," she said. He sighed and turned the key.

It was not a long drive, an hour and a half at most. When they had gone half the distance Rachel opened the window and threw the painting into a field. It was very good and had been painted by a very talented hand, but there were many reasons why she didn't want it either.

35

The night was clear, cool, and very quiet. At first they saw a few other cars on the road, but later none at all. As the traffic thinned the old man seemed to drive more slowly, reluctant perhaps to be cut off from humanity. Once Rachel asked him to go faster; he pressed down on the accelerator for a minute or two, then eased off and drove even slower than before.

Rachel did not bother him again. She knew that no speed could satisfy: her mind was racing faster than any car. She thought of Angela telling her of Dan's recurring nightmare—his mother and father, towering over him, screaming at each other. They had a quarrel about the war, Lily Gris said. And she thought of Dan in Lily Gris's arms on the bridge over the Seine, in the first hours of 1948, watching his mother falling a long fall into the cold dark water. Had the path of his studies, his whole career, been determined somehow in that moment? He had become an expert on the war, one of the two or three leading men on the subject of the French collaboration. He had discovered new evidence, developed new theories. Had it all been an unconscious but unrelenting effort to unlock his memory of that night? What did you do in the war, Daddy? Was that what he really wanted to know? Mummy found out. If not everything, at least enough to arouse suspicion. And she was too high spirited and independent to forget about it. Had she overheard him talking with DePoe, reliving the good old days of Mhamid? Or had he mumbled in his sleep, drunk and unguarded? Mummy found out so he pushed her off a bridge.

As Lily Gris had said, it was a long time ago. Long before Xavier Monette had even heard of a man named Simon Calvi. How had it happened? Had he, like Hans Kopple, seen a photograph in a newspaper? A photograph of a man he knew as Victor Reinhardt. Private Victor Reinhardt of the Wehrmacht. Missing and presumed dead. Only he wasn't dead; he had turned up in the new state of Israel, the reborn homeland for the Jews, the ones who were left, and was becoming a successful politician. A spokesman in the beginning for the Moroccan Jews, but later for all who were not of European origin. A useful man to know.

Then he would wait. Wait and watch the course of Simon Calvi's career. And at the right moment, the moment when Simon Calvi had progressed to the point where he had too much to lose, he would go to his house at night, or meet him in a cafe, and say, much as she had said, Hello, Victor Reinhardt. And when they had finished discussing old times he would say, Here are some interesting political ideas you may want to adopt. Nothing very dishonorable in the beginning of course: just carry on with what you are already doing, build your power base.

Later he would make greater demands, and greater still, driving Calvi like a wedge into the new state. When had he brought in the Arabs? Surely they were not partners from the beginning; he would bide his time until he was certain Calvi was well hooked. There would never be any reason to even let Calvi suspect that the Arabs were involved. Which probably suited the Arabs perfectly: how

delighted they must have been at the whole divisive affair.
They would pay, and pay well.

And Calvi would be allowed to go on believing, if he
could, that he was a legitimate spokesman for a repressed
minority. They would keep him on a loose rein, not push
too hard. But in the end they had pushed him too hard.
No longer content to play the patient long-term game,
they had raised the stakes. Higher than Simon Calvi could
stomach. So they had lost, and the game was over.
Grunberg was right. For Israel it had finished very well.
With a jolt she realized that was partly due to her.

They entered Orange. The old driver slowed the taxi
until it crept along at not much more than a walking pace.
The town showed no sign of life. No insomniac walked the
streets, no dog prowled the alleys for garbage. The houses
were dark. The inhabitants were sleeping, the way normal
people do in the dead of night. Instead of riding ninety
miles in a taxi with a gun stuck to your thigh. Grunberg
had been right about Israel, Calvi had been right about
innocence. She had given up parts of herself which were
gone forever. Tonight she wanted something to show for
it. Adam, yes, if he were alive, and she was more sure than
ever that he must be; revenge simply if he were not. She
directed the driver to the rue de St. Jean-Baptiste.

For the others it was over. Even for Xavier Monette.
Simon Calvi had been his only card, and he had played it
for the last time. Why had he become involved at all? To
that she had no answer, but an understanding of the
man was forming in her brain, a man who would kill
his son but keep his grandson alive.

The taxi followed the rue de St. Jean-Baptiste to the
edge of the town. "Stop," Rachel said to the driver.

"Here?"

"Yes."

He steered the car to the side of the road and stopped.
He turned to look at her. "You have to piss?"

"No. I'm getting out." She preferred to keep her
destination secret.

He shrugged. "If that's what you want." Rachel gave him a fifty-franc tip, not in appreciation of his services, but for luck, although she did not believe in that sort of thing. Taking her suitcase and handbag she got out of the taxi. It backed across the road, turned and drove off in the direction from which it had come. It left her alone with the silence and a billion stars.

Quietly she walked through the grass at the side of the road, past the last houses of the town and into the country. Vineyards lay on both sides: the leafless stalks of early spring looked like poor bent gravemarkers. The distance to the house seemed much greater than before. Rachel resisted the temptation to break into a run. She shifted the suitcase and the handbag to opposite hands and kept walking.

From a slight rise a few hundred yards away she saw the high stone walls emerge from the darkness. She set the suitcase on the ground and took off her skirt. She unwound the tape from her leg, pulled on a pair of jeans from the suitcase and stuck the gun in her belt.

"It's very simple," Pinchas Levy had said, "if you don't mind killing a dog."

"I do."

Rachel emptied the suitcase and piled everything on the ground. Then she ripped out the inner lining. Underneath were a screwdriver, a small flashlight, a length of nylon rope with a hook attached to one end, a lead apron of the kind used by dentists to protect their patients during X rays, and a leather muzzle. Rachel repacked the suitcase, closed it and hid it and her handbag behind a tree, safe from any passing headlights. She wound the lead apron around her left forearm, fastening it tightly with the straps which were meant to fit over the shoulders. Then, putting the screwdriver and flashlight in her pockets and carrying the rope and muzzle in her right hand, she advanced toward the gate in the wall, where Xavier Monette had thrown a dead fox to the dog with no name.

The gates were locked and bolted from the inside. The

iron railings were spaced about four inches apart, and ended in spear points a couple of feet above her head. Inside the gravel lane reflected the starlight and her eyes followed it easily to the shadows of the peach grove in front of the house. No lights showed. The thought came to her for the first time that she might be too late: he had reason to leave this place, in a hurry. She forced the idea from her mind.

Rachel squatted in front of the gate, placing the muzzle at her feet and holding the hook in her right hand. She poked her left arm through the railings and whistled once in a low tone. Somewhere in the darkness a cicada made a shrill reply. Then the silence returned. Rachel held her breath and listened carefully, but she heard no bark, no paws running through the grass. She was about to whistle again when she felt a soft breeze, and then a vise closed on her forearm with tremendous force.

The Doberman jerked her forward sharply, knocking her head against the gate, and dragging her to her knees. His yellow eyes glowed cold and opaque, and a deep savage growl rumbled in his throat. Despite the layers of lead around her arm she could feel the pressure of his teeth. He would let go only if he had the chance to sink them into a more vital spot. "Remember that a dog in combat is very direct," Pinchas Levy had said. "It has no guile."

Rachel struggled into a sitting position and braced her feet against the railing. Using the muscles in her legs she tried to pull the Doberman forward. He dug his paws into the ground and leaned back; she felt that her arm would be torn from the shoulder. But very slowly the dog's head was drawn closer to the gate. He growled more fiercely than ever but did not let go. With all her might Rachel straightened her legs, slowly pulling the dog forward another inch, perhaps two. Her shoulder could bear no more. With her right hand she reached quickly through the railing and slipped the hook under the dog's leather collar. Then she jerked hard on the nylon rope, bringing the dog's head tightly against the gate. In response he bit deeper into the lead. Rachel wound the rope around one of the railings and then several times around the dog's neck.

She tied the rope to the gate, leaving several feet beyond the knot. This free end she wound again around the dog's neck, and began to pull. The dog didn't like it. He choked and gasped and struggled for breath. Finally he released her arm. Rachel grabbed the muzzle and slipped it over his head. She fastened the leather straps very tightly so he could not bark. Then she stood up and unwrapped the lead protector from her arm. One sharp tooth had penetrated all the way, through to her skin. A little wetness had oozed from the hole and already coagulated. She took a few steps away from the gate. The Doberman began to growl again, but could not even turn his head to watch Rachel put her hands on top of the wall and climb over.

She dropped to the ground on the other side. Suddenly she thought of the possibility that she had arrived ahead of him, that he would come along the road any minute and see the dog with his head stuck in the gate. But it wasn't likely: he had a comfortable head start, at least six or seven hours.

She walked toward the peach grove, her feet making little sound in the soft grass. By the time she reached the trees she could not hear the dog's growling at all. Ahead she saw the dark bulk of the house, and beside it and slightly in front the smaller shadow of the miniature Greek temple the olive oil merchant had built for his homesick mistress. A little marble building with no windows and a brass padlock on the door. She remembered Xavier Monette's call from the telephone box at the gate. "Please be quick," he had ordered the thick-necked housekeeper. Mademoiselle Hoff. And the coffee had been ready.

But she had also seen Mademoiselle Hoff hurrying toward the temple with a heavy washtub in her arms. "We

use it for storage and laundry," he had said of the temple.
But the washtub had been big enough to hide a five-year-
old boy.

She walked around to the heavy wooden door at the
rear of the temple. Not a sound came from within, or from
the house nearby. Rachel took her pencil flashlight from
her pocket and shone it for a moment on the door. The
brass padlock was in place; the hasp was sturdy. But the
screws yielded to her screwdriver, and she dropped them
one by one into her pocket where they could make no
noise. The hasp swung free. Rachel drew the gun from her
belt and slowly pushed the door open.

Cool air touched her skin as she stepped inside. She
closed the door behind her and ran the narrow beam of
light in a sweeping arc. A man stood against the far wall.
She jerked the light back on to him, and dropped to one
knee, pointing the gun as Levy had told her. But she did
not fire: the man had no face. He was a manikin, a
manikin with a black round-rimmed hat and a long black
coat. Rachel crossed the cold hard floor and lifted the hat
off the plastic head. A black furry thing fell out of the hat
and dropped to her feet like a dead animal. She did not
bother to pick it up; it had to be a false beard. She turned
the hat in her hands and sniffed inside. It smelled faintly
of mint and stale sweat.

Slowly Rachel shone the light around the room. The
walls were hung with heavy red drapes. In the center of
each drape was a white circle, outlined in black, and
within each circle a black swastika. Gold-framed photographs were displayed on the drapes. A few were portraits
of Adolf Hitler; some showed him addressing large
crowds. There were photographs of other Nazis she did
not recognize. One picture, smaller than the rest, caught
her eye. She went over to the wall and looked at it closely.

Two young men were standing on flat sandy ground,
one tall and thin, the other shorter and already growing
plump. They wore képis, the flat, round-topped, stiff-
brimmed hat of the French soldier. The tall one was

smiling, the shorter one seemed less relaxed. The smiling man was Xavier Monette and there was little doubt that his companion was DePoe. Behind them stood a long low windowless building which appeared to be made of concrete blocks.

Near the door was a steel file cabinet with two drawers. The top one was empty. In the bottom drawer Rachel found a worn German edition of *Mein Kampf*. She turned quickly through the pages. Some of the passages were underlined in blue ink. Rachel did not know German, but in most of the underlined sections she noticed the word Juden.

In the back of the book was an envelope, addressed to Xavier Monette. She recognized the handwriting and began to tremble as she withdrew its contents. It was a Xerox copy of the letter Dan had written to his father six days before he died, a letter she thought he had never mailed.

". . . I have received one letter with which you may be able to help me," she read. "Not a letter at all, really—it's a document that seems to pertain to North Africa. I know you were there during the war and you may have come across information that might help to explain it. I will make a copy of it in the morning when the secretary arrives, and enclose it with this letter." From that she had assumed he had not sent the letter. Attached to the last page was a copy of the document. He had copied the letter as well, mailing it and keeping the original. Rachel had never kept a copy of a letter in her life.

Barely aware of what she was doing Rachel neatly folded the letter, returned it to the envelope, placed it in the book and put the book in the drawer as she had found it. Xavier Monette had come for the original document. Had he intended to kill Dan from the beginning, or had there been an argument? He had begun to search the study for it but had been stopped by Mrs. Flores's arrival. He came to the funeral hoping for a chance to continue the search. She remembered leaving him alone in Dan's office, and finding him in the study in the middle of the night. He had to have that document: he could not risk having Calvi exposed.

So he had sent the blond man to try for a third time. The blond man who bore such a strong resemblance to the housekeeper, Mademoiselle Hoff. And the blond man had almost succeeded. Monette would have tried again. She knew that if she hadn't started moving she would be dead. It would take more than a few such setbacks to make him give up. He had been fighting his one-man war for a long time; a war against the Jews. A war, she suddenly thought, that he had been forced to wage finally within his own family, against a wife who knew his secret and a son who wrote books in support of the enemy. And married one.

Rachel closed the door of the filing cabinet and went outside. A thin gray crescent showed on the eastern horizon, as if a giant eyelid was slowly opening. In front of the door she knelt and replaced the hasp. She spent more time than she should have driving in the screws: her hands were unsteady. Inside the house she heard a toilet flush. The sound made her heart pound so hard she feared it would seize and stop forever. She ran to the other side of the temple, where she could not be seen from the house.

Leaning horizontally against the wall was a short ladder of the kind used in harvesting fruit trees. Rachel stood it upright and climbed onto the flat roof of the temple. She crawled across to the edge which faced the front of the house.

She lay on the roof as dawn slowly spread color over the earth. The grass became green, the gravel lane rust, the house white with black trim and an orange tile roof. In front of the house was parked a long black car which the night had hidden from her. She was about to lower herself from the roof and try to disable it when the front door opened.

Mademoiselle Hoff appeared on the threshold. She wore a light coat and a formal black hat on her broad head. Sticking two fingers between her lips she whistled loudly. The harsh sound echoed over the fields, but brought no dog running. Mademoiselle Hoff scanned the ground, while Rachel crept back on the roof. She whistled again, waited for a few moments, and reentered the house.

A minute later she came out again, carrying three large suitcases. She opened the trunk of the car and lifted them in. From the open doorway came the sound of footsteps on the tile floor. Two sets of footsteps, Rachel thought, one of them very light. She knew those light footsteps, and the knowledge made her as still as a corpse; a corpse with tears in its eyes.

Xavier Monette walked through the door. And there beside him was Adam. Rachel bit her lip to keep from calling out his name.

They were dressed for traveling; Monette in a dark suit and dark coat and Adam in beige shorts, a beige shirt, and a black necktie.

"Is everything ready?" Monette asked Mademoiselle Hoff in French.

"I can't find the dog."

Monette made a short gesture of dismissal. "It's not important." He began walking toward the car. Adam hung back. Shoot him now, she thought. But Monette turned. "Come," he said in English to Adam. "We are in a hurry."

"Are we going to see Mummy and Daddy?"

"Come when I call you," Monette said sharply.

Adam came. Monette took him by the arm as they went to the car. Mademoiselle Hoff opened the passenger door. Monette and Adam approached the other side, closer to Rachel. Monette reached for the door handle.

Rachel jumped to her feet and pointed the gun at Monette. "Stop." Three heads jerked up to look at her. Two with fear and the other with wonder.

"It's her." Mademoiselle Hoff spoke with hatred. "The bitch who killed Rudi."

Monette's arm snapped out as quickly as a snake; he

grabbed Adam and raised him up as a shield. Mademoiselle Hoff slowly closed the door and put her hands in the pockets of her coat.

"I've come for my son. Put him down."

Monette smiled reasonably. "He's not yours. He is mine."

"You madman. You killed your son. You stuck a God-damned letter opener into his chest."

Monette's smile ebbed from his face, leaving it for an instant without expression. Then as if a tidal wave had surged up from his heart, Monette's face turned red and swollen. The pressure made a muscle in his cheek twitch.

"Imbecile," he shouted. "There are more important things than human life. Much more important." He was squeezing Adam's arms so hard that his knuckles went as white as dried bones. "But why should I explain myself to a Jew?"

Adam began to cry. Rachel felt a rage more powerful than any she had ever imagined sweep over her; every cell in her body seemed to quiver with it.

Monette noticed and it brought a smile once more to his face, a mocking smile. "You want to kill me, don't you?" He held Adam higher. "Then shoot."

Rachel thought of aiming low, at his legs which were not covered by Adam's body. It wouldn't kill him, but he might drop Adam. She aimed the gun at his knees. But her hand was shaking so badly she did not dare fire. "Give him to me."

Monette laughed a short barking laugh. It almost kept her from catching the brief flicker of his eyes. She glanced quickly at Mademoiselle Hoff on the far side of the car.

The woman was drawing a black gun from her coat pocket. Rachel aimed at her and pulled the trigger. The explosion almost kicked the gun from her hand. Pinchas had warned her, but she had forgotten. There was a sharp whining sound, and a ragged silver tear appeared in the black roof of the car. She lifted her gaze beyond the car, right into the barrel of Mademoiselle Hoff's gun.

Rachel dropped face down and rolled. She heard the crack of another shot and felt the tiny breeze an insect might make, close to her neck. She kept rolling until she reached the edge of the roof. There was nowhere else to go.

She raised her head and looked down. Mademoiselle Hoff swung the gun in a short arc. Point, don't aim, Pinchas had said. Rachel pointed and squeezed. This time she was ready for the explosion.

Mademoiselle Hoff fell backward with a hoarse grunt. Her gun went off as she hit the ground, a last shot at the bright blue sky.

The car door slammed. Rachel saw that Monette had jumped into the front seat, pushing Adam ahead of him. Before she could react he had started the engine and wheeled the car around in the lane. The tires fired gravel in the air as it sped away.

Rachel leaped off the roof, fell, rolled to her feet and ran. She could catch him at the gate. It was locked, and he would have trouble opening it because of the dog. She ran along the lane, through the peach orchard and toward the gate. She ran with all her heart.

The car was already there. Quickly Monette got out, opened the lock and slid back the bolt. One side of the gate he threw open easily, but she could see he was having difficulty with the other. The animal, whining in fear, had dug its paws into the ground. Monette drew back his leg and kicked it in the head. Then he pushed the door open.

Rachel was very close, but not close enough. Monette scrambled back into the car. In a moment they would be gone. Don't fire while moving, Pinchas had told her. She forced herself to stop and kneel.

Through the rear window she saw the back of Monette's head. He had no shield now. She pointed the gun. Suddenly her hand was very steady, steadier than it had ever been or than a human hand could be; as steady as something old and immovable, like the earth itself. She pulled the trigger.

The black car rolled through the gate, across the road, and stopped against the trunk of an olive tree. The passenger door opened. Adam stepped down to the ground. He looked toward the house.

"Adam."

Rachel dropped the gun. She ran to him, lifted him up and held him in her arms. His fine hair touched the skin of her face and slowly grew damp with her tears.

"Mummy," he said very softly, almost to himself. As she rocked him to and fro she felt the tension ebb gradually from his little body until at last he was at peace. In that moment Rachel was aware of a faint quickening of pride within her, pride in what she had done.

It died stillborn. Adam's lips moved against her breast, "Where's Daddy?"

She opened her mouth to tell him, but the sounds that came out were beyond her control. Sobbing she clung to him, and Adam sobbed too.

"But Daddy said he wouldn't die for ages and ages."

"My brave little boy. My brave little boy."

It was no good. Rachel felt completely helpless. She could not begin to make his pain go away. And for a long time after, what she had done meant nothing to her at all.